SHORT STORIES FROM
THE NINETEENTH CENTURY

10 – 15 elderflower heads, depending on size
2 unwaxed lemons
500g sugar

- Wash the elderflowers carefully, and place them in a large saucepan with the flowers facing downwards.
- Add the peel of your lemons to them, followed by the juice and the sugar.
- Pour over 1 litre boiling water, and bring the pan to the boil stirring to dissolve the sugar.
- Turn off the heat, cover with a lid, and leave steeping for 24 hours.
- Strain through muslin into clean bottles. It's wise to release the lids every 3 days, just to make sure it's not fermenting. If it doesn't fizz after a fortnight, you're probably safe.

Sloe Gin

You can pick sloes all along West Beach in the autumn (although you have to get in quick – they soon vanish), and I like to make a batch of sloe gin every year. This is not a drink for the impatient. It needs at least a year to mature, and if you can't wait, you'll get a thin, over-sweet liqueur that's hardly worth the effort.

This is more of a rule of thumb than a recipe, as sloe gin is an imprecise art. First of all, you're supposed to wait until after the first frosts to pick your sloes, but that's no use anymore. Instead, only pick your sloes when they're ripe (i.e. not hard like bullets), then wash them at home and freeze them for 24 hours before use. This breaks up the skins and means you don't have to prick each one with a pin.

Find a wide-necked bottle or Kilner jar, and pour in caster sugar until it's 1/3 full. Then add your sloes (I find it easiest if they're still frozen), filling up another 1/3 of the jar. Now pour in your gin (honestly: I buy the cheapest that the supermarket will sell me) to the top. Before you seal the lid, add two almonds, then shake until most of the sugar has dissolved. You'll need to give it a few more shakes over the next couple of days, but when you can no longer see sugar, hide it from yourself until the following Christmas, when it will come as a nice surprise.

Sloe Gin Negroni

I mean, obviously you're supposed to sip your sloe gin from a dainty little glass in a civilised manner. Or you could do this, which somehow manages to be even more alcoholic than a normal negroni.

1 measure gin
1 measure sloe gin
1 measure Campari
Orange bitters
1 Strip orange zest

Fill a tumbler with ice. Pour over the gin, sloe gin and Campari (in that order), and then a shake of the orange bitters if you have them. Garnish with a good, long strip of orange zest and you're good to go.

Short Stories from the Nineteenth Century

Selected and introduced by
DAVID STUART DAVIES

WORDSWORTH CLASSICS

For my husband
ANTHONY JOHN RANSON
with love from your wife, the publisher.
Eternally grateful for your unconditional love,
not just for me but for our children,
Simon, Andrew and Nichola Trayler

Readers who are interested in other titles from
Wordsworth Editions are invited to visit our website at
www.wordsworth-editions.com

For our latest list and a full mail-order service contact
Bibliophile Books, 5 Thomas Road, London E14 7BN
TEL: +44 (0) 207 515 9222 FAX: +44 (0) 207 538 4115
E-MAIL: orders@bibliophilebooks.com

This edition published 2000 by Wordsworth Editions Limited
8B East Street, Ware, Hertfordshire SG12 9ET

ISBN 978-1-84022-407-8

Text © Wordsworth Editions Limited 2000

Permission was granted by A. P. Watts on behalf of the
literary executors of the estate of H. G. Wells
to reprint 'The Stolen Bacillus'

Wordsworth® is a registered trademark of
Wordsworth Editions Limited,
the company founded by Michael Trayler in 1987

Typeset by Antony Gray
Printed and bound in Great Britain by
Clays Ltd, St Ives plc

To

MARCUS & CLIVE

INTRODUCTION

The telling of stories is as old as time. The urge for mankind to relate incidents from life has been with us since we learned to walk upright and live in communities. The cave paintings created by early man that can still be seen in various locations around the world, with their graphic depictions of family life, the hunt and the kill, bear witness to our innate desire to tell and be told stories.

It was in the nineteenth century that storytelling as a formalised art came to prominence. There are many reasons for this. The growth of education ensured that a greater number of people were able to read. Until then this facility had been mainly restricted to the wealthy. As the century progressed, more and more individuals from all walks of life began to enjoy the pleasures of literature. Developments in printing techniques gave rise to cheap periodicals that could be afforded by the middle and lower-middle classes. By the mid-nineteenth century, novels were still very expensive and prohibitive to all but the comfortably off. For example, when Charlotte Brontë's *Jane Eyre* was first published in 1847, it cost one pound and eleven shillings. This was at a time when a housemaid's annual income was less than twenty pounds a year. However, especially in Britain, periodicals like *Household Words*, founded by Charles Dickens, *Tinsley's Magazine*, which serialised an early Thomas Hardy novel, *A Pair of Blue Eyes*, *Harper's New Weekly Review*, *The Cornhill Magazine*, *The Idler*, *Pearson's Weekly Magazine*, *The Strand Magazine*, *et al.* brought literature into the lowliest of homes. Many of the great British novels of the second half of the nineteenth century were published in serialised form in such magazines before they appeared in hard covers in the bookshops. But, perhaps more importantly, the nineteenth century was the golden age of the storyteller, those magicians who can take the raw material of life, enhance it and mould it into something that both entertains and provokes thought.

As well as serialising novels, the new popular publications required complete tales – short stories – to feature within their pages. Little did the publishers of such magazines realise at the time that they were in fact providing a springboard for the golden age of short-story writing which spilled over into the early part of twentieth century.

Creating a short story requires a different technique from that used when writing a full-blown novel. The obvious assumption is that because a story is shorter and contains fewer scenes and characters, it is easier to write. However, because there are fewer scenes and characters – and indeed fewer words – it becomes incumbent upon the short-story writer to make each of these elements count all the more. There is a need to aim at a kind of literary perfection in a short story. Novelists can get away with the odd dull chapter or a disappointing incident which fails to ring true emotionally or dramatically. They have another two hundred pages or so in which to make amends for such weaknesses. This is not the case with short-story writers. They have to get it right in two dozen or so pages. Their canvas is small. They are working on a miniature and therefore the brushstrokes have to be all the more carefully applied.

This painting metaphor is appropriate for a short story like a painting captures, in a written dramatic form, a vivid, colourful moment from the lives of a set of characters – sometimes just one character. Often there will be a surprise ending or a 'sting in the tale' which prompts the reader to reconsider the situation and characters within the piece. A good short story should make us reflect on our own lives and consider the issues raised in the tale. True literature is not just there to entertain – although it certainly should do that – it is there to help us understand ourselves and the world in which we live that little bit better. That is not to say that one has to be an intellectual to appreciate the stories in this collection. They were written to be read by a large number of readers and as such dealt with themes and issues that were, and indeed remain, of considerable importance and relevance to the majority.

It is interesting to note that many of the great Victorian novelists who created fat, labyrinthine plots, like Charles Dickens, Thomas Hardy, Wilkie Collins, Anthony Trollope and Elizabeth Gaskell, could also create short stories with the same amount of power and finesse. They could practise economy with as much success as they exercised largesse. On the other hand, there were those writers who never went beyond the short story form or arguably were more effective in this format than in their longer works. This category includes writers such as Guy de Maupassant, Anton Chekov, O. Henry, Charlotte Perkins Gilman and Arthur Conan Doyle.

A question that is often raised when dealing with literature of a past age is – why should we bother with it now when it is old-fashioned and out of date? This query raises an important point but the response is a simple one: we have much to learn from the past. Old does not equate with *passé*. Because the stories come from a different era, it does not mean that they have nothing to offer the modern reader. Human nature with its nobility, its foibles, its reactions to love, death, fear and hate does not change, whether one wears a crinoline or a mini skirt; and that's what gives power to these stories. The problems, concerns and interests of our great-grandfathers and great-grandmothers are very similar to those that involve us today.

It is also true to say that writers of the nineteenth century created tales which made unparalleled use of the written language. They delighted in the beauty and the power of words. Sadly, this approach to storytelling has deteriorated in general fiction in the last sixty years or so and this is one reason why reading these tales of yesterday is such a pleasure. One must remember that the cinema and television were far away when the stories in this volume were written and therefore many of them are strong in imagery and description. They create pictures which stimulate the imagination.

This selection includes some of the greatest British writers spanning that remarkable era of the nineteenth century. Some, like Charles Dickens, Robert Louis Stevenson and Wilkie Collins, died before the century ended. Others, like Arthur Conan Doyle, H. G. Wells, Bram Stoker and Thomas Hardy, continued writing well into the twentieth century. Also included is a small group of writers from other countries whose work helps to widen our view of yesterday's canvas. From France there is Guy de Maupassant, one of the greatest short-story writers of all. From America we have one of their most accomplished exponents of this form, O. Henry; also from America I have chosen a story by Charlotte Perkins Gilman, one of the rare women writers to succeed in a profession which was seen as a male preserve; a woman found it hard to find a publisher or be taken seriously as a writer. The Russian Anton Chekhov, better known for his plays, also features in this collection.

This then is a heady mix of excellent tales by excellent tellers of tales, but because this crop has been taken from the time of the great golden harvest in short-story writing, it is but a sample – a mere taster of the riches available from the tales of yesterday.

Each story is prefaced with concise biographical details concerning its author and a brief discussion of the themes in the story and other issues of interest that, it is hoped, will stimulate your thoughts as you read the story. There is also a set of notes that explain any words or phrases that may prove puzzling for the modern reader. Time now to leave the world of explanation and enter the wonderful realm of fiction.

DAVID STUART DAVIES

CONTENTS

CHARLES DICKENS

CHARLES DICKENS (1812–70) was perhaps the greatest novelist of the nineteenth century. All his novels are still in print and they present a rich canvas of life and behaviour at all levels of contemporary society. Many of his works, such as *Oliver Twist*, *Great Expectations*, *David Copperfield*, *A Tale of Two Cities* and *A Christmas Carol*, have been filmed, televised and presented as both straight plays and musicals, revealing the power and the timelessness of his writing.

Dickens was born on the south coast of England, near Portsmouth, but the family had moved to London by the time he was seven. In London the Dickens family fell on hard times and Charles's father was imprisoned for debt in the notoriously bleak Marshalsea Prison. The poverty and lack of home comforts that the young Dickens experienced at this time were to haunt him for the rest of his life.

Charles Dickens began writing in his early twenties. In 1832 he became a journalist and his work brought him into close contact with the grimmer facets of society. Before long he began to contribute sketches of London life to the *Monthly Magazine*. These pieces appeared under the pseudonym of 'Boz', but gradually everyone learned the real name of the author. 'The Black Veil' is one of Dickens's *Sketches by Boz*.

Charles Dickens wrote his first novel, *The Pickwick Papers*, in 1836. The success of this comic account of the doings of the Pickwick Club ensured that further novels followed – novels which became darker in tone and content as he grew older.

Dickens saw himself as a crusading novelist. He had great sympathy for the poor and downtrodden and many of his books highlight the injustices to be found in the society of the time. For example, *Nicholas Nickleby* exposed the cruelty of the board schools, and in *Bleak House* the ludicrous workings of the British legal system were satirised to great effect.

'The Black Veil' contains scenes that brilliantly illustrate the poverty and terrible living conditions to be found in the poorer quarters of London. Dickens's detailed description of Walworth in its decrepitude is wonderful. With an artist's eyes, he creates pictures with words which are every bit as vivid as a colourful painting.

The events related in the story are simple and it is a credit to his genius that Dickens can use them to construct a compelling tale. We are drawn into the story, having had our curiosity stimulated by the strange behaviour and equally strange request made by the lady in the black veil. It is a request which not only creates a mystery but also eventually exposes the complex nature of human feelings and emotions.

The storyteller is a young doctor who has just set up in practice and is awaiting his first patient. Little does he know that the events surrounding his 'first professional visit' will stay with him for the rest of his life. For the reader, too, the revelations provoke not only sympathy but also provide a memorable conclusion.

The Black Veil

ONE WINTER'S EVENING, towards the close of the year 1800, or within a year or two of that time, a young medical practitioner, recently established in business, was seated by a cheerful fire in his little parlour, listening to the wind which was beating the rain in pattering drops against the window or rumbling dismally in the chimney. The night was wet and cold; he had been walking through mud and water the whole day, and was now comfortably reposing in his dressing-gown and slippers, more than half asleep and less than half awake, revolving a thousand matters in his wandering imagination. First, he thought how hard the wind was blowing and how the cold, sharp rain would be at that moment beating in his face if he were not comfortably housed at home. Then, his mind reverted to his annual Christmas visit to his native place[1] and dearest friends; he thought how glad they would all be to see him, and how happy it would make Rose if he could only tell her that he had found a patient at last, and hoped to have more and to come down again, in a few months' time, and marry her, and take her home to gladden his lonely fireside and stimulate him to fresh exertions. Then he began to wonder when his first patient would appear or whether he was destined, by a special dispensation of providence, never to have any patients at all; and then he thought about Rose again, and dropped to sleep and dreamed about her, till the tones of her sweet merry voice sounded in his ears and her soft tiny hand rested on his shoulder.

There *was* a hand upon his shoulder, but it was neither soft nor tiny, its owner being a corpulent round-headed boy who, in consideration of the sum of one shilling per week and his food, was let out by the parish to carry medicine and messages. As there was no demand for the medicine, however, and no necessity for the messages, he usually occupied his unemployed hours – averaging fourteen a day – in abstracting peppermint drops, taking animal nourishment and going to sleep.

'A lady, sir – a lady!' whispered the boy, rousing his master with a shake.

'What lady?' cried our friend, starting up, not quite certain that his dream was an illusion and half expecting that it might be Rose herself. 'What lady? Where?'

'*There*, sir!' replied the boy, pointing to the glass door leading into the surgery, with an expression of alarm which the very unusual apparition of a customer might have tended to excite.

The surgeon looked towards the door and started himself, for an instant, on beholding the appearance of his unlooked-for visitor.

It was a singularly tall woman, dressed in deep mourning and standing so close to the door that her face almost touched the glass. The upper part of her figure was carefully muffled in a black shawl, as if for the purpose of concealment; and her face was shrouded by a thick black veil. She stood perfectly erect; her figure was drawn up to its full height, and though the surgeon *felt* that the eyes beneath the veil were fixed on him, she stood perfectly motionless, and evinced, by no gesture whatever, the slightest consciousness of his having turned towards her.

'Do you wish to consult me?' he enquired, with some hesitation, holding open the door. It opened inwards, and therefore the action did not alter the position of the figure, which still remained motionless on the same spot.

She slightly inclined her head, in token of acquiescence.

'Pray walk in,' said the surgeon.

The figure moved a step forward; and then, turning its head in the direction of the boy – to his infinite horror – appeared to hesitate.

'Leave the room, Tom,' said the young man, addressing the boy, whose large round eyes had been extended to their utmost width during this brief interview. 'Draw the curtain, and shut the door.'

The boy drew a green curtain across the glass part of the door, retired into the surgery, closed the door after him, and immediately applied one of his large eyes to the keyhole on the other side.

The surgeon drew a chair to the fire and motioned the visitor to a seat. The mysterious figure slowly moved towards it. As the blaze shone upon the black dress, the surgeon observed that the bottom of it was saturated with mud and rain.

'You are very wet,' he said.

'I am,' said the stranger, in a low deep voice.

'And you are ill?' added the surgeon, compassionately, for the tone was that of a person in pain.

'I am,' was the reply – 'very ill; not bodily, but mentally. It is not for myself, or on my own behalf,' continued the stranger, 'that I come to you. If I laboured under bodily disease, I should not be out, alone, at such an hour or on such a night as this; and if I were afflicted with it, twenty-four hours hence, God knows how gladly I would lie down and pray to die. It is for another that I beseech your aid, sir. I may be mad to ask it for him – I think I am; but, night after night, through the long dreary hours of watching and weeping, the thought has been ever present to my mind; and though even I see the hopelessness of human assistance availing him, the bare thought of laying him in his grave without it makes my blood run cold!' And a shudder, such as the surgeon well knew art could not produce, trembled through the speaker's frame.

There was a desperate earnestness in this woman's manner that went to the young man's heart. He was young in his profession and had not yet witnessed enough of the miseries which are daily presented before the eyes of its members to have grown comparatively callous to human suffering.

'If,' he said, rising hastily, 'the person of whom you speak be in so hopeless a condition as you describe, not a moment is to be lost. I will go with you instantly. Why did you not obtain medical advice before?'

'Because it would have been useless before – because it is useless even now,' replied the woman, clasping her hands passionately.

The surgeon gazed, for a moment, on the black veil, as if to ascertain the expression of the features beneath it: its thickness, however, rendered such a result impossible.

'You *are* ill,' he said, gently, 'although you do not know it. The fever which has enabled you to bear, without feeling it, the fatigue you have evidently undergone, is burning within you now. Put that to your lips,' he continued, pouring out a glass of water – 'compose yourself for a few moments, and then tell me, as calmly as you can, what the disease of the patient is and how long he has been ill. When

I know what it is necessary I should know to render my visit
serviceable to him, I am ready to accompany you.'

The stranger lifted the glass of water to her mouth, without raising
the veil; put it down again untasted; and burst into tears.

'I know,' she said, sobbing aloud, 'that what I say to you now seems
like the ravings of fever. I have been told so before, less kindly than
by you. I am not a young woman; and they do say that as life steals on
towards its final close, the last short remnant, worthless as it may
seem to all beside, is dearer to its possessor than all the years that
have gone before, connected though they be with the recollection of
old friends long since dead and young ones – children perhaps – who
have fallen off² from and forgotten one as completely as if they had
died too. My natural term of life cannot be many years longer and
should be dear on that account; but I would lay it down without a
sigh – with cheerfulness – with joy – if what I tell you now were only
false or imaginary. Tomorrow morning he of whom I speak will be I
know, though I would fain think otherwise, beyond the reach of
human aid; and yet, tonight, though he is in deadly peril, you must
not see and could not serve him.'

'I am unwilling to increase your distress,' said the surgeon, after a
short pause, 'by making any comment on what you have just said, or
appearing desirous to investigate a subject you are so anxious to
conceal; but there is an inconsistency in your statement which I
cannot reconcile with probability. This person is dying tonight, and
I cannot see him when my assistance might possibly avail; you
apprehend it will be useless tomorrow, and yet you would have me
see him then! If he be, indeed, as dear to you as your words and
manner would imply, why not try to save his life before delay and the
progress of his disease render it impracticable?'

'God help me!' exclaimed the woman, weeping bitterly, 'how can I
hope strangers will believe what appears incredible, even to myself?
You will *not* see him then, sir?' she added, rising suddenly.

'I did not say that I declined to see him,' replied the surgeon; 'but I
warn you, that if you persist in this extraordinary procrastination,
and the individual dies, a fearful responsibility rests with you.'

'The responsibility will rest heavily somewhere,' replied the
stranger bitterly. 'Whatever responsibility rests with me, I am
content to bear and ready to answer.'

'As I incur none,' continued the surgeon, 'by acceding to your
request, I will see him in the morning, if you leave me the address. At
what hour can he be seen?'

'*Nine*,' replied the stranger.

'You must excuse my pressing these enquiries,' said the surgeon, 'but is he in your charge now?'

'He is not,' was the rejoinder.

'Then if I gave you instructions for his treatment through the night, you could not assist him?'

The woman wept bitterly, as she replied, 'I could not.'

Finding that there was but little prospect of obtaining more information by prolonging the interview, and anxious to spare the woman's feelings, which, subdued at first by a violent effort, were now irrepressible and most painful to witness, the surgeon repeated his promise of calling in the morning at the appointed hour. His visitor, after giving him a direction to an obscure part of Walworth, left the house in the same mysterious manner in which she had entered it.

It will be readily believed that so extraordinary a visit produced a considerable impression on the mind of the young surgeon; and that he speculated a great deal and to very little purpose on the possible circumstances of the case. In common with the generality of people, he had often heard and read of singular instances in which a presentiment of death, at a particular day or even minute, had been entertained and realised. At one moment he was inclined to think that the present might be such a case; but, then, it occurred to him that all the anecdotes of the kind he had ever heard were of persons who had been troubled with a foreboding of their own death. This woman, however, spoke of another person – a man; and it was impossible to suppose that a mere dream or delusion of fancy would induce her to speak of his approaching dissolution[3] with such terrible certainty as she had spoken. It could not be that the man was to be murdered in the morning, and that the woman, originally a consenting party, and bound to secrecy by an oath, had relented, and, though unable to prevent the commission of some outrage on the victim, had determined to prevent his death if possible by the timely interposition of medical aid? The idea of such things happening within two miles of the metropolis appeared too wild and preposterous to be entertained beyond the instant. Then his original impression that the woman's intellects were disordered recurred; and, as it was the only mode of solving the difficulty with any degree of satisfaction, he obstinately made up his mind to believe that she was mad. Certain misgivings upon this point, however, stole upon his thoughts at the time, and presented themselves again and again through the long dull course of a sleepless night; during which, in spite of all his efforts to the contrary, he was unable to banish the black veil from his disturbed imagination.

The back part of Walworth, at its greatest distance from town, is a straggling miserable place enough, even in these days; but, five-and-thirty years ago, the greater portion of it was little better than a dreary waste, inhabited by a few scattered people of questionable character, whose poverty prevented their living in any better neighbourhood or whose pursuits and mode of life rendered its solitude desirable. Very many of the houses which have since sprung up on all sides were not built until some years afterwards; and the great majority even of those which were sprinkled about, at irregular intervals, were of the rudest and most miserable description.

The appearance of the place through which he walked in the morning was not calculated to raise the spirits of the young surgeon, or to dispel any feeling of anxiety or depression which the singular kind of visit he was about to make had awakened. Striking off from the high road, his way lay across a marshy common, through irregular lanes, with here and there a ruinous and dismantled cottage fast falling to pieces with decay and neglect. A stunted tree or pool of stagnant water, roused into a sluggish action by the heavy rain of the preceding night, skirted the path occasionally; and, now and then, a miserable patch of garden-ground, with a few old boards knocked together for a summerhouse and old palings imperfectly mended with stakes pilfered from the neighbouring hedges, bore testimony at once to the poverty of the inhabitants and the little scruple they entertained in appropriating the property of other people to their own use. Occasionally, a filthy-looking woman would make her appearance from the door of a dirty house, to empty the contents of some cooking utensil into the gutter in front or to scream after a little slipshod girl who had contrived to stagger a few yards from the door under the weight of a sallow infant almost as big as herself; but scarcely anything was stirring around; and so much of the prospect as could be faintly traced through the cold damp mist which hung heavily over it presented a lonely and dreary appearance perfectly in keeping with the objects we have described.

After plodding wearily through the mud and mire, making many enquiries for the place to which he had been directed; and receiving as many contradictory and unsatisfactory replies in return; the young man at length arrived before the house which had been pointed out to him as the object of his destination. It was a small low building, one storey above the ground, with even a more desolate and unpromising exterior than any he had yet passed. An old yellow curtain was closely drawn across the window upstairs, and the parlour shutters were closed, but not fastened. The house was detached from any other, and, as it stood at an angle of a narrow lane, there was no other habitation in sight.

When we say that the surgeon hesitated and walked a few paces beyond the house before he could prevail upon himself to lift the knocker, we say nothing that need raise a smile upon the face of the boldest reader. The police of London were a very different body in that day; the isolated position of the suburbs, when the rage for building and the progress of improvement had not yet begun to connect them with the main body of the city and its environs, rendered many of them (and this in particular) a place of resort for the worst and most depraved characters. Even the streets in the gayest parts of London were imperfectly lighted at that time; and such places as these were left entirely to the mercy of the moon and stars. The chances of detecting desperate characters, or of tracing them to their haunts, were thus rendered very few, and their offences naturally increased in boldness as the consciousness of comparative security became the more impressed upon them by daily experience. Added to these considerations, it must be remembered that the young man had spent some time in the public hospitals of the metropolis; and, although neither Burke nor Bishop[4] had then gained a horrible notoriety, his own observation might have suggested to him how easily the atrocities to which the former has since given his name might be committed. Be this as it may, whatever reflection made him hesitate, he *did* hesitate: but, being a young man of strong mind and great personal courage, it was only for an instant – he stepped briskly back and knocked gently at the door.

A low whispering was audible, immediately afterwards, as if some person at the end of the passage were conversing stealthily with another on the landing above. It was succeeded by the noise of a pair of heavy boots upon the bare floor. The door-chain was softly unfastened; the door opened; and a tall, ill-favoured man, with black hair and a face, as the surgeon often declared afterwards, as pale and haggard as the countenance of any dead man he ever saw, presented himself.

'Walk in, sir,' he said in a low tone.

The surgeon did so, and the man having secured the door again, by the chain, led the way to a small back parlour at the extremity of the passage.

'Am I in time?'

'Too soon!' replied the man. The surgeon turned hastily round, with a gesture of astonishment not unmixed with alarm, which he found it impossible to repress.

'If you'll step in here, sir,' said the man, who had evidently noticed the action – 'if you'll step in here, sir, you won't be detained five minutes, I assure you.'

The surgeon at once walked into the room. The man closed the door and left him alone.

It was a little cold room, with no other furniture than two deal chairs and a table of the same material. A handful of fire, unguarded by any fender, was burning in the grate, which brought out the damp if it served no more comfortable purpose, for the unwholesome moisture was stealing down the walls in long slug-like tracks. The window, which was broken and patched in many places, looked into a small enclosed piece of ground almost covered with water. Not a sound was to be heard, either within the house or without. The young surgeon sat down by the fireplace to await the result of his first professional visit.

He had not remained in this position many minutes when the noise of some approaching vehicle struck his ear. It stopped; the street-door was opened; a low talking succeeded, accompanied with a shuffling noise of footsteps along the passage and on the stairs, as if two or three men were engaged in carrying some heavy body to the room above. The creaking of the stairs, a few seconds afterwards, announced that the newcomers having completed their task, what-ever it was, were leaving the house. The door was again closed, and the former silence was restored.

Another five minutes had elapsed, and the surgeon had resolved to explore the house in search of someone to whom he might make his errand known, when the room-door opened and his last night's visitor, dressed in exactly the same manner, with the veil lowered as before, motioned him to advance. The singular height of her form, coupled with the circumstance of her not speaking, caused the idea to pass across his brain for an instant that it might be a man disguised in woman's attire. The hysteric sobs which issued from beneath the veil, and the convulsive attitude of grief of the whole figure, however, at once exposed the absurdity of the suspicion; and he hastily followed.

The woman led the way upstairs to the front room and paused at the door to let him enter first. It was scantily furnished with an old deal box, a few chairs, and a tent bedstead, without hangings or cross-rails, which was covered with a patchwork counterpane. The dim light admitted through the curtain which he had noticed from the outside rendered the objects in the room so indistinct, and communicated to all of them so uniform a hue, that he did not, at first, perceive the object on which his eye at once rested when the woman rushed frantically past him and flung herself on her knees by the bedside.

Stretched upon the bed, closely enveloped in a linen wrapper and covered with blankets, lay a human form, stiff and motionless. The head and face, which were those of a man, were uncovered, save by a bandage which passed over the head and under the chin. The eyes were closed. The left arm lay heavily across the bed and the woman held the passive hand.

The surgeon gently pushed the woman aside and took the hand in his.

'My God!' he exclaimed, letting it fall involuntarily – 'the man is dead!'

The woman started to her feet and beat her hands together.

'Oh! don't say so, sir,' she exclaimed, with a burst of passion amounting almost to frenzy. 'Oh! don't say so, sir! I can't bear it! Men have been brought to life before, when unskilful people have given them up for lost; and men have died who might have been restored if proper means had been resorted to. Don't let him lie here, sir, without one effort to save him! This very moment life may be passing away. Do try, sir – do, for heaven's sake!' – And while speaking, she hurriedly chafed[5] first the forehead and then the breast of the senseless form before her; and then wildly beat the cold hands, which, when she ceased to hold them, fell listlessly and heavily back on the coverlet.

'It is of no use, my good woman,' said the surgeon, soothingly, as he withdrew his hand from the man's breast. 'Stay – undraw that curtain!'

'Why?' said the woman, starting up.

'Undraw that curtain!' repeated the surgeon in an agitated tone.

'I darkened the room on purpose,' said the woman, throwing herself before him as he rose to undraw it. – 'Oh! sir, have pity on me! If it can be of no use, and he is really dead, do not expose that form to other eyes than mine!'

'This man died no natural or easy death,' said the surgeon. 'I *must* see the body!' With a motion so sudden that the woman hardly knew that he had slipped from beside her, he tore open the curtain, admitted the full light of day and returned to the bedside.

'There has been violence here,' he said, pointing towards the body and gazing intently on the face from which the black veil was now, for the first time, removed. In the excitement of a minute before, the female had thrown off the bonnet and veil, and now stood with her eyes fixed upon him. Her features were those of a woman about fifty, who had once been handsome. Sorrow and weeping had left traces upon them which not time itself would ever have produced without their aid; her face was deadly pale; and there was a nervous contortion of the lip and an unnatural fire in her eye which showed too plainly that her bodily and mental powers had nearly sunk beneath an accumulation of misery.

'There has been violence here,' said the surgeon, preserving his searching glance.

'There has!' replied the woman.

'This man has been murdered.'

'That I call God to witness he has,' said the woman, passionately; 'pitilessly, inhumanly murdered!'

'By whom?' said the surgeon, seizing the woman by the arm.

'Look at the butchers' marks, and then ask me!' she replied.

The surgeon turned his face towards the bed and bent over the body which now lay full in the light of the window. The throat was swollen and a livid mark encircled it. The truth flashed suddenly upon him.

'This is one of the men who were hanged this morning!' he exclaimed, turning away with a shudder.

'It is,' replied the woman, with a cold, unmeaning stare.

'Who was he?' enquired the surgeon.

'*My son*,' rejoined the woman; and fell senseless at his feet.

It was true. A companion, equally guilty with himself, had been acquitted for want of evidence; and this man had been left for death, and executed. To recount the circumstances of the case, at this distant period, must be unnecessary, and might give pain to some persons still alive. The history was an everyday one. The mother was a widow without friends or money, and had denied herself necessaries to bestow them on her orphan boy. That boy, unmindful of her prayers and forgetful of the sufferings she had endured for him – incessant anxiety of mind and voluntary starvation of body – had plunged into a career of dissipation and crime. And this was the result; his own death by the hangman's hands, and his mother's shame and incurable insanity.

For many years after this occurrence, and when profitable and arduous avocations[6] would have led many men to forget that such a miserable being existed, the young surgeon was a daily visitor at the side of the harmless madwoman; not only soothing her by his presence and kindness, but alleviating the rigour of her condition by pecuniary donations for her comfort and support, bestowed with no

sparing hand. In the transient gleam of recollection and consciousness which preceded her death, a prayer for his welfare and
protection, as fervent as mortal ever breathed, rose from the lips of
this poor friendless creature. That prayer flew to heaven and was
heard. The blessings he was instrumental in conferring have been
repaid to him a thousandfold; but, amid all the honours of rank and
station which have since been heaped upon him, and which he has so
well earned, he can have no reminiscence more gratifying to his heart
than that connected with the black veil.

THOMAS HARDY

THOMAS HARDY (1840–1928) was born and lived the greater part of his life near Dorchester, the county town of Dorset. Most of his stories and novels were set in this predominantly rural area which he renamed, for fictional purposes, Wessex. 'The Withered Arm' is one of his *Wessex Tales*.

Hardy was the son of a small builder and mason and at the age of sixteen he became an apprentice to John Hicks, a Dorchester architect and church restorer. With remarkable discipline, which involved him getting up in the early hours of the morning to study, Hardy developed his classical education by studying Greek. In 1862 he moved to London to work as an architect and it was here that he began to write seriously – poetry at first and then novels. His first published novel, *Desperate Remedies*, appeared in 1871 and by this time he had given up his life to writing. Great novels followed including *Far from the Madding Crowd*, *The Mayor of Casterbridge* and *Jude the Obscure*. All his writing reflected the skilful symmetry and careful planning influenced by his practice as an architect.

From an early age Hardy loved listening to stories that were told by his father and other relations, usually around the fireside after the evening meal. Storytelling was a popular form of domestic entertainment in Victorian times. These tales would be country anecdotes, stories of dramatic incident, tragedy, comedy and superstition. Later in life, many of his short stories would echo the ideas, themes and even plots that he heard in his youth. For example, while he was still a boy, Hardy knew of an old woman who, in an attempt to cure her of some wasting disease when she was a young girl, had been taken to have her blood 'turned' by a convict's corpse. He was later to use this incident in his story 'The Withered Arm'.

Hardy was a great believer in fate as the ruler of our destiny and in 'The Withered Arm' fate – or we could call it coincidence – plays an important part in the lives of the three main characters. Hardy was of the opinion that, no matter what our actions in life, we could not change our preordained future, and in this story we are convinced by his clever writing that the bright young bride who arrives at Holmbrook is doomed from the start.

Traditions of witches and witchcraft lasted a long time in the Dorset villages. In Hardy's own village there was a man known as the Planet Ruler. He was an astrologer and one of Hardy's aunts consulted him regularly about her future. This mystic would seem to be the model for Trendle the 'white wizard' or 'conjuror' who recommends the grisly cure to Gertrude in the story.

In the later novels, like *Tess of the D'Urbervilles* and *Jude the Obscure*, Hardy directs his sympathies towards the central character; but in 'The Withered Arm' he records the proceedings in a neutral fashion, allowing the reader to react personally, without authorial persuasion, to the characters and events. At the end, we have to ask ourselves whom do we feel most sorry for and then, more importantly, why?

The Withered Arm

I

A LORN MILKMAID

IT WAS AN EIGHTY-COW DAIRY, and the troop of milkers, regular and supernumerary,[1] were all at work; for, though the time of year was as yet but early April, the feed lay entirely in water meadows and the cows were 'in full pail'. The hour was about six in the evening, and three-fourths of the large, red, rectangular animals having been finished off, there was opportunity for a little conversation.

'He do bring home his bride tomorrow, I hear. They've come as far as Anglebury today.'

The voice seemed to proceed from the belly of the cow called Cherry, but the speaker was a milking-woman, whose face was buried in the flank of that motionless beast.

'Hav' anybody seen her?' said another.

There was a negative response from the first. 'Though they say she's a rosy-cheeked, tisty-tosty[2] little body enough,' she added; and as the milkmaid spoke she turned her face so that she could glance past her cow's tail to the other side of the barton,[3] where a thin fading woman of thirty milked somewhat apart from the rest.

'Years younger than he, they say,' continued the second, with also a glance of reflectiveness in the same direction.

'How old do you call him, then?'

'Thirty or so.'

'More like forty,' broke in an old milkman near, in a long white pinafore or 'wropper', and with the brim of his hat tied down, so that he looked like a woman. ' 'A was born before our Great Weir was builded, and I hadn't man's wages when I laved[4] water there.'

The discussion waxed so warm that the purr of the milk-streams became jerky, till a voice from another cow's belly cried with authority, 'Now, then, what the Turk do it matter to us about Farmer Lodge's age, or Farmer Lodge's new mis'ess! I shall have to pay him nine pound a year for the rent of every one of these milchers, whatever his age or hers. Get on with your work, or 'twill be dark afore we have done. The evening is pinking in a'ready.' This speaker was the dairyman himself, by whom the milkmaids and men were employed.

Nothing more was said publicly about Farmer Lodge's wedding; but the first woman murmured under her cow to her next neighbour, ' 'Tis hard for *she*,' signifying the thin worn milkmaid aforesaid.

'Oh no,' said the second. 'He ha'n't spoke to Rhoda Brook for years.'

When the milking was done they washed their pails and hung them on a many-forked stand made as usual of the peeled limb of an oak tree, set upright in the earth, and resembling a colossal antlered horn. The majority then dispersed in various directions homeward. The thin woman who had not spoken was joined by a boy of twelve or thereabout, and the twain went away up the field also.

Their course lay apart from that of the others, to a lonely spot high above the water-meads and not far from the border of Egdon Heath, whose dark countenance was visible in the distance as they drew nigh to their home.

'They've just been saying down in barton that your father brings his young wife home from Anglebury tomorrow,' the woman observed. 'I shall want to send you for a few things to market, and you'll be pretty sure to meet 'em.'

'Yes, mother,' said the boy. 'Is father married, then?'

'Yes .. You can give her a look, and tell me what she's like, if you do see her.'

'Yes, mother.'

'If she's dark or fair, and if she's tall – as tall as I. And if she seems like a woman who has ever worked for a living or one that has been always well off, and has never done anything, and shows marks of the lady on her, as I expect she do.'

'Yes.'

They crept up the hill in the twilight, and entered the cottage. It was built of mud walls, the surface of which had been washed by many rains into channels and depressions that left none of the original flat face visible; while here and there in the thatch above a rafter showed like a bone protruding through the skin.

She was kneeling down in the chimney-corner, before two pieces of turf laid together with the heather inwards, blowing at the red-hot ashes with her breath till the turves flamed. The radiance lit her pale cheek, and made her dark eyes, that had once been handsome, seem handsome anew. 'Yes,' she resumed, 'see if she is dark or fair, and if you can, notice if her hands be white; if not, see if they look as though she had ever done housework, or are milker's hands like mine.'

The boy again promised, inattentively this time, his mother not observing that he was cutting a notch with his pocket-knife in the beech-backed chair.

II

THE YOUNG WIFE

The road from Anglebury to Holmstoke is in general level; but there is one place where a sharp ascent breaks its monotony. Farmers homeward-bound from the former market-town, who trot all the rest of the way, walk their horses up this short incline.

The next evening, while the sun was yet bright, a handsome new gig, with a lemon-coloured body and red wheels, was spinning westward along the level highway at the heels of a powerful mare. The driver was a yeoman in the prime of life, cleanly shaven like an actor, his face being toned to that bluish-vermilion hue which so often graces a thriving farmer's features when returning home after successful dealings in the town. Beside him sat a woman, many years his junior – almost, indeed, a girl. Her face too was fresh in colour, but it was of a totally different quality – soft and evanescent, like the light under a heap of rose-petals.

Few people travelled this way, for it was not a main road; and the long white riband of gravel that stretched before them was empty, save of one small scarce-moving speck, which presently resolved itself into the figure of a boy, who was creeping on at a snail's pace, and continually looking behind him – the heavy bundle he carried being some excuse for, if not the reason of, his dilatoriness. When the bouncing gig-party slowed at the bottom of the incline above mentioned, the pedestrian was only a few yards in front. Supporting the large bundle by putting one hand on his hip, he turned and looked straight at the farmer's wife as though he would read her through and through, pacing along abreast of the horse.

The low sun was full in her face, rendering every feature, shade, and contour distinct, from the curve of her little nostril to the colour of her eyes. The farmer, though he seemed annoyed at the boy's persistent presence, did not order him to get out of the way; and thus the lad preceded them, his hard gaze never leaving her, till they reached the top of the ascent, when the farmer trotted on with relief in his lineaments[5] – having taken no outward notice of the boy whatever.

'How that poor lad stared at me!' said the young wife.

'Yes, dear; I saw that he did.'

'He is one of the village, I suppose?'

'One of the neighbourhood. I think he lives with his mother a mile or two off.'

'He knows who we are, no doubt?'

'Oh yes. You must expect to be stared at just at first, my pretty Gertrude.'

'I do – though I think the poor boy may have looked at us in the hope we might relieve him of his heavy load, rather than from curiosity.'

'Oh no,' said her husband, off-handedly. 'These country lads will carry a hundredweight once they get it on their backs; besides, his pack had more size than weight in it. Now, then, another mile and I shall be able to show you our house in the distance – if it is not too dark before we get there.' The wheels spun round, and particles flew from their periphery as before, till a white house of ample dimensions revealed itself, with farm-buildings and ricks at the back.

Meanwhile the boy had quickened his pace, and turning up a by lane some mile and half short of the white farmstead, ascended towards the leaner pastures, and so on to the cottage of his mother.

She had reached home after her day's milking at the outlying dairy, and was washing cabbage at the doorway in the declining light. 'Hold up the net a moment,' she said, without preface, as the boy came up.

He flung down his bundle, held the edge of the cabbage-net, and as she filled its meshes with the dripping leaves she went on, 'Well, did you see her?'

'Yes; quite plain.'

'Is she ladylike?'

'Yes; and more. A lady complete.'

'Is she young?'

'Well, she's growed up, and her ways be quite a woman's.'

'Of course. What colour is her hair and face?'

'Her hair is lightish, and her face as comely as a live doll's.'

'Her eyes, then, are not dark like mine?'

'No – of a bluish turn, and her mouth is very nice and red; and when she smiles, her teeth show white.'

'Is she tall?' said the woman sharply.

'I couldn't see. She was sitting down.'

'Then do you go to Holmstoke church tomorrow morning: she's sure to be there. Go early and notice her walking in, and come home and tell me if she's taller than I.'

'Very well, mother. But why don't you go and see for yourself?'

'I go to see her! I wouldn't look up at her if she were to pass my window this instant. She was with Mr Lodge, of course. What did he say or do?'

'Just the same as usual.'

'Took no notice of you?'

'None.'

Next day the mother put a clean shirt on the boy, and started him off for Holmstoke church. He reached the ancient little pile when the door was just being opened, and he was the first to enter. Taking his seat by the font, he watched all the parishioners file in. The well-to-do Farmer Lodge came nearly last; and his young wife, who accompanied him, walked up the aisle with the shyness natural to a modest woman who had appeared thus for the first time. As all other eyes were fixed upon her, the youth's stare was not noticed now.

When he reached home his mother said 'Well?' before he had entered the room.

'She is not tall. She is rather short,' he replied.

'Ah!' said his mother, with satisfaction.

'But she's very pretty – very. In fact, she's lovely.' The youthful freshness of the yeoman's wife had evidently made an impression even on the somewhat hard nature of the boy.

'That's all I want to hear,' said his mother quickly. 'Now, spread the tablecloth. The hare you wired is very tender; but mind that nobody catches you. – You've never told me what sort of hands she had.'

'I have never seen 'em. She never took off her gloves.'

'What did she wear this morning?'

'A white bonnet and a silver-coloured gownd. It whewed and whistled so loud when it rubbed against the pews that the lady coloured up more than ever for very shame at the noise, and pulled it in to keep it from touching; but when she pushed into her seat, it whewed more than ever. Mr Lodge, he seemed pleased, and his waistcoat stuck out, and his great golden seals hung like a lord's; but she seemed to wish her noisy gownd anywhere but on her.'

'Not she! However, that will do now.'

These descriptions of the newly married couple were continued from time to time by the boy at his mother's request, after any chance encounter he had had with them. But Rhoda Brook, though she might easily have seen young Mrs Lodge for herself by walking a couple of miles, would never attempt an excursion towards the quarter where the farmhouse lay. Neither did she, at the daily milking in the dairyman's yard on Lodge's outlying second farm, ever speak on the subject of the recent marriage. The dairyman, who rented the cows of Lodge, and knew perfectly the tall milkmaid's history, with manly kindliness always kept the gossip in the cow-barton from annoying Rhoda. But the atmosphere thereabout was full of the subject during the first days of Mrs Lodge's arrival; and from her boy's description and the casual words of the other milkers, Rhoda Brook could raise a mental image of the unconscious Mrs Lodge that was realistic as a photograph.

III

A VISION

One night, two or three weeks after the bridal return, when the boy was gone to bed, Rhoda sat a long time over the turf ashes that she had raked out in front of her to extinguish them. She contemplated so intently the new wife, as presented to her in her mind's eye over the embers, that she forgot the lapse of time. At last, wearied with her day's work, she too retired.

But the figure which had occupied her so much during this and the previous days was not to be banished at night. For the first time Gertrude Lodge visited the supplanted woman in her dreams. Rhoda Brook dreamed – since her assertion that she really saw, before falling asleep, was not to be believed – that the young wife, in the pale silk dress and white bonnet, but with features shockingly distorted, and wrinkled as by age, was sitting upon her chest as she lay. The pressure of Mrs Lodge's person grew heavier; the blue eyes peered cruelly into her face; and then the figure thrust forward its left hand mockingly, so as to make the wedding-ring it wore glitter in Rhoda's eyes. Maddened mentally, and nearly suffocated by pressure, the sleeper struggled; the incubus,[6] still regarding her, withdrew to the foot of the bed, only, however, to come forward by degrees, resume her seat, and flash her left hand as before.

Gasping for breath, Rhoda, in a last desperate effort, swung out her right hand, seized the confronting spectre by its obtrusive left arm, and whirled it backward to the floor, starting up herself as she did so with a low cry.

'Oh, merciful heaven!' she cried, sitting on the edge of the bed in a cold sweat, 'that was not a dream – she was here!'

She could feel her antagonist's arm within her grasp even now – the very flesh and bone of it, as it seemed. She looked on the floor whither she had whirled the spectre, but there was nothing to be seen.

Rhoda Brook slept no more that night, and when she went milking at the next dawn they noticed how pale and haggard she looked. The milk that she drew quivered into the pail; her hand had not calmed even yet, and still retained the feel of the arm. She came home to breakfast as wearily as if it had been supper-time.

'What was that noise in your chimmer,[7] mother, last night?' said her son. 'You fell off the bed, surely?'

'Did you hear anything fall? At what time?'

'Just when the clock struck two.'

She could not explain, and when the meal was done went silently about her household work, the boy assisting her, for he hated going afield on the farms, and she indulged his reluctance. Between eleven and twelve the garden-gate clicked, and she lifted her eyes to the window. At the bottom of the garden, within the gate, stood the woman of her vision. Rhoda seemed transfixed.

'Ah, she said she would come!' exclaimed the boy, also observing her.

'Said so – when? How does she know us?'

'I have seen and spoken to her. I talked to her yesterday.'

'I told you,' said the mother, flushing indignantly, 'never to speak to anybody in that house, or go near the place.'

'I did not speak to her till she spoke to me. And I did not go near the place. I met her in the road.'

'What did you tell her?'

'Nothing. She said, "Are you the poor boy who had to bring the heavy load from market?" And she looked at my boots, and said they would not keep my feet dry if it came on wet, because they were so cracked. I told her I lived with my mother, and we had enough to do to keep ourselves, and that's how it was; and she said then, "I'll come and bring you some better boots, and see your mother." She gives away things to other folks in the meads besides us.'

Mrs Lodge was by this time close to the door – not in her silk, as Rhoda had dreamt of in the bedchamber, but in a morning hat, and gown of common light material, which became her better than silk. On her arm she carried a basket.

The impression remaining from the night's experience was still strong. Brook had almost expected to see the wrinkles, the scorn, and the cruelty on her visitor's face. She would have escaped an interview, had escape been possible. There was, however, no back-door to the cottage, and in an instant the boy had lifted the latch to Mrs Lodge's gentle knock.

'I see I have come to the right house,' said she, glancing at the lad, and smiling. 'But I was not sure till you opened the door.'

The figure and action were those of the phantom; but her voice was so indescribably sweet, her glance so winning, her smile so tender, so unlike that of Rhoda's midnight visitant, that the latter could hardly believe the evidence of her senses. She was truly glad that she had not hidden away in sheer aversion, as she had been inclined to do. In her basket Mrs Lodge brought the pair of boots that she had promised to the boy, and other useful articles.

At these proofs of a kindly feeling towards her and hers, Rhoda's heart reproached her bitterly. This innocent young thing should have her blessing and not her curse. When she left them a light seemed gone from the dwelling. Two days later she came again to know if the boots fitted; and less than a fortnight after that paid Rhoda another call. On this occasion the boy was absent.

'I walk a good deal,' said Mrs Lodge, 'and your house is the nearest outside our own parish. I hope you are well. You don't look quite well.'

Rhoda said she was well enough; and indeed, though the paler of the two, there was more of the strength that endures in her well-defined features and large frame, than in the soft-cheeked young woman before her. The conversation became quite confidential as regarded their powers and weaknesses; and when Mrs Lodge was leaving, Rhoda said, 'I hope you will find this air agree with you, ma'am, and not suffer from the damp of the water-meads.'

The younger one replied that there was not much doubt of it, her general health being usually good. 'Though, now you remind me,' she added, 'I have one little ailment which puzzles me. It is nothing serious, but I cannot make it out.'

She uncovered her left hand and arm; and their outline confronted Rhoda's gaze as the exact original of the limb she had beheld and seized in her dream. Upon the pink round surface of the arm were faint marks of an unhealthy colour, as if produced by a rough grasp. Rhoda's eyes became riveted on the discolorations; she fancied that she discerned in them the shape of her own four fingers.

'How did it happen?' she said mechanically.

'I cannot tell,' replied Mrs Lodge, shaking her head. 'One night when I was sound asleep, dreaming I was away in some strange place, a pain suddenly shot into my arm there, and was so keen as to awaken me. I must have struck it in the daytime, I suppose, though I don't remember doing so.' She added, laughing, 'I tell my dear husband that it looks just as if he had flown into a rage and struck me there. Oh, I dare say it will soon disappear.'

'Ha, ha! Yes . . . On what night did it come?'

Mrs Lodge considered, and said it would be a fortnight ago on the morrow. 'When I awoke, I could not remember where I was,' she added, 'till the clock striking two reminded me.'

She had named the night and the hour of Rhoda's spectral encounter, and Brook felt like a guilty thing. The artless disclosure startled her; she did not reason on the freaks of coincidence; and all the scenery of that ghastly night returned with double vividness to her mind.

'Oh, can it be,' she said to herself, when her visitor had departed, 'that I exercise a malignant power over people against my own will?' She knew that she had been slyly called a witch since her fall; but never having understood why that particular stigma had been attached to her, it had passed disregarded. Could this be the explanation, and had such things as this ever happened before?

IV

A SUGGESTION

The summer drew on, and Rhoda Brook almost dreaded to meet Mrs Lodge again, notwithstanding that her feeling for the young wife amounted wellnigh to affection. Something in her own individuality seemed to convict Rhoda of crime. Yet a fatality sometimes would direct the steps of the latter to the outskirts of Holmstoke whenever she left her house for any other purpose than her daily work; and hence it happened that their next encounter was out of doors. Rhoda could not avoid the subject which had so mystified her, and after the first few words she stammered, 'I hope your – arm is well again, ma'am?' She had perceived with consternation that Gertrude Lodge carried her left arm stiffly.

'No; it is not quite well. Indeed it is no better at all; it is rather worse. It pains me dreadfully sometimes.'

'Perhaps you had better go to a doctor, ma'am.'

She replied that she had already seen a doctor. Her husband had insisted upon her going to one. But the surgeon had not seemed to understand the afflicted limb at all; he had told her to bathe it in hot water, and she had bathed it, but the treatment had done no good.

'Will you let me see it?' said the milkwoman.

Mrs Lodge pushed up her sleeve and disclosed the place, which was a few inches above the wrist. As soon as Rhoda Brook saw it, she could hardly preserve her composure. There was nothing of the nature of a wound, but the arm at that point had a shrivelled look, and the outline of the four fingers appeared more distinct than at the former time. Moreover, she fancied that they were imprinted in precisely the relative position of her clutch upon the arm in the trance; the first finger towards Gertrude's wrist, and the fourth towards her elbow.

What the impress resembled seemed to have struck Gertrude herself since their last meeting. 'It looks almost like finger marks,' she said; adding with a faint laugh, 'my husband says it is as if some witch, or the devil himself, had taken hold of me there, and blasted the flesh.'

Rhoda shivered. 'That's fancy,' she said hurriedly. 'I wouldn't mind it, if I were you.'

'I shouldn't so much mind it,' said the younger, with hesitation, 'if – if I hadn't a notion that it makes my husband – dislike me – no, love me less. Men think so much of personal appearance.'

'Some do – he for one.'

'Yes; and he was very proud of mine, at first.'

'Keep your arm covered from his sight.'

'Ah – he knows the disfigurement is there!' She tried to hide the tears that filled her eyes.

'Well, ma'am, I earnestly hope it will go away soon.'

And so the milkwoman's mind was chained anew to the subject by a horrid sort of spell as she returned home. The sense of having been guilty of an act of malignity increased, affect as she might to ridicule her superstition. In her secret heart Rhoda did not altogether object to a slight diminution of her successor's beauty, by whatever means it had come about; but she did not wish to inflict upon her physical pain. For though this pretty young woman had rendered impossible any reparation which Lodge might have made Rhoda for his past conduct, everything like resentment at the unconscious usurpation[8] had quite passed away from the elder's mind.

If the sweet and kindly Gertrude Lodge only knew of the dream-scene in that bedchamber, what would she think? Not to inform her of it seemed treachery in the presence of her friendliness; but tell she could not of her own accord – neither could she devise a remedy.

She mused upon the matter the greater part of the night; and the next day, after the morning milking, set out to obtain another glimpse of Gertrude Lodge if she could, being held to her by a gruesome fascination. By watching the house from a distance the milkmaid was presently able to discern the farmer's wife in a ride she was taking alone – probably to join her husband in some distant field. Mrs Lodge perceived her, and cantered in her direction.

'Good-morning, Rhoda!' Gertrude said, when she had come up. 'I was going to call.'

Rhoda noticed that Mrs Lodge held the reins with some difficulty.

'I hope – the bad arm . . . ' said Rhoda.

'They tell me there is possibly one way by which I might be able to find out the cause, and so perhaps the cure, of it,' replied the other anxiously. 'It is by going to some clever man over in Egdon Heath. They did not know if he was still alive – and I cannot remember his name at this moment; but they said that you knew more of his movements than anybody else hereabout, and could tell me if he were still to be consulted. Dear me – what was his name? But you know.'

'Not Conjuror Trendle?' said her thin companion, turning pale.

'Trendle – yes. Is he alive?'

'I believe so,' said Rhoda, with reluctance.

'Why do you call him conjuror?'

'Well – they say – they used to say he was a – he had powers other folks have not.'

'Oh, how could my people be so superstitious as to recommend a man of that sort! I thought they meant some medical man. I shall think no more of him.'

Rhoda looked relieved, and Mrs Lodge rode on. The milkwoman had inwardly seen, from the moment she heard of her having been mentioned as a reference for this man, that there must exist a sarcastic feeling among the workfolk that a sorceress would know the whereabouts of the exorcist. They suspected her, then. A short time ago this would have given no concern to a woman of her common sense. But she had a haunting reason to be superstitious now; and she had been seized with sudden dread that this Conjuror Trendle might name her as the malignant influence which was blasting the fair person of Gertrude, and so lead her friend to hate her for ever, and to treat her as some fiend in human shape.

But all was not over. Two days after, a shadow intruded into the window-pattern thrown on Rhoda Brook's floor by the afternoon sun. The woman opened the door at once, almost breathlessly.

'Are you alone?' said Gertrude. She seemed to be no less harassed and anxious than Brook herself.

'Yes,' said Rhoda.

'The place on my arm seems worse, and troubles me!' the young farmer's wife went on. 'It is so mysterious! I do hope it will not be an incurable wound. I have again been thinking of what they said about Conjuror Trendle. I don't really believe in such men, but I should not mind just visiting him, from curiosity – though on no account must my husband know. Is it far to where he lives?'

'Yes – five miles,' said Rhoda, backwardly. 'In the heart of Egdon.'

'Well, I should have to walk. Could not you go with me to show me the way – say tomorrow afternoon?'

'Oh, not I – that is,' the milkwoman murmured, with a start of dismay. Again the dread seized her that something to do with her fierce act in the dream might be revealed, and her character in the eyes of the most useful friend she had ever had be ruined irretrievably.

Mrs Lodge urged, and Rhoda finally assented, though with much misgiving. Sad as the journey would be to her, she could not conscientiously stand in the way of a possible remedy for her patron's[9] strange affliction. It was agreed that, to escape suspicion of their mystic intent, they should meet at the edge of the heath, at the corner of a plantation which was visible from the spot where they now stood.

V

CONJUROR TRENDLE

By the next afternoon, Rhoda would have done anything to escape this inquiry. But she had promised to go. Moreover, there was a horrid fascination at times in becoming instrumental in throwing such possible light on her own character as would reveal her to be something greater in the occult world than she had ever herself suspected.

She started just before the time of day mentioned between them, and half an hour's brisk walking brought her to the south-eastern extension of the Egdon tract of country, where the fir plantation was. A slight figure, cloaked and veiled, was already there. Rhoda recognised, almost with a shudder, that Mrs Lodge bore her left arm in a sling.

They hardly spoke to each other, and immediately set out on their climb into the interior of this solemn country, which stood high above the rich alluvial soil they had left half an hour before. It was a long walk; thick clouds made the atmosphere dark, though it was as yet only early afternoon; and the wind howled dismally over the slopes of the heath – not improbably the same heath which had witnessed the agony of the Wessex King Ina, presented to after-ages as Lear. Gertrude Lodge talked most, Rhoda replying with monosyllabic preoccupation. She had a strange dislike to walking on the side of her companion where hung the afflicted arm, moving round to the other when inadvertently near it. Much heather had been brushed by their feet when they descended upon a cart track, beside which stood the house of the man they sought.

He did not profess his remedial practices openly, or care anything about their continuance, his direct interests being those of a dealer in furze,[10] turf, 'sharp sand' and other local products. Indeed, he affected not to believe largely in his own powers, and when warts that had been shown him for cure miraculously disappeared – which it must be owned they infallibly did – he would say lightly, 'Oh, I only drink a glass of grog upon 'em at your expense – perhaps it's all chance,' and immediately turn the subject.

He was at home when they arrived, having in fact seen them descending into his valley. He was a grey-bearded man, with a reddish face, and he looked singularly at Rhoda the first moment he beheld her. Mrs Lodge told him her errand; and then with words of self-disparagement he examined her arm.

'Medicine can't cure it,' he said, promptly. ' 'Tis the work of an enemy.'

Rhoda shrank into herself, and drew back.

'An enemy? What enemy?' asked Mrs Lodge.

He shook his head. 'That's best known to yourself,' he said. 'If you like I can show the person to you, though I shall not myself know who it is. I can do no more; and don't wish to do that.'

She pressed him; on which he told Rhoda to wait outside where she stood, and took Mrs Lodge into the room. It opened immediately from the door; and, as the latter remained ajar, Rhoda Brook could see the proceedings without taking part in them. He brought a tumbler from the dresser, nearly filled it with water, and fetching an egg, prepared it in some private way; after which he broke it on the edge of the glass, so that the white went in and the yolk remained. As it was getting gloomy, he took the glass and its contents to the window, and told Gertrude to watch the mixture closely. They leant over the table together, and the milkwoman could see the opaline hue of the egg fluid changing form as it sank in the water, but she was not near enough to define the shape that it assumed.

'Do you catch the likeness of any face or figure as you look?' demanded the conjuror of the young woman.

She murmured a reply, in tones so low as to be inaudible to Rhoda, and continued to gaze intently into the glass. Rhoda turned, and walked a few steps away.

When Mrs Lodge came out, and her face was met by the light, it appeared exceedingly pale – as pale as Rhoda's – against the sad dun shades of the upland's garniture.[11] Trendle shut the door behind her, and they at once started homeward together. But Rhoda perceived that her companion had quite changed.

'Did he charge much?' she asked, tentatively.

'Oh no – nothing. He would not take a farthing,' said Gertrude.

'And what did you see?' inquired Rhoda.

'Nothing I – care to speak of.' The constraint in her manner was remarkable, her face was so rigid as to wear an oldened aspect, faintly suggestive of the face in Rhoda's bedchamber.

'Was it you who first proposed coming here?' Mrs Lodge suddenly enquired, after a long pause. 'How very odd, if you did.'

'No. But I am not sorry we have come, all things considered,' she replied. For the first time a sense of triumph possessed her, and she did not altogether deplore that the young thing at her side should learn that their lives had been antagonised by other influences than their own.

The subject was no more alluded to during the long and dreary walk home. But in some way or other a story was whispered about the many-dairied lowland that winter that Mrs Lodge's gradual loss of the use of her left arm was owing to her being 'over-looked' by Rhoda Brook. The latter kept her own counsel about the incubus, but her face grew sadder and thinner; and in the spring she and her boy disappeared from the neighbourhood of Holmstoke.

VI

A SECOND ATTEMPT

Half a dozen years passed away, and Mr and Mrs Lodge's married experience sank into prosiness,[12] and worse. The farmer was usually gloomy and silent: the woman whom he had wooed for her grace and beauty was contorted and disfigured in the left limb; moreover, she had brought him no child, which rendered it likely that he would be the last of a family who had occupied that valley for some two hundred years. He thought of Rhoda Brook and her son; and feared this might be a judgement from heaven upon him.

The once blithe-hearted and enlightened Gertrude was changing into an irritable, superstitious woman, whose whole time was given to experimenting upon her ailment with every quack remedy she came across. She was honestly attached to her husband, and was ever secretly hoping against hope to win back his heart again by regaining some at least of her personal beauty. Hence it arose that her closet was lined with bottles, packets, and ointment-pots of every description – nay, bunches of mystic herbs, charms, and books of necromancy, which in her schoolgirl time she would have ridiculed as folly.

'Damned if you won't poison yourself with these apothecary messes and witch mixtures some time or other,' said her husband, when his eye chanced to fall upon the multitudinous array.

She did not reply, but turned her sad soft glance upon him in such heart-swollen reproach that he looked sorry for his words, and added, 'I only meant it for your good, you know, Gertrude.'

'I'll clear out the whole lot, and destroy them,' said she, huskily, 'and try such remedies no more!'

'You want somebody to cheer you,' he observed. 'I once thought of adopting a boy; but he is too old now. And he is gone away I don't know where.'

She guessed to whom he alluded; for Rhoda Brook's story had in the course of years become known to her; though not a word had ever passed between her husband and herself on the subject. Neither had she ever spoken to him of her visit to Conjuror Trendle, and of what was revealed to her, or she thought was revealed to her, by that solitary heath-man.

She was now five-and-twenty; but she seemed older. 'Six years of marriage, and only a few months of love,' she sometimes whispered to herself. And then she thought of the apparent cause, and said, with a tragic glance at her withering limb, 'If I could only again be as I was when he first saw me!'

She obediently destroyed her nostrums[13] and charms; but there remained a hankering wish to try something else – some other sort of cure altogether. She had never revisited Trendle since she had been conducted to the house of the solitary by Rhoda against her will; but it now suddenly occurred to Gertrude that she would, in a last desperate effort at deliverance from this seeming curse, again seek out the man, if he yet lived. He was entitled to a certain credence, for the indistinct form he had raised in the glass had undoubtedly resembled the only woman in the world who – as she now knew, though not then – could have a reason for bearing her ill-will. The visit should be paid.

This time she went alone, though she nearly got lost on the heath, and roamed a considerable distance out of her way. Trendle's house was reached at last, however: he was not indoors, and instead of waiting at the cottage she went to where his bent figure was pointed out to her at work a long way off. Trendle remembered her, and laying down the handful of furze-roots which he was gathering and throwing into a heap, he offered to accompany her in her homeward direction, as the distance was considerable and the days were short. So they walked together, his head bowed nearly to the earth, and his form of a colour with it.

'You can send away warts and other excrescences, I know,' she said; 'why can't you send away this?' And the arm was uncovered.

'You think too much of my powers!' said Trendle; 'and I am old and weak now, too. No, no; it is too much for me to attempt in my own person. What have ye tried?'

She named to him some of the hundred medicaments and counter-spells which she had adopted from time to time. He shook his head.

'Some were good enough,' he said, approvingly; 'but not many of them for such as this. This is of the nature of a blight, not of the nature of a wound; and if you ever do throw it off, it will be all at once.'

'If I only could!'

'There is only one chance of doing it known to me. It has never failed in kindred afflictions – that I can declare. But it is hard to carry out, and especially for a woman.'

'Tell me!' said she.

'You must touch with the limb the neck of a man who's been hanged.'

She started a little at the image he had raised.

'Before he's cold – just after he's cut down,' continued the conjuror, impassively.

'How can that do good?'

'It will turn the blood and change the constitution. But, as I say, to do it is hard. You must go to the jail when there's a hanging, and wait for him when he's brought off the gallows. Lots have done it, though perhaps not such pretty women as you. I used to send dozens for skin complaints. But that was in former times. The last I sent was in '13 – near twelve years ago.'

He had no more to tell her; and, when he had put her into a straight track homeward, turned and left her, refusing all money as at first.

VII

A RIDE

The communication sank deep into Gertrude's mind. Her nature was rather a timid one; and probably of all remedies that the white wizard could have suggested there was not one which would have filled her with so much aversion as this, not to speak of the immense obstacles in the way of its adoption.

Casterbridge, the county-town, was a dozen or fifteen miles off; and though in those days, when men were executed for horse-stealing, arson and burglary, an assize seldom passed without a hanging, it was not likely that she could get access to the body of the criminal unaided. And the fear of her husband's anger made her reluctant to breathe a word of Trendle's suggestion to him or to anybody about him.

She did nothing for months, and patiently bore her disfigurement as before. But her woman's nature, craving for renewed love, through the medium of renewed beauty (she was but twenty-five), was ever stimulating her to try what, at any rate, could hardly do her any harm. 'What came by a spell will go by a spell surely,' she would say. Whenever her imagination pictured the act she shrank in terror from the possibility of it; when the words of the conjuror, 'It will turn your blood,' were seen to be capable of a scientific no less than a ghastly interpretation, the mastering desire returned, and urged her on again.

There was at this time but one county paper, and that her husband only occasionally borrowed. But old-fashioned days had old-fashioned means, and news was extensively conveyed by word of mouth from market to market or from fair to fair; so that, whenever such an event as an execution was about to take place, few within a radius of twenty miles were ignorant of the coming sight; and, so far as Holmstoke was concerned, some enthusiasts had been known to walk all the way to Casterbridge and back in one day, solely to witness the spectacle. The next assizes were in March; and when Gertrude Lodge heard that they had been held, she enquired stealthily at the inn as to the result, as soon as she could find opportunity.

She was, however, too late. The time at which the sentences were to be carried out had arrived, and to make the journey and obtain admission at such short notice required at least her husband's assistance. She dared not tell him, for she had found by delicate experiment that these smouldering village beliefs made him furious if mentioned, partly because he half entertained them himself. It was therefore necessary to wait for another opportunity.

Her determination received a fillip from learning that two epileptic children had attended from this very village of Holmstoke many years before with beneficial results, though the experiment had been strongly condemned by the neighbouring clergy. April, May, June passed; and it is no overstatement to say that by the end of the last-named month Gertrude wellnigh longed for the death of a fellow-creature. Instead of her formal prayers each night, her unconscious prayer was, 'O Lord, hang some guilty or innocent person soon!'

This time she made earlier enquiries, and was altogether more systematic in her proceedings. Moreover, the season was summer, between the haymaking and the harvest, and in the leisure thus afforded him her husband had been holiday-taking away from home.

The assizes were in July, and she went to the inn as before. There was to be one execution – only one, for arson.

Her greatest problem was not how to get to Casterbridge, but what means she should adopt for obtaining admission to the jail. Though access for such purposes had formerly never been denied, the custom had fallen into desuetude;[14] and in contemplating her possible difficulties, she was again almost driven to fall back upon her husband. But, on sounding him about the assizes, he was so uncommunicative, so more than usually cold, that she did not proceed, and decided that whatever she did she would do alone.

Fortune, obdurate hitherto, showed her unexpected favour. On the Thursday before the Saturday fixed for the execution, Lodge remarked to her that he was going away from home for another day or two on business at a fair, and that he was sorry he could not take her with him.

She exhibited on this occasion so much readiness to stay at home that he looked at her in surprise. Time had been when she would have shown deep disappointment at the loss of such a jaunt. However, he lapsed into his usual taciturnity, and on the day named left Holmstoke.

It was now her turn. She at first had thought of driving, but on reflection held that driving would not do, since it would necessitate her keeping to the turnpike-road, and so increase by tenfold the risk of her ghastly errand being found out. She decided to ride, and avoid the beaten track, notwithstanding that in her husband's stables there was no animal just at present which by any stretch of imagination could be considered a lady's mount, in spite of his promise before marriage always to keep a mare for her. He had, however, many cart-horses, fine ones of their kind; and among the rest was a serviceable creature, an equine Amazon, with a back as broad as a sofa, on which Gertrude had occasionally taken an airing when unwell. This horse she chose.

On Friday afternoon one of the men brought it round. She was dressed, and before going down looked at her shrivelled arm. 'Ah!' she said to it, 'if it had not been for you this terrible ordeal would have been saved me!'

When strapping up the bundle in which she carried a few articles of clothing, she took occasion to say to the servant, 'I take these in case I should not get back tonight from the person I am going to visit. Don't be alarmed if I am not in by ten, and close up the house as usual. I shall be at home tomorrow for certain.' She meant then to tell her husband privately: the deed accomplished was not like the deed projected. He would almost certainly forgive her.

And then the pretty palpitating Gertrude Lodge went from her husband's homestead; but though her goal was Casterbridge she did not take the direct route thither through Stickleford. Her cunning course at first was in precisely the opposite direction. As soon as she was out of sight, however, she turned to the left, by a road which led into Egdon, and on entering the heath wheeled round, and set out in the true course, due westerly. A more private way down the county could not be imagined; and as to direction, she had merely to keep her horse's head to a point a little to the right of the sun. She knew that she would light upon a furze-cutter or cottager of some sort from time to time, from whom she might correct her bearing.

Though the date was comparatively recent, Egdon was much less fragmentary in character than now. The attempts – successful and otherwise – at cultivation on the lower slopes, which intrude and break up the original heath into small detached heaths, had not been carried far: Enclosure Acts had not taken effect, and the banks and fences which now exclude the cattle of those villagers who formerly enjoyed rights of commonage[15] thereon, and the carts of those who had turbary[16] privileges which kept them in firing all the year round, were not erected. Gertrude therefore rode along with no other obstacles than the prickly furze-bushes, the mats of heather, the white watercourses, and the natural steeps and declivities of the ground.

Her horse was sure, if heavy-footed and slow, and though a draught animal,[17] was easy-paced; had it been otherwise, she was not a woman who could have ventured to ride over such a bit of country with a half-dead arm. It was therefore nearly eight o'clock when she drew rein to breathe her bearer on the last outlying high point of heathland towards Casterbridge, previous to leaving Egdon for the cultivated valleys.

She halted before a pool called Rushy Pond, flanked by the ends of two hedges; a railing ran through the centre of the pond, dividing it in half. Over the railing she saw the low green country; over the green trees the roofs of the town; over the roofs a white flat façade, denoting the entrance to the county jail. On the roof of this front, specks were moving about; they seemed to be workmen erecting something. Her flesh crept. She descended slowly, and was soon amid cornfields and pastures. In another half-hour, when it was almost dusk, Gertrude reached the White Hart, the first inn of the town on that side.

Little surprise was excited by her arrival: farmers' wives rode on horseback then more than they do now; though for that matter, Mrs Lodge was not imagined to be a wife at all; the innkeeper supposed her some harum-scarum young woman who had come to attend 'hang-fair' next day. Neither her husband nor herself ever dealt in Casterbridge market, so that she was unknown. While dismounting she beheld a crowd of boys standing at the door of a harness-maker's shop just above the inn, looking inside it with deep interest.

'What is going on there?' she asked of the ostler.

'Making the rope for tomorrow.'

She throbbed responsively, and contracted her arm.

' 'Tis sold by the inch afterwards,' the man continued. 'I could get you a bit, miss, for nothing, if you'd like?'

She hastily repudiated any such wish, all the more from a curious creeping feeling that the condemned wretch's destiny was becoming interwoven with her own; and having engaged a room for the night, sat down to think.

Up to this time she had formed but the vaguest notions about her means of obtaining access to the prison. The words of the cunning man returned to her mind. He had implied that she should use her beauty, impaired though it was, as a pass-key. In her inexperience she knew little about jail functionaries; she had heard of a high sheriff and an under-sheriff, but dimly only. She knew, however, that there must be a hangman, and to the hangman she determined to apply.

VIII

A WATERSIDE HERMIT

At this date, and for several years after, there was a hangman to almost every jail. Gertrude found, on enquiry, that the Casterbridge official dwelt in a lonely cottage by a deep slow river flowing under the cliff on which the prison buildings were situate – the stream being the self-same one, though she did not know it, which watered the Stickleford and Holmstoke meads lower down in its course.

Having changed her dress, and before she had eaten or drunk – for she could not take her ease till she had ascertained some particulars – Gertrude pursued her way by a path along the waterside to the cottage indicated. Passing thus the outskirts of the jail, she discerned on the level roof over the gateway three rectangular lines against the sky, where the specks had been moving in her distant view; she recognised what the erection was, and passed quickly on. Another hundred yards brought her to the executioner's house, which a boy pointed out. It stood close to the same stream, and was hard by a weir, the waters of which emitted a steady roar.

While she stood hesitating the door opened, and an old man came forth shading a candle with one hand. Locking the door on the outside, he turned to a flight of wooden steps fixed against the end of the cottage, and began to ascend them, this being evidently the staircase to his bedroom. Gertrude hastened forward, but by the time she reached the foot of the ladder he was at the top. She called to him loudly enough to be heard above the roar of the weir; he looked down and said, 'What d'ye want here?'

'To speak to you a minute.'

The candlelight, such as it was, fell upon her imploring, pale, up-turned face, and Davies (as the hangman was called) backed down the ladder. 'I was just going to bed,' he said; ' "Early to bed and early to rise," but I don't mind stopping a minute for such a one as you. Come into house.' He reopened the door, and preceded her to the room within.

The implements of his daily work, which was that of a jobbing gardener, stood in a corner, and seeing probably that she looked rural, he said, 'If you want me to undertake country work I can't come, for I never leave Casterbridge for gentle nor simple – not I. My real calling is officer of justice,' he added formally.

'Yes, yes! That's it! Tomorrow!'

'Ah! I thought so. Well, what's the matter about that? 'Tis no use to come here about the knot – folks do come continually, but I tell 'em one knot is as merciful as another if ye keep it under the ear. Is the unfortunate man a relation; or, I should say, perhaps' (looking at her dress) 'a person who's been in your employ?'

'No. What time is the execution?'

'The same as usual – twelve o'clock, or as soon after as the London mail-coach gets in. We always wait for that, in case of a reprieve.'

'Oh – a reprieve – I hope not!' she said involuntarily.

'Well – hee, hee! – as a matter of business, so do I! But still, if ever a young fellow deserved to be let off, this one does; only just turned eighteen, and only present by chance when the rick was fired. Howsomever, there's not much risk of it, as they are obliged to make an example of him, there having been so much destruction of property that way lately.'

'I mean,' she explained, 'that I want to touch him for a charm, a cure of an affliction, by the advice of a man who has proved the virtue of the remedy.'

'Oh yes, miss! Now I understand. I've had such people come in past years. But it didn't strike me that you looked of a sort to require blood-turning. What's the complaint? The wrong kind for this, I'll be bound.'

'My arm.' She reluctantly showed the withered skin.

'Ah! – 'tis all a-scram!' said the hangman, examining it.

'Yes,' said she.

'Well,' he continued with interest, 'that *is* the class o' subject, I'm bound to admit. I like the look of the wownd; it is truly as suitable for the cure as any I ever saw. 'Twas a knowing man that sent 'ee, whoever he was.'

'You can contrive for me all that's necessary?' she said, breathlessly.

'You should really have gone to the governor of the jail, and your doctor with 'ee, and given your name and address – that's how it used to be done, if I recollect. Still, perhaps, I can manage it for a trifling fee.'

'Oh, thank you! I would rather do it this way, as I should like it kept private.'

'Lover not to know, eh?'

'No – husband.'

'Aha! Very well. I'll get 'ee a touch of the corpse.'

'Where is it now?' she said, shuddering.

'It? – *he*, you mean; he's living yet. Just inside that little small winder up there in the glum.' He signified the jail on the cliff above.

She thought of her husband and her friends. 'Yes, of course,' she said; 'and how am I to proceed?'

He took her to the door. 'Now, do you be waiting at the little wicket in the wall, that you'll find up there in the lane, not later than one o'clock. I will open it from the inside, as I shan't come home to dinner till he's cut down. Good-night. Be punctual; and if you don't want anybody to know 'ee, wear a veil. Ah – once I had such a daughter as you!'

She went away, and climbed the path above, to assure herself that she would be able to find the wicket next day. Its outline was soon visible to her – a narrow opening in the outer wall of the prison precincts. The steep was so great that, having reached the wicket, she stopped a moment to breathe; and looking back upon the waterside cot, saw the hangman again ascending his outdoor staircase. He entered the loft or chamber to which it led, and in a few minutes extinguished his light.

The town clock struck ten, and she returned to the White Hart as she had come.

IX

A RENCOUNTER[18]

It was one o'clock on Saturday. Gertrude Lodge, having been admitted to the jail as above described, was sitting in a waiting-room within the second gate, which stood under a classic archway of ashlar, then comparatively modern, and bearing the inscription, 'COVNTY GAOL: 1793'. This had been the façade she saw from the heath the day before. Near at hand was a passage to the roof on which the gallows stood.

The town was thronged, and the market suspended; but Gertrude had seen scarcely a soul. Having kept her room till the hour of the appointment, she had proceeded to the spot by a way which avoided the open space below the cliff where the spectators had gathered; but she could, even now, hear the multitudinous babble of their voices, out of which rose at intervals the hoarse croak of a single voice, uttering the words, 'Last dying speech and confession!' There had been no reprieve, and the execution was over; but the crowd still waited to see the body taken down.

Soon the persistent woman heard a trampling overhead, then a hand beckoned to her, and, following directions, she went out and crossed the inner paved court beyond the gatehouse, her knees trembling so that she could scarcely walk. One of her arms was out of its sleeve, and only covered by her shawl.

On the spot at which she had now arrived were two trestles, and before she could think of their purpose she heard heavy feet descending stairs somewhere at her back. Turn her head she would not, or could not, and, rigid in this position, she was conscious of a rough coffin passing her shoulder, borne by four men. It was open, and in it lay the body of a young man, wearing the smockfrock of a rustic, and fustian breeches. The corpse had been thrown into the coffin so hastily that the skirt of the smockfrock was hanging over. The burden was temporarily deposited on the trestles.

By this time the young woman's state was such that a grey mist seemed to float before her eyes, on account of which, and the veil she wore, she could scarcely discern anything: it was as though she had nearly died, but was held up by a sort of galvanism.

'Now,' said a voice close at hand, and she was just conscious that the word had been addressed to her.

By a last strenuous effort she advanced, at the same time hearing persons approaching behind her. She bared her poor curst arm; and Davies, uncovering the face of the corpse, took Gertrude's hand, and held it so that her arm lay across the dead man's neck, upon a line the colour of an unripe blackberry, which surrounded it.

Gertrude shrieked; 'the turn o' the blood', predicted by the conjuror, had taken place. But at that moment a second shriek rent the air of the enclosure: it was not Gertrude's, and its effect upon her was to make her start round.

Immediately behind her stood Rhoda Brook, her face drawn, and her eyes red with weeping. Behind Rhoda stood Gertrude's own husband: his countenance lined, his eyes dim, but without a tear.

'Damn you! what are you doing here?' he said, hoarsely.

'Hussy – to come between us and our child now!' cried Rhoda. 'This is the meaning of what Satan showed me in the vision! You are like her at last!' And clutching the bare arm of the younger woman, she pulled her unresistingly back against the wall. Immediately Brook had loosened her hold the fragile young Gertrude slid down against the feet of her husband. When he lifted her up she was unconscious.

The mere sight of the twain had been enough to suggest to her that the dead young man was Rhoda's son. At that time the relatives of an executed convict had the privilege of claiming the body for burial, if they chose to do so; and it was for this purpose that Lodge was awaiting the inquest with Rhoda. He had been summoned by her as soon as the young man was taken in the crime, and at different times since; and he had attended in court during the trial. This was the 'holiday' he had been indulging in of late. The two wretched parents had wished to avoid exposure; and hence had come themselves for the body, a waggon and sheet for its conveyance and covering being in waiting outside.

Gertrude's case was so serious that it was deemed advisable to call to her the surgeon who was at hand. She was taken out of the jail into the town; but she never reached home alive. Her delicate vitality, sapped perhaps by the paralysed arm, collapsed under the double shock that followed the severe strain, physical and mental, to which she had subjected herself during the previous twenty-four hours. Her blood had been 'turned' indeed – too far. Her death took place in the town three days after.

Her husband was never seen in Casterbridge again; once only in the old market-place at Anglebury, which he had so much frequented, and very seldom in public anywhere. Burdened at first with moodiness and remorse, he eventually changed for the better, and appeared as a chastened and thoughtful man. Soon after attending the funeral of his poor young wife, he took steps towards giving up the farms in Holmstoke and the adjoining parish, and, having sold every head of his stock, he went away to Port-Bredy, at the other end of the county, living there in solitary lodgings till his death two years later of a painless decline. It was then found that he had bequeathed the whole of his not inconsiderable property to a reformatory for boys, subject to the payment of a small annuity to Rhoda Brook, if she could be found to claim it.

For some time she could not be found; but eventually she reappeared in her old parish – absolutely refusing, however, to have anything to do with the provision made for her. Her monotonous milking at the dairy was resumed, and followed for many long years, till her form became bent, and her once abundant dark hair white and worn away at the forehead – perhaps by long pressure against the cows. Here, sometimes, those who knew her experiences would stand and observe her, and wonder what sombre thoughts were beating inside that impassive, wrinkled brow, to the rhythm of the alternating milk-streams.

WILKIE COLLINS

WILLIAM WILKIE COLLINS (1824–89) was the eldest son of the
landscape painter William Collins. In 1846, having spent five years in
the tea business, he entered the legal profession and read for the bar
at Lincoln's Inn. It was here that he gained the experience of the law,
the practitioners of it and those individuals who fall under its power,
which gave him much of his material for his writing.

He became a close friend of Charles Dickens, contributing stories
to Dickens's own magazine, *Household Words*. Wilkie Collins was the
first Englishman to write a full-length detective novel, *The Moon-
stone*. His other most famous work, *The Woman in White*, is a mystery
novel with the kind of bizarre elements and strange characters that
appealed to the author. The same nightmarish quality which
pervades much of this novel can be found in 'A Terribly Strange
Bed', which is set on the seamier side of Paris in the middle of the
nineteenth century.

The story begins casually enough: the narrator, a young
Englishman who has finished his formal education, seeks excitement
in one of the gambling houses in Paris. He does not want the artificial
glamour of the more fashionable upmarket establishments but
prefers the appeal of the rough and ready houses where 'they don't
mind letting a man in with a ragged coat'. We would call this kind of
behaviour 'slumming'. However, in rejecting one form of
artificiality, he is lured into accepting another. He persuades his
friend to accompany him and we know as soon as they enter this
lowly gaming house that things are not as they should be. By his
careful description of the place and the characters the young men
encounter there, Collins creates a mood of unease and strangeness
that both intrigues and repels the reader. We know that the narrator
is in peril but we cannot fathom which form it will take until it is
almost too late.

The oddness of the situation, the apparent innocence of the
storyteller and the sense of menace draw the reader into this surreal
tale until he is completely engrossed and cannot put it down until it is

finished. Ideas on the nature of friendship, risk and gullibility are all explored in this deceptively simple but unsettling short story.

The Terribly Strange Bed

SHORTLY AFTER MY EDUCATION at college was finished, I happened to be staying at Paris with an English friend. We were both young men then, and lived, I am afraid, rather a wild life, in the delightful city of our sojourn. One night we were idling about the neighbourhood of the Palais Royal, doubtful to what amusement we should next betake ourselves. My friend proposed a visit to Frascati's; but his suggestion was not to my taste. I knew Frascati's, as the French saying is, by heart; had lost and won plenty of five-franc pieces there, merely for amusement's sake, until it was amusement no longer, and was thoroughly tired, in fact, of all the ghastly respectabilities of such a social anomaly as a respectable gambling-house. 'For heaven's sake,' said I to my friend, 'let us go somewhere where we can see a little genuine, blackguard,[1] poverty-stricken gaming, with no false gingerbread glitter thrown over it at all. Let us get away from fashionable Frascati's to a house where they don't mind letting in a man with a ragged coat, or a man with no coat, ragged or otherwise.'

'Very well,' said my friend, 'we needn't go out of the Palais Royal to find the sort of company you want. Here's the place just before us: as blackguard a place, by all report, as you could possibly wish to see.' In another minute we arrived at the door, and entered the house,

When we got upstairs, and had left our hats and sticks with the doorkeeper, we were admitted into the chief gambling-room. We did not find many people assembled there. But, few as the men were who looked up at us on our entrance, they were all types – lamentably true types – of their respective classes.

We had come to see blackguards; but these men were something worse. There is a comic side, more or less appreciable, in all blackguardism – here there was nothing but tragedy – mute, weird tragedy. The quiet in the room was horrible. The thin, haggard, long-haired young man, whose sunken eyes fiercely watched the turning up of the cards, never spoke; the flabby, fat-faced, pimply player who pricked his piece of pasteboard[2] perseveringly, to register how often black won and how often red – never spoke; the dirty, wrinkled old man, with the vulture eyes and the darned greatcoat, who had lost his last *sou* [3] and still looked on desperately after he could play no longer – never spoke. Even the voice of the croupier sounded as if it were strangely dulled and thickened in the atmosphere of the room. I had entered the place to laugh, but the spectacle before me was something to weep over. I soon found it necessary to take refuge in excitement from the depression of spirits which was fast stealing on me. Unfortunately I sought the nearest excitement, by going to the table, and beginning to play. Still more unfortunately, as the event will show, I won – won prodigiously; won incredibly; won at such a rate that the regular players at the table crowded round me, and, staring at my stakes with hungry, superstitious eyes, whispered to one another that the English stranger was going to break the bank.

The game was Rouge et Noir. I had played at it in every city in Europe, without, however, the care or the wish to study the Theory of Chances – that philosopher's stone of all gamblers! And a gambler, in the strict sense of the word, I had never been. I was heart-whole from the corroding passion for play. My gaming was a mere idle amusement. I never resorted to it by necessity, because I never knew what it was to want money. I never practised it so incessantly as to lose more than I could afford, or to gain more than I could coolly pocket without being thrown off my balance by my good luck. In short, I had hitherto frequented gambling-tables just as I frequented ballrooms and opera-houses – because they amused me, and because I had nothing better to do with my leisure hours.

But on this occasion it was very different – now, for the first time in my life, I felt what the passion for play really was. My success first bewildered, and then, in the most literal meaning of the word, intoxicated me. Incredible as it may appear, it is nevertheless true that I only lost when I attempted to estimate chances and played according to previous calculation. If I left everything to luck, and staked without any care or consideration, I was sure to win – to win in the face of every recognised probability in favour of the bank. At first, some of the men present ventured their money safely enough on my colour; but I speedily increased my stakes to sums which they dared not risk. One after another they left off playing, and breathlessly looked on at my game.

Still, time after time, I staked higher and higher, and still won. The excitement in the room rose to fever pitch. The silence was interrupted by a deep-muttered chorus of oaths and exclamations in different languages every time the gold was shovelled across to my side of the table – even the imperturbable croupier dashed his rake to the floor in a (French) fury of astonishment at my success. But one man present preserved his self-possession; and that man was my friend. He came to my side and, whispering in English, begged me to leave the place, satisfied with what I had already gained. I must do him the justice to say that he repeated his warnings and entreaties several times, and only left me and went away after I had rejected his advice (I was to all intents and purposes gambling-drunk) in terms which rendered it impossible for him to address me again that night.

Shortly after he had gone, a hoarse voice behind me cried: 'Permit me, my dear sir! – permit me to restore to their proper place two Napoleons which you have dropped. Wonderful luck, sir! I pledge you my word of honour, as an old soldier, in the course of my long experience in this sort of thing, I never saw such luck as yours! – never! Go on, sir – *sacré mille bombes!*[4] Go on boldly, and break the bank!'

I turned round and saw, nodding and smiling at me with inveterate civility, a tall man, dressed in a frogged and braided surtout.[5]

If I had been in my senses, I should have considered him, personally, as being rather a suspicious specimen of an old soldier. He had goggling bloodshot eyes, mangy mustachios and a broken nose. His voice betrayed a barrack-room intonation of the worst order, and he had the dirtiest pair of hands I ever saw – even in France. These little personal peculiarities exercised, however, no repelling influence on me.

In the mad excitement, the reckless triumph of that moment, I was ready to 'fraternise' with anybody who encouraged me in my game. I accepted the old soldier's offered pinch of snuff, clapped him on the back, and swore he was the honestest fellow in the world – the most glorious relic of the Grand Army that I had ever met with, 'Go on!' cried my military friend, snapping his fingers in ecstasy – 'Go on and win! Break the bank – *mille tonnerres!* my gallant English comrade, break the bank!'

And I *did* go on – went on at such a rate that in another quarter of an hour the croupier called out: 'Gentlemen the bank has discontinued for tonight.' All the notes, all the gold in that 'bank' now lay in a heap under my hands; the whole floating capital of the gambling-house was waiting to pour into my pockets!

'Tie up the money in your pocket-handkerchief, my worthy sir,' said the old soldier, as I wildly plunged my hands into my heap of gold. 'Tie it up, as we used to tie up a bit of dinner in the Grand Army; your winnings are too heavy for any breeches pockets that ever were sewed. There! that's it! – shovel them in, notes and all! *Crediê!*

what luck – Stop! another Napoleon on the floor! *Ah! sacré petit polisson de Napoléon!* have I found thee at last? Now then, sir – two tight double knots each way with your honourable permission, and the money's safe. Feel it! feel it, fortunate sir! hard and round as a cannon ball – *ah, bah!* if they had only fired such cannon balls at us at Austerlitz – *nom d'une pipe!* if they only had! And now, as an ancient grenadier, as an ex-brave of the French Army, what remains for me to do? I ask what? Simply this: to entreat my valued English friend to drink a bottle of champagne with me and toast the goddess Fortune in foaming goblets before we part!'

Excellent ex-brave! Convivial ancient grenadier! Champagne by all means! An English cheer for an old soldier! Hurrah! hurrah! Another English cheer for the goddess Fortune! Hurrah! hurrah! hurrah!

'Bravo! the Englishman; the amiable, gracious Englishman, in whose veins circulates the vivacious blood of France! Another glass? *Ah, bah!* – the bottle is empty! Never mind! *Vive le vin!* I, the old soldier, order another bottle, and half a pound of *bonbons* with it!'

'No, no, ex-brave; never – ancient grenadier! *Your* bottle last time; *my* bottle this. Behold it! Toast away! The French Army! – the great Napoleon! – the present company! the croupier! the honest croupier's wife and daughters – if he has any! the Ladies generally! Everybody in the world!'

By the time the second bottle of champagne was emptied, I felt as if I had been drinking liquid fire – my brain seemed all aflame. No excess in wine ever had this effect on me before in my life. Was it the result of a stimulant acting upon my system when I was in a highly excited state? Was my stomach in a particularly disordered condition? Or was the champagne amazingly strong?

'Ex-brave of the French Army!' cried I, in a mad state of exhilaration, '*I* am on fire! how are *you?* You have set me on fire! Do you hear, my hero of Austerlitz? Let us have a third bottle of champagne to put the flame out!'

The old soldier wagged his head; rolled his goggle eyes, until I expected to see them slip out of their sockets; placed his dirty forefinger by the side of his broken nose; solemnly ejaculated, 'Coffee!' and immediately ran off into an inner room.

The word pronounced by the eccentric veteran seemed to have a magical effect on the rest of the company present. With one accord they all rose to depart. Probably they had expected to profit by my intoxication; but, finding that my new friend was benevolently bent on preventing me from getting dead drunk, had now abandoned all hope of thriving pleasantly on my winnings. Whatever their motive might be, at any rate they went away in a body. When the old soldier returned, and sat down again opposite to me at the table, we had the room to ourselves. I could see the croupier, in a sort of vestibule which opened out of it, eating his supper in solitude. The silence was now deeper than ever.

A sudden change, too, had come over the 'ex-brave'. He assumed a portentously solemn look and, when he spoke to me again, his speech was ornamented by no oaths, enforced by no finger-snapping, enlivened by no apostrophes or exclamations.

'Listen, my dear sir,' said he, in mysteriously confidential tones – 'listen to an old soldier's advice. I have been to the mistress of the house (a very charming woman, with a genius for cookery!) to impress on her the necessity of making us some particularly strong and good coffee. You must drain this coffee in order to get rid of your little amiable exaltation of spirits before you think of going home – you *must*, my good and gracious friend! With all that money to take home tonight, it is a sacred duty to yourself to have your wits about you. You are known to be a winner to an enormous extent by several gentlemen present tonight, who, in a certain point of view, are very worthy and excellent fellows, but they are mortal men, my dear sir, and they have their amiable weaknesses! Need I say more? Ah, no, no! you understand me! Now this is what you must do – send for a cabriolet when you feel quite well again – draw up all the windows when you get into it – and tell the driver to take you home only through the large and well-lighted thoroughfares. Do this; and you and your money will be safe. Do this; and tomorrow you will thank an old soldier for giving you a word of honest advice.'

Just as the ex-brave ended his oration in very lachrymose tones, the coffee came in, ready poured out in two cups. My attentive friend handed me one of the cups with a bow. I was parched with thirst, and drank it off at a draught. Almost instantly afterwards, I was seized with a fit of giddiness, and felt more completely intoxicated than ever. The room whirled round and round furiously; the old soldier seemed to be regularly bobbing up and down before me like the piston of a steam-engine. I was half deafened by a violent singing in my ears; a feeling of utter bewilderment, helplessness, idiocy, overcame me. I rose from my chair, holding on by the table to keep my balance, and stammered out that I felt dreadfully unwell – so unwell that I did not know how I was to get home.

'My dear friend,' answered the old soldier – and even his voice seemed to be bobbing up and down as he spoke – 'my dear friend, it would be madness to go home in *your* state; you would be sure to lose your money; you might be robbed and murdered with the greatest ease. *I* am going to sleep here. Do *you* sleep here, too – they make up capital beds in this house – take one; sleep off the effects of the wine, and go home safely with your winnings tomorrow – tomorrow, in broad daylight.'

I had but two ideas left – one, that I must never let go hold of my handkerchief full of money; the other, that I must lie down somewhere immediately, and fall off into comfortable sleep. So I agreed to the proposal about the bed and took the offered arm of the old soldier, carrying my money with my disengaged hand. Preceded by the croupier, we passed along some passages and up a flight of stairs into the bedroom which I was to occupy. The ex-brave shook me warmly by the hand, proposed that we should breakfast together, and then, followed by the croupier, left me for the night.

I ran to the wash-hand stand; drank some of the water in my jug; poured the rest out, and plunged my face into it; then sat down in a chair and tried to compose myself. I soon felt better. The change for my lungs, from the fetid atmosphere of the gambling-room to the cool air of the apartment I now occupied; the almost equally refreshing change for my eyes, from the glaring gaslights of the *salon* to the dim, quiet flicker of one bedroom candle, aided wonderfully the restorative effects of cold water. The giddiness left me, and I began to feel a little like a reasonable being again. My first thought was of the risk of sleeping all night in a gambling-house; my second, of the still greater risk of trying to get out after the house was closed, and of going home alone at night, through the streets of Paris, with a large sum of money about me. I had slept in worse places than this on my travels; so I determined to lock, bolt, and barricade my door, and take my chance till the next morning.

Accordingly, I secured myself against all intrusion; looked under the bed, and into the cupboard; tried the fastening of the window; and then, satisfied that I had taken every proper precaution, pulled off my upper clothing, put my light, which was a dim one, on the hearth among a feathery litter of wood ashes, and got into bed, with the handkerchief full of money under my pillow.

I soon felt not only that I could not go to sleep, but that I could not even close my eyes. I was wide awake, and in a high fever. Every nerve in my body trembled – every one of my senses seemed to be preternaturally sharpened. I tossed and rolled, and tried every kind of position, and perseveringly sought out the cold corners of the bed, and all to no purpose. Now, I thrust my arms over the clothes; now, I poked them under the clothes; now, I violently shot my legs straight out down to the bottom of the bed; now, I convulsively coiled them up as near my chin as they would go; now, I shook out my crumpled pillow, changed it to the cool side, patted it flat, and lay down quietly on my back; now, I fiercely doubled it in two, set it up on end, thrust it against the board of the bed, and tried a sitting posture. Every effort was in vain; I groaned with vexation, as I felt that I was in for a sleepless night.

What could I do? I had no book to read. And yet, unless I found out some method of diverting my mind, I felt certain that I was in the condition to imagine all sorts of horrors; to rack my brain with forebodings of every possible and impossible danger; in short, to pass the night in suffering all conceivable varieties of nervous terror.

I raised myself on my elbow, and looked about the room – which was brightened by a lovely moonlight pouring straight through the window – to see if it contained any pictures or ornaments that I could at all clearly distinguish. While my eyes wandered from wall to wall, a remembrance of Le Maistre's delightful little book, *Voyage autour de ma Chambre*,[6] occurred to me. I resolved to imitate the French author and find occupation and amusement enough to relieve the tedium of my wakefulness by making a mental inventory of every article of furniture I could see, and by following up to their sources the multitude of associations which even a chair, a table, or a wash-hand stand may be made to call forth.

In the nervous unsettled state of my mind at that moment, I found it much easier to make my inventory than to make my reflections, and thereupon soon gave up all hope of thinking in Le Maistre's fanciful track – or, indeed, of thinking at all. I looked about the room at the different articles of furniture, and did nothing more.

There was, first, the bed I was lying in: a four-post bed, of all things in the world to meet with in Paris! – yes, a thoroughly clumsy British four-poster, with the regular top lined with chintz – the regular fringed valance all around – the regular stifling unwholesome curtains, which I remembered having mechanically drawn back against the posts without particularly noticing the bed when I first got into the room. Then there was the marble-topped wash-hand stand, from which the water I had spilt, in my hurry to pour it out, was still dripping, slowly and more slowly, on to the brick floor. Then two small chairs, with my coat, waistcoat and trousers flung on them. Then a large elbow-chair covered with dirty-white dimity, with my cravat and shirt-collar thrown over the back. Then a chest of drawers, with two of the brass handles off and a tawdry, broken china inkstand placed on it by way of ornament for the top. Then the dressing-table, adorned by a very small looking-glass and a very large pin-cushion. Then the window – an unusually large window. Then a dark old picture, which the feeble candle dimly showed me. It was the picture of a fellow in a high Spanish hat, crowned with a plume of towering feathers. A swarthy sinister ruffian, looking upward, shading his eyes with his hand and looking intently upward – it might be at some tall gallows at which he was going to be hanged. At any rate, he had the appearance of thoroughly deserving it.

This picture put a kind of constraint upon me to look upward too – at the top of the bed. It was a gloomy and not an interesting object, and I looked back at the picture. I counted the feathers in the man's hat – they stood out in relief – three white, two green. I observed the crown of his hat, which was of a conical shape, according to the fashion supposed to have been favoured by Guido Fawkes. I wondered what he was looking up at. It couldn't be at the stars; such a desperado was neither astrologer nor astronomer. It must be at the high gallows, and he was going to be hanged presently. Would the executioner come into possession of his conical-crowned hat and plume of feathers? I counted the feathers again three white, two green.

While I still lingered over this very improving intellectual employment, my thoughts insensibly began to wander. The moonlight shining into the room reminded me of a certain moonlight night in England – the night after a picnic party in a Welsh valley. Every incident of the drive homeward, through lovely scenery, which the moonlight made lovelier than ever, came back to my remembrance, though I had never given the picnic a thought for years; though, if I had *tried* to recollect it, I could certainly have recalled little or nothing of that scene long past. Of all the wonderful faculties that help to tell us we are immortal, which speaks the sublime truth more eloquently than memory? Here was I, in a strange house of the most suspicious character, in a situation of uncertainty, and even of peril, which might seem to make the cool exercise of my recollection almost out of the question; nevertheless, remembering, quite involuntarily, places, people, conversations, minute circumstances of every kind, which I had thought forgotten for ever; which I could not possibly have recalled at will, even under the most favourable auspices. And what cause had produced in a moment the whole of this strange, complicated, mysterious effect? Nothing but some rays of moonlight shining in at my bedroom window.

I was still thinking of the picnic – of our merriment on the drive home – of the sentimental young lady who *would* quote *Childe Harold*[7] because it was moonlight. I was absorbed by these past scenes and past amusements, when, in an instant, the thread on which my memories hung snapped asunder; my attention immediately came back to present things more vividly than ever, and I found myself, I neither knew why nor wherefore, looking hard at the picture again.

Looking for what?

Good God! the man had pulled his hat down on his brows! – No! the hat itself was gone! Where was the conical crown? Where the feathers – three white, two green? Not there! In place of the hat and feathers, what dusky object was it that now hid his forehead, his eyes, his shading hand?

Was the bed moving?

I turned on my back and looked up. Was I mad? drunk? dreaming? giddy again? or was the top of the bed really moving down – sinking slowly, regularly, silently, horribly, right down throughout the whole of its length and breadth – right down upon me, as I lay underneath?

My blood seemed to stand still. A deadly paralysing coldness stole all over me as I turned my head round on the pillow and determined to test whether the bed-top was really moving or not by keeping my eye on the man in the picture.

The next look in that direction was enough. The dull, black, frowsy outline of the valance above me was within an inch of being parallel with his waist. I still looked breathlessly. And steadily, and slowly – very slowly – I saw the figure, and the line of frame below the figure, vanish, as the valance moved down before it.

I am, constitutionally, anything but timid. I have been on more than one occasion in peril of my life, and have not lost my self-possession for an instant; but when the conviction first settled on my mind that the bed-top was really moving, was steadily and continuously sinking down upon me, I looked up shuddering, helpless, panic-stricken, beneath the hideous machinery for murder which was advancing closer and closer to suffocate me where I lay.

I looked up, motionless, speechless, breathless. The candle, fully spent, went out; but the moonlight still brightened the room. Down and down, without pausing and without sounding, came the bed-top, and still my panic-terror seemed to bind me faster and faster to the mattress on which I lay – down and down it sank, till the dusty odour from the lining of the canopy came stealing into my nostrils.

At that final moment the instinct of self-preservation startled me out of my trance, and I moved at last. There was just room for me to roll myself sideways off the bed. As I dropped noiselessly to the floor, the edge of the murderous canopy touched me on the shoulder.

Without stopping to draw my breath, without wiping the cold

sweat from my face, I rose instantly on my knees to watch the bed-top. I was literally spellbound by it. If I had heard footsteps behind me, I could not have turned round; if a means of escape had been miraculously provided for me, I could not have moved to take advantage of it. The whole life in me was, at that moment, concentrated in my eyes.

It descended – the whole canopy, with the fringe round it, came down – down – close down; so close that there was not room now to squeeze my finger between the bed-top and the bed. I felt at the sides, and discovered that what had appeared to me from beneath to be the ordinary light canopy of a four-poster bed, was in reality a thick, broad mattress, the substance of which was concealed by the valance and its fringe. I looked up and saw the four posts rising, hideously bare. In the middle of the bed-top was a huge wooden screw that had evidently worked it down through a hole in the ceiling, just as ordinary presses are worked down on the substance selected for compression. The frightful apparatus moved without making the faintest noise. There had been no creaking as it came down; there was now not the faintest sound from the room above. Amid a dead and awful silence I beheld before me – in the nineteenth century, and in the civilised capital of France – such a machine for secret murder by suffocation as might have existed in the worst days of the Inquisition, in the lonely inns among the Hartz Mountains, in the mysterious tribunals of Westphalia! Still, as I looked on it, I could not move, I could hardly breathe, but I began to recover the power of thinking, and in a moment I discovered the murderous conspiracy framed against me in all its horror.

My cup of coffee had been drugged, and drugged too strongly. I had been saved from being smothered by having taken an overdose of some narcotic. How I had chafed and fretted at the fever-fit which had preserved my life by keeping me awake! How recklessly I had confided myself to the two wretches who had led me into this room, determined, for the sake of my winnings, to kill me in my sleep by the surest and most horrible contrivance for secretly accomplishing my destruction! How many men, winners like me, had slept, as I had proposed to sleep, in that bed, and had never been seen or heard of more! I shuddered at the bare idea of it.

But, ere long, all thought was again suspended by the sight of the murderous canopy moving once more. After it had remained on the bed – as nearly as I could guess – about ten minutes, it began to move up again. The villains who worked it from above evidently believed that their purpose was now accomplished. Slowly and silently, as it had descended, that horrible bed-top rose towards its former place. When it reached the upper extremities of the four posts, it reached the ceiling too. Neither hole nor screw could be seen; the bed became in appearance an ordinary bed again – the canopy an ordinary canopy – even to the most suspicious eyes.

Now, for the first time, I was able to move – to rise from my knees – to dress myself in my upper clothing – and to consider of how I should escape. If I betrayed, by the smallest noise, that the attempt to suffocate me had failed, I was certain to be murdered. Had I made any noise already? I listened intently, looking towards the door.

No! no footsteps in the passage outside – no sound of a tread, light or heavy, in the room above – absolute silence everywhere. Besides locking and bolting my door, I had moved an old wooden chest against it, which I had found under the bed. To remove this chest (my blood ran cold as I thought of what its contents might be!) without making some disturbance was impossible; and, moreover, to think of escaping through the house, now barred up for the night, was sheer insanity. Only one chance was left me – the window. I stole to it on tiptoe.

My bedroom was on the first floor, above an *entresol*,[8] and looked into the back street. I raised my hand to open the window, knowing that on that action hung, by the merest hair's-breadth, my chance of safety. They keep vigilant watch in a House of Murder. If any part of the frame cracked, if the hinge creaked, I was a lost man! It must have occupied me at least five minutes, reckoning by time – five *hours*, reckoning by suspense – to open that window. I succeeded in doing it silently – in doing it with all the dexterity of a housebreaker—and then looked down into the street. To leap the distance beneath me would be almost certain destruction! Next, I looked round at the sides of the house. Down the left side ran a thick waterpipe – it passed close by the outer edge of the window. The moment I saw the pipe, I knew I was saved. My breath came and went freely for the first time since I had seen the canopy of the bed moving down upon me!

To some men the means of escape which I had discovered might have seemed difficult and dangerous enough – to *me* the prospect of slipping down the pipe into the street did not suggest even a thought of peril. I had always been accustomed, by the practice of gymnastics, to keep up my schoolboy powers as a daring and expert climber; and knew that my head, hands and feet would serve me faithfully in any hazards of ascent or descent. I had already got one leg over the windowsill, when I remembered the handkerchief filled with money under my pillow. I could well have afforded to leave it behind me, but I was revengefully determined that the miscreants of the gambling-house should miss their plunder as well as their victim. So I went back to the bed and tied the heavy handkerchief at my back by my cravat.

Just as I had made it tight and fixed it in a comfortable place, I thought I heard a sound of breathing outside the door. The chill feeling of horror ran through me again as I listened. No! dead silence still in the passage – I had only heard the night air blowing softly into the room. The next moment I was on the windowsill – and the next I had a firm grip on the waterpipe with my hands and knees.

I slid down into the street easily and quietly, as I thought I should, and immediately set off at the top of my speed to a branch Prefecture[9] of Police, which I knew was situated in the immediate neighbourhood. A sub-prefect,[10] and several picked men among his subordinates, happened to be up, maturing, I believe, some scheme for discovering the perpetrator of a mysterious murder which all Paris was talking of just then. When I began my story, in a breathless hurry and in very bad French, I could see that the sub-prefect suspected me of being a drunken Englishman who had robbed somebody; but he soon altered his opinion as I went on, and before I had anything like concluded, he shoved all the papers before him into a drawer, put on his hat, supplied me with another (for I was bare-headed), ordered a file of soldiers, desired his expert followers to get ready all sorts of tools for breaking open doors and ripping up brick-flooring, and took my arm, in the most friendly and familiar manner possible, to lead me with him out of the house. I will venture to say that when the sub-prefect was a little boy, and was taken for the first time to the play, he was not half as much pleased as he was now at the job in prospect for him at the gambling-house!

Away we went through the streets, the sub-prefect cross-examining and congratulating me in the same breath as we marched at the head of our formidable *posse comitatus*.[11] Sentinels were placed at the back and front of the house the moment we got to it; a tremendous battery of knocks was directed against the door; a light appeared at a window; I was told to conceal myself behind the police – then came more knocks, and a cry of 'Open in the name of the law!' At that terrible summons, bolts and locks gave way before an invisible hand, and the moment after the sub-prefect was in the passage, confronting a waiter half-dressed and ghastly pale. This was the short dialogue which immediately took place –

'We want to see the Englishman who is sleeping in this house.'

'He went away hours ago.'

'He did no such thing. His friend went away; *he* remained. Show us to his bedroom!'

'I swear to you, Monsieur le Sous-Préfet, he is not here! he – '

'I swear to you, Monsieur le Garçon, he is. He slept here – he didn't find your bed comfortable – he came to us to complain of it – here he is among my men – and here am I ready to look for a flea or two in his bedstead. Renaudin!' (calling to one of the subordinates, and pointing to the waiter) 'collar that man, and tie his hands behind him. Now, then, gentlemen, let us walk upstairs!'

Every man and woman in the house was secured – the 'old soldier' the first. Then I identified the bed in which I had slept, and then we went into the room above.

No object that was at all extraordinary appeared in any part of it. The sub-prefect looked round the place, commanded everybody to be silent, stamped twice on the floor, called for a candle, looked attentively at the spot he had stamped on, and ordered the flooring there to be carefully taken up. This was done in no time. Lights were produced, and we saw a deep raftered cavity between the floor of this room and the ceiling of the room beneath. Through this cavity there ran perpendicularly a sort of case of iron thickly greased; and inside the case appeared the screw, which communicated with the bed-top below. Extra lengths of screw, freshly oiled; levers covered with felt; all the complete upper works of a heavy press – constructed with infernal ingenuity so as to join the fixtures below, and when taken to pieces again to go into the smallest possible compass – were next discovered and pulled out on the floor. After some little difficulty, the sub-prefect succeeded in putting the machinery together, and, leaving his men to work it, descended with me to the bedroom. The smothering canopy was then lowered, but not so noiselessly as I had seen it lowered. When I mentioned this to the sub-prefect, his answer, simple as it was, had a terrible significance. 'My men,' said he, 'are working down the bed-top for the first time—the men whose money you won were in better practice.'

We left the house in the sole possession of two police agents – every one of the inmates being removed to prison on the spot. The sub-prefect, after taking down my *procès-verbal*[12] in his office, returned with me to my hotel to get my passport. 'Do you think,' I asked, as I gave it to him, 'that any men have really been smothered in that bed, as they tried to smother *me*?'

'I have seen dozens of drowned men laid out at the morgue,' answered the sub-prefect, 'in whose pocketbooks were found letters stating that they had committed suicide in the Seine, because they had lost everything at the gaming-table. Do I know how many of those men entered the same gambling-house that *you* entered? won as *you* won? took that bed as *you* took it? slept in it? were smothered in it? and were privately thrown into the river, with a letter of explanation written by the murderers and placed in their pocket-books? No man can say how many or how few have suffered the fate from which you have escaped. The people of the gambling-house kept their bedstead machinery a secret from *us* – even from the police! The dead kept the rest of the secret for them. Good-night, or rather good-morning, Monsieur Faulkner! Be at my office again at nine o'clock – in the meantime, *au revoir*!'

The rest of my story is soon told. I was examined and re-examined; the gambling-house was strictly searched all through from top to bottom; the prisoners were separately interrogated; and two of the less guilty among them made a confession. *I* discovered that the old soldier was the master of the gambling-house – *justice* discovered that he had been drummed out of the army as a vagabond years ago; that he had been guilty of all sorts of villainies since; that he was in possession of stolen property, which the owners identified; and that he, the croupier, another accomplice and the woman who had made my cup of coffee were all in the secret of the bedstead. There appeared some reason to doubt whether the inferior persons attached to the house knew anything of the suffocating machinery; and they received the benefit of that doubt by being treated simply as thieves and vagabonds. As for the old soldier and his two head-myrmidons, they went to the galleys; the woman who had drugged my coffee was imprisoned for I forget how many years; the regular attendants at the gambling-house were considered 'suspicious' and placed under 'surveillance'; and I became, for one whole week (which is a long time), the head 'lion' in Parisian society. My adventure was drama-tised by three illustrious playmakers, but never saw theatrical daylight, for the censorship forbade the introduction on the stage of a correct copy of the gambling-house bedstead.

One good result was produced by my adventure, which any censorship must have approved – it cured me of ever again trying Rouge et Noir as an amusement. The sight of a green cloth, with packs of cards and heaps of money on it, will henceforth be forever associated in my mind with the sight of a bed-canopy descending to suffocate me in the silence and darkness of the night.

ROBERT LOUIS STEVENSON

ROBERT LOUIS STEVENSON (1850–94) was born in Edinburgh, the son of a prosperous civil engineer. It was planned that Stevenson should follow in his father's career but his weak constitution and ill health meant that he had to enter a less physically demanding profession. He chose the law, but by the time Stevenson was called to the bar in 1875 he had already determined to be a writer. While still in his twenties he began to suffer respiratory problems. In an attempt to alleviate his suffering, Stevenson spent much of his life travelling to warmer countries. These trips abroad – to Europe, America and ultimately Samoa – provided him with experience and material for his writings, as well as a wife whom he met in Europe, followed to California, and married in 1880. He finally settled in Samoa where he became known as 'Tusitala', the teller of tales. He died of a brain haemorrhage while working on his unfinished novel *Weir of Hermiston*.

In his comparatively short life Stevenson created a wide range of novels and stories which have assured that his work will continue to be found on the shelves of bookshops and libraries. From his pen came such classics as *Treasure Island, The Strange Case of Dr Jekyll and Mr Hyde, Kidnapped* and *The Black Arrow*.

'The Bottle Imp' is steeped in the glamour and mystery of the Southern Seas where Stevenson spent the last years of his life. At first glance the story has all the elements of an *Arabian Nights* tale: the gift of wishes, an imp trapped in a bottle, a beautiful heroine and an ill-fated hero. It is told simply as such a tale or parable would be. However, the story does raise questions about personal happiness and contentment – questions that are very relevant today. It is a general conception that the sudden acquisition of wealth – like a lottery win – would immediately wipe out one's problems. Common sense should tell us that this is not so. And even if many of our current worries would be eliminated if a fortune suddenly landed in our lap, it is more than likely that our unexpected wealth would bring with it a fresh set of problems. The story explores this dilemma very effectively.

'The Bottle Imp' is also a love story which shows us that perhaps true wealth is a selfless and caring partner who is prepared to make great sacrifices for our happiness, something that money cannot buy.

The Bottle Imp

THERE WAS A MAN of the island of Hawaii, whom I shall call Keawe; for the truth is, he still lives, and his name must be kept secret; but the place of his birth was not far from Honaunau, where the bones of Keawe the Great lie hidden in a cave. This man was poor, brave, and active; he could read and write like a schoolmaster; he was a first-rate mariner besides, sailed for some time in the island steamers, and steered a whaleboat on the Kamakua coast. At length it came in Keawe's mind to have a sight of the great world and foreign cities, and he shipped on a vessel bound to San Francisco.

This is a fine town, with a fine harbour, and rich people uncountable; and, in particular, there is one hill which is covered with palaces. Upon this hill Keawe was one day taking a walk, with his pocket full of money, viewing the great houses upon either hand with pleasure. 'What fine houses they are!' he was thinking, 'and how happy must these people be who dwell in them, and take no care for the morrow!' The thought was in his mind when he came abreast of a house that was smaller than some others, but all finished and beautified like a toy; the steps of that house shone like silver, and the borders of the garden bloomed like garlands, and the windows were bright like diamonds; and Keawe stopped and wondered at the excellence of all he saw. So stopping, he was aware of a man that looked forth upon him through a window, so clear that Keawe could see him as you see a fish in a pool upon the reef. The man was elderly, with a bald head and a black beard; and his face was heavy with sorrow, and he bitterly sighed. And the truth of it is, that as Keawe looked in upon the man and the man looked out upon Keawe, each envied the other.

All of a sudden the man smiled and nodded, and beckoned Keawe to enter, and met him at the door of the house.

'This is a fine house of mine,' said the man, and bitterly sighed. 'Would you not care to view the chambers?'

So he led Keawe all over it, from the cellar to the roof, and there was nothing there that was not perfect of its kind, and Keawe was astonished.

'Truly,' said Keawe, 'this is a beautiful house; if I lived in the like of it, I should be laughing all day long. How comes it, then, that you should be sighing?'

'There is no reason,' said the man, 'why you should not have a house in all points similar to this, and finer, if you wish. You have some money, I suppose?'

'I have fifty dollars,' said Keawe; 'but a house like this will cost more than fifty dollars.'

The man made a computation. 'I am sorry you have no more,' said he, 'for it may raise you trouble in the future; but it shall be yours at fifty dollars.'

'The house?' asked Keawe.

'No, not the house,' replied the man; 'but the bottle. For I must tell you, although I appear to you so rich and fortunate, all my fortune, and this house itself and its garden, came out of a bottle not much bigger than a pint. This is it.'

And he opened a lockfast[1] place, and took out a round-bellied bottle with a long neck; the glass of it was white like milk, with changing rainbow colours in the grain. Withinsides something obscurely moved, like a shadow and a fire.

'This is the bottle,' said the man; and, when Keawe laughed, 'You do not believe me?' he added. 'Try, then for yourself. See if you can break it.'

So Keawe took the bottle up and dashed it on the floor till he was weary; but it jumped on the floor like a child's ball, and was not injured.

'This is a strange thing,' said Keawe, 'for by the touch of it, as well as by the look, the bottle should be of glass.'

'Of glass it is,' replied the man, sighing more heavily than ever; 'but the glass of it was tempered in the flames of hell. An imp lives in it, and that is the shadow we behold there moving; or, so I suppose. If any man buy this bottle the imp is at his command; all that he desires – love, fame, money, houses like this house, ay, or a city like this city – all are his at the word uttered. Napoleon had this bottle, and by it he grew to be the king of the world; but he sold it at the last and fell. Captain Cook[2] had this bottle, and by it he found his way to so many islands; but he too sold it, and was slain upon Hawaii. For, once it is sold, the power goes and the protection; and unless a man remain content with what he has, ill will befall him.'

'And yet you talk of selling it yourself?' Keawe said.

'I have all I wish, and I am growing elderly,' replied the man. 'There is one thing the imp cannot do – he cannot prolong life; and it would not be fair to conceal from you there is a drawback to the bottle; for if a man die before he sells it, he must burn in hell for ever.'

'To be sure, that is a drawback and no mistake,' cried Keawe. 'I would not meddle with the thing. I can do without a house, thank God; but there is one thing I could not be doing with one particle, and that is to be damned.'

'Dear me, you must not run away with things,' returned the man. 'All you have to do is to use the power of the imp in moderation, and then sell it to someone else, as I do to you, and finish your life in comfort.'

'Well, I observe two things,' said Keawe. 'All the time you keep sighing like a maid in love that is one; and for the other, you sell this bottle very cheap.'

'I have told you already why I sigh,' said the man. 'It is because I fear my health is breaking up; and, as you said yourself, to die and go to the devil is a pity for anyone. As for why I sell so cheap, I must explain to you there is a peculiarity about the bottle. Long ago, when the devil brought it first upon earth, it was extremely expensive, and was sold first of all to Prester John[3] for many millions of dollars; but it cannot be sold at all, unless sold at a loss. If you sell it for as much as you paid for it, back it comes to you again like a homing pigeon. It follows that the price has kept falling in these centuries, and the bottle is now remarkably cheap. I bought it myself from one of my great neighbours on this hill, and the price I paid was only ninety dollars. I could sell it for as high as eighty-nine dollars and ninety-nine cents, but not a penny dearer, or back the thing must come to me. Now, about this there are two bothers. First, when you offer a bottle so singular for eighty-odd dollars, people suppose you to be jesting. And second – but there is no hurry about that – and I need not go into it. Only remember it must be coined money that you sell it for.'

'How am I to know that this is all true?' asked Keawe

'Some of it you can try at once,' replied the man. 'Give me your fifty dollars, take the bottle, and wish your fifty dollars back into your pocket. If that does not happen, I pledge you my honour I will cry off the bargain and restore your money.'

'You are not deceiving me?' said Keawe

The man bound himself with a great oath.

'Well, I will risk that much,' said Keawe, 'for that can do no harm,' and he paid over his money to the man, and the man handed him the bottle.

'Imp of the bottle,' said Keawe, 'I want my fifty dollars back.' And sure enough, he had scarce said the word before his pocket was as heavy as ever.

'To be sure this is a wonderful bottle,' said Keawe

'And now good-morning to you, my fine fellow, and the devil go with you for me,' said the man.

'Hold on,' said Keawe, 'I don't want any more of this fun. Here, take your bottle back.'

'You have bought it for less than I paid for it,' replied the man, rubbing his hands. 'It is yours now; and, for my part, I am only concerned to see the back of you.' And with that he rang for his Chinese servant, and had Keawe shown out of the house.

Now, when Keawe was in the street, with the bottle under his arm, he began to think. 'If all is true about this bottle, I may have made a losing bargain,' thinks he. 'But perhaps the man was only fooling me.' The first thing he did was to count his money; the sum was exact – forty-nine dollars American money, and one Chile piece. 'That looks like the truth,' said Keawe. 'Now I will try another part.'

The streets in that part of the city were as clean as a ship's decks, and though it was noon, there were no passengers. Keawe set the bottle in the gutter and walked away. Twice he looked back, and there was the milky, round-bellied bottle where he had left it. A third time he looked back and turned a corner; but he had scarce done so, when something knocked upon his elbow, and behold! it was the long neck sticking up; and as for the round belly, it was jammed into the pocket of his pilot-coat.[4]

'And that looks like the truth,' said Keawe.

The next thing he did was to buy a corkscrew in a shop, and go apart into a secret place in the fields. And there he tried to draw the cork, but as often as he put the screw in, out it came again, and the cork was as whole as ever.

'This is some new sort of cork,' said Keawe, and all at once he began to shake and sweat, for he was afraid of that bottle.

On his way back to the port-side he saw a shop where a man sold shells and clubs from the wild islands, old heathen deities, old coined money, pictures from China and Japan, and all manner of things that sailors bring in their sea-chests. And here he had an idea. So he went in and offered the bottle for a hundred dollars. The man of the shop laughed at him at first, and offered him five; but, indeed, it was a curious bottle, such glass was never blown in any human glassworks, so prettily the colours shone under the milky way, and so strangely the shadow hovered in the midst; so, after he had disputed a while after the manner of his kind, the shopman gave Keawe sixty silver dollars for the thing and set it on a shelf in the midst of his window.

'Now,' said Keawe, 'I have sold that for sixty which I bought for fifty – or, to say truth, a little less, because one of my dollars was from Chile. Now I shall know the truth upon another point.'

So he went back on board his ship, and when he opened his chest, there was the bottle, which had come more quickly than himself. Now Keawe had a mate on board whose name was Lopaka.

'What ails you,' said Lopaka, 'that you stare in your chest?'

They were alone in the ship's forecastle,[5] and Keawe bound him to secrecy, and told all.

'This is a very strange affair,' said Lopaka; 'and I fear you will be in trouble about this bottle. But there is one point very clear – that you are sure of the trouble, and you had better have the profit in the bargain. Make up your mind what you want with it; give the order, and when it is done as you desire, I will buy the bottle myself; for I have an idea of my own to get a schooner, and go trading through the islands.'

'That is not my idea,' said Keawe; 'but to have a beautiful house and garden on the Kona Coast, where I was born, the sun shining in at the door, flowers in the garden, glass in the windows, pictures on the walls, and fine carpets and toys on the tables, for all the world like the house I was in this day – only a storey higher, and with balconies all about like the king's palace; and to live there without care and make merry with my friends and relatives.'

'Well,' said Lopaka, 'let us carry it back with us to Hawaii; and if all comes true as you suppose, I will buy the bottle, as I said, and ask for a schooner.'

Upon that they were agreed, and it was not long before the ship returned to Honolulu, carrying Keawe and Lopaka, and the bottle. They were scarce come ashore when they met a friend upon the beach, who began at once to condole with Keawe.

'I do not know what I am to be condoled about,' said Keawe.

'Is it possible you have not heard,' said the friend, 'that your uncle – that good old man – is dead, and your cousin – that beautiful boy – was drowned at sea?'

Keawe was filled with sorrow, and, beginning to weep and to lament, he forgot about the bottle. But Lopaka was thinking to himself, and presently, when Keawe's grief was a little abated, 'I have been thinking,' said Lopaka, 'had not your uncle lands in Hawaii, in the district of Kaü?'

'No,' said Keawe, 'not in Kaü; they are on the mountainside – a little be-south Kookena.'

'These lands will now be yours?' asked Lopaka.

'And so they will,' says Keawe, and began again to lament for his relatives.

'No,' said Lopaka, 'do not lament at present. I have a thought in my mind. How if this should be the doing of the bottle? For here is the place ready for your house.'

'If this be so,' cried Keawe, 'it is a very ill way to serve me by killing my relatives. But it may be, indeed; for it was in just such a station that I saw the house with my mind's eye.'

'The house, however, is not yet built,' said Lopaka.

'No, nor like to be!' said Keawe; 'for though my uncle has some coffee and ava[6] and bananas, it will not be more than will keep me in comfort; and the rest of that land is the black lava.'

'Let us go to the lawyer,' said Lopaka; 'I have still this idea in my mind.'

Now, when they came to the lawyer's, it appeared Keawe's uncle had grown monstrous rich in the last days, and there was a fund of money.

'And here is the money for the house!' cried Lopaka.

'If you are thinking of a new house,' said the lawyer, 'here is the card of a new architect of whom they tell me great things.'

'Better and better!' cried Lopaka 'Here is all made plain for us. Let us continue to obey orders.'

So they went to the architect, and he had drawings of houses on his table.

'You want something out of the way,' said the architect. 'How do you like this?' and he handed a drawing to Keawe.

Now, when Keawe set eyes on the drawing, he cried out aloud, for it was the picture of his thought exactly drawn.

'I am in for this house,' thought he. 'Little as I like the way it comes to me, I am in for it now, and I may as well take the good along with the evil.'

So he told the architect all that he wished, and how he would have that house furnished, and about the pictures on the wall and the knick-knacks on the tables; and he asked the man plainly for how much he would undertake the whole affair.

The architect put many questions, and took his pen and made a computation; and when he had done he named the very sum that Keawe had inherited.

Lopaka and Keawe looked at one another and nodded.

'It is quite clear,' thought Keawe, 'that I am to have this house, whether or no. It comes from the devil, and I fear I will get little good by that; and of one thing I am sure. I will make no more wishes as long as I have this bottle. But with the house I am saddled, and I may as well take the good along with the evil.'

So he made his terms with the architect, and they signed a paper; and Keawe and Lopaka took ship again and sailed to Australia; for it was concluded between them they should not interfere at all, but leave the architect and the bottle imp to build and to adorn the house at their own pleasure.

The voyage was a good voyage, only all the time Keawe was holding in his breath, for he had sworn he would utter no more wishes and take no more favours from the devil. The time was up when they got back. The architect told him that the house was ready, and Keawe and Lopaka took a passage in the *Hall*, and went down Kona way to view the house, and see if all had been done fitly according to the thought that was in Keawe's mind.

Now, the house stood on the mountainside, visible to ships. Above, the forest ran up into the clouds of rain; below, the black lava fell in cliffs, where the kings of old lay buried. A garden bloomed about the house with every hue of flowers; and there was an orchard of papaia[7] on the one hand and an orchard of breadfruit on the other, and right in front, towards the sea, a ship's mast had been rigged up and bore a flag. As for the house, it was three storeys high, with great chambers and broad balconies on each. The windows were of glass, so excellent that it was as clear as water and as bright as day. All manner of furniture adorned the chambers. Pictures hung upon the walls in golden frames – pictures of ships, and men fighting, and of the most beautiful women, and of singular places; nowhere in the world are there pictures of so bright a colour as those Keawe found hanging in his house. As for the knick-knacks, they were extraordinarily fine: chiming clocks and musical boxes, little men with nodding heads, books filled with pictures, weapons of price from all quarters of the world, and the most elegant puzzles to entertain the leisure of a solitary man. And as no one would care to live in such chambers, only to walk through and view them, the balconies were made so broad that a whole town might have lived upon them in delight; and Keawe knew not which to prefer, whether the back porch, where you got the land breeze and looked upon the orchards and the flowers, or the front balcony, where you could drink the wind off the sea, and look down the steep wall of the mountain and see the *Hall* going by once a week or so between Hookena and the hills of Pele, or the schooners plying up the coast for wood and ava and bananas.

When they had viewed all, Keawe and Lopaka sat on the porch.

'Well,' asked Lopaka, 'is it all as you designed?'

'Words cannot utter it,' said Keawe. 'It is better than I dreamed, and I am sick with satisfaction.'

'There is but one thing to consider,' said Lopaka, 'all this may be quite natural, and the bottle imp have nothing whatever to say to it. If I were to buy the bottle, and got no schooner after all, I should have put my hand in the fire for nothing. I gave you my word, I know; but yet I think you would not grudge me one more proof.'

'I have sworn I would take no more favours,' said Keawe. 'I have gone already deep enough.'

'This is no favour I am thinking of,' replied Lopaka. 'It is only to see the imp himself. There is nothing to be gained by that, and so nothing to be ashamed of, and yet, if I once saw him, I should be sure of the whole matter. So indulge me so far, and let me see the imp; and, after that, here is the money in my hand, and I will buy it.'

'There is only one thing I am afraid of,' said Keawe. 'The imp may be very ugly to view, and if you once set eyes upon him you might be very undesirous of the bottle.'

'I am a man of my word,' said Lopaka. 'And here is the money betwixt us.'

'Very well,' replied Keawe, 'I have a curiosity myself. So come, let us have one look at you, Mr Imp.'

Now, as soon as that was said, the imp looked out of the bottle, and in again, swift as a lizard; and there sat Keawe and Lopaka turned to stone. The night had quite come before either found a thought to say or voice to say it with; and then Lopaka pushed the money over and took the bottle.

'I am a man of my word,' said he, 'and had need to be so, or I would not touch this bottle with my foot. Well, I shall get my schooner and a dollar or two for my pocket; and then I will be rid of this devil as fast as I can. For, to tell you the plain truth, the look of him has cast me down.'

'Lopaka,' said Keawe, 'do not you think any worse of me than you can help; I know it is night, and the roads bad, and the pass by the tombs an ill place to go by so late, but I declare since I have seen that little face, I cannot eat or sleep or pray till it is gone from me. I will give you a lantern, and a basket to put the bottle in, and any picture or fine thing in all my house that takes your fancy, but be gone at once, and go sleep at Hookena with Nahinu.'

'Keawe,' said Lopaka, 'many a man would take this ill; above all, when I am doing you a turn so friendly as to keep my word and buy the bottle; and for that matter, the night and the dark, and the way by the tombs, must be all tenfold more dangerous to a man with such a sin upon his conscience and such a bottle under his arm. But for my part, I am so extremely terrified myself, I have not the heart to blame you. Here I go, then; and I pray God you may be happy in your house, and I fortunate with my schooner, and both get to heaven in the end in spite of the devil and his bottle.'

So Lopaka went down the mountain; and Keawe stood on his front balcony, and listened to the clink of the horse's shoes, and watched the lantern go shining down the path and along the cliff of caves where the old dead are buried; and all the time he trembled and clasped his hands, and prayed for his friend, and gave glory to God that he himself was escaped out of that trouble.

But the next day came very brightly, and that new house of his was so delightful to behold that he forgot his terrors. One day followed another, and Keawe dwelt there in perpetual joy. He had his place on the back porch; it was there he ate and lived, and read the stories in the Honolulu newspapers; but when anyone came by they would go in and view the chambers and the pictures. And the fame of the house went far and wide; it was called Ka-Hale Ntu – the Great House – in all Kona; and sometimes the Bright House, for Keawe kept a Chinaman, who was all day dusting and furbishing; and the glass, and the gilt, and the fine stuffs, and the pictures, shone as bright as the morning. As for Keawe himself, he could not walk in the chambers without singing, his heart was so enlarged; and when ships sailed by upon the sea, he would fly his colours on the mast.

So time went by, until one day Keawe went upon a visit as far as Kailua to certain of his friends. There he was well feasted; and left as soon as he could the next morning, and rode hard, for he was impatient to behold his beautiful house; and, besides, the night then coming on was the night in which the dead of old days go abroad in the sides of Kona; and having already meddled with the devil, he was the more chary of meeting with the dead. A little beyond Honaunau, looking far ahead, he was aware of a woman bathing in the edges of the sea; and she seemed a well-grown girl, but he thought no more of it. Then he saw her white shift flutter as she put it on, and then her red *holoku*; and by the time he came abreast of her she was done with her toilet, and had come up from the sea, and stood by the track-side in her red *holoku*, and she was all freshened with the bath, and her eyes shone and were kind. Now Keawe no sooner beheld her than he drew rein.

'I thought I knew everyone in this country,' said he. 'How comes it that I do not know you?'

'I am Kokua, daughter of Kiano,' said the girl, 'and I have just returned from Oahu. Who are you?'

'I will tell you who I am in a little,' said Keawe, dismounting from his horse, 'but not now. For I have a thought in my mind, and if you knew who I was, you might have heard of me, and would not give me a true answer. But tell me, first of all, one thing: are you married?'

At this Kokua laughed out aloud. 'It is you who ask questions,' she said. 'Are you married yourself?'

'Indeed, Kokua, I am not,' replied Keawe, 'and never thought to be until this hour. But here is the plain truth. I have met you here at the roadside, and I saw your eyes, which are like the stars, and my heart went to you as swift as a bird. And so now, if you want none of me, say so, and I will go on to my own place; but if you think me no worse than any other young man, say so, too, and I will turn aside to your father's for the night, and tomorrow I will talk with the good man.'

Kokua said never a word, but she looked at the sea and laughed.

'Kokua,' said Keawe, 'if you say nothing, I will take that for the good answer; so let us be stepping to your father's door.'

She went on ahead of him, still without speech; only sometimes she glanced back and glanced away again, and she kept the strings of her hat in her mouth.

Now, when they had come to the door, Kiano came out on his veranda, and cried out and welcomed Keawe by name. At that the girl looked over, for the fame of the great house had come to her ears; and, to be sure, it was a great temptation. All that evening they were very merry together; and the girl was as bold as brass under the eyes of her parents, and made a mark of Keawe, for she had a quick wit. The next day he had a word with Kiano, then found the girl alone.

'Kokua,' said he, 'you made a mark of me all the evening; and there is still time to bid me go. I would not tell you who I was, because I have so fine a house, and I feared you would think too much of that house and too little of the man that loves you. Now you know all, and if you wish to have seen the last of me, say so at once.'

'No,' said Kokua, but this time she did not laugh, nor did Keawe ask for more.

This was the wooing of Keawe; things had gone quickly; but so an arrow goes, and the ball of a rifle swifter still, and yet both may strike the target. Things had gone fast, but they had gone far also, and the thought of Keawe rang in the maiden's head; she heard his voice in the breach of the surf upon the lava, and for this young man that she had seen but twice she would have left father and mother and her native islands. As for Keawe himself, his horse flew up the path of the mountain under the cliff of tombs, and the sound of the hoofs, and the sound of Keawe singing to himself for pleasure, echoed in the caverns of the dead. He came to the Bright House, and still he was singing. He sat and ate on the broad balcony, and the Chinaman wondered at his master to hear how he sang between the mouthfuls. The sun went down into the sea, and the night came; and Keawe walked the balconies by lamplight, high on the mountains, and the voice of his singing startled men on ships.

'Here am I now upon my high place,' he said to himself. 'Life may be no better; this is the mountain top; and all shelves about me towards the worse. For the first time I will light up the chambers, and bathe in my fine bath with the hot water and the cold, and sleep above in the bed of my bridal chamber.'

So the Chinaman had word, and he must rise from sleep and light the furnaces; and as he walked below, beside the boilers, he heard his master singing and rejoicing above him in the lighted chambers. When the water began to be hot the Chinaman cried to his master: and Keawe went into the bathroom; and the Chinaman heard him sing as he filled the marble basin; and heard him sing, and the singing broken, as he undressed; until of a sudden, the song ceased. The Chinaman listened, and listened; he called up the house to Keawe to ask if all were well, and Keawe answered him, 'Yes,' and bade him go to bed; but there was no more singing in the Bright House; and all night long the Chinaman heard his master's feet go round and round the balconies without repose.

Now, the truth of it was this: as Keawe undressed for his bath, he spied upon his flesh a patch like a patch of lichen on a rock, and it was then that he stopped singing. For he knew the likeness of that patch, and knew that he was fallen in the Chinese Evil.[8]

Now, it is a sad thing for any man to fall into this sickness. And it would be a sad thing for anyone to leave a house so beautiful and so commodious, and depart from all his friends to the north coast of Molokai, between the mighty cliff and the sea-breakers. But what was that to the case of the man Keawe, he who had met his love but yesterday and won her but that morning, and now saw all his hopes break, in a moment, like a piece of glass?

A while he sat upon the edge of the bath, then sprang, with a cry, and ran outside; and to and fro, to and fro, along the balcony, like one despairing.

'Very willingly could I leave Hawaii, the home of my fathers,' Keawe was thinking. 'Very lightly could I leave my house, the high-placed, the many-windowed, here upon the mountains. Very bravely could I go to Molokai, to Kalaupapa by the cliffs, to live with the smitten and to sleep there, far from my fathers. But what wrong have I done, what sin lies upon my soul, that I should have encountered Kokua coming cool from the sea-water in the evening? Kokua, the soul ensnarer! Kokua, the light of my life! Her may I never wed, her may I look upon no longer, her may I no more handle with my loving hand; and it is for this, it is for you, O Kokua! that I pour out my lamentations!'

Now you are to observe what sort of a man Keawe was, for he might have dwelt there in the Bright House for years, and no one been the wiser of his sickness; but he reckoned nothing of that, if he must lose Kokua. And again he might have wed Kokua even as he was; and so many would have done, because they have the souls of pigs; but Keawe loved the maid manfully, and he would do her no hurt and bring her in no danger.

A little beyond the midst of the night, there came in his mind the recollection of that bottle. He went round to the back porch, and called to memory the day when the devil had looked forth; and at the thought ice ran in his veins.

'A dreadful thing is in the bottle,' thought Keawe, 'and dreadful is the imp, and it is a dreadful thing to risk the flames of hell. But what other hope have I to cure my sickness or to wed Kokua? What!' he thought, 'would I beard the devil once, only to get me a house, and not face him again to win Kokua?'

Thereupon he called to mind it was the next day the *Hall* went by on her return to Honolulu. 'There must I go first,' he thought, 'and see Lopaka. For the best hope that I have now is to find that same bottle I was so pleased to be rid of.'

Never a wink could he sleep; the food stuck in his throat; but he sent a letter to Kiano, and about the time when the steamer would be coming, rode down beside the cliff of the tombs. It rained; his horse went heavily; he looked up at the black mouths of the caves, and he envied the dead that slept there and were done with trouble; and called to mind how he had galloped by the day before, and was astonished. So he came down to Hookena, and there was all the country gathered for the steamer as usual. In the shed before the store they sat and jested and passed the news; but there was no matter of speech in Keawe's bosom, and he sat in their midst and looked without on the rain falling on the houses, and the surf beating among the rocks, and the sighs arose in his throat.

'Keawe of the Bright House is out of spirits,' said one to another. Indeed, and so he was, and little wonder.

Then the *Hall* came, and the whaleboat carried him on board. The afterpart of the ship was full of Haoles[9] – who had been to visit the volcano, as their custom is; and the midst was crowded with Kanakas, and the forepart with wild bulls from Hilo and horses from Kaü; but Keawe sat apart from all in his sorrow, and watched for the house of Kiano. There it sat low upon the shore in the black rocks, shaded by the cocoa-palms, and there by the door was a red *holoku*, no greater than a fly, and going to and fro with a fly's busyness. 'Ah, queen of my heart,' he cried, 'I'll venture my dear soul to win you!'

Soon after, darkness fell and the cabins were lit up and the Haoles sat and played at the cards and drank whisky as their custom is; but Keawe walked the deck all night; and all the next day, as they steamed under the lee of Maui and of Molokai, he was still pacing to and fro like a wild animal in a menagerie.

Towards evening they passed Diamond Head, and came to the pier of Honolulu. Keawe stepped out among the crowd and began to ask for Lopaka. It seemed he had become the owner of a schooner – none better in the islands – and was gone upon an adventure as far as Pola-Pola or Kahiki; so there was no help to be looked for from Lopaka. Keawe called to mind a friend of his, a lawyer in the town (I must not tell his name), and enquired of him. They said he was grown suddenly rich, and had a fine new house upon Waikiki shore; and this put a thought in Keawe's head, and he called a hack and drove to the lawyer's house.

The house was all brand new, and the trees in the garden no greater than walking-sticks, and the lawyer, when he came, had the air of a man well pleased.

'What can I do to serve you?' said the lawyer.

'You are a friend of Lopaka's,' replied Keawe, 'and Lopaka purchased from me a certain piece of goods that I thought you might enable me to trace.'

The lawyer's face became very dark. 'I do not profess to misunderstand you, Mr Keawe,' said he, 'though this is an ugly business to be stirring in. You may be sure I know nothing, but yet I have a guess, and if you would apply in a certain quarter I think you might have news.'

And he named the name of a man, which, again, I had better not repeat. So it was for days, and Keawe went from one to another, finding everywhere new clothes and carriages, and fine new houses, and men everywhere in great contentment, although, to be sure, when he hinted at his business their faces would cloud over.

'No doubt I am upon the track,' thought Keawe. 'These new

clothes and carriages are all the gifts of the little imp, and these glad faces are the faces of men who have taken their profit and got rid of the accursed thing in safety. When I see pale cheeks and hear sighing, I shall know that I am near the bottle.'

So it befell at last he was recommended to a Haole in Beritania Street. When he came to the door, about the hour of the evening meal, there were the usual marks of the new house, and the young garden, and the electric light shining in the windows; but when the owner came, a shock of hope and fear ran through Keawe; for here was a young man, white as a corpse and black about the eyes, the hair shedding from his head and such a look in his countenance as a man may have when he is waiting for the gallows.

'Here it is, to be sure,' thought Keawe, and so with this man he noways veiled his errand. 'I am come to buy the bottle,' said he.

At the word, the young Haole of Beritania Street reeled against the wall. 'The bottle!' he gasped. 'To buy the bottle!' Then he seemed to choke, and seizing Keawe by the arm, carried him into a room and poured out wine in two glasses.

'Here is my respects,' said Keawe, who had been much about with Haoles in his time. 'Yes,' he added, 'I am come to buy the bottle. What is the price by now?'

At that word the young man let his glass slip through his fingers, and looked upon Keawe like a ghost. 'The price,' says he; 'the price! You do not know the price?'

'It is for that I am asking you,' returned Keawe. 'But why are you so much concerned? Is there anything wrong about the price?'

'It has dropped a great deal in value since your time, Mr Keawe,' said the young man, stammering.

'Well, well, I shall have the less to pay for it,' said Keawe 'How much did it cost you?'

The young man was as white as a sheet.

'Two cents,' said he.

'What!' cried Keawe, 'two cents? Why, then, you can only sell it for one. And he who buys it – ' The words died upon Keawe's tongue; he who bought it could never sell it again, the bottle and the bottle imp must abide with him until he died, and when he died must carry him to the red end of hell.

The young man of Beritania Street fell upon his knees. 'For God's sake, buy it!' he cried. 'You can have all my fortune in the bargain. I was mad when I bought it at that price. I had embezzled money at my store; I was lost else; I must have gone to jail.'

'Poor creature,' said Keawe, 'you would risk your soul upon so desperate an adventure, and to avoid the proper punishment of your own disgrace; and you think I could hesitate with love in front of me. Give me the bottle, and the change which I make sure you have all ready. Here is a five-cent piece.'

It was as Keawe supposed; the young man had the change ready in a drawer; the bottle changed hands, and Keawe's fingers were no sooner clasped upon the stalk than he had breathed his wish to be a clean man. And sure enough, when he got home to his room, and stripped himself before a glass, his flesh was whole like an infant's. And here was the strange thing: he had no sooner seen this miracle than his mind was changed within him, and he cared naught for the Chinese Evil, and little enough for Kokua; and had but the one thought, that here he was bound to the bottle imp for time and for eternity, and had no better hope but to be a cinder for ever in the flames of hell. Away ahead of him he saw them blaze with his mind's eye, and his soul shrank, and darkness fell upon the light.

When Keawe came to himself a little, he was aware it was the night when the band played at the hotel. Thither he went, because he feared to be alone; and there, among happy faces, walked to and fro, and heard the tunes go up and down, and saw Berger beat the measure, and all the while he heard the flames crackle and saw the red fire burning in the bottomless pit. Of a sudden the band played *Hiki-ao-ao*; that was a song that he had sung with Kokua, and at the strain courage returned to him.

'It is done now,' he thought, 'and once more let me take the good along with the evil.'

So it befell that he returned to Hawaii by the first steamer, and as soon as it could be managed he was wedded to Kokua, and carried her up the mountainside to the Bright House.

Now it was so with these two, that when they were together Keawe's heart was stilled; but as soon as he was alone he fell into a brooding horror, and heard the flames crackle, and saw the red fire burn in the bottomless pit. The girl, indeed, had come to him wholly; her heart leaped in her side at sight of him, her hand clung to his; and she was so fashioned, from the hair upon her head to the nails upon her toes, that none could see her without joy. She was pleasant in her nature. She had the good word always. Full of song she was, and went to and fro in the Bright House, the brightest thing in its three storeys, carolling like the birds. And Keawe beheld and heard her with delight, and then must shrink upon one side, and weep and groan to think upon the price that he had paid for her; and then he must dry his eyes, and wash his face, and go and sit with her on the broad balconies, joining in her songs, and, with a sick spirit, answering her smiles.

There came a day when her feet began to be heavy and her songs more rare; and now it was not Keawe only that would weep apart, but each would sunder[10] from the other and sit in opposite balconies with the whole width of the Bright House betwixt. Keawe was so sunk in his despair, he scarce observed the change, and was only glad he had more hours to sit alone and brood upon his destiny and was not so frequently condemned to pull a smiling face on a sick heart. But one day, coming softly through the house, he heard the sound of a child sobbing, and there was Kokua rolling her face upon the balcony floor and weeping like the lost.

'You do well to weep in this house, Kokua,' he said. 'And yet I would give the head off my body that you (at least) might have been happy.'

'Happy!' she cried. 'Keawe, when you lived alone in your Bright House you were the word of the island for a happy man; laughter and song were in your mouth, and your face was as bright as the sunrise. Then you wedded poor Kokua; and the good God knows what is amiss in her – but from that day you have not smiled. Oh!' she cried, 'what ails me? I thought I was pretty, and I knew I loved my husband. What ails me, that I throw this cloud upon him?'

'Poor Kokua,' said Keawe. He sat down by her side, and sought to take her hand; but that she plucked away, 'Poor Kokua,' he said again. 'My poor child – my pretty. And I had thought all this while to spare you! Well, you shall know all. Then, at least, you will pity poor Keawe; then you will understand how much he loved you in the past – that he dared hell for your possession – and how much he loves you still (the poor condemned one), that he can yet call up a smile when he beholds you.'

With that he told her all, even from the beginning.

'You have done this for me?' she cried. 'Ah, well, then what do I care!' and she clasped and wept upon him.

'Ah, child!' said Keawe, 'and yet, when I consider of the fire of hell, I care a good deal!'

'Never tell me,' said she, 'that a man can be lost because he loved Kokua, and no other fault. I tell you, Keawe, I shall save you with these hands, or perish in your company. What! you loved me and gave your soul, and you think I will not die to save you in return?'

'Ah, my dear, you might die a hundred times: and what difference would that make?' he cried, 'except to leave me lonely till the time comes for my damnation?'

'You know nothing,' said she. 'I was educated in a school in Honolulu; I am no common girl. And I tell you I shall save my lover. What is this you say about a cent? But all the world is not American. In England they have a piece they call a farthing,[11] which is about half a cent. Ah! sorrow!' she cried, 'that makes it scarcely better, for the buyer must be lost, and we shall find none so brave as my Keawe! But, then, there is France; they have a small coin there which they call a centime, and these go five to the cent, or thereabout. We could not do better. Come, Keawe, let us go to the French islands; let us go to Tahiti as fast as ships can bear us. There we have four centimes, three centimes, two centimes, one centime; four possible sales to come and go on; and two of us to push the bargain. Come, my Keawe! kiss me, and banish care. Kokua will defend you.'

'Gift of God!' he cried. 'I cannot think that God will punish me for desiring aught so good. Be it as you will then, take me where you please: I put my life and my salvation in your hands.'

Early the next day Kokua went about her preparations. She took Keawe's chest that he went with sailoring; and first she put the bottle in a corner, and then packed it with the richest of their clothes and the bravest of the knick-knacks in the house. 'For,' said she, 'we must seem to be rich folks, or who would believe in the bottle?' All the time of her preparation she was as gay as a bird; only when she looked upon Keawe the tears would spring in her eye, and she must run and kiss him. As for Keawe, a weight was off his soul; now that he had his secret shared, and some hope in front of him, he seemed like a new man, his feet went lightly on the earth, and his breath was good to him again. Yet was terror still at his elbow; and ever and again, as the wind blows out a taper, hope died in him, and he saw the flames toss and the red fire burn in hell.

It was given out in the country they were gone pleasuring in the States, which was thought a strange thing, and yet not so strange as the truth, if any could have guessed it. So they went to Honolulu in the *Hall*, and thence in the *Umatilla* to San Francisco with a crowd of Haoles, and at San Francisco took their passage by the mail brigantine, the *Tropic Bird*, for Papeete, the chief place of the French in the south islands. Thither they came, after a pleasant voyage, on a fair day of the Trade Wind, and saw the reef with the surf breaking, and Motuiti with its palms, and the schooner riding withinside and the white houses of the town low down along the shore among green trees, and overhead the mountains and the clouds of Tahiti, the wise island.

It was judged the most wise to hire a house, which they did accordingly, opposite the British Consul's, to make a great parade of money, and themselves conspicuous with carriages and horses. This it was very easy to do, so long as they had the bottle in their possession; for Kokua was more bold than Keawe and whenever she had a mind called on the imp for twenty or a hundred dollars. At this rate they soon grew to be remarked in the town; and the strangers from Hawaii, their riding and their driving, the fine *holokus* and the rich lace of Kokua, became the matter of much talk.

They got on well after the first with the Tahiti language, which is indeed like to the Hawaiian, with a change of certain letters; and as soon as they had any freedom of speech, began to push the bottle. You are to consider it was not an easy subject to introduce; it is not easy to persuade people you are in earnest, when you offer to sell them for four centimes the spring of health and riches inexhaustible. It was necessary besides to explain the dangers of the bottle; and either people disbelieved the whole thing and laughed, or they thought the more of the darker part, became overcast with gravity, and drew away from Keawe and Kokua, as from persons who had dealings with the devil. So far from gaining ground, these two began to find they were avoided in the town; the children ran away from them screaming, a thing intolerable to Kokua; Catholics crossed themselves as they went by; and all persons began with one accord to disengage themselves from their advances.

Depression fell upon their spirits. They would sit at night in their new house, after a day's weariness, and not exchange one word, or the silence would be broken by Kokua bursting suddenly into sobs. Sometimes they would pray together; sometimes they would have the bottle out upon the floor, and sit all evening watching how the shadow hovered in the midst. At such times they would be afraid to go to rest. It was long ere slumber came to them, and, if either dozed off, it would be to wake and find the other silently weeping in the dark, or, perhaps, to wake alone, the other having fled from the house, and the neighbourhood of that bottle, to pace under the bananas in the little garden or to wander on the beach by moonlight.

One night it was so when Kokua awoke. Keawe was gone. She felt in the bed and his place was cold. Then fear fell upon her, and she sat up in bed. A little moonshine filtered through the shutters. The room was bright, and she could spy the bottle on the floor. Outside it blew high, the great trees of the avenue cried aloud, and the fallen leaves rattled in the veranda. In the midst of this Kokua was aware of another sound: whether of a beast or of a man she could scarce tell, but it was as sad as death, and cut her to the soul. Softly she arose, set the door ajar, and looked forth into the moonlit yard. There, under the bananas, lay Keawe, his mouth in the dust, and as he lay he moaned.

It was Kokua's first thought to run forward and console him; her second potently withheld her. Keawe had borne himself before his wife like a brave man; it became her little in the hour of weakness to intrude upon his shame. With the thought she drew back into the house.

'Heaven,' she thought, 'how careless have I been – how weak! It is he, not I, that stands in this eternal peril; it was he, not I that took the curse upon his soul. It is for my sake, and for the love of a creature of so little worth and such poor help, that he now beholds so close to him the flames of hell – ay, and smells the smoke of it, lying without there in the wind and moonlight. Am I so dull of spirit that never till now have I surmised my duty, or have I seen it before and turned aside? But now, at least, I take up my soul in both the hands of my affection; now I say farewell to the white steps of heaven and the waiting faces of my friends. A love for a love, and let mine be equalled with Keawe's! A soul for a soul, and be it mine to perish!'

She was a deft woman with her hands, and was soon apparelled. She took in her hands the charge – the precious centimes they kept ever at their side; for this coin is little used, and they had made provision at a government office. When she was forth in the avenue clouds came on the wind, and the moon was blackened. The town slept, and she knew not whither to turn till she heard one coughing in the shadow of the trees.

'Old man,' said Kokua, 'what do you here abroad in the cold night?'

The old man could scarce express himself for coughing, but she made out that he was old and poor, and a stranger in the island.

'Will you do me a service?' said Kokua. 'As one stranger to another, and as an old man to a young woman, will you help a daughter of Hawaii?'

'Ah,' said the old man. 'So you are the witch from the Eight Islands, and even my old soul you seek to entangle. But I have heard of you, and defy your wickedness.'

'Sit down here,' said Kokua, 'and let me tell you a tale.' And she told him the story of Keawe from the beginning to the end.

'And now,' said she, 'I am his wife, whom he bought with his soul's welfare. And what should I do? If I went to him myself and offered to buy it, he would refuse. But if you go, he will sell it eagerly; I will await you here; you will buy it for four centimes, and I will buy it again for three. And the Lord strengthen a poor girl!'

'If you meant falsely,' said the old man, 'I think God would strike you dead.'

'He would!' cried Kokua. 'Be sure He would. I could not be so treacherous; God would not suffer it.'

'Give me the four centimes and await me here,' said the old man.

Now, when Kokua stood alone in the street, her spirit died. The wind roared in the trees, and it seemed to her the rushing of the flames of hell; the shadows towered in the light of the street lamp, and they seemed to her the snatching hands of evil ones. If she had had the strength, she must have run away, and if she had had the breath, she must have screamed aloud; but, in truth, she could do neither, and stood and trembled in the avenue, like an affrighted child.

Then she saw the old man returning, and he had the bottle in his hand.

'I have done your bidding,' said he. 'I left your husband weeping like a child; tonight he will sleep easy.' And he held the bottle forth.

'Before you give it me,' Kokua panted, 'take the good with the evil – ask to be delivered from your cough.'

'I am an old man,' replied the other, 'and too near the gate of the grave to take a favour from the devil. But what is this? Why do you not take the bottle? Do you hesitate?'

'Not hesitate!' cried Kokua. 'I am only weak. Give me a moment. It is my hand resists, my flesh shrinks back from the accursed thing. One moment only!'

The old man looked upon Kokua kindly. 'Poor child!' said he, 'you fear; your soul misgives you. Well, let me keep it. I am old, and can never more be happy in this world, and as for the next – '

'Give it me!' gasped Kokua. 'There is your money. Do you think I am so base as that? Give me the bottle.'

'God bless you, child,' said the old man.

Kokua concealed the bottle under her *holoku*, said farewell to the old man, and walked off along the avenue, she cared not whither. For all roads were now the same to her, and led equally to hell. Sometimes she walked, and sometimes ran; sometimes she screamed out loud in the night, and sometimes lay by the wayside in the dust and wept. All that she had heard of hell came back to her; she saw the flames blaze, and she smelled the smoke, and her flesh withered on the coals.

Near day she came to her mind again, and returned to the house. It was even as the old man had said – Keawe slumbered like a child. Kokua stood and gazed upon his face.

'Now, my husband,' said she, 'it is your turn to sleep. When you wake it will be your turn to sing and laugh. But for poor Kokua, alas! that meant no evil – for poor Kokua no more sleep, no more singing, no more delight, whether in earth or heaven.'

With that she lay down in the bed by his side, and her misery was so extreme that she fell in a deep slumber instantly.

Late in the morning her husband woke her and gave her the good news. It seemed he was silly with delight, for he paid no heed to her distress, ill though she dissembled it. The words stuck in her mouth, it mattered not; Keawe did the speaking. She ate not a bite, but who was to observe it? For Keawe cleared the dish. Kokua saw and heard him, like some strange thing in a dream; there were times when she forgot or doubted, and put her hands to her brow; to know herself doomed and hear her husband babble seemed so monstrous.

All the while Keawe was eating and talking, and planning the time of their return, and thanking her for saving him and fondling her, and calling her the true helper after all. He laughed at the old man that was fool enough to buy that bottle

'A worthy man he seemed,' Keawe said. 'But no one can judge by appearances. For why did the old reprobate require the bottle?'

'My husband,' said Kokua humbly, 'his purpose may have been good.'

Keawe laughed like an angry man.

'Fiddle-de-dee!' cried Keawe. 'An old rogue, I tell you; and an old ass to boot. For the bottle was hard enough to sell at four centimes; and at three it will be quite impossible. The margin is not broad enough, the thing begins to smell of scorching – brrr!' said he, and shuddered. 'It is true I bought it myself at a cent, when I knew not there were smaller coins. I was a fool for my pains; there will never be found another, and whoever has that bottle now will carry it to the pit.'

'Oh, my husband!' said Kokua. 'Is it not a terrible thing to save oneself by the eternal ruin of another? It seems to me I could not laugh. I would be humbled. I would be filled with melancholy. I would pray for the poor holder.'

Then Keawe, because he felt the truth of what she said, grew the more angry. 'Hoity-toity!' cried he. 'You may be filled with melancholy if you please. It is not the mind of a good wife. If you thought at all of me, you would sit shamed.'

Thereupon he went out, and Kokua was alone.

What chance had she to sell that bottle at two centimes? None, she perceived. And if she had any, here was her husband hurrying her away to a country where there was nothing lower than a cent. And here – on the morrow of her sacrifice – was her husband leaving her and blaming her.

She would not even try to profit by what time she had, but sat in the house, and now had the bottle out and viewed it with unutterable fear, and now, with loathing, hid it out of sight.

By and by Keawe came back, and would have her take a drive.

'My husband, I am ill,' she said. 'I am out of heart. Excuse me, I can take no pleasure.'

Then was Keawe more wroth[12] than ever. With her, because he thought she was brooding over the case of the old man; and with himself, because he thought she was right and was ashamed to be so happy.

'This is your truth,' cried he, 'and this your affection! Your husband is just saved from eternal ruin, which he encountered for the love of you – and you can take no pleasure! Kokua, you have a disloyal heart.'

He went forth again furious, and wandered in the town all day. He met friends, and drank with them; they hired a carriage and drove into the country, and there drank again. All the time Keawe was ill at ease, because he was taking this pastime while his wife was sad, and because he knew in his heart that she was more right than he; and the knowledge made him drink the deeper.

Now there was an old brutal Haole drinking with him, one that had been a boatswain of a whaler – a runaway, a digger in gold mines, a convict in prisons. He had a low mind and a foul mouth; he loved to drink and to see others drunken; and he pressed the glass upon Keawe. Soon there was no more money in the company.

'Here, you!' says the boatswain, 'you are rich, you have been always saying. You have a bottle or some foolishness.'

'Yes,' says Keawe, 'I am rich; I will go back and get some money from my wife, who keeps it.'

'That's a bad idea, mate,' said the boatswain. 'Never you trust a petticoat with dollars. They're all as false as water; you keep an eye on her.'

Now this word struck in Keawe's mind; for he was muddled with what he had been drinking.

'I should not wonder but she was false, indeed,' thought he. 'Why else should she be so cast down at my release? But I will show her I am not the man to be fooled. I will catch her in the act.'

Accordingly, when they were back in town, Keawe bade the boatswain wait for him at the corner by the old calaboose,[13] and went forward up the avenue alone to the door of his house. The night had come again; there was a light within, but never a sound;

and Keawe crept about the corner, opened the back door softly, and looked in.

There was Kokua on the floor, the lamp at her side; before her was a milk-white bottle, with a round belly and a long neck; and as she viewed it, Kokua wrung her hands.

A long time Keawe stood and looked in the doorway. At first he was struck stupid; and then fear fell upon him that the bargain had been made amiss, and the bottle had come back to him as it came at San Francisco; and at that his knees were loosened, and the fumes of the wine departed from his head like mists off a river in the morning. And then he had another thought; and it was a strange one, that made his cheeks to burn.

'I must make sure of this,' thought he.

So he closed the door, and went softly round the corner again, and then came noisily in, as though he were but now returned. And, lo! by the time he opened the front door no bottle was to be seen; and Kokua sat in a chair and started up like one awakened out of sleep.

'I have been drinking all day and making merry,' said Keawe. 'I have been with good companions, and now I only came back for money, and return to drink and carouse with them again.'

Both his face and voice were as stern as judgment, but Kokua was too troubled to observe.

'You do well to use your own, my husband,' said she and her words trembled.

'Oh, I do well in all things,' said Keawe, and he went straight to the chest and took out money. But he looked besides in the corner where they kept the bottle, and there was no bottle there.

At that the chest heaved upon the floor like a sea-billow, and the house spun about him like a wreath of smoke, for he saw she was lost now, and there was no escape. 'It is what I feared,' he thought. 'It is she who has bought it.'

And then he came to himself a little and rose up; but the sweat streamed on his face as thick as the rain and as cold as the well-water.

'Kokua,' said he, 'I said to you today what ill became me. Now I return to carouse with my jolly companions,' and at that he laughed a little quietly. 'I will take more pleasure in the cup if you forgive me.'

She clasped his knees in a moment; she kissed his knees with flowing tears.

'Oh,' she cried, 'I ask but a kind word!'

'Let us never one think hardly of the other,' said Keawe, and was gone out of the house.

Now, the money that Keawe had taken was only some of that store of centime pieces they had laid in at their arrival. It was very sure he had no mind to be drinking. His wife had given her soul for him, now he must give his for hers; no other thought was in the world with him.

At the corner, by the old calaboose, there was the boatswain waiting.

'My wife has the bottle,' said Keawe, 'and, unless you help me to recover it, there can be no more money and no more liquor tonight.'

'You do not mean to say you are serious about that bottle?' cried the boatswain.

'There is the lamp,' said Keawe. 'Do I look as if I was jesting?'

'That is so,' said the boatswain. 'You look as serious as a ghost.'

'Well, then,' said Keawe, 'here are two centimes; you just go to my wife in the house, and offer her these for the bottle, which (if I am not much mistaken) she will give you instantly. Bring it to me here, and I will buy it back from you for one; for that is the law with this bottle, that it still must be sold for a less sum. But whatever you do, never breathe a word to her that you have come from me.'

'Mate, I wonder are you making a fool of me?' asked the boatswain.

'It will do you no harm if I am,' returned Keawe.

'That is so, mate,' said the boatswain.

'And if you doubt me,' added Keawe, 'you can try. As soon as you are clear of the house, wish to have your pocket full of money, or a bottle of the best rum, or what you please, and you will see the virtue of the thing.'

'Very well, Kanaka,' says the boatswain. 'I will try; but if you are having your fun out of me, I will take my fun out of you with a belaying pin.'[14]

So the whaler-man went off up the avenue; and Keawe stood and waited. It was near the same spot where Kokua had waited the night before; but Keawe was more resolved, and never faltered in his purpose; only his soul was bitter with despair.

It seemed a long time he had to wait before he heard a voice singing in the darkness of the avenue. He knew the voice to be the boatswain's; but it was strange how drunken it appeared upon a sudden.

Next the man himself came stumbling into the light of the lamp. He had the devil's bottle buttoned in his coat; another bottle was in his hand; and even as he came in view he raised it to his mouth and drank.

'You have it,' said Keawe. 'I see that.'

'Hands off!' cried the boatswain, jumping back. 'Take a step near me, and I'll smash your mouth. You thought you could make a catspaw[15] of me, did you?'

'What do you mean?' cried Keawe.

'Mean?' cried the boatswain. 'This is a pretty good bottle, this is; that's what I mean. How I got it for two centimes, I can't make out; but I am sure you shan't have it for one.'

'You mean you won't sell?' gasped Keawe.

'No, sir,' cried the boatswain. 'But I'll give you a drink of the rum, if you like.'

'I tell you,' said Keawe, 'the man who has that bottle goes to hell.'

'I reckon I'm going anyway,' returned the sailor; 'and this bottle's the best thing to go with I've struck yet. No, sir!' he cried again, 'this is my bottle now, and you can go and fish for another.'

'Can this be true?' Keawe cried. 'For your own sake, I beseech you, sell it me!'

'I don't value any of your talk,' replied the boatswain. 'You thought I was flat,[16] now you see I'm not; and there's an end. If you won't have a swallow of the rum, I'll have one myself. Here's your health, and good-night to you!'

So off he went down the avenue towards town, and there goes the bottle out of the story.

But Keawe ran to Kokua light as the wind; and great was their joy that night; and great, since then, has been the peace of all their days in the Bright House.

ARTHUR CONAN DOYLE

ARTHUR CONAN DOYLE (1859–1930) was a prolific writer whose fiction covered a wide range of subjects from ghost stories and science-fiction adventures to tales of the Crusades and the Napoleonic Wars. However his greatest claim to fame is his creation of the detective Sherlock Holmes. This character, with the deerstalker hat, curly pipe and caped travelling coat, is known throughout the world. Even those who have never read a Holmes story recognise his image.

It was Doyle's intention in creating Sherlock Holmes to present the reading public with a scientific detective who solved cases by deduction rather than by guesswork or by relying on the carelessness of the criminal. He first appeared in two novels, *A Study in Scarlet* and *The Sign of Four*. These books provoked little interest from the reading public, but when Doyle began writing short stories featuring his detective hero for the new monthly publication *The Strand Magazine*, Sherlock Holmes rapidly became popular and very famous. Readers were so eager to devour the latest adventure of this fascinating detective that there were queues outside bookstalls on the day *The Strand Magazine* was published.

Ironically, the more popular Holmes became with the readers, the less interested the author grew in writing the stories. He really felt that in completing a dozen of the tales (known today as *The Adventures of Sherlock Holmes*) he had gone as far as he could with the format and character. He now wanted to turn his hand to writing serious works of historical fiction. The offer of the enormous fee of fifty pounds per story persuaded him to continue and he wrote a further twelve stories, known as *The Memoirs of Sherlock Holmes*. However, in the last story in this collection, Doyle killed Holmes off. He was made to fall over a cliff into the terrible chasm created by the Reichenbach Falls in Switzerland. The detective plunged to his supposed death in the icy waters below, taking with him his arch-enemy, the master criminal Professor Moriarty.

Readers were outraged at Doyle for killing their hero but he took no notice and got on with his other writing projects. In time, his resolve weakened. First he wrote *The Hound of the Baskervilles*, featuring Holmes in what the author claimed was an investigation that took place before the Reichenbach incident. This was such a success that his publishers offered him great sums of money to resurrect Holmes properly and at last he gave in and did just that.

By the time Doyle died in 1930, Holmes and his good friend Dr Watson, who acts as the storyteller, were established icons of popular culture. Since then they have appeared regularly on stage, in films and on television.

'The Red-Headed League' is one of the early Holmes stories and features the detective in sparkling form. The plot is a wonderful mixture of the bizarre and comic. Doyle carefully plants clues in the story that Jabez Wilson tells to Sherlock Holmes and it is possible for the reader to form a theory and play detective too.

The Red-Headed League

I HAD CALLED UPON MY FRIEND, Mr Sherlock Holmes, one day in the autumn of last year, and found him in deep conversation with a very stout, florid-faced, elderly gentleman, with fiery red hair. With an apology for my intrusion, I was about to withdraw, when Holmes pulled me abruptly into the room and closed the door behind me.

'You could not possibly have come at a better time, my dear Watson,' he said cordially.

'I was afraid that you were engaged.'

'So I am. Very much so.'

'Then I can wait in the next room.'

'Not at all. This gentleman, Mr Wilson, has been my partner and helper in many of my most successful cases, and I have no doubt that he will be of the utmost use to me in yours also.'

The stout gentleman half rose from his chair, and gave a bob of greeting, with a quick little questioning glance from his small, fat-encircled eyes.

'Try the settee,' said Holmes, relapsing into his armchair, and putting his fingertips together, as was his custom when in judicial moods. 'I know, my dear Watson, that you share my love of all that is bizarre and outside the conventions and humdrum routine of everyday life. You have shown your relish for it by the enthusiasm which has prompted you to chronicle, and, if you will excuse my saying so, somewhat to embellish so many of my own little adventures.'

'Your cases have indeed been of the greatest interest to me,' I observed.

'You will remember that I remarked the other day, just before we went into the very simple problem presented by Miss Mary Sutherland, that for strange effects and extraordinary combinations we must go to life itself, which is always far more daring than any effort of the imagination.'

'A proposition which I took the liberty of doubting.'

'You did, doctor, but none the less you must come round to my view, for otherwise I shall keep piling fact upon fact on you until your reason breaks down under them and acknowledges me to be right. Now, Mr Jabez Wilson here has been good enough to call upon me this morning, and to begin a narrative which promises to be one of the most singular which I have listened to for some time. You have heard me remark that the strangest and most unique things are very often connected not with the larger but with the smaller crimes, and occasionally, indeed, are those where there is room for doubt whether any positive crime has been committed. As far as I have heard, it is impossible for me to say whether the present case is an instance of crime or not, but the course of events is certainly among the most singular that I have ever listened to. Perhaps, Mr Wilson, you would have the great kindness to recommence your narrative. I ask you not merely because my friend Dr Watson has not heard the opening part, but also because the peculiar nature of the story makes me anxious to have every possible detail from your lips. As a rule, when I have heard some slight indication of the course of events, I am able to guide myself by the thousands of other similar cases which occur to my memory. In the present instance I am forced to admit that the facts are, to the best of my belief, unique.'

The portly client puffed out his chest with an appearance of some little pride, and pulled a dirty and wrinkled newspaper from the inside pocket of his greatcoat. As he glanced down the advertisement column, with his head thrust forward, and the paper flattened out upon his knee, I took a good look at the man, and endeavoured after the fashion of my companion to read the indications which might be presented by his dress or appearance.

I did not gain very much, however, by my inspection. Our visitor bore every mark of being an average commonplace British tradesman, obese, pompous and slow. He wore rather baggy grey shepherd's check trousers, a not over-clean black frock-coat, unbuttoned in the front, and a drab waistcoat with a heavy brassy Albert chain, and a square pierced bit of metal dangling down as an ornament. A frayed top-hat and a faded brown overcoat with a wrinkled velvet collar lay upon a chair beside him. Altogether, look as I would, there was nothing remarkable about the man save his blazing red head, and the expression of extreme chagrin and discontent upon his features.

Sherlock Holmes's quick eye took in my occupation and he shook his head with a smile as he noticed my questioning glances. 'Beyond the obvious facts that he has at some time done manual labour, that he takes snuff, that he is a Freemason, that he has been in China, and that he has done a considerable amount of writing lately, I can deduce nothing else.'

Mr Jabez Wilson started up in his chair, with his forefinger upon the paper, but his eyes upon my companion.

'How, in the name of good fortune, did you know all that, Mr Holmes?' he asked. 'How did you know, for example, that I did manual labour? It's as true as gospel, for I began as a ship's carpenter.'

'Your hands, my dear sir. Your right hand is quite a size larger than your left. You have worked with it, and the muscles are more developed.'

'Well, the snuff, then, and the Freemasonry?'

'I won't insult your intelligence by telling you how I read that, especially as, rather against the strict rules of your order, you use an arc and compass breastpin.'

'Ah, of course, I forgot that. But the writing?'

'What else can be indicated by that right cuff, so very shiny for five inches, and the left one with the smooth patch near the elbow where you rest it upon the desk.'

'Well, but China?'

'The fish which you have tattooed immediately above your right wrist could only have been done in China. I have made a small study of tattoo marks, and have even contributed to the literature of the subject. That trick of staining the fishes' scales a delicate pink is quite peculiar to China. When, in addition, I see a Chinese coin hanging from your watch-chain, the matter becomes even more simple.'

Mr Jabez Wilson laughed heavily. 'Well, I never!' said he. 'I thought at first you had done something clever, but I see that there was nothing in it after all.'

'I begin to think, Watson,' said Holmes, 'that I make
explaining. *Omne ignotum pro magnifico,*[1] you know, a
little reputation, such as it is, will suffer shipwreck if I a
Can you not find the advertisement, Mr Wilson?'

'Yes, I have got it now,' he answered, with his thick, red finge
planted halfway down the column. 'Here it is. This is what began it
all. You just read it for yourself, sir.'

I took the paper from him and read as follows:

> To the Red-Headed League – On account of the bequest of
> the late Ezekiah Hopkins, of Lebanon, Penn., USA, there is now
> another vacancy open which entitles a member of the league to a
> salary of four pounds a week for purely nominal services. All red-
> headed men who are sound in body and mind, and above the age
> of twenty-one years, are eligible. Apply in person on Monday, at
> eleven o'clock, to Duncan Ross, at the offices of the league, 7
> Pope's Court, Fleet Street.

'What on earth does this mean?' I ejaculated, after I had twice read
over the extraordinary announcement.

Holmes chuckled, and wriggled in his chair, as was his habit when
in high spirits. 'It is a little off the beaten track, isn't it?' said he. 'And
now, Mr Wilson, off you go at scratch,[2] and tell us all about yourself,
your household, and the effect which this advertisement had upon
your fortunes. You will first make a note, doctor, of the paper and the
date.'

'It is the *Morning Chronicle* of 27 April 1890. Just two months ago.'

'Very good. Now, Mr Wilson?'

'Well, it is just as I have been telling you, Mr Sherlock Holmes,'
said Jabez Wilson, mopping his forehead, 'I have a small pawnbroker's business in Saxe-Coburg Square, near the City. It's not a
very large affair, and of late years it has not done more than just give
me a living. I used to be able to keep two assistants, but now I only
keep one; and I would have a job to pay him, but that he is willing to
come for half wages, so as to learn the business.'

'What is the name of this obliging youth?' asked Sherlock Holmes.

'His name is Vincent Spaulding, and he's not such a youth either.
It's hard to say his age. I should not wish a smarter assistant, Mr
Holmes; and I know very well that he could better himself, and earn
twice what I am able to give him. But after all, if he is satisfied, why
should I put ideas in his head?'

'Why, indeed? You seem most fortunate in having an employee
who comes under the full market price. It is not a common

NINETEENTH CENTURY SHORT STORIES

xperience among employers in this age. I don't know that your assistant is not as remarkable as your advertisement.'

'Oh, he has his faults, too,' said Mr Wilson. 'Never was such a fellow for photography. Snapping away with a camera when he ought to be improving his mind, and then diving down into the cellar like a rabbit into its hole to develop his pictures. That is his main fault; but on the whole, he's a good worker. There's no vice in him.'

'He is still with you, I presume?'

'Yes, sir. He and a girl of fourteen, who does a bit of simple cooking, and keeps the place clean – that's all I have in the house, for I am a widower, and never had any family. We live very quietly, sir, the three of us; and we keep a roof over our heads, and pay our debts, if we do nothing more.

'The first thing that put us out was that advertisement. Spaulding, he came down into the office just this day eight weeks with this very paper in his hand, and he says: "I wish to the Lord, Mr Wilson, that I was a red-headed man."

' "Why's that?" I asks.

' "Why," says he, "here's another vacancy in the League of the Red-Headed Men. It's worth quite a little fortune to any man who gets it, and I understand that there are more vacancies than there are men, so that the trustees are at their wits' end what to do with the money. If my hair would only change colour, here's a nice little crib all ready for me to step into."

' "Why, what is it, then?" I asked. You see, Mr Holmes, I am a very stay-at-home man, and, as my business came to me instead of my having to go to it, I was often weeks on end without putting my foot over the doormat. In that way I didn't know much of what was going on outside, and I was always glad of a bit of news.

' "Have you never heard of the League of the Red-Headed Men?" he asked, with his eyes open.

' "Never."

' "Why, I wonder at that, for you are eligible yourself for one of the vacancies."

' "And what are they worth?" I asked.

' "Oh, merely a couple of hundred a year, but the work is slight, and it need not interfere much with one's other occupations."

'Well, you can easily think that that made me prick up my ears, for the business has not been over good for some years, and an extra couple of hundred would have been very handy.

' "Tell me all about it," said I.

' "Well," said he, showing me the advertisement, "you can see for yourself that the league has a vacancy, and there is the address where you should apply for particulars. As far as I can make out, the league was founded by an American millionaire, Ezekiah Hopkins, who was very peculiar in his ways. He was himself red-headed, and he had a great sympathy for all red-headed men; so, when he died, it was found that he had left his enormous fortune in the hands of trustees, with instructions to apply the interest to the providing of easy berths to men whose hair is of that colour. From all I hear it is splendid pay, and very little to do."

' "But," said I, "there would be millions of red-headed men who would apply."

' "Not so many as you might think," he answered. "You see, it is really confined to Londoners, and to grown men. This American had started from London when he was young, and he wanted to do the old town a good turn. Then, again, I have heard it is no use your applying if your hair is light red, or dark red, or anything but real, bright, blazing, fiery red. Now, if you cared to apply, Mr Wilson, you would just walk in; but perhaps it would hardly be worth your while to put yourself out of the way for the sake of a few hundred pounds."

'Now, it is a fact, gentlemen, as you may see for yourselves, that my hair is of a very full and rich tint, so that it seemed to me that, if there was to be any competition in the matter, I stood as good a chance as any man that I had ever met. Vincent Spaulding seemed to know so much about it that I thought he might prove useful, so I just ordered him to put up the shutters for the day, and to come right away with me. He was very willing to have a holiday, so we shut the business up, and started off for the address that was given us in the advertisement.

'I never hope to see such a sight as that again, Mr Holmes. From north, south, east and west every man who had a shade of red in his hair had tramped into the City to answer the advertisement. Fleet Street was choked with red-headed folk, and Pope's Court looked like a coster's orange barrow. I should not have thought there were so many in the whole country as were brought together by that single advertisement. Every shade of colour they were – straw, lemon, orange, brick, Irish setter, liver, clay; but, as Spaulding said, there were not many who had the real vivid flame-coloured tint. When I saw how many were waiting, I would have given it up in despair; but Spaulding would not hear of it. How he did it I could not imagine, but he pushed and pulled and butted until he got me through the crowd, and right up to the steps which led to the office. There was a double stream upon the stair, some going up in hope, and some coming back dejected; but we wedged in as well as we could, and soon found ourselves in the office.'

'Your experience has been a most entertaining one,' remarked Holmes, as his client paused and refreshed his memory with a huge pinch of snuff. 'Pray continue your very interesting statement.'

'There was nothing in the office but a couple of wooden chairs and a deal table, behind which sat a small man, with a head that was even redder than mine. He said a few words to each candidate as he came up, and then he always managed to find some fault in them which would disqualify them. Getting a vacancy did not seem to be such a very easy matter after all. However, when our turn came, the little man was more favourable to me than to any of the others, and he closed the door as we entered, so that he might have a private word with us.

' "This is Mr Jabez Wilson," said my assistant, "and he is willing to fill a vacancy in the league."

' "And he is admirably suited for it," the other answered. "He has every requirement. I cannot recall when I have seen anything so fine." He took a step backwards, cocked his head on one side, and gazed at my hair until I felt quite bashful. Then suddenly he plunged forward, wrung my hand, and congratulated me warmly on my success. "It would be injustice to hesitate," said he. "You will, however, I am sure, excuse me for taking an obvious precaution." With that he seized my hair in both his hands, and tugged until I yelled with the pain. "There is water in your eyes," said he, as he released me. "I perceive that all is as it should be. But we have to be careful, for we have twice been deceived by wigs and once by paint. I could tell you tales of cobbler's wax which would disgust you with human nature." He stepped over to the window, and shouted through it at the top of his voice that the vacancy was filled. A groan of disappointment came up from below, and the folk all trooped away in different directions, until there was not a red head to be seen except my own and that of the manager.

' "My name," said he, "is Mr Duncan Ross, and I am myself one of the pensioners upon the fund left by our noble benefactor. Are you a married man, Mr Wilson? Have you a family?"

'I answered that I had not.

'His face fell immediately.

' "Dear me!" he said gravely, "that is very serious indeed! I am sorry to hear you say that. The fund was, of course, for the propagation and spread of red-heads as well as for their maintenance. It is exceedingly unfortunate that you should be a bachelor."

'My face lengthened at this, Mr Holmes, for I thought that I was not to have the vacancy after all; but after thinking it over for a few minutes, he said that it would be all right.

' "In the case of another," said he, "the objection might be fatal, but we must stretch a point in favour of a man with such a head of hair as yours. When shall you be able to enter upon your new duties?"

' "Well, it is a little awkward, for I have a business already," said I.

' "Oh, never mind about that, Mr Wilson!" said Vincent Spaulding. "I shall be able to look after that for you."

' "What would be the hours?" I asked.

' "Ten to two."

'Now a pawnbroker's business is mostly done of an evening, Mr Holmes, especially Thursday and Friday evening, which is just before pay-day; so it would suit me very well to earn a little in the mornings. Besides, I knew that my assistant was a good man, and that he would see to anything that turned up.

' "That would suit me very well," said I. "And the pay?"

' "Is four pounds a week."

' "And the work?"

' "Is purely nominal."

' "What do you call purely nominal?"

' "Well, you have to be in the office, or at least in the building, the whole time. If you leave, you forfeit your whole position for ever. The will is very clear upon that point. You don't comply with the conditions if you budge from the office during that time."

' "It's only four hours a day, and I should not think of leaving," said I.

' "No excuse will avail," said Mr Duncan Ross, "neither sickness, nor business, nor anything else. There you must stay, or you lose your billet."[3]

' "And the work?"

' "Is to copy out the *Encyclopaedia Britannica*. There is the first volume of it in that press. You must find your own ink, pens and blotting-paper, but we provide this table and chair. Will you be ready tomorrow?"

' "Certainly," I answered.

' "Then, goodbye, Mr Jabez Wilson, and let me congratulate you once more on the important position which you have been fortunate enough to gain." He bowed me out of the room, and I went home with my assistant, hardly knowing what to say or do, I was so pleased at my own good fortune.

'Well, I thought over the matter all day, and by evening I was in low spirits again; for I had quite persuaded myself that the whole affair must be some great hoax or fraud, though what its object might be I could not imagine. It seemed altogether past belief that anyone could make such a will, or that they would pay such a sum for doing anything so simple as copying out the *Encyclopaedia Britannica*. Vincent Spaulding did what he could to cheer me up, but by bedtime I had reasoned myself out of the whole thing. However, in the morning I determined to have a look at it anyhow, so I bought a penny bottle of ink, and with a quill pen and seven sheets of foolscap paper, I started off for Pope's Court.

'Well, to my surprise and delight everything was as right as possible. The table was set out ready for me and Mr Duncan Ross was there to see that I got fairly to work. He started me off upon the letter A, and then he left me; but he would drop in from time to time to see that all was right with me. At two o'clock he bade me good-day, complimented me upon the amount that I had written, and locked the door of the office after me.

'This went on day after day, Mr Holmes, and on Saturday the manager came in and planked down four golden sovereigns for my week's work. It was the same next week, and the same the week after. Every morning I was there at ten, and every afternoon I left at two. By degrees Mr Duncan Ross took to coming in only once of a morning, and then, after a time, he did not come in at all. Still, of course, I never dared to leave the room for an instant, for I was not sure when he might come, and the billet was such a good one, and suited me so well, that I would not risk the loss of it.

'Eight weeks passed away like this, and I had written about Abbots, and Archery, and Armour, and Architecture, and Attica, and hoped with diligence that I might get on to the Bs before very long. It cost me something in foolscap, and I had pretty nearly filled a shelf with my writings. And then suddenly the whole business came to an end.'

'To an end?'

'Yes, sir. And no later than this morning. I went to my work as usual at ten o'clock, but the door was shut and locked, with a little square of cardboard hammered on to the middle of the panel with a tack. Here it is, and you can read for yourself.'

He held up a piece of white cardboard, about the size of a sheet of notepaper. It read in this fashion:

THE RED-HEADED
LEAGUE IS DISSOLVED
9 OCT 1890

Sherlock Holmes and I surveyed this curt announcement and the rueful face behind it until the comical side of the affair so completely over-topped every other consideration that we both burst out into a roar of laughter.

'I cannot see that there is anything very funny,' cried our client, flushing up to the roots of his flaming head. 'If you can do nothing better than laugh at me, I can go elsewhere.'

'No, no,' cried Holmes, shoving him back into the chair from which he had half risen. 'I really wouldn't miss your case for the world. It is most refreshingly unusual. But there is, if you will excuse me saying so, something just a little funny about it. Pray what steps did you take when you found the card upon the door?'

'I was staggered, sir. I did not know what to do. Then I called at the offices round, but none of them seemed to know anything about it. Finally, I went to the landlord, who is an accountant living on the ground floor, and I asked him if he could tell me what had become of the Red-Headed League. He said that he had never heard of any such body. Then I asked him who Mr Duncan Ross was. He answered that the name was new to him.

' "Well," said I, "the gentleman at No. 4."

' "What, the red-headed man?"

' "Yes."

' "Oh," said he, "his name was William Morris. He was a solicitor, and was using my room as a temporary convenience until his new premises were ready. He moved out yesterday.'

' "Where could I find him?"

' "Oh, at his new offices. He did tell me the address. Yes, 17 King Edward Street, near St Paul's."

'I started off, Mr Holmes, but when I got to that address it was a manufactory of artificial knee-caps, and no one in it had ever heard of either Mr William Morris or Mr Duncan Ross.'

'And what did you do then?' asked Holmes.

'I went home to Saxe-Coburg Square, and I took the advice of my assistant. But he could not help me in any way. He could only say that if I waited I should hear by post. But that was not quite good enough, Mr Holmes. I did not wish to lose such a place without a struggle, so, as I had heard that you were good enough to give advice to poor folk who were in need of it, I came right away to you.'

'And you did very wisely,' said Holmes. 'Your case is an exceedingly remarkable one, and I shall be happy to look into it. From what you have told me I think that it is possible that graver issues hang from it than might at first sight appear.'

'Grave enough!' said Mr Jabez Wilson. 'Why, I have lost four pounds a week.'

'As far as you are personally concerned,' remarked Holmes, 'I do not see that you have any grievance against this extraordinary league. On the contrary, you are, as I understand, richer by some thirty pounds, to say nothing of the minute knowledge which you have gained on every subject which comes under the letter A. You have lost nothing by them.'

'No, sir. But I want to find out about them, and who they are, and what their object was in playing this prank – if it was a prank – upon me. It was a pretty expensive joke for them, for it cost them two-and-thirty pounds.'

'We shall endeavour to clear up these points for you. And, first, one or two questions, Mr Wilson. This assistant of yours who first called your attention to the advertisement – how long had he been with you?'

'About a month then.'

'How did he come?'

'In answer to an advertisement.'

'Was he the only applicant?'

'No, I had a dozen.'

'Why did you pick him?'

'Because he was handy, and would come cheap.'

'At half wages, in fact.'

'Yes.'

'What is he like, this Vincent Spaulding?'

'Small, stout-built, very quick in his ways, no hair on his face, though he's not short of thirty. Has a white splash of acid upon his forehead.'

Holmes sat up in his chair in considerable excitement.

'I thought as much,' said he. 'Have you ever observed that his ears are pierced for ear-rings?'

'Yes, sir. He told me that a gypsy had done it for him when he was a lad.'

'Hum!' said Holmes, sinking back in deep thought. 'He is still with you?'

'Oh, yes, sir; I have only just left him.'

'And has your business been attended to in your absence?'

'Nothing to complain of, sir. There's never very much to do of a morning.'

'That will do, Mr Wilson. I shall be happy to give you an opinion upon the subject in the course of a day or two. Today is Saturday, and I hope that by Monday we may come to a conclusion.

'Well, Watson,' said Holmes, when our visitor had left us, 'what do you make of it all?'

'I make nothing of it,' I answered, frankly. 'It is a most mysterious business.'

'As a rule,' said Holmes, 'the more bizarre a thing is the less mysterious it proves to be. It is your commonplace, featureless crimes which are really puzzling, just as a commonplace face is the most difficult to identify. But I must be prompt over this matter.'

'What are you going to do then?' I asked.

'To smoke,' he answered. 'It is quite a three-pipe problem, and I beg that you won't speak to me for fifty minutes.' He curled himself up in his chair, with his thin knees drawn up to his hawk-like nose, and there he sat with his eyes closed and his black clay pipe thrusting out like the bill of some strange bird. I had come to the conclusion that he had dropped asleep, and indeed was nodding myself, when he suddenly sprang out of his chair with the gesture of a man who had made up his mind, and put his pipe down upon the mantelpiece.

'Sarasate plays at the St James's Hall this afternoon,' he remarked. 'What do you think, Watson? Could your patients spare you for a few hours?'

'I have nothing to do today. My practice is never very absorbing.'

'Then put on your hat, and come. I am going through the City first, and we can have some lunch on the way. I observe that there is a good deal of German music on the programme, which is rather more to my taste than Italian or French. It is introspective, and I want to introspect. Come along!'

We travelled by the Underground as far as Aldersgate; and a short walk took us to Saxe-Coburg Square, the scene of the singular story which we had listened to in the morning. It was a pokey little shabby-genteel place, where four lines of dingy two-storeyed brick houses looked out into a small railed-in enclosure, where a lawn of weedy grass and a few clumps of faded laurel bushes made a hard fight against a smoke-laden and uncongenial atmosphere. Three gilt balls and a brown board with Jabez Wilson in white letters, upon a corner house, announced the place where our red-headed client carried on his business. Sherlock Holmes stopped in front of it with his head on one side, and looked it all over, with his eyes shining brightly between puckered lids. Then he walked slowly up the street and then down again to the corner, still looking keenly at the houses. Finally he returned to the pawnbroker's, and, having thumped vigorously upon the pavement with his stick two or three times, he went up to the door and knocked. It was instantly opened by a bright-looking, clean-shaven young fellow, who asked him to step in.

'Thank you,' said Holmes, 'I only wished to ask you how you would go from here to the Strand.'

'Third right, fourth left,' answered the assistant promptly, closing the door.

'Smart fellow, that,' observed Holmes as we walked away. 'He is, in my judgement, the fourth smartest man in London, and for daring I am not sure that he has not a claim to be third. I have known something of him before.'

'Evidently,' said I, 'Mr Wilson's assistant counts for a good deal in this mystery of the Red-Headed League. I am sure that you enquired your way merely in order that you might see him.'

'Not him.'

'What then?'

'The knees of his trousers.'

'And what did you see?'

'What I expected to see.'

'Why did you beat the pavement?'

'My dear doctor, this is a time for observation, not for talk. We are spies in an enemy's country. We know something of Saxe-Coburg Square. Let us now explore the paths which lie behind it.'

The road in which we found ourselves as we turned round the corner from the retired Saxe-Coburg Square presented as great a contrast to it as the front of a picture does to the back. It was one of the main arteries which convey the traffic of the City to the north and west. The roadway was blocked with the immense stream of commerce flowing in a double tide inwards and outwards, while the footpaths were black with the hurrying swarm of pedestrians. It was difficult to realise as we looked at the line of fine shops and stately business premises that they really abutted on the other side upon the faded and stagnant square which we had just quitted.

'Let me see,' said Holmes, standing at the corner, and glancing along the line, 'I should like just to remember the order of the houses here. It is a hobby of mine to have an exact knowledge of London. There is Mortimer's, the tobacconist, the little newspaper shop, the Coburg branch of the City and Suburban Bank, the Vegetarian Restaurant and McFarlane's carriage-building depot. That carries us right on to the other block. And now, doctor, we've done our work, so it's time we had some play. A sandwich, and a cup of coffee, and then off to violin land, where all is sweetness and delicacy and harmony and there are no red-headed clients to vex us with their conundrums.'

My friend was an enthusiastic musician, being himself not only a very capable performer, but a composer of no ordinary merit. All the afternoon he sat in the stalls wrapped in the most perfect happiness, gently waving his long thin fingers in time to the music, while his gently smiling face and his languid, dreamy eyes were as unlike those of Holmes the sleuth-hound, Holmes the relentless, keen-witted, ready-handed criminal agent, as it was possible to conceive. In his singular character the dual nature alternately asserted itself, and his extreme exactness and astuteness represented, as I have often thought, the reaction against the poetic and contemplative mood which occasionally predominated in him. The swing of his nature took him from extreme languor to devouring energy; and, as I knew well, he was never so truly formidable as when, for days on end, he had been lounging in his armchair amid his improvisations and his black-letter editions. Then it was that the lust of the chase would suddenly come upon him, and that his brilliant reasoning power would rise to the level of intuition, until those who were unacquainted with his methods would look askance at him as on a man whose knowledge was not that of other mortals. When I saw him that afternoon so enwrapped in the music at St James's Hall I felt that an evil time might be coming upon those whom he had set himself to hunt down.

'You want to go home, no doubt, doctor,' he remarked, as we emerged.

'Yes, it would be as well.'

'And I have some business to do which will take some hours. This business at Coburg Square is serious.'

'Why serious?'

'A considerable crime is in contemplation. I have every reason to believe that we shall be in time to stop it. But today being Saturday rather complicates matters. I shall want your help tonight.'

'At what time?'

'Ten will be early enough.'

'I shall be at Baker Street at ten.'

'Very well. And, I say, doctor! there may be some little danger, so kindly put your army revolver in your pocket.' He waved his hand, turned on his heel, and disappeared in an instant among the crowd.

I trust that I am not more dense than my neighbours, but I was always oppressed with a sense of my own stupidity in my dealings with Sherlock Holmes. Here I had heard what he had heard, I had seen what he had seen, and yet from his words it was evident that he saw clearly not only what had happened, but what was about to happen, while to me the whole business was still confused and grotesque. As I drove home to my house in Kensington I thought over it all, from the extraordinary story of the red-headed copier of the *Encyclopaedia* down to the visit to Saxe-Coburg Square, and the ominous words with which he had parted from me. What was this nocturnal expedition, and why should I go armed? Where were we going, and what were we to do? I had the hint from Holmes that this smooth-faced pawnbroker's assistant was a formidable man – a man who might play a deep game. I tried to puzzle it out, but gave it up in despair, and set the matter aside until night should bring an explanation.

It was a quarter past nine when I started from home and made my way across the park, and so through Oxford Street to Baker Street. Two hansoms were standing at the door, and, as I entered the passage, I heard the sound of voices from above. On entering his room, I found Holmes in animated conversation with two men, one of whom I recognised as Peter Jones, the official police agent, while the other was a long, thin, sad-faced man, with a very shiny hat and oppressively respectable frock-coat.

'Ha! our party is complete,' said Holmes, buttoning up his pea-jacket, and taking his heavy hunting-crop from the rack. 'Watson, I think you know Mr Jones, of Scotland Yard? Let me introduce you to Mr Merryweather, who is to be our companion in tonight's adventure.'

'We're hunting in couples again, doctor, you see,' said Jones in his consequential way. 'Our friend here is a wonderful man for starting a chase. All he wants is an old dog to help him to do the running down.'

'I hope a wild goose may not prove to be the end of our chase,' observed Mr Merryweather gloomily.

'You may place considerable confidence in Mr Holmes, sir,' said the police agent loftily. 'He has his own little methods, which are, if he won't mind my saying so, just a little too theoretical and fantastic, but he has the makings of a detective in him. It is not too much to say that once or twice, as in that business of the Sholto murder and the Agra treasure, he has been more nearly correct than the official force.'

'Oh, if you say so, Mr Jones, it is all right!' said the stranger, with deference. 'Still, I confess that I miss my rubber.[4] It is the first Saturday night for seven-and-twenty years that I have not had my rubber.'

'I think you will find,' said Sherlock Holmes, 'that you will play for a higher stake tonight than you have ever done yet, and that the play will be more exciting. For you, Mr Merryweather, the stake will be some thirty thousand pounds; and for you, Jones, it will be the man upon whom you wish to lay your hands.'

'John Clay, the murderer, thief, smasher[5] and forger. He's a young man, Mr Merryweather, but he is at the head of his profession, and I would rather have my bracelets on him than on any criminal in London. He's a remarkable man, is young John Clay. His grandfather was a royal duke, and he himself has been to Eton and Oxford. His brain is as cunning as his fingers, and though we meet signs of him at every turn, we never know where to find the man himself. He'll crack a crib[6] in Scotland one week, and be raising money to build an orphanage in Cornwall the next. I've been on his track for years, and have never set eyes on him yet.'

'I hope that I may have the pleasure of introducing you tonight. I've had one or two little turns also with Mr John Clay, and I agree with you that he is at the head of his profession. It is past ten, however, and quite time that we started. If you two will take the first hansom, Watson and I will follow in the second.'

Sherlock Holmes was not very communicative during the long drive, and lay back in the cab humming the tunes which he had heard in the afternoon. We rattled through an endless labyrinth of gaslit streets until we emerged into Farringdon Street.

'We are close there now,' my friend remarked. 'This fellow Merryweather is a bank director and personally interested in the matter. I thought it as well to have Jones with us also. He is not a bad fellow, though an absolute imbecile in his profession. He has one positive virtue. He is as brave as a bulldog, and as tenacious as a lobster if he gets his claws upon anyone. Here we are, and they are waiting for us.'

We had reached the same crowded thoroughfare in which we had found ourselves in the morning. Our cabs were dismissed, and, following the guidance of Mr Merryweather, we passed down a narrow passage, and through a side door, which he opened for us. Within there was a small corridor, which ended in a very massive iron gate. This also was opened, and led down a flight of winding stone steps, which terminated at another formidable gate. Mr Merryweather stopped to light a lantern, and then conducted us down a dark, earth-smelling passage, and so, after opening a third door, into a huge vault or cellar, which was piled all round with crates and massive boxes.

'You are not very vulnerable from above,' Holmes remarked, as he held up the lantern and gazed about him.

'Nor from below,' said Mr Merryweather, striking his stick upon the flags which lined the floor. 'Why, dear me, it sounds quite hollow!' he remarked, looking up in surprise.

'I must really ask you to be a little more quiet,' said Holmes severely. 'You have already imperilled the whole success of our expedition. Might I beg that you would have the goodness to sit down upon one of those boxes, and not to interfere?'

The solemn Mr Merryweather perched himself upon a crate, with a very injured expression upon his face, while Holmes fell upon his knees upon the floor and, with the lantern and a magnifying lens, began to examine minutely the cracks between the stones. A few seconds sufficed to satisfy him, for he sprang to his feet again, and put his glass in his pocket.

'We have at least an hour before us,' he remarked, 'for they can hardly take any steps until the good pawnbroker is safely in bed. Then they will not lose a minute, for the sooner they do their work the longer time they will have for their escape. We are at present, doctor – as no doubt you have divined – in the cellar of the City branch of one of the principal London banks. Mr Merryweather is the chairman of the directors, and he will explain to you that there are reasons why the more daring criminals of London should take a considerable interest in this cellar at present.'

'It is our French gold,' whispered the director. 'We have had several warnings that an attempt might be made upon it.'

'Your French gold?'

'Yes. We had occasion some months ago to strengthen our resources, and borrowed, for that purpose, thirty thousand napoleons[7] from the Bank of France. It has become known that we have never had occasion to unpack the money, and that it is still lying in our cellar. The crate upon which I sit contains two thousand napoleons packed between layers of lead foil. Our reserve of bullion is much larger at present than is usually kept in a single branch office, and the directors have had misgivings upon the subject.'

'Which were very well justified,' observed Holmes. 'And now it is time that we arranged our little plans. I expect that within an hour matters will come to a head. In the meantime, Mr Merryweather, we must put the screen over that dark lantern.'

'And sit in the dark?'

'I am afraid so. I had brought a pack of cards in my pocket, and I thought that, as we were a *partie carrée*,[8] you might have your rubber after all. But I see that the enemy's preparations have gone so far that we cannot risk the presence of a light. And, first of all, we must choose our positions. These are daring men, and, though we shall take them at a disadvantage, they may do us some harm unless we are careful. I shall stand behind this crate, and do you conceal yourself behind those. Then, when I flash a light upon them, close in swiftly. If they fire, Watson, have no compunction about shooting them down.'

I placed my revolver, cocked, upon the top of the wooden case behind which I crouched. Holmes shot the slide across the front of his lantern, and left us in pitch darkness – such an absolute darkness as I had never before experienced. The smell of hot metal remained to assure us that the light was still there, ready to flash out at a moment's notice. To me, with my nerves worked up to a pitch of expectancy, there was something depressing and subduing in the sudden gloom, and in the cold, dank air of the vault.

'They have but one retreat,' whispered Holmes. 'That is back through the house into Saxe-Coburg Square. I hope that you have done what I asked you, Jones?'

'I have an inspector and two officers waiting at the front door.'

'Then we have stopped all the holes. And now we must be silent and wait.'

What a time it seemed! From comparing notes afterwards it was but an hour and a quarter, yet it appeared to me that the night must have almost gone, and the dawn be breaking above us. My limbs were weary and stiff, for I feared to change my position, yet my nerves were worked up to the highest pitch of tension, and my hearing was so acute that I could not only hear the gentle breathing of my companions, but I could distinguish the deeper, heavier in-breath of the bulky Jones from the thin sighing note of the bank director. From my position I could look over the case in the direction of the floor. Suddenly my eyes caught the glint of a light.

At first it was but a lurid spark upon the stone pavement. Then it lengthened out until it became a yellow line, and then, without any warning or sound, a gash seemed to open and a hand appeared, a white, almost womanly hand, which felt about in the centre of the little area of light. For a minute or more the hand, with its writhing fingers, protruded out of the floor. Then it was withdrawn as suddenly as it appeared, and all was dark again save the single lurid spark, which marked a chink between the stones.

Its disappearance, however, was but momentary. With a rending, tearing sound, one of the broad, white stones turned over upon its side, and left a square, gaping hole, through which streamed the light of a lantern. Over the edge there peeped a clean-cut, boyish face, which looked keenly about it, and then, with a hand on either side of the aperture, drew itself shoulder high and waist high, until one knee rested upon the edge. In another instant he stood at the side of the hole and was hauling after him a companion, lithe and small like himself, with a pale face and a shock of very red hair.

'It's all clear,' he whispered. 'Have you the chisel, and the bags. Great Scott! Jump, Archie, jump, and I'll swing for it!'

Sherlock Holmes had sprung out and seized the intruder by the collar. The other dived down the hole, and I heard the sound of rending cloth as Jones clutched at his skirts.[9] The light flashed upon the barrel of a revolver, but Holmes's hunting-crop came down on the man's wrist, and the pistol clinked upon the stone floor.

'It's no use, John Clay,' said Holmes blandly; 'you have no chance at all.'

'So I see,' the other answered with the utmost coolness. 'I fancy that my pal is all right, though I see you have got his coat-tails.'

'There are three men waiting for him at the door,' said Holmes.

'Oh, indeed. You seem to have done the thing very completely. I must compliment you.'

'And I you,' Holmes answered. 'Your red-headed idea was very new and effective.'

'You'll see your pal again presently,' said Jones. 'He's quicker at climbing down holes than I am. Just hold out while I fix the derbies.'

'I beg that you will not touch me with your filthy hands,' remarked our prisoner, as the handcuffs clattered upon his wrists. 'You may not be aware that I have royal blood in my veins. Have the goodness also when you address me always to say "sir" and "please".'

'All right,' said Jones, with a stare and a snigger. 'Well, would you please, sir, march upstairs, where we can get a cab to carry your highness to the police station.'

'That is better,' said John Clay serenely. He made a sweeping bow to the three of us, and walked quietly off in the custody of the detective.

'Really, Mr Holmes,' said Mr Merryweather, as we followed them from the cellar, 'I do not know how the bank can thank you or repay you. There is no doubt that you have detected and defeated in the most complete manner one of the most determined attempts at bank robbery that have ever come within my experience.'

'I have one or two little scores of my own to settle with Mr John Clay,' said Holmes. 'I have been at some small expense over this matter, which I shall expect the bank to refund, but beyond that I am amply repaid by having had an experience which is in many ways unique, and by hearing the very remarkable narrative of the Red-Headed League.'

'You see, Watson,' he explained in the early hours of the morning, as we sat over a glass of whisky and soda in Baker Street, 'it was perfectly obvious from the first that the only possible object of this rather fantastic business of the advertisement of the league, and the copying of the *Encyclopaedia*, must be to get this not over-bright pawnbroker out of the way for a number of hours every day. It was a curious way of managing it, but really it would be difficult to suggest a better. The method was no doubt suggested to Clay's ingenious mind by the colour of his accomplice's hair. The four pounds a week was a lure which must draw him, and what was it to them, who were playing for thousands? They put in the advertisement; one rogue has the temporary office, the other rogue incites the man to apply for it, and together they manage to secure his absence every morning in the week. From the time that I heard of the assistant having come for half-wages, it was obvious to me that he had some strong motive for securing the situation.'

'But how could you guess what the motive was?'

'Had there been women in the house, I should have suspected a mere vulgar intrigue. That, however, was out of the question. The man's business was a small one, and there was nothing in his house which could account for such elaborate preparations and such an expenditure as they were at. It must then be something out of the house. What could it be? I thought of the assistant's fondness for photography, and his trick of vanishing into the cellar. The cellar! There was the end of this tangled clue. Then I made enquiries as to this mysterious assistant, and found that I had to deal with one of the coolest and most daring criminals in London. He was doing something in the cellar – something which took many hours a day for months on end. What could it be, once more? I could think of nothing save that he was running a tunnel to some other building.

'So far I had got when we went to visit the scene of action. I surprised you by beating upon the pavement with my stick. I was ascertaining whether the cellar stretched out in front or behind. It was not in front. Then I rang the bell, and, as I hoped, the assistant answered it. We have had some skirmishes, but we had never set eyes on each other before. I hardly looked at his face. His knees were what I wished to see. You must yourself have remarked how worn, wrinkled and stained they were. They spoke of those hours of burrowing. The only remaining point was what they were burrowing for. I walked round the corner, saw that the City and Suburban Bank abutted on our friend's premises, and felt that I had solved my problem. When you drove home after the concert I called upon Scotland Yard, and upon the chairman of the bank directors, with the result that you have seen.'

'And how could you tell that they would make their attempt tonight?' I asked.

'Well, when they closed their league offices that was a sign that they cared no longer about Mr Jabez Wilson's presence; in other words, that they had completed their tunnel. But it was essential that they should use it soon, as it might be discovered, or the bullion might be removed. Saturday would suit them better than any other day, as it would give them two days for their escape. For all these reasons I expected them to come tonight.'

'You reasoned it out beautifully,' I exclaimed in unfeigned admiration. 'It is so long a chain, and yet every link rings true.'

'It saved me from ennui,'[10] he answered, yawning. 'Alas, I already feel it closing in upon me! My life is spent in one long effort to escape from the commonplaces of existence. These little problems help me to do so.'

'And you are a benefactor of the race,' said I.

He shrugged his shoulders. 'Well, perhaps, after all, it is of some little use,' he remarked. '*L'homme c'est rien – l'oeuvre c'est tout,*[11] as Gustave Flaubert wrote to George Sand.'

H. G. WELLS

HERBERT GEORGE WELLS (1866–1946) was the youngest of three sons. His father Joseph ran a general shop and played professional cricket. When Joseph Wells broke his leg and could no longer earn a proper living, thirteen-year-old Herbert was sent to work in a draper's shop. His mother became a housekeeper at a large country house, and on his visits to her, the young Herbert would study books in the library secretly. His love was for literature and science. After a brief spell as an apprentice to a pharmacist, H. G. Wells won a scholarship to study at the Normal School of Science (now the Imperial College) in 1884. It was about this time that he began to write – essays and short stories at first. Then in 1895, the year after he wrote 'The Stolen Bacillus', he published *The Time Machine* and became a celebrity overnight. Other works, which we today might call science fiction but Wells referred to as 'scientific romances', followed. *The Island of Doctor Moreau, The Invisible Man, The War of the Worlds* and *The First Men in the Moon*. Wells also wrote books about the lives and struggles of ordinary people, such as *Kipps* and *The History of Mr Polly*. He was concerned about social justice and became a member of the Fabian Society, a group of intellectuals who sought to bring about a fairer society by planning for a gradual system of reforms.

We can see a coming together of Wells's main interests and concerns in 'The Stolen Bacillus': science, politics and the well-being of society. Certainly, there are elements within this short story which are relevant today. There is the research scientist working to understand and control a dangerous disease and yet ultimately with the power to destroy his world; and there is the anarchist – the political rebel who wishes to make his mark on society at whatever cost to innocent lives. These characters are still with us. The climax of the story is presented as a comic chase and there is a final amusing twist, but these come as a sugar coating to what is essentially a very dark story.

The Stolen Bacillus

'THIS AGAIN,' said the bacteriologist,[1] slipping a glass slide under the miscroscope, 'is a preparation of the celebrated bacillus of cholera – the cholera germ.'

The pale-faced man peered down the microscope. He was evidently not accustomed to that kind of thing, and held a limp white hand over his disengaged eye. 'I see very little,' he said.

'Touch this screw,' said the bacteriologist; 'perhaps the microscope is out of focus for you. Eyes vary so much. Just the fraction of a turn this way or that.'

'Ah! now I see,' said the visitor. 'Not so very much to see after all. Little streaks and shreds of pink. And yet those little particles, those mere atomies, might multiply and devastate a city! Wonderful!'

He stood up, and releasing the glass slip from the microscope, held it in his hand towards the window. 'Scarcely visible,' he said, scrutinising the preparation. He hesitated, 'Are these – alive? Are they dangerous now?'

'Those have been stained and killed,' said the bacteriologist. 'I wish, for my own part, we could kill and stain every one of them in the universe.'

'I suppose,' the pale man said with a slight smile, 'that you scarcely care to have such things about you in the living – in the active state?'

'On the contrary, we are obliged to,' said the bacteriologist. 'Here, for instance – ' He walked across the room and took up one of several sealed tubes. 'Here is the living thing. This is a cultivation of the actual living disease bacteria.' He hesitated. 'Bottled cholera, so to speak.'

A slight gleam of satisfaction appeared momentarily in the face of the pale man. 'It's a deadly thing to have in your possession,' he said, devouring the little tube with his eyes. The bacteriologist watched the morbid pleasure in his visitor's expression. This man, who had visited him that afternoon with a note of introduction from an old friend, interested him from the very contrast of their dispositions. The lank black hair and deep grey eyes, the haggard expression and nervous manner, the fitful yet keen interest in his visitor, were a novel change from the phlegmatic deliberations of the ordinary scientific worker with whom the bacteriologist chiefly associated. It was perhaps natural, with a hearer evidently so impressionable to the lethal nature of his topic, to take the most effective aspect of the matter.

He held the tube in his hand thoughtfully. 'Yes, here is the pestilence imprisoned. Only break such a little tube as this into a supply of drinking-water, say to these minute particles of life that one must needs stain and examine with the highest powers of the microscope even to see, and that one can neither smell nor taste – say to them, "Go forth, increase and multiply, and replenish the cisterns," and death – mysterious, untraceable death, death swift and terrible, death full of pain and indignity – would be released upon this city, and go hither and thither seeking his victims. Here he would take the husband from the wife, here the child from its mother, here the statesman from his duty, and here the toiler from his trouble. He would follow the water-mains, creeping along streets, picking out and punishing a house here and a house there where they did not boil their drinking-water, creeping into the wells of the mineral-water makers, getting washed into salad and lying dormant in ices. He would wait ready to be drunk in the horse-troughs and by unwary children in the public fountains. He would soak into the soil, to reappear in springs and wells at a thousand unexpected places. Once start him at the water supply, and before we could ring him in, and catch him again, he would have decimated the metropolis.' He stopped abruptly. He had been told rhetoric[2] was his weakness. 'But he is quite safe here, you know – quite safe.'

The pale-faced man nodded. His eyes shone. He cleared his throat. 'These anarchist – rascals,' said he, 'are fools, blind fools – to use bombs when this kind of thing is attainable. I think – '

A gentle rap, a mere light touch of the fingernails was heard at the door. The bacteriologist opened it.

'Just a minute, dear,' whispered his wife.

When he re-entered the laboratory his visitor was looking at his watch. 'I had no idea I had wasted an hour of your time,' he said. 'Twelve minutes to four. I ought to have left here by half-past three. But your things were really too interesting. No, positively I cannot stop a moment longer. I have an engagement at four.'

He passed out of the room, reiterating his thanks, and the bacteriologist accompanied him to the door, and then returned thoughtfully along the passage to his laboratory. He was musing on the ethnology[3] of his visitor. Certainly the man was not a Teutonic type nor a common Latin one. 'A morbid product, anyhow, I am afraid,' said the bacteriologist to himself. 'How he gloated on those cultivations of disease-germs!' A disturbing thought struck him. He turned to the bench by the vapour-bath, and then very quickly to his writing-table. Then he felt hastily in his pockets, and then rushed to the door. 'I may have put it down on the hall table,' he said.

'Minnie!' he shouted hoarsely in the hall.

'Yes, dear,' came a remote voice.

'Had I anything in my hand when I spoke to you, dear, just now?'

Pause.

'Nothing, dear, because I remember – '

'Blue ruin!' cried the bacteriologist, and incontinently[4] ran to the front door and down the steps of his house to the street.

Minnie, hearing the door slam violently, ran in alarm to the window. Down the street a slender man was getting into a cab. The bacteriologist, hatless, and in his carpet slippers, was running and gesticulating wildly towards this group. One slipper came off, but he did not wait for it. 'He has gone *mad*!' said Minnie; 'it's that horrid science of his;' and, opening the window, would have called after him. The slender man, suddenly glancing round, seemed struck with the same idea of mental disorder. He pointed hastily to the bacteriologist, said something to the cabman, the apron of the cab slammed, the whip swished, the horse's feet clattered, and in a moment the cab, bacteriologist hotly in pursuit, had receded up the vista of the roadway and disappeared round the corner.

Minnie remained straining out of the window for a minute. Then she drew her head back into the room again. She was dumbfounded. 'Of course he is eccentric,' she meditated. 'But running about London – in the height of the season, too – in his socks!' A happy thought struck her. She hastily put her bonnet on, seized his shoes, went into the hall, took down his hat and light overcoat from the pegs, emerged upon the doorstep, and hailed a cab that opportunely crawled by. 'Drive me up the road and round Havelock Crescent, and see if we can find a gentleman running about in a velveteen coat and no hat.'

'Velveteen coat, ma'am and no 'at. Very good, ma'am.' And the cabman whipped up at once in the most matter-of-fact way, as if he drove to this address every day in his life.

Some few minutes later the little group of cabmen and loafers that collects round the cabmen's shelter at Haverstock Hill were startled by the passing of a cab with a ginger-coloured screw of a horse,[5] driven furiously

They were silent as it went by, and then as it receded – 'That's 'Arry

'Icks. Wot's *he* got?' said the stout gentleman known as Old Tootles.

'He's a-using his whip, he is, *to* rights,' said the ostler boy.[6]

'Hallo!' said poor old Tommy Byles; 'here's another bloomin'' loonatic. Blowed if there ain't.'

'It's Old George,' said Old Tootles, 'and he's drivin' a loonatic, *as* you say. Ain't he a-clawin' out of the keb? Wonder if he's after 'Arry 'Icks?'

The group round the cabmen's shelter became animated. Chorus: 'Go it, George!' 'It's a race!' 'You'll ketch 'em!' 'Whip up!'

'She's a goer, she is!' said the ostler boy.

'Strike me giddy!' cried Old Tootles. 'Here! *I'm* a-goin' to begin in a minute. Here's another comin'. If all the kebs in Hampstead ain't gone mad this morning!'

'It's a female this time,' said the ostler boy.

'She's a-following *him*,' said Old Tootles. 'Usually the other way about.'

'What's she got in her 'and?'

'Looks like a 'igh 'at.'

'What a bloomin' lark it is! Three to one on old George,' said the ostler boy. 'Next!'

Minnie went by in a perfect roar of applause. She did not like it but she felt that she was doing her duty, and whirled on down Haverstock Hill and Camden Town High Street with her eyes ever intent on the animated back of Old George, who was driving her vagrant husband so incomprehensively away from her.

The man in the foremost cab sat crouched in the corner, his arms tightly folded, and the little tube that contained such vast possibilities of destruction gripped in his hand. His mood was a singular mixture of fear and exultation. Chiefly he was afraid of being caught before he could accomplish his purpose, but behind this was a vaguer but larger fear of the awfulness of his crime. But his exultation far exceeded his fear. No anarchist before him had ever approached this conception of his. Ravachol, Vaillant, all those distinguished persons whose fame he had envied, dwindled into insignificance beside him. He had only to make sure of the water-supply, and break the little tube into a reservoir. How brilliantly he had planned it, forged the letter of introduction, and got into the laboratory, and how brilliantly he had seized his opportunity! The world should hear of him at last. All those people who had sneered at him, neglected him, preferred other people to him, found his company undesirable, should consider him at last. Death, death, death! They had always treated him as a man of no importance. All the world had been in a conspiracy to keep him under. He would teach them yet what it is to isolate a man. What was this familiar street? Great St Andrew's Street, of course! How fared the chase? He craned out of the cab. The bacteriologist was scarcely fifty yards behind. That was bad. He would be caught and stopped yet. He felt in his pocket for money, and found half a sovereign. This he thrust up through the trap in the top of the cab into the man's face. 'More,' he shouted, 'if only we get away.'

The money was snatched out of his hand. 'Right you are,' said the cabman, and the trap slammed, and the lash lay along the glistening side of the horse. The cab swayed, and the anarchist, half-standing under the trap, put the hand containing the little glass tube upon the apron to preserve his balance. He felt the brittle thing crack, and the broken half of it rang upon the floor of the cab. He fell back into the seat with a curse, and stared dismally at the two or three drops of moisture on the apron.

He shuddered.

'Well! I suppose I shall be the first. *Phew!* Anyhow, I shall be a martyr. That's something. But it is a filthy death, nevertheless. I wonder if it hurts as much as they say.'

Presently a thought occurred to him – he groped between his feet. A little drop was still in the broken end of the tube, and he drank that to make sure. It was better to make sure. At any rate, he would not fail.

Then it dawned upon him that there was no further need to escape the bacteriologist. In Wellington Street he told the cabman to stop and got out. He slipped on the step, his head felt queer. It was rapid stuff this cholera poison. He waved his cabman out of existence, so to speak, and stood on the pavement with his arms folded upon his breast, awaiting the arrival of the bacteriologist. There was something tragic in his pose. The sense of imminent death gave him a certain dignity. He greeted his pursuer with a defiant laugh.

'*Vive l'anarchie!*[7] You are too late, my friend. I have drunk it. The cholera is abroad!'

The bacteriologist from his cab beamed curiously at him through his spectacles. 'You have drunk it! An anarchist! I see now.' He was about to say something more, and then checked himself. A smile hung in the corner of his mouth. He opened the apron of his cab as if to descend, at which the anarchist waved him a dramatic farewell and strode off towards Waterloo Bridge, carefully jostling his infected body against as many people as possible.

The bacteriologist was so preoccupied with the vision of him that he scarcely manifested the slightest surprise at the appearance of

Minnie upon the pavement with his hat and shoes and overcoat. 'Very good of you to bring my things,' he said, and remained lost in contemplation of the receding figure of the anarchist. 'You had better get in,' he said, still staring. Minnie felt absolutely convinced now that he was mad, and directed the cabman home on her own responsibility.

'Put on my shoes? Certainly, dear,' said he, as the cab began to turn and hid the strutting black figure, now small in the distance, from his eyes. Then suddenly something grotesque struck him, and he laughed. Then he remarked, 'It is really very serious, though. You see, that man came to my house to see me, and he is an anarchist. No – don't faint, or I cannot possibly tell you the rest. And I wanted to astonish him, not knowing he was an anarchist, and took up a cultivation of that new species of bacterium I was telling you of, that infests, and I think causes the blue patches upon, various monkeys; and, like a fool, I said it was Asiatic cholera. And he ran away with it to poison the water of London, and he certainly might have made things look blue for this civilised city. But instead he has swallowed it. Of course, I cannot say what will happen, but you know it turned that kitten blue, and the three puppies – in patches, and the sparrow – bright blue. But the bother is, I shall have all the trouble and expense of preparing some more.

'Put on my coat on this hot day! Why? Because we might meet Mrs Jabber? My dear, Mrs Jabber is not a draught. But why should I wear a coat on a hot day because of Mrs – ? Oh! *very* well.'

ELIZABETH GASKELL

ELIZABETH GASKELL *née* Stevenson (1810–65), better known as Mrs Gaskell, was adopted by her aunt after her mother died when she was just over a year old. As a result Elizabeth moved from London, the place of her birth, and was brought up and educated in Knutsford in Cheshire. As a teenager she also studied at Stratford-upon-Avon and at the age of seventeen she had an excellent knowledge of modern and classical languages. In 1832 she married the Reverend William Gaskell, and went to live in Manchester. She was happy in her marriage, which produced four daughters and one son, who died of scarlet fever in infancy. She also found time to write. At first she penned articles and short stories and then, partly to console herself for the loss of her son, she wrote a novel of industrial life and strife in Manchester called *Mary Barton*. Although published anonymously, it was a great success. Both Dickens and Charlotte Brontë admired her work and encouraged her. Other stories and novels followed, including her most famous work, *Cranford*, that deals with the lives of a set of characters dwelling in a small northern town modelled on Knutsford. As well as her novels, she also wrote a biography of her close friend Charlotte Brontë. Mrs Gaskell died suddenly of a heart attack in Leeds and was buried in Knutsford.

Elizabeth Gaskell was an expert at exploring and examining the complexities of relationships within a small community, as she does in 'The Squire's Story'. The story itself is set between 1768 and 1775, and so in essence she created an historical tale, but she was clever enough to know that the manners and behaviour of her characters were timeless and that is why the story still appeals to readers today. The arrival of a rich and personable man in a small village is still guaranteed to intrigue its inhabitants, especially when there is no obvious source of his wealth. This essentially grim tale unfolds in a simple fashion and through a series of subtle revelations we are slowly led to realise that there is something that is not quite right about Mr Higgins. And when, in the closing moments of the story, we learn the truth, we are perhaps reminded of how, at the beginning of the tale, Higgins treated the village children.

There are also moments of satire in 'The Squire's Story'. Mr Dudgeon represents the aspiring middle-class man who attempts to mimic the aristocracy by building a house that is a smaller version of the grander houses he serves. He called it 'a cottage' but it 'spread out far and wide' and had 'exquisite gardens' and 'exquisitely clean rooms'.

'The Squire's Story' is a rich offering, presenting a vivid picture of the times in which it is set, but also revealing the eternal weaknesses of humankind.

The Squire's Story

IN THE YEAR 1769 the little town of Barford was thrown into a state of great excitement by the intelligence that a gentleman (and 'quite the gentleman,' said the landlord of the George Inn) had been looking at Mr Clavering's old house. This house was neither in the town nor in the country. It stood on the outskirts of Barford, on the roadside leading to Derby. The last occupant had been a Mr Clavering – a Northumberland gentleman of good family – who had come to live in Barford while he was but a younger son; but when some elder branches of the family died, he had returned to take possession of the family estate. The house of which I speak was called the White House, from its being covered with a greyish kind of stucco. It had a good garden to the back, and Mr Clavering had built capital stables, with what were then considered the latest improvements. The point of good stabling was expected to let the house, as it was in a hunting county; otherwise it had few recommendations. There were many bedrooms – some entered through others, even to the number of five, leading one beyond the other; several sitting-rooms of the small and poky kind, wainscoted[1] round with wood, and then painted a heavy slate colour; one good dining-room, and a drawing-room over it, both looking into the garden, with pleasant bow-windows.

Such was the accommodation offered by the White House. It did not seem to be very tempting to strangers, though the good people of Barford rather piqued[2] themselves on it as the largest house in the town and as a house in which 'townspeople' and 'county people' had often met at Mr Clavering's friendly dinners. To appreciate this circumstance of pleasant recollection, you should have lived some

years in a little country town, surrounded by gentlemen's seats. You
would then understand how a bow or a courtsey from a member of a
county family elevates the individuals who receive it almost as much,
in their own eyes, as the pair of blue garters fringed with silver did
Mr Bickerstaff's ward. They trip lightly on air for a whole day
afterwards. Now Mr Clavering was gone, where could town and
county mingle?

I mention these things that you may have an idea of the
desirability of the letting of the White House in the Barfordites'
imagination; and to make the mixture thick and slab, you must add
for yourselves the bustle, the mystery, and the importance which
every little event either causes or assumes in a small town; and then,
perhaps, it will be no wonder to you that twenty ragged little urchins
accompanied the 'gentleman' aforesaid to the door of the White
House; and that, although he was above an hour inspecting it under
the auspices of Mr Jones, the agent's clerk, thirty more had joined
themselves on to the wondering crowd before his exit, and awaited
such crumbs of intelligence as they could gather before they were
threatened or whipped out of hearing distance. Presently out came
the 'gentleman' and the lawyer's clerk. The latter was speaking as he
followed the former over the threshold. The gentleman was tall,
well dressed, handsome; but there was a sinister cold look in his
quick-glancing, light blue eyes, which a keen observer might not
have liked. There were no keen observers among the boys and ill-
conditioned gaping girls. But they stood too near; inconveniently
close; and the gentleman, lifting up his right hand, in which he
carried a short riding-whip, dealt one or two sharp blows to the
nearest, with a look of savage enjoyment on his face as they moved
away whimpering and crying. An instant after, his expression of
countenance had changed.

'Here!' said he, drawing out a handful of money, partly silver,
partly copper, and throwing it into the midst of them. 'Scramble for
it! fight it out, my lads! Come this afternoon, at three, to the George,
and I'll throw you out some more.'

So the boys hurrahed for him as he walked off with the agent's
clerk. He chuckled to himself, as over a pleasant thought. 'I'll have
some fun with those lads,' he said; 'I'll teach 'em to be prowling and
prying about me. I'll tell you what I'll do. I'll make the money so hot
in the fire-shovel that it shall burn their fingers. You come and see
the faces and the howling. I shall be very glad if you will dine with
me at two; and by that time I may have made up my mind respecting
the house.'

Mr Jones, the agent's clerk, agreed to come to the George at two, but, somehow, he had a distaste for his entertainer. Mr Jones would not like to have said, even to himself, that a man with a purse full of money, who kept many horses and spoke familiarly of noblemen – above all, who thought of taking the White House – could be anything but a gentleman; but still the uneasy wonder as to who this Mr Robinson Higgins could be filled the clerk's mind long after Mr Higgins, Mr Higgins's servants and Mr Higgins's stud had taken possession of the White House.

The White House was re-stuccoed (this time of a pale yellow colour) and put into thorough repair by the accommodating and delighted landlord; while his tenant seemed inclined to spend any amount of money on internal decorations, which were showy and effective in their character, enough to make the White House a nine days' wonder to the good people of Barford. The slate-coloured paints became pink, and were picked out with gold; the old-fashioned banisters were replaced by newly gilt ones; but, above all, the stables were a sight to be seen. Since the days of the Roman Emperor never was there such provision made for the care, the comfort and the health of horses. But everyone said it was no wonder, when they were led through Barford, covered up to their eyes, but curving their arched and delicate necks and prancing with short high steps in repressed eagerness.

Only one groom came with them; yet they required the care of three men. Mr Higgins, however, preferred engaging two lads out of Barford; and Barford highly approved of his preference. Not only was it kind and thoughtful to give employment to the lounging lads themselves, but they were receiving such a training in Mr Higgins's stables as might fit them for Doncaster or Newmarket.

The district of Derbyshire in which Barford was situated was too close to Leicestershire not to support a hunt and a pack of hounds. The master of the hounds was a certain Sir Harry Manley, who was *aut* a huntsman *aut nullus*.[3] He measured a man by the 'length of his fork', not by the expression of his countenance or the shape of his head. But, as Sir Harry was wont to observe, there was such a thing as too long a fork, so his approbation was withheld until he had seen a man on horseback; and if his seat there was square and easy, his hand light and his courage good Sir Harry hailed him as a brother.

Mr Higgins attended the first meet of the season, not as a subscriber but as an amateur. The Barford huntsmen piqued themselves on their bold riding; and their knowledge of the country came by nature; yet this new strange man, whom nobody knew, was in at the death, sitting on his horse, both well breathed and calm, without a hair turned on the sleek skin of the latter, supremely addressing the old huntsman as he hacked off the tail of the fox; and he, the old man, who was testy even under Sir Harry's slightest rebuke, and flew out on any other member of the hunt that dared to utter a word against his sixty years' experience as stable-boy, groom, poacher, and what not – he, old Isaac Wormeley, was meekly listening to the wisdom of this stranger, only now and then giving one of his quick, up-turning, cunning glances, not unlike the sharp o'er-canny looks of the poor deceased Reynard,[4] round whom the hounds were howling, unadmonished by the short whip which was now tucked into Wormeley's well-worn pocket.

When Sir Harry rode into the copse – full of dead brushwood and wet tangled grass – and was followed by the members of the hunt, as one by one they cantered past, Mr Higgins took off his cap and bowed – half deferentially, half insolently – with a lurking smile in the corner of his eye at the discomfited looks of one or two of the laggards.[5]

'A famous run, sir,' said Sir Harry. 'The first time you have hunted in our country; but I hope we shall see you often.'

'I hope to become a member of the hunt, sir,' said Mr Higgins.

'Most happy – proud, I'm sure, to receive so daring a rider among us. You took the Cropper Gate, I fancy; while some of our friends here – ', scowling at one or two cowards by way of finishing his speech. 'Allow me to introduce myself – master of the hounds.' He fumbled in his waistcoat pocket for the card on which his name was formally inscribed. 'Some of our friends here are kind enough to come home with me to dinner; might I ask for the honour?'

'My name is Higgins,' replied the stranger, bowing low. 'I am only lately come to occupy the White House at Barford, and I have not as yet presented my letters of introduction.'

'Hang it!' replied Sir Harry; 'a man with a seat like yours, and that good brush in your hand, might ride up to any door in the county (I'm a Leicestershire man!) and be a welcome guest. Mr Higgins, I shall be proud to become better acquainted with you over my dinner-table.'

Mr Higgins knew pretty well how to improve the acquaintance thus begun. He could sing a good song, tell a good story, and was well up in practical jokes; with plenty of that keen worldly sense, which seems like an instinct in some men, and which in this case taught him on whom he might play off such jokes, with impunity from their resentment, and with a security of applause from the more boisterous, vehement or prosperous. At the end of twelve months Mr Robinson Higgins was, out-and-out, the most popular member of the Barford hunt; had beaten all the others by a couple of lengths, as his first patron, Sir Harry, observed one evening, when they were just leaving the dinner-table of an old hunting squire in the neighbourhood.

'Because, you know,' said Squire Hearn, holding Sir Harry by the button – 'I mean, you see, this young spark is looking sweet upon Catherine; and she's a good girl, and will have ten thousand pounds down, the day she's married, by her mother's will; and excuse me, Sir Harry – but I should not like my girl to throw herself away.'

Though Sir Harry had a long ride before him, and but the early and short light of a new moon to take it in, his kind heart was so much touched by Squire Hearn's trembling, tearful anxiety, that he stopped and turned back into the dining-room to say, with more asseverations[6] than I care to give: 'My good squire, I may say I know that man pretty well by this time, and a better fellow never existed. If I had twenty daughters he should have the pick of them.'

Squire Hearn never thought of asking the grounds for his old friend's opinion of Mr Higgins; it had been given with too much earnestness for any doubts to cross the old man's mind as to the possibility of its not being well founded. Mr Hearn was not a doubter, or a thinker, or suspicious by nature; it was simply love for Catherine, his only daughter, that prompted his anxiety in this case; and, after what Sir Harry had said, the old man could totter with an easy mind, though not with very steady legs, into the drawing-room, where his bonny, blushing daughter Catherine and Mr Higgins stood close together on the hearth-rug – he whispering, she listening with downcast eyes.

She looked so happy, so like what her dead mother had looked when the squire was a young man, that all his thought was how to please her most. His son and heir was about to be married, and bring his wife to live with the squire; Barford and the White House were not distant an hour's ride; and, even as these thoughts passed through his mind, he asked Mr Higgins if he could not stay all night – the young moon was already set – the roads would be dark – and Catherine looked up with a pretty anxiety, which, however, had not much doubt in it, for the answer.

With every encouragement of this kind from the old squire, it took everybody rather by surprise when one morning it was discovered that Miss Catherine Hearn was missing; and when, according to the usual fashion in such cases, a note was found, saying that she had eloped with 'the man of her heart', and gone to Gretna Green, no one could imagine why she could not quietly have stopped at home and been married in the parish church. She had always been a romantic, sentimental girl; very pretty and very affectionate, and very much spoiled, and very much wanting in common sense. Her indulgent father was deeply hurt at this want of confidence in his never-varying affection; but when his son came, hot with indignation from the baronet's (his future father-in-law's house, where every form of law and of ceremony was to accompany his own impending marriage), Squire Hearn pleaded the cause of the young couple with imploring cogency, and protested that it was a piece of spirit in his daughter, which he admired and was proud of.

However, it ended with Mr Nathaniel Hearn's declaring that he and his wife would have nothing to do with his sister and her husband.

'Wait till you've seen him, Nat!' said the old squire, trembling with his distressful anticipations of family discord; 'he's an excuse for any girl. Only ask Sir Harry's opinion of him.'

'Confound Sir Harry! So that a man sits his horse well, Sir Harry cares nothing about anything else. Who is this man – this fellow? Where does he come from? What are his means? Who are his family?'

'He comes from the south – Surrey or Somersetshire, I forget which; and he pays his way well and liberally. There's not a tradesman in Barford but says he cares no more for money than for water; he spends like a prince, Nat. I don't know who his family are, but he seals with a coat of arms, which may tell you if you want to know – and he goes regularly to collect his rents from his estates in the south. Oh, Nat! if you would but be friendly, I should be as well pleased with Kitty's marriage as any father in the county.'

Mr Nathaniel Hearn gloomed, and muttered an oath or two to himself. The poor old father was reaping the consequences of his weak indulgence to his two children. Mr and Mrs Nathaniel Hearn kept apart from Catherine and her husband; and Squire Hearn durst never ask them to Levison Hall, though it was his own house. Indeed, he stole away as if he were a culprit whenever he went to visit the White House, and if he passed a night there, he was fain to equivocate[7] when he returned home the next day; an equivocation which was well interpreted by the surly, proud Nathaniel. But the younger Mr and Mrs Hearn were the only people who did not visit at the White House.

Mr and Mrs Higgins were decidedly more popular than their

brother and sister-in-law. She made a very pretty, sweet-tempered hostess, and her education had not been such as to make her intolerant of any want of refinement in the associates who gathered round her husband. She had gentle smiles for townspeople as well as county people; and unconsciously played an admirable second in her husband's project of making himself universally popular.

But there is someone to make ill-natured remarks, and draw ill-natured conclusions from very simple premises, in every place; and in Barford this bird of ill-omen was a Miss Pratt. She did not hunt – so Mr Higgins's admirable riding did not call out her admiration. She did not drink – so the well-selected wines, so lavishly dispensed among his guests, could never mollify Miss Pratt. She could not bear comic songs, or buffo stories[8] – so, in that way, her approbation was impregnable. And these three secrets of popularity constituted Mr Higgins's great charm.

Miss Pratt sat and watched. Her face looked immovably grave at the end of any of Mr Higgins's best stories; but there was a keen, needle-like glance of her unwinking little eyes which Mr Higgins felt rather than saw, and which made him shiver, even on a hot day, when it fell upon him. Miss Pratt was a dissenter,[9] and, to propitiate this female Mordecai,[10] Mr Higgins asked the dissenting minister, whose services she attended, to dinner; kept himself and his company in good order; gave a handsome donation to the poor of the chapel. All in vain – Miss Pratt stirred not a muscle more of her face towards graciousness; and Mr Higgins was conscious that, in spite of all his open efforts to captivate Mr Davis, there was a secret influence on the other side, throwing in doubts and suspicions, and evil interpretations of all he said or did. Miss Pratt, the little, plain old maid, living on eighty pounds a year, was the thorn in the popular Mr Higgins's side, although she had never spoken one uncivil word to him; indeed, on the contrary, had treated him with a stiff and elaborate civility.

The thorn – the grief to Mrs Higgins was this. They had no children! Oh! how she would stand and envy the careless, busy motion of half a dozen children; and then, when observed, move on with a deep, deep sigh of yearning regret. But it was as well.

It was noticed that Mr Higgins was remarkably careful of his health. He ate, drank, took exercise, rested, by some secret rules of his own; occasionally bursting into an excess, it is true, but only on rare occasions – such as when he returned from visiting his estates in the south, and collecting his rents. That unusual exertion and fatigue – for there were no stage-coaches within forty miles of Barford, and he, like most country gentlemen of that day, would have preferred riding if there had been – seemed to require some strange excess to compensate for it; and rumours went through the town that he shut himself up, and drank enormously for some days after his return. But no one was admitted to these orgies.

One day – they remembered it well afterwards – the hounds met not far from the town; and the fox was found in a part of the wild heath which was beginning to be enclosed by a few of the more wealthy townspeople, who were desirous of building themselves houses rather more in the country than those they had hitherto lived in.

Among these the principal was a Mr Dudgeon, the attorney of Barford, and the agent for all the county families about. The firm of Dudgeon had managed the leases, the marriage settlements, and the wills of the neighbourhood for generations. Mr Dudgeon's father had the responsibility of collecting the landowners' rents just as the present Mr Dudgeon had at the time of which I speak: and as his son and his son's son have done since. Their business was an hereditary estate to them; and with something of the old feudal feeling was mixed a kind of proud humility at their position towards the squires whose family secrets they had mastered, and the mysteries of whose fortunes and estates were better known to the Messrs Dudgeon than to themselves.

Mr John Dudgeon had built himself a house on Wildbury Heath – a mere cottage, as he called it; but though only two storeys high, it spread out far and wide, and work people from Derby had been sent for on purpose to make the inside as complete as possible. The gardens too were exquisite in arrangement, if not very extensive; and not a flower was grown in them but of the rarest species.

It must have been somewhat of a mortification to the owner of this dainty place when, on the day of which I speak, the fox, after a long race, during which he had described a circle of many miles, took refuge in the garden; but Mr Dudgeon put a good face on the matter when a gentleman hunter, with the careless insolence of the squires of those days and that place, rode across the velvet lawn, and tapping at the window of the dining-room with his whip-handle, asked permission – no! that is not it – rather, informed Mr Dudgeon of their intention – to enter his garden in a body, and have the fox unearthed. Mr Dudgeon compelled himself to smile assent with the grace of a masculine Griselda;[11] and then he hastily gave orders to have all that the house afforded of provision set out for luncheon, guessing rightly enough that a six hours' run would give even homely fare an acceptable welcome.

He bore without wincing the entrance of the dirty boots into his exquisitely clean rooms; he only felt grateful for the care with which Mr Higgins strode about, laboriously and noiselessly moving on the tip of his toes, as he reconnoitred the rooms with a curious eye.

'I'm going to build a house myself, Dudgeon; and, upon my word, I don't think I could take a better model than yours.'

'Oh! my poor cottage would be too small to afford any hints for such a house as you would wish to build, Mr Higgins,' replied Mr Dudgeon, gently rubbing his hands nevertheless at the compliment.

'Not at all! not at all! Let me see. You have dining-room, drawing-room' – he hesitated, and Mr Dudgeon filled up the blank as he expected.

'Four sitting-rooms and the bedrooms. But allow me to show you over the house. I confess I took some pains in arranging it, and, though far smaller than what you would require, it may, nevertheless, afford you some hints.'

So they left the eating gentlemen with their mouths and their plates quite full, and the scent of the fox overpowering that of the hasty rashers of ham; and they carefully inspected all the ground-floor rooms. Then Mr Dudgeon said: 'If you are not tired, Mr Higgins – it is rather my hobby, so you must pull me up if you are – we will go upstairs, and I will show you my sanctum.'

Mr Dudgeon's sanctum was the centre room, over the porch, which formed a balcony, and which was carefully filled with choice flowers in pots. Inside, there were all kinds of elegant contrivances for hiding the real strength of all the boxes and chests required by the particular nature of Mr Dudgeon's business: for although his office was in Barford, he kept (as he informed Mr Higgins) what was the most valuable here, as being safer than an office which was locked up and left every night.

But, as Mr Higgins reminded him with a sly poke in the side, when next they met, his own house was not over-secure. A fortnight after the gentlemen of the Barford hunt lunched there, Mr Dudgeon's strong-box – in his sanctum upstairs, with the mysterious spring-bolt to the window invented by himself, the secret of which was only known to the inventor and a few of his most intimate friends, to whom he had proudly shown it – this strong-box, containing the collected Christmas rents of half a dozen landlords (there was then no bank nearer than Derby), was rifled; and the secretly rich Mr Dudgeon had to stop his agent in his purchases of paintings by Flemish artists, because the money was required to make good the missing rents.

The Dogberries and Verges[12] of those days were quite incapable of obtaining any clue to the robber or robbers; and though one or two vagrants were taken up and brought before Mr Dunover and Mr Higgins, the magistrates who usually attended in the courtroom at Barford, there was no evidence brought against them, and after a couple of nights' durance[13] in the lock-ups they were set at liberty. But it became a standing joke with Mr Higgins to ask Mr Dudgeon, from time to time, whether he would recommend him a place of safety for his valuables; or if he had made any more inventions lately for securing houses from robbers.

About two years after this time about seven years after Mr Higgins had been married – one Tuesday evening, Mr Davis was sitting reading the news in the coffee-room of the George Inn. He belonged to a club of gentlemen who met there occasionally to play at whist, to read what few newspapers and magazines were published in those days, to chat about the market at Derby, and prices all over the country.

This Tuesday night it was a black frost; and few people were in the room. Mr Davis was anxious to finish an article in the *Gentleman's Magazine*; indeed, he was making extracts[14] from it, intending to answer it, and yet unable with his small income to purchase a copy. So he stayed late; it was past nine, and at ten o'clock the room was closed.

But while he wrote, Mr Higgins came in. He was pale and haggard with cold; Mr Davis, who had had for some time sole possession of the fire, moved politely on one side, and handed to the newcomer the sole London newspaper which the room afforded.

Mr Higgins accepted it, and made some remark on the intense coldness of the weather; but Mr Davis was too full of his article, and intended reply, to fall into conversation readily. Mr Higgins hitched his chair nearer to the fire, and put his feet on the fender, giving an audible shudder. He put the newspaper on one end of the table near him, and sat gazing into the red embers of the fire, crouching down over them as if his very marrow were chilled. At length he said: 'There is no account of the murder at Bath in that paper?'

Mr Davis, who had finished taking his notes, and was preparing to go, stopped short, and asked: 'Has there been a murder at Bath? No! I have not seen anything of it – who was murdered?'

'Oh! it was a shocking, terrible murder!' said Mr Higgins, not raising his look from the fire, but gazing on with his eyes dilated till the whites were seen all round them. 'A terrible, terrible murder! I wonder what will become of the murderer? I can fancy the red glowing centre of that fire – look and see how infinitely distant it seems, and how the distance magnifies it into something awful and unquenchable.'

'My dear sir, you are feverish; how you shake and shiver!' said Mr Davis, thinking privately that his companion had symptoms of fever, and that he was wandering in his mind.

'Oh, no!' said Mr Higgins, 'I am not feverish. It is the night which is so cold.' And for a time he talked with Mr Davis about the article in the *Gentleman's Magazine*, for he was rather a reader himself, and could take more interest in Mr Davis's pursuits than most of the people at Barford.

At length it drew near to ten, and Mr Davis rose up to go home to his lodgings.

'No, Davis, don't go. I want you here. We will have a bottle of port together, and that will put Saunders into good humour. I want to tell you about this murder,' he continued, dropping his voice, and speaking hoarse and low. 'She was an old woman, and he killed her, sitting reading her Bible by her own fireside!' He looked at Mr Davis with a strange searching gaze, as if trying to find some sympathy in the horror which the idea presented to him.

'Who do you mean, my dear sir? What is this murder you are so full of? No one has been murdered here.'

'No, you fool! I tell you it was in Bath!' said Mr Higgins, with sudden passion; and then calming himself to most velvet-smoothness of manner, he laid his hand on Mr Davis's knee, there, as they sat by the fire, and gently detaining him, began the narration of the crime he was so full of; but his voice and manner were constrained to a stony quietude: he never looked in Mr Davis's face; once or twice, as Mr Davis remembered afterwards, his grip tightened like a compressing vice.

'She lived in a small house in a quiet old-fashioned street, she and her maid. People said she was a good old woman; but for all that she hoarded and hoarded, and never gave to the poor. Mr Davis, it is wicked not to give to the poor – wicked – wicked, is it not? I always give to the poor, for once I read in the Bible that "Charity covereth a multitude of sins". The wicked old woman never gave, but hoarded her money, and saved, and saved. Someone heard of it; I say she threw a temptation in his way, and God will punish her for it. And this man – or it might be a woman, who knows? – and this person – heard also that she went to church in the mornings, and her maid in the afternoons; and so – while the maid was at church, and the street and the house quite still, and the darkness of a winter afternoon coming on she was nodding over the Bible – and that, mark you! is a sin, and one that God will avenge sooner or later; and a step came in the dusk up the stair, and that person I told you of stood in the room.

At first he – no! At first, it is supposed for, you understand, all this is mere guesswork – it is supposed that he asked her civilly enough to give him her money, or to tell him where it was; but the old miser defied him, and would not ask for mercy and give up her keys, even when he threatened her, but looked him in the face as if he had been a baby – Oh, God! Mr Davis, I once dreamt when I was a little innocent boy that I should commit a crime like this, and I wakened up crying; and my mother comforted me – that is the reason I tremble so now – that and the cold, for it is very very cold!'

'But did he murder the old lady?' asked Mr Davis. 'I beg your pardon, sir, but I am interested by your story.'

'Yes! he cut her throat; and there she lies yet in her quiet little parlour, with her face upturned and all ghastly white, in the middle of a pool of blood. Mr Davis, this wine is no better than water; I must have some brandy!'

Mr Davis was horror-struck by the story, which seemed to have fascinated him as much as it had done his companion.

'Have they got any clue to the murderer?' said he. Mr Higgins drank down half a tumbler of raw brandy before he answered.

'No! no clue whatever. They will never be able to discover him, and I should not wonder – Mr Davis – I should not wonder if he repented after all, and did bitter penance for his crime; and if so – will there be mercy for him at the last day?'

'God knows!' said Mr Davis, with solemnity. 'It is an awful story,' continued he, rousing himself; 'I hardly like to leave this warm light room and go out into the darkness after hearing it. But it must be done,' buttoning on his greatcoat – 'I can only say I hope and trust they will find out the murderer and hang him. – If you'll take my advice, Mr Higgins, you'll have your bed warmed, and drink a treacle posset[15] just the last thing.

The next morning Mr Davis went to call on Miss Pratt, who was not very well; and by way of being agreeable and entertaining, he related to her all he had heard the night before about the murder at Bath; and really he made a very pretty connected story out of it, and interested Miss Pratt very much in the fate of the old lady – partly because of a similarity in their situations; for she also privately hoarded money, and had but one servant, and stopped at home alone on Sunday afternoons to allow her servant to go to church.

'And when did all this happen?' she asked.

'I don't know if Mr Higgins named the day; and yet I think it must have been on this very last Sunday.'

'And today is Wednesday. Ill news travels fast.'

'Yes, Mr Higgins thought it might have been in the London newspaper.'

'That it could never be. Where did Mr Higgins learn all about it?'

'I don't know, I did not ask; I think he only came home yesterday; he had been south to collect his rents, somebody said.'

Miss Pratt grunted. She used to vent her dislike and suspicions of Mr Higgins in a grunt whenever his name was mentioned. 'Well, I shan't see you for some days. Godfrey Merton has asked me to go and stay with him and his sister; and I think it will do me good. Besides,' added she, 'these winter evenings – and these murderers at large in the country – I don't quite like living with only Peggy to call to in case of need.'

Miss Pratt went to stay with her cousin, Mr Merton. He was an active magistrate, and enjoyed his reputation as such. One day he came in, having just received his letters

'Bad account of the morals of your little town here, Jessy!' said he, touching one of his letters. 'You've either a murderer among you, or some friend of a murderer. Here's a poor old lady at Bath had her throat cut last Sunday week; and I've a letter from the Home Office, asking to lend them "my very efficient aid", as they are pleased to call it, towards finding out the culprit. It seems he must have been thirsty, and of a comfortable jolly turn; for before going to his horrid work he tapped a barrel of ginger wine the old lady had set by to work; and he wrapped the spigot round with a piece of a letter taken out of his pocket, as may be supposed; and this piece of a letter was found afterwards; there are only these letters on the outside, "—ns, Esq., —arford, —egworth", which someone has ingeniously made out to mean Barford, near Kegworth. On the other side there is some allusion to a racehorse, I conjecture, though the name is singular, enough: "Church-and-King-and-down-with-the-Rump".'[16]

Miss Pratt caught at this name immediately; it had hurt her feelings as a dissenter only a few months ago, and she remembered it well.

'Mr Nat Hearn has – or had (as I am speaking in the witness-box, as it were, I must take care of my tenses) – a horse with that ridiculous name.'

'Mr Nat Hearn,' repeated Mr Merton, making a note of the intelligence; then he recurred to his letter from the Home Office again. 'There is also a piece of a small key, broken in the futile attempt to open a desk – well, well. Nothing more of consequence. The letter is what we must rely upon.'

'Mr Davis said that Mr Higgins told him – ' Miss Pratt began.

'Higgins!' exclaimed Mr Merton, '*ns*. Is it Higgins, the blustering fellow that ran away with Nat Hearn's sister?'

'Yes!' said Miss Pratt. 'But though he has never been a favourite of mine – '

'*ns*,' repeated Mr Merton. 'It is too horrible to think of; a member of the hunt – kind old Squire Hearn's son-in-law! Who else have you in Barford with names that end in *ns*?'

'There's Jackson, and Higginson, and Blenkinsop, and Davis, and Jones. Cousin! One thing strikes me – how did Mr Higgins know all about it to tell Mr Davis on Tuesday what had happened on Sunday afternoon?'

There is no need to add much more. Those curious in lives of the highwaymen may find the name of Higgins as conspicuous among those annals as that of Claude Duval. Kate Hearn's husband collected his rents on the highway, like many another 'gentleman' of the day; but, having been unlucky in one or two of his adventures, and hearing exaggerated accounts of the hoarded wealth of the old lady at Bath, he was led on from robbery to murder, and was hanged for his crime at Derby in 1775.

He had not been an unkind husband; and his poor wife took lodgings in Derby to be near him in his last moments – his awful last moments. Her old father went with her everywhere but into her husband's cell; and wrung her heart by constantly accusing himself of having promoted her marriage with a man of whom he knew so little. He abdicated his squireship in favour of his son Nathaniel. Nat was prosperous, and the helpless silly father could be of no use to him; but to his widowed daughter the foolish old man was all in all; her knight, her protector, her companion – her most faithful loving companion. Only he ever declined assuming the office of her counsellor – shaking his head sadly, and saying: 'Ah! Kate, Kate! if I had had more wisdom to have advised thee better, thou need'st not have been an exile here in Brussels, shrinking from the sight of every English person as if they knew thy story.'

I saw the White House not a month ago; it was to let, perhaps for the twentieth time since Mr Higgins occupied it; but still the tradition goes in Barford that once upon a time a highwayman lived there, and amassed untold treasures; and that the ill-gotten wealth yet remains walled up in some unknown concealed chamber; but in what part of the house no one knows.

ANTHONY TROLLOPE

ANTHONY TROLLOPE (1815–82) is still a very popular writer today. His novels set in the fictitious county of Barsetshire, *The Barchester Chronicles*, are perhaps his most enduring works and have been adapted for radio and television. However, Trollope has another claim to fame that has nothing to do with literature. For most of his working life he was a government official attached to the Post Office and was responsible for many reforms of the service, in particular the introduction of the pillar box into the British Isles.

His career in the civil service might make him appear ill-fitted to be a successful writer whose stories provide a fascinating analysis of Victorian life, morals and behaviour, but he came from a family of writers – his mother, sister and eldest brother also wrote novels – so one could say that storytelling was in his blood. Perhaps his masterpiece was the novel *The Way We Live Now* (1875), a bitter satire which attacks the all-pervading dishonesty in all sections of Victorian society, from the literary to the commercial world.

The basic plot of 'The Journey to Panama', like that of so many of the stories in this collection, is quite simple. The skill comes in the actual writing that presents both characters and ideas with a subtle and telling precision. The notion of a holiday romance is as appealing today for the young and unattached as it must have been in the nineteenth century. Away from the routine of everyday existence, mixing with strangers in glamorous surroundings, it is easy to see how one can fall in love with someone one does not really know. Trollope charts the progress of such an infatuation in this story, noting the various stages of its development. He treats the situation in a wittily wry and sophisticated manner at first, but gradually we are conscious that a dark tragedy is unfolding before us. The climax of the story exposes a kind of formalised and accepted cruelty which existed for certain women at this time and reveals the brave stoicism they exhibited in accepting that their married fate was arranged for them and they could never expect to find fulfilment in true love.

The modern reader should not be put off by the first three or four paragraphs which, at first glance, seem to be rather abstract and long-winded. They follow the fashion of the time, with the author discussing the general situation before focusing on the particular. I can assure you, once you have met Ralph Forrest and Miss Viner you will be desperate to know the outcome of their relationship.

The Journey to Panama

THERE IS PERHAPS no form of life in which men and women of the present day frequently find themselves for a time existing so unlike their customary conventional life as that experienced on board the large ocean steamers. On the voyages so made, separate friendships are formed and separate enmities are endured. Certain lines of temporary politics are originated by the energetic, and intrigues, generally innocent in their conclusions, are carried on with the keenest spirit by those to whom excitement is necessary; whereas the idle and torpid sink into insignificance and general contempt – as it is their lot to do on board ship as in other places. But the enjoyments and activity of such a life do not display themselves till the third or fourth day of the voyage. The men and women at first regard each with distrust and ill-concealed dislike. They by no means anticipate the strong feelings which are to arise, and look forward to ten, fifteen or twenty days of gloom or seasickness. Seasickness disappears, as a general condition, on the evening of the second day, and the gloom about noon on the fourth. Then the men begin to think that the women are not so ugly, vulgar and insipid; and the women drop their monosyllables, discontinue the close adherence to their own niches, which they first observed, and become affable, perhaps even beyond their wont[1] on shore. And alliances spring up among the men themselves. On their first entrance to this new world, they generally regard each other with marked aversion, each thinking that those nearest to him are low fellows, or perhaps worse; but by the fourth day, if not sooner, every man has his two or three intimate friends with whom he talks and smokes, and to whom he communicates those peculiar politics, and perhaps intrigues, of his own voyage. The female friendships are slower in their growth, for the suspicion of women is perhaps stronger than that of men; but when grown they also are stronger, and exhibit themselves sometimes in instances of feminine affection.

But the most remarkable alliances are those made between gentlemen and ladies. This is a matter of course on board ship quite as much as on shore, and it is of such an alliance that the present tale purports to tell the story. Such friendships, though they may be very dear, can seldom be very lasting. Though they may be full of sweet romance – for people become very romantic among the discomforts of a sea voyage – such romance is generally short-lived and delusive, and occasionally is dangerous.

There are several of these great ocean routes, of which, by the common consent, as it seems, of the world, England is the centre. There is the Great Eastern line, running from Southampton across the Bay of Biscay and up the Mediterranean. It crosses the Isthmus of Suez, and branches away to Australia, to India, to Ceylon, and to China. There is the great American line, traversing the Atlantic to New York and Boston with the regularity of clockwork. The voyage here is so much a matter of everyday routine, that romance has become scarce upon the route. There are one or two other North American lines, perhaps open to the same objection. Then there is the line of packets to the African coast – very romantic as I am given to understand; and there is the great West Indian route, to which the present little history is attached – great, not on account of our poor West Indian Islands, which cannot at the present moment make anything great, but because it spreads itself out from thence to Mexico and Cuba, to Guiana and the republics of Grenada and Venezuela, to Central America, the Isthmus of Panama, and from thence to California, Vancouver's Island, Peru and Chili.

It may be imagined how various are the tribes which leave the shores of Great Britain by this route. There are Frenchmen for the French sugar islands, as a rule not very romantic; there are old Spaniards, Spaniards of Spain, seeking to renew their fortunes amidst the ruins of their former empire; and new Spaniards – Spaniards, that is, of the American republics, who speak Spanish, but are unlike the Don both in manners and physiognomy[2] – men and women with a touch perhaps of Indian blood, very keen after dollars, and not much given to the graces of life. There are Dutchmen too, and Danes, going out to their own islands. There are citizens of the stars and stripes, who find their way everywhere – and, alas! perhaps, now also citizens of the new Southern flag,[3] with the palmetto leaf. And there are Englishmen of every shade and class, and Englishwomen also.

It is constantly the case that women are doomed to make the long voyage alone. Some are going out to join their husbands, some to find a husband, some few peradventure to leave a husband. Girls who have been educated at home in England, return to their distant homes across the Atlantic, and others follow their relatives who have gone before them as pioneers into a strange land. It must not be supposed that these females absolutely embark in solitude, putting their feet upon the deck without the aid of any friendly arm. They are generally consigned to some prudent elder, and appear as they first show themselves on the ship to belong to a party. But as often as not their real loneliness shows itself after a while. The prudent elder is not, perhaps, congenial; and by the evening of the fourth day a new friendship is created.

Not a long time since, such a friendship was formed under the circumstances which I am now about to tell. A young man – not very young, for he had turned his thirtieth year, but still a young man – left Southampton by one of the large West Indian steamboats, purposing to pass over the Isthmus[4] of Panama, and thence up to California and Vancouver's Island. It would be too long to tell the cause which led to these distant voyagings. Suffice to say, it was not the accursed hunger after gold – *auri sacra fames*[5] – which so took him; nor had he any purpose of permanently settling himself in those distant colonies of Great Britain. He was at the time a widower, and perhaps his home was bitter to him without the young wife whom he had early lost. As he stepped on board he was accompanied by a gentleman some fifteen years his senior, who was to be the companion of his sleeping apartment as far as St Thomas. The two had been introduced to each other, and therefore appeared as friends on board the *Serrapiqui*; but their acquaintance had commenced in Southampton, and my hero, Ralph Forrest by name, was alone in the world as he stood looking over the side of the ship at the retreating shores of Hampshire.

'I say, old fellow, we'd better see about our places,' said his new friend, slapping him on his back. Mr Matthew Morris was an old traveller, and knew how to become intimate with his temporary allies at a very short notice. A long course of travelling had knocked all bashfulness out of him, and when he had a mind to do so he could make any man his brother in half an hour, and any woman his sister in ten minutes.

'Places? what places?' said Forrest.

'A pretty fellow you are to go to California. If you don't look sharper than that you'll get little to drink and nothing to eat till you come back again. Don't you know the ship's as full as ever she can hold?'

Forrest acknowledged that she was full.

'There are places at table for about a hundred, and we have a hundred and thirty on board. As a matter of course those who don't look sharp will have to scramble. However, I've put cards on the plates and taken the seats. We had better go down and see that none of these Spanish fellows ousts us.' So Forrest descended after his friend, and found that the long tables were already nearly full of expectant dinner eaters. When he took his place a future neighbour informed him, not in the most gracious voice, that he was encroaching on a lady's seat; and when he immediately attempted to leave that which he held, Mr Matthew Morris forbade him to do so. Thus a little contest arose, which, however, happily was brought to a close without bloodshed. The lady was not present at the moment, and the grumpy gentleman agreed to secure for himself a vacant seat on the other side.

For the first three days the lady did not show herself. The grumpy gentleman, who, as Forrest afterwards understood, was the owner of stores in Bridgetown, Barbados, had other ladies with him also. First came forth his daughter, creeping down to dinner on the second day, declaring that she would be unable to eat a morsel, and prophesying that she would be forced to retire in five minutes. On this occasion, however, she agreeably surprised herself and her friends. Then came the grumpy gentleman's wife, and the grumpy gentleman's wife's brother – on whose constitution the sea seemed to have an effect quite as violent as on that of the ladies; and lastly, at breakfast on the fourth day, appeared Miss Viner, and took her place as Mr Forrest's neighbour at his right hand.

He had seen her before on deck, as she lay on one of the benches, vainly endeavouring to make herself comfortable, and had remarked to his companion that she was very unattractive and almost ugly. Dear young ladies, it is thus that men always speak of you when they first see you on board ship! She was disconsolate, sick at heart, and ill at ease in body also. She did not like the sea. She did not in the least like the grumpy gentleman, in whose hands she was placed. She did not especially like the grumpy gentleman's wife; and she altogether hated the grumpy gentleman's daughter, who was the partner of her berth. That young lady had been very sick and very selfish; and Miss Viner had been very sick also, and perhaps equally selfish. They might have been angels, and yet have hated each other under such circumstances. It was no wonder that Mr Forrest thought her ugly as she twisted herself about on the broad bench, vainly striving to be comfortable.

'She'll brighten up wonderfully before we're in the Tropics,' said

Mr Morris. 'And you won't find her so bad then. It's she that is to sit next you.'

'Heaven forbid!' said Forrest. But, nevertheless, he was very civil to her when she did come down on the fourth morning. On board the West Indian packets, the world goes down to its meals. In crossing between Liverpool and the States, the world goes up to them.

Miss Viner was by no means a very young lady. She also was nearly thirty. In guessing her age on board the ship the ladies said that she was thirty-six, but the ladies were wrong. She was an Irishwoman, and when seen on shore, in her natural state, and with all her wits about her, was by no means without attraction. She was bright-eyed, with a clear dark skin, and good teeth; her hair was of a dark brown and glossy, and there was a touch of feeling and also of humour about her mouth, which would have saved her from Mr Forrest's ill-considered criticism had he first met her under more favourable circumstances.

'You'll see a good deal of her,' Mr Morris said to him, as they began to prepare themselves for luncheon by a cigar immediately after breakfast. 'She's going across the Isthmus and down to Peru.'

'How on earth do you know?'

'I pretty well know where they're all going by this time. Old Grumpy told me so. He has her in tow as far as St Thomas, but knows nothing about her. He gives her up there to the captain. You'll have a chance of making yourself very agreeable as you run across with her to the Spanish Main.'

Mr Forrest replied that he did not suppose he should know her much better than he did now; but he made no further remark as to her ugliness. She had spoken a word or two to him at table, and he had seen that her eyes were bright, and had found that her tone was sweet.

'I also am going to Panama,' he said to her, on the morning of the fifth day. The weather at that time was very fine, and the October sun as it shone on them, while hour by hour they made more towards the south, was pleasant and genial. The big ship lay almost without motion on the bosom of the Atlantic, as she was driven through the waters at the rate of twelve miles per hour. All was as pleasant now as things can be on board a ship, and Forrest had forgotten that Miss Viner had seemed so ugly to him when he first saw her. At this moment, as he spoke to her, they were running through the Azores, and he had been assisting her with his field-glass to look for orange-groves on their sloping shores, orange-groves they had not succeeded in seeing, but their failure had not disturbed their peace.

'I also am going to Panama.'

'Are you, indeed?' said she. 'Then I shall not feel so terribly alone and disconsolate. I have been looking forward with such fear to that journey on from St Thomas.'

'You shall not be disconsolate, if I can help it,' he said. 'I am not much of a traveller myself, but what I can do I will.'

'Oh, thank you!'

'It is a pity Mr Morris is not going on with you. He's at home everywhere, and knows the way across the Isthmus as well as he does down Regent Street.'

'Your friend, you mean?'

'My friend, if you call him so; and indeed I hope he is, for I like him. But I don't know more of him than I do of you. I am as much alone as you are. Perhaps more so.'

'But,' she said, 'a man never suffers in being alone.'

'Oh! does he not? Don't think me uncivil, Miss Viner, if I say that you may be mistaken in that. You feel your own shoe when it pinches, but do not realise the tight boot of your neighbour.'

'Perhaps not,' said she. And then there was a pause, during which she pretended to look again for the orange groves. 'But there are worse things, Mr Forrest, than being alone in the world. It is often a woman's lot to wish that she were let alone.' Then she left him and retreated to the side of the grumpy gentleman's wife, feeling perhaps that it might be prudent to discontinue a conversation which, seeing that Mr Forrest was quite a stranger to her, was becoming particular.

'You're getting on famously, my dear,' said the lady from Barbadoes.

'Pretty well, thank you, ma'am,' said Miss Viner.

'Mr Forrest seems to be making himself quite agreeable. I tell Amelia' – Amelia was the young lady to whom in their joint cabin Miss Viner could not reconcile herself – 'I tell Amelia that she is wrong not to receive attentions from gentlemen on board ship. If it is not carried too far,' and she put great emphasis on the 'too far' – 'I see no harm in it.'

'Nor I, either,' said Miss Viner.

'But then Amelia is so particular.'

'The best way is to take such things as they come,' said Miss Viner – perhaps meaning that such things never did come in the way of Amelia. 'If a lady knows what she is about she need not fear a gentleman's attentions.'

'That's just what I tell Amelia; but then, my dear, she has not had so much experience as you and I.'

Such being the amenities which passed between Miss Viner and the prudent lady who had her in charge, it was not wonderful that the former should feel ill at ease with her own 'party', as the family of the Grumpy Barbadian was generally considered to be by those on board.

'You're getting along like a house on fire with Miss Viner,' said Matthew Morris to his young friend.

'Not much fire I can assure you,' said Forrest.

'She ain't so ugly as you thought her?'

'Ugly! – no; she's not ugly. I don't think I ever said she was. But she is nothing particular as regards beauty.'

'No; she won't be lovely for the next three days to come, I dare say. By the time you reach Panama, she'll be all that is perfect in woman. I know how these things go.'

'Those sort of things don't go at all quickly with me,' said Forrest, gravely. 'Miss Viner is a very interesting young woman, and as it seems that her route and mine will be together for some time, it is well that we should be civil to each other. And the more so, seeing that the people she is with are not congenial to her.'

'No; they are not. There is no young man with them. I generally observe that on board ship no one is congenial to unmarried ladies except unmarried men. It is a recognised nautical rule. Uncommon hot, isn't it? We are beginning to feel the tropical air. I shall go and cool myself with a cigar in the fiddle.' The 'fiddle' is a certain part of the ship devoted to smoking, and thither Mr Morris betook himself. Forrest, however, did not accompany him, but going forward into the bow of the vessel, threw himself along upon the sail, and meditated on the loneliness of his life.

On board the *Serrapiqui*, the upper tier of cabins opened on to a long gallery, which ran round that part of the ship immediately over the saloon, so that from thence a pleasant inspection could be made of the viands[6] as they were being placed on the tables. The custom on board these ships is for two bells to ring preparatory to dinner, at an internal of half an hour. At the sound of the first, ladies would go to their cabins to adjust their toilets; but as dressing for dinner is not carried to an extreme at sea, these operations are generally over before the second bell, and the lady passengers would generally assemble in the balcony for some fifteen minutes before dinner. At first they would stand here alone, but by degrees they were joined by some of the more enterprising of the men, and so at last a kind of little drawing-room was formed. The cabins of Miss Viner's party opened to one side of this gallery, and that of Mr Morris and Forrest on the other. Hitherto Forrest had been contented to remain on his own side, occasionally throwing a word across to the ladies on the other; but on this day he boldly went over as soon as he had washed his hands and took his place between Amelia and Miss Viner.

'We are dreadfully crowded here, ma'am,' said Amelia.

'Yes, my dear, we are,' said her mother. 'But what can one do?'

'There's plenty of room in the ladies' cabin,' said Miss Viner. Now if there be one place on board a ship more distasteful to ladies than another, it is the ladies' cabin. Mr Forrest stood his ground, but it may be doubted whether he would have done so had he fully understood all that Amelia had intended.

Then the last bell rang. Mr Grumpy gave his arm to Mrs Grumpy. The brother-in-law gave his arm to Amelia, and Forrest did the same to Miss Viner. She hesitated for a moment, and then took it, and by so doing transferred herself mentally and bodily from the charge of the prudent and married Mr Grumpy to that of the perhaps imprudent, and certainly unmarried Mr Forrest. She was wrong. A kind-hearted, motherly old lady from Jamaica, who had seen it all, knew that she was wrong, and wished that she could tell her so.

But there are things of this sort which kind-hearted old ladies cannot find it in their hearts to say. After all, it was only for the voyage. Perhaps Miss Viner was imprudent, but who in Peru would be the wiser? Perhaps, indeed, it was the world that was wrong, and not Miss Viner. *Honi soit qui mal y pense,*[7] she said to herself, as she took his arm, and leaning on it, felt that she was no longer so lonely as she had been. On that day she allowed him to give her a glass of wine out of his decanter. 'Hadn't you better take mine, Miss Viner?' asked Mr Grumpy, in a loud voice, but before he could be answered, the deed had been done.

'Don't go too fast, old fellow,' Morris said to our hero that night, as they were walking the deck together before they turned in. 'One gets into a hobble in such matters before one knows where one is.'

'I don't think I have anything particular to fear,' said Forrest.

'I dare say not, only keep your eyes open. Such harridans as Mrs Grumpy allow any latitude to their tongues out in these diggings. You'll find that unpleasant tidings will be put on board the ship going down to Panama, and everybody's eye will be upon you.' So warned, Mr Forrest did put himself on his guard, and the next day and a half his intimacy with Miss Viner progressed but little. These were, probably, the dullest hours that he had on the whole voyage.

Miss Viner saw this and drew back. On the afternoon of that second day she walked a turn or two on deck with the weak brother-in-law, and when Mr Forrest came near her, she applied herself to her book. She meant no harm; but if she were not afraid of what people might say, why should he be so? So she turned her shoulder towards him at dinner, and would not drink of his cup.

'Have some of mine, Miss Viner,' said Mr Grumpy, very loudly. But on that day Miss Viner drank no wine.

The sun sets quickly as one draws near to the Tropics, and the day was already gone, and the dusk had come on, when Mr Forrest walked out upon the deck that evening a little after six. But the night was beautiful and mild, and there was a hum of many voices from the benches. He was already uncomfortable, and sore with a sense of being deserted. There was but one person on board the ship that he liked, and why should he avoid her and be avoided? He soon perceived where she was standing. The Grumpy family had a bench to themselves, and she was opposite to it, on her feet, leaning against the side of the vessel. 'Will you walk this evening, Miss Viner?' he asked.

'I think not,' she answered.

'Then I shall persevere in asking till you are sure. It will do you good, for I have not seen you walking all day.'

'Have you not? Then I will take a turn. Oh, Mr Forrest, if you knew what it was to have to live with such people as those.' And then, out of that, on that evening, there grew up between them something like the confidence of real friendship. Things were told such as none but friends do tell to one another, and warm answering words were spoken such as the sympathy of friendship produces. Alas, they were both foolish; for friendship and sympathy should have deeper roots.

She told him all her story. She was going out to Peru to be married to a man who was nearly twenty years her senior. It was a long engagement, of ten years' standing. When first made, it was made as being contingent on certain circumstances. An option of escaping from it had then been given to her, but now there was no longer an option. He was rich, and she was penniless. He had even paid her passage-money and her outfit. She had not at last given way and taken these irrevocable steps till her only means of support in England had been taken from her. She had lived the last two years with a relative who was now dead. 'And he also is my cousin – a distant cousin – you understand that.'

'And do you love him?'

'Love him! What; as you loved her whom you have lost? – as she loved you when she clung to you before she went? No; certainly not. I shall never know anything of that love.'

'And is he good?'

'He is a hard man. Men become hard when they deal in money as he has done. He was home five years since, and then I swore to myself that I would not marry him. But his letters to me are kind.'

Forrest sat silent for a minute or two, for they were up in the bow again, seated on the sail that was bound round the bowsprit, and then he answered her, 'A woman should never marry a man unless she loves him.'

'Ah,' says she, 'of course you will condemn me. That is the way in which women are always treated. They have no choice given them, and are then scolded for choosing wrongly.'

'But you might have refused him.'

'No; I could not. I cannot make you understand the whole – how it first came about that the marriage was proposed, and agreed to by me under certain conditions. Those conditions have come about, and I am now bound to him. I have taken his money and have no escape. It is easy to say that a woman should not marry without love, as easy as it is to say that a man should not starve. But there are men who starve – starve although they work hard.'

'I did not mean to judge you, Miss Viner.'

'But I judge myself, and condemn myself so often. Where should I be in half an hour from this if I were to throw myself forward into the sea? I often long to do it. Don't you feel tempted sometimes to put an end to it all?'

'The waters look cool and sweet, but I own I am afraid of the bourne beyond.'

'So am I, and that fear will keep me from it.'

'We are bound to bear our burden of sorrow. Mine, I know, is heavy enough.'

'Yours, Mr Forrest! Have you not all the pleasures of memory to fall back on, and every hope for the future? What can I remember, or what can I hope? But, however, it is near eight o'clock, and they have all been at tea this hour past. What will my Cerberus[8] say to me? I do not mind the male mouth, if only the two feminine mouths could be stopped.' Then she rose and went back to the stern of the vessel; but as she slid into a seat, she saw that Mrs Grumpy was standing over her.

From thence to St Thomas the voyage went on in the customary manner. The sun became very powerful, and the passengers in the lower part of the ship complained loudly of having their portholes closed. The Spaniards sat gambling in the cabin all day, and the ladies prepared for the general move which was to be made at St Thomas. The alliance between Forrest and Miss Viner went on much the same as ever, and Mrs Grumpy said very ill-natured things. On one occasion she ventured to lecture Miss Viner; but that lady knew how to take her own part, and Mrs Grumpy did not get the best of it. The dangerous alliance, I have said, went on the same as ever; but it must not be supposed that either person in any way committed aught that was wrong. They sat together and talked together, each now knowing the other's circumstances; but had it not been for the prudish caution of some of the ladies there would have been nothing amiss. As it was there was not much amiss. Few of the passengers really cared whether or no Miss Viner had found an admirer. Those who were going down to Panama were mostly Spaniards, and as the great separation became nearer, people had somewhat else of which to think.

And then the separation came. They rode into that pretty harbour of St Thomas early in the morning, and were ignorant, the most of them, that they were lying in the very worst centre of yellow fever among all those plague-spotted islands. St Thomas is very pretty as seen from the ships; and when that has been said, all has been said that can be said in its favour. There was a busy, bustling time of it then. One vessel after another was brought up alongside of the big ship that had come from England, and each took its separate freight of passengers and luggage. First started the boat that ran down the Leeward Islands to Demerara, taking with her Mr Grumpy and all his family.

'Goodbye, Miss Viner,' said Mrs Grumpy. 'I hope you'll get quite safely to the end of your voyage; but do take care.'

'I'm sure I hope everything will be right,' said Amelia, as she absolutely kissed her enemy. It is astonishing how well young women can hate each other, and yet kiss at parting.

'As to everything being right,' said Miss Viner, 'that is too much to hope. But I do not know that anything is going especially wrong – Goodbye, sir,' and then she put out her hand to Mr Grumpy. He was at the moment leaving the ship laden with umbrellas, sticks, and coats, and was forced to put them down in order to free his hand.

'Well, goodbye,' he said. 'I hope you'll do, till you meet your friends at the Isthmus.'

'I hope I shall, sir,' she replied; and so they parted.

Then the Jamaica packet started.

'I dare say we shall never see each other again,' said Morris, as he shook his friend's hand heartily. 'One never does. Don't interfere with the rights of that gentleman in Peru, or he might run a knife into you.'

'I feel no inclination to injure him on that point.'

'That's well; and now goodbye.' And thus they also were parted. On the following morning the branch ship was dispatched to Mexico; and then on the afternoon of the third day that for Colon – as we Englishmen call the town on this side of the Isthmus of Panama. Into that vessel Miss Viner and Mr Forrest moved themselves and their effects; and now that the three-headed Cerberus was gone, she had no longer hesitated in allowing him to do for her all those little things which it is well that men should do for women when they are travelling. A woman without assistance under such circumstances is very forlorn, very apt to go to the wall, very ill able to assert her rights as to accommodation; and I think that few can blame Miss Viner for putting herself and her belongings under the care of the only person who was disposed to be kind to her.

Late in the evening the vessel steamed out of St Thomas's harbour, and as she went Ralph Forrest and Emily Viner were standing together at the stern of the boat looking at the retreating lights of the Danish town. If there be a place on the earth's surface odious to me, it is that little Danish isle to which so many of our young seamen are sent to die – there being no good cause whatever for such sending. But the question is one which cannot well be argued here.

'I have five more days of self and liberty left me,' said Miss Viner. 'That is my life's allowance.'

'For heaven's sake do not say words that are so horrible.'

'But am I to lie for heaven's sake, and say words that are false; or shall I be silent for heaven's sake, and say nothing during these last hours that are allowed to me for speaking? It is so. To you I can say that it is so, and why should you begrudge me the speech?'

'I would begrudge you nothing that I could do for you.'

'No, you should not. Now that my incubus[9] has gone to Barbados, let me be free for a day or two. What chance is there, I wonder, that the ship's machinery should all go wrong, and that we should be tossed about in the seas here for the next six months? I suppose it would be very wicked to wish it?'

'We should all be starved; that's all.'

'What, with a cow on board, and a dozen live sheep, and thousands of cocks and hens! But we are to touch at Santa Martha and Cartagena. What would happen to me if I were to run away at Santa Martha?'

'I suppose I should be bound to run with you.'

'Oh, of course. And therefore, as I would not wish to destroy you, I won't do it. But it would not hurt you much to be shipwrecked, and wait for the next packet.'

'Miss Viner,' he said after a pause – and in the meantime he had drawn nearer to her, too near to her considering all things – 'in the name of all that is good, and true, and womanly, go back to England. With your feelings, if I may judge of them by words which are spoken half in jest – '

'Mr Forrest, there is no jest.'

'With your feelings, a poorhouse in England would be better than a palace in Peru.'

'An English workhouse would be better, but an English poorhouse is not open to me. You do not know what it is to have friends – no, not friends, but people belonging to you – just so near as to make your respectability a matter of interest to them, but not so near that they should care for your happiness. Emily Viner married to Mr Gorloch in Peru is put out of the way respectably. She will cause no further trouble, and her name may be mentioned in family circles without annoyance. The fact is, Mr Forrest, that there are people who have no business to live at all.'

'I would go back to England,' he added, after another pause. 'When you talk to me with such bitterness of five more days of living liberty you scare my very soul. Return, Miss Viner, and brave the worst. He is to meet you at Panama. Remain on this side of the Isthmus, and send him word that you must return. I will be the bearer of the message.'

'And shall I walk back to England?' said Miss Viner.

'I had not quite forgotten all that,' he replied, very gently. 'There are moments when a man may venture to propose that which under ordinary circumstances would be a liberty. Money, in a small moderate way, is not greatly an object to me. As a return for my valiant defence of you against your West Indian Cerberus, you shall allow me to arrange that with the agent at Colon.'

'I do so love plain English, Mr Forrest. You are proposing, I think, to give me something about fifty guineas.'

'Well, call it so if you will,' said he, 'if you will have plain English that is what I mean.'

'So that by my journey out here, I should rob and deceive the man I do know, and also rob the man I don't know. I am afraid of that bourne beyond the waters of which we spoke but I would rather face that than act as you suggest.'

'Of the feelings between him and you, I can of course be no judge.'

'No; no; you cannot. But what a beast I am not to thank you! I do thank you. That which it would be mean in me to take, it is noble, very noble, in you to offer. It is a pleasure to me – I cannot tell why – but it is a pleasure to me to have had the offer. But think of me as a sister, and you will feel that it would not be accepted – could not be accepted, I mean, even if I could bring myself to betray that other man.'

Thus they ran across the Caribbean Sea, renewing very often such conversations as that just given. They touched at Santa Martha and Cartagena on the coast of the Spanish Main and at both places he went with her on shore. He found that she was fairly well educated, and anxious to see and to learn all that might be seen and learned in the course of her travels. On the last day, as they neared the Isthmus, she became more tranquil and quiet in the expression of her feelings than before, and spoke with less of gloom than she had done.

'After all ought I not to love him?' she said. 'He is coming all the way up from Callao merely to meet me. What man would go from London to Moscow to pick up a wife?'

'I would – and thence round the world to Moscow again – if she were the wife I wanted.'

'Yes; but a wife who has never said that she loved you! It is purely a matter of convenience. Well; I have locked my big box, and I shall give the key to him before it is ever again unlocked. He has a right to it, for he has paid for nearly all that it holds.'

'You look at things from such a mundane point of view.'

'A woman should, or she will always be getting into difficulty. Mind, I shall introduce you to him, and tell him all that you have done for me. How you braved Cerberus and the rest of it.'

'I shall certainly be glad to meet him.'

'But I shall not tell him of your offer – not yet at least. If he be good and gentle with me, I shall tell him that too after a time. I am very bad at keeping secrets – as no doubt you have perceived. We go across the Isthmus at once, do we not?'

'So the captain says.'

'Look!' – and she handed him back his own field-glass. 'I can see the men on the wooden platform. Yes; and I can see the smoke of an engine.' And then, in little more than an hour from that time, the ship had swung round on her anchor.

Colon, or Aspinwall as it should be called, is a place in itself as detestable as St Thomas. It is not so odious to an Englishman, for it is not used by Englishmen more than is necessary. We have no great depot of traffic there, which we might with advantage move elsewhere. Taken, however, on its own merits, Aspinwall is not a detestable place. Luckily, however, travellers across the Isthmus to the Pacific are never doomed to remain there long. If they arrive early in the day, the railway thence to Panama takes them on at once.

If it be not so, they remain on board ship till the next morning. Of course it will be understood that the transit line chiefly affects Americans, as it is the highroad from New York to California.

In less than an hour from their landing, their baggage had been examined by the Custom House officers of New Grenada, and they were on the railway cars, crossing the Isthmus. The officials in those out-of-the-way places always seem like apes imitating the doings of men. The officers at Aspinwall open and look at the trunks just as monkeys might do, having clearly no idea of any duty to be performed, nor any conception that goods of this or that class should not be allowed to pass. It is the thing in Europe to examine luggage going into a new country; and why should not they be as good as Europeans?

'I wonder whether he will be at the station?' she said, when the three hours of the journey had nearly passed. Forrest could perceive that her voice trembled as she spoke, and that she was becoming nervous.

'If he has already reached Panama, he will be there. As far as I could learn the arrival up from Peru had not been telegraphed.'

'Then I have another day – perhaps two. We cannot say how many. I wish he were there. Nothing is so intolerable as suspense.'

'And the box must be opened again.'

When they reached the station at Panama they found that the vessel from the South American coast was in the roads, but that the passengers were not yet on shore. Forrest, therefore, took Miss Viner down to the hotel, and there remained with her, sitting next to her in the common drawing-room of the house, when she had come back from her own bedroom. It would be necessary that they should remain there four or five days, and Forrest had been quick in securing a room for her. He had assisted in taking up her luggage, had helped her in placing her big box, and had thus been recognised by the crowd in the hotel as her friend. Then came the tidings that the passengers were landing, and he became nervous as she was. 'I will go down and meet him,' said he, 'and tell him that you are here. I shall soon find him by his name.' And so he went out.

Everybody knows the scrambling manner in which passengers arrive at an hotel out of a big ship. First come two or three energetic, heated men, who, by dint of screeching and bullying, have gotten themselves first disposed. They always get the worst rooms at the inns, the housekeepers having a notion that the richest people, those with the most luggage, must be more tardy in their movements. Four or five of this nature passed by Forrest in the hall, but he was not tempted to ask questions of them. One, from his age, might have been Mr

Gorloch, but he instantly declared himself to be Count Sapparello. Then came an elderly man alone, with a small bag in his hand. He was one of those who pride themselves on going from Pole to Pole without encumbrance, and who will be behoved to no one for the carriage of their luggage. To him, as he was alone in the street, Forrest addressed himself. 'Gorloch?' said he.

'Gorloch: are you a friend of his?'

'A friend of mine is so,' said Forrest.

'Ah, indeed; yes,' said the other. And then he hesitated. 'Sir,' he then said, 'Mr Gorloch died at Callao, just seven days before the ship sailed. You had better see Mr Cox.' And then the elderly man passed in with his little bag.

Mr Gorloch was dead. 'Dead!' said Forrest, to himself, as he leaned back against the wall of the hotel, still standing on the street pavement. 'She has come out here; and now he is gone!'And then a thousand thoughts crowded on him. Who should tell her? And how would she bear it? Would it in truth be a relief to her to find that that liberty for which she had sighed had come to her? Or now that the testing of her feelings had come to her, would she regret the loss of home and wealth, and such position as life in Peru would give her? And above all would this sudden death of one who was to have been so near to her, strike her to the heart?

But what was he to do? How was he now to show his friendship? He was returning slowly in at the hotel door, where crowds of men and women were now thronging, when he was addressed by a middle-aged, good-looking gentleman, who asked him whether his name was Forrest. 'I am told,' said the gentleman, when Forrest had answered him, 'that you are a friend of Miss Viner's. Have you heard the sad tidings from Callao?' It then appeared that this gentleman had been a stranger to Mr Gorloch, but had undertaken to bring a letter up to Miss Viner. This letter was handed to Mr Forrest, and he found himself burdened with the task of breaking the news to his poor friend. Whatever he did do, he must do at once, for all those who had come up by the Pacific steamer knew the story, and it was incumbent on him that Miss Viner should not hear the tidings in a sudden manner and from a stranger's mouth.

He went up into the drawing-room, and found Miss Viner seated there in the midst of a crew of women. He went up to her, and taking her hand, asked her in a whisper whether she would come out with him for a moment.

'Where is he?' said she. 'I know that something is the matter. What is it?'

'There is such a crowd here. Step out for a moment.' And he led her away to her own room.

'Where is he?' said she. 'What is the matter? He has sent to say that he no longer wants me. Tell me; am I free from him?'

'Miss Viner, you are free.'

Though she had asked the question herself, she was astounded by the answer; but, nevertheless, no idea of the truth had yet come upon her. 'It is so,' she said. 'Well, what else? Has he written? He has bought me, as he would a beast of burden, and has, I suppose, a right to treat me as he pleases.'

'I have a letter; but, dear Miss Viner – '

'Well, tell me all – out at once. Tell me everything.'

'You are free, Miss Viner; but you will be cut to the heart when you learn the meaning of your freedom.'

'He has lost everything in trade. He is ruined.'

'Miss Viner, he is dead!'

She stood staring at him for a moment or two, as though she could not realise the information which he gave her. Then gradually she retreated to the bed, and sat upon it. 'Dead, Mr Forrest!' she said. He did not answer her, but handed her the letter, which she took and read as though it were mechanically. The letter was from Mr Gorloch's partner, and told her everything which it was necessary that she should know.

'Shall I leave you now?' he said, when he saw that she had finished reading it.

'Leave me; yes – no. But you had better leave me, and let me think about it. Alas me, that I should have so spoken of him!'

'But you have said nothing unkind.'

'Yes; much that was unkind. But spoken words cannot be recalled. Let me be alone now, but come to me soon. There is no one else here that I can speak to.'

He went out, and finding that the hotel dinner was ready, he went in and dined. Then he strolled into the town, among the hot, narrow, dilapidated streets; and then, after two hours' absence, returned to Miss Viner's room. When he knocked, she came and opened the door, and he found that the floor was strewn with clothes.

'I am preparing, you see, for my return. The vessel starts back for St Thomas the day after tomorrow.'

'You are quite right to go – to go at once. Oh, Miss Viner! Emily, now at least you must let me help you.'

He had been thinking of her most during those last two hours, and her voice had become pleasant to his ears, and her eyes very bright to his sight.

'You shall help me,' she said. 'Are you not helping me when at such a time you come to speak to me?'

'And you will let me think that I have a right to act as your protector?'

'My protector! I do know that I want such aid as that. During the days that we are here together you shall be my friend.'

'You shall not return alone. My journeys are nothing to me. Emily, I will return with you to England.'

Then she rose up from her seat and spoke to him.

'Not for the world,' she said. 'Putting out of question the folly of your forgetting your own objects, do you think it possible that I should go with you, now that he is dead? To you I have spoken of him harshly; and now that it is my duty to mourn for him, could I do so heartily if you were with me? While he lived, it seemed to me that in those last days I had a right to speak my thoughts plainly. You and I were to part and meet no more, and I regarded us both as people apart, who for a while might drop the common usages of the world. It is so no longer. Instead of going with you farther, I must ask you to forget that we were ever together.'

'Emily, I shall never forget you.'

'Let your tongue forget me. I have given you no cause to speak good of me, and you will be too kind to speak evil.'

After that she explained to him all that the letter had contained. The arrangements for her journey had all been made; money also had been sent to her; and Mr Gorloch in his will had provided for her, not liberally, seeing that he was rich, but still sufficiently.

And so they parted at Panama. She would not allow him even to cross the Isthmus with her, but pressed his hand warmly as he left her at the station.

'God bless you!' he said.

'And may God bless you, my friend!' she answered.

Thus alone she took her departure for England, and he went on his way to California.

OSCAR WILDE

Oscar Wilde (1854–1900) is one of the greatest playwrights of the nineteenth or any century. His plays were comedies filled with witty lines and jokes and they exposed the empty and facile lives of the aristocracy and the well-to-do. His most popular comedies, *The Importance of Being Earnest*, *A Woman of No Importance*, *An Ideal Husband* and *Lady Windemere's Fan* are being revived constantly. A poet also, his verse, filled with rich fancy, was much admired. Wilde's only full-length novel, *The Picture of Dorian Gray*, is both a superb supernatural tale and a vivid evocation of aristocratic and artistic life in the late Victorian era.

In 1895, at the height of his fame, Oscar Wilde's career collapsed when he became involved in an ill-advised and unsuccessful libel suit against the Marquis of Queensberry and was exposed as a practising homosexual. As a result he was jailed for two years' hard labour. On his release he fled to Paris where he died prematurely three years later. It was a very sad end for an artist of great sensitivity, wit and perception.

There is a slang expression that has become popular within the last decade – 'get a life'. The suggestion behind this injunction is that the person to whom it is addressed is rather boring and lacks an interesting personality. Some people will go to great lengths to appear interesting, as it seems does the central character in Wilde's story 'The Sphinx Without a Secret'. The original Sphinx was a mythical creature, with the body of a lion and the head of a woman, which posed a cunning riddle and killed all those who could not solve it. As a result the term sphinx can be used to refer to anyone who appears enigmatic or who holds a mysterious secret. Again, in this tale Wilde seems to be exposing the triviality of aristocratic society. And when you have read the story, consider this question: was the handkerchief dropped on purpose?

The Sphinx Without a Secret

ONE AFTERNOON I was sitting outside the Café de la Paix, watching the splendour and shabbiness of Parisian life, and wondering over my vermouth at the strange panorama of pride and poverty that was passing before me, when I heard someone call my name. I turned round and saw Lord Murchison. We had not met since we had been at college together, nearly ten years before, so I was delighted to come across him again, and we shook hands warmly. At Oxford we had been great friends. I had liked him immensely, he was so handsome, so high-spirited, and so honourable. We used to say of him that he would be the best of fellows if he did not always speak the truth, but I think we really admired him all the more for his frankness. I found him a good deal changed. He looked anxious and puzzled, and seemed to be in doubt about something. I felt it could not be modern scepticism, for Murchison was the stoutest of Tories, and believed in the Pentateuch as firmly as he believed in the House of Peers; so I concluded that it was a woman, and asked him if he was married yet.

'I don't understand women well enough,' he answered.

'My dear Gerald,' I said, 'women are meant to be loved, not to be understood.'

'I cannot love where I cannot trust,' he replied.

'I believe you have a mystery in your life, Gerald,' I exclaimed; 'tell me about it.'

'Let us go for a drive,' he answered, 'it is too crowded here. No, not a yellow carriage, any other colour – there, that dark green one will do;' and in a few moments we were trotting down the boulevard in the direction of the Madeleine.

'Where shall we go to?' I said.

'Oh, anywhere you like!' he answered – 'to the restaurant in the Bois; we will dine there, and you shall tell me all about yourself.'

'I want to hear about you first,' I said. 'Tell me your mystery.'

He took from his pocket a little silver-clasped morocco case, and handed it to me. I opened it. Inside there was the photograph of a woman. She was tall and slight, and strangely picturesque with her large vague eyes and loosened hair. She looked like a *clairvoyante*,[1] and was wrapped in rich furs.

'What do you think of that face?' he said; 'is it truthful?'

I examined it carefully. It seemed to me the face of someone who had a secret, but whether that secret was good or evil I could not say. Its beauty was a beauty moulded out of many mysteries – the beauty, in fact, which is psychological, not plastic – and the faint smile that just played across the lips was far too subtle to be really sweet.

'Well,' he cried impatiently, 'what do you say?'

'She is the Gioconda[2] in sables,' I answered. 'Let me know all about her.'

'Not now,' he said; 'after dinner,' and began to talk of other things.

When the waiter brought us our coffee and cigarettes I reminded Gerald of his promise. He rose from his seat, walked two or three times up and down the room, and, sinking into an armchair, told me the following story:

'One evening,' he said, 'I was walking down Bond Street about five o'clock. There was a terrific crush of carriages, and the traffic was almost stopped. Close to the pavement was standing a little yellow brougham, which, for some reason or other, attracted my attention. As I passed by there looked out from it the face I showed you this afternoon. It fascinated me immediately. All that night I kept thinking of it, and all the next day. I wandered up and down that wretched Row, peering into every carriage, and waiting for the yellow brougham; but I could not find *ma belle inconnue*,[3] and at last I began to think she was merely a dream. About a week afterwards I was dining with Madame de Rastail. Dinner was for eight o'clock; but at half-past eight we were still waiting in the drawing-room. Finally the servant threw open the door and announced Lady Alroy. It was the woman I had been looking for. She came in very slowly, looking like a moonbeam in grey lace, and, to my intense delight, I was asked to take her in to dinner. After we had sat down, I remarked quite innocently, "I think I caught sight of you in Bond Street some time ago, Lady Alroy." She grew very pale, and said to me in a low voice, "Pray do not talk so loud; you may be overheard." I felt miserable at having made such a bad beginning, and plunged recklessly into the subject of the French plays. She spoke very little, always in the same low musical voice, and seemed as if she was afraid of someone listening. I fell passionately, stupidly in love, and the indefinable atmosphere of mystery that surrounded her excited my most ardent curiosity. When she was going away, which she did very soon after dinner, I asked her if I might call and see her. She hesitated for a moment, glanced round to see if anyone was near us, and then said, "Yes; tomorrow at a quarter to five." I begged Madame de Rastail to tell me about her; but all that I could learn was that she was a widow with a beautiful house in Park Lane, and as some scientific bore began a dissertation on widows, as exemplifying the survival of the matrimonially fittest, I left and went home.

'The next day I arrived at Park Lane punctual to the moment, but was told by the butler that Lady Alroy had just gone out. I went down to the club quite unhappy and very much puzzled, and after long consideration wrote her a letter, asking if I might be allowed to try my chance some other afternoon. I had no answer for several days, but at last I got a little note saying she would be at home on Sunday at four and with this extraordinary postscript: "Please do not write to me here again; I will explain when I see you." On Sunday she received me, and was perfectly charming; but when I was going away she begged of me, if I ever had occasion to write to her again, to address my letter to Mrs Knox, care of Whittaker's Library, Green Street. 'There are reasons," she said, "why I cannot receive letters in my own house."

'All through the season I saw a great deal of her, and the atmosphere of mystery never left her. Sometimes I thought that she was in the power of some man, but she looked so unapproachable that I could not believe it. It was really very difficult for me to come to any conclusion, for she was like one of those strange crystals that one sees in museums, which are at one moment clear, and at another clouded. At last I determined to ask her to be my wife: I was sick and tired of the incessant secrecy that she imposed on all my visits, and on the few letters I sent her. I wrote to her at the library to ask her if she could see me the following Monday at six. She answered yes, and I was in the seventh heaven of delight. I was infatuated with her: in spite of the mystery, I thought then – in consequence of it, I see now. No; it was the woman herself I loved. The mystery troubled me, maddened me. Why did chance put me in its track?'

'You discovered it, then?' I cried.

'I fear so,' he answered. 'You can judge for yourself. When Monday came round I went to lunch with my uncle, and about four o'clock found myself in the Marylebone Road. My uncle, you know, lives in Regent's Park. I wanted to get to Piccadilly, and took a short cut through a lot of shabby little streets. Suddenly I saw in front of me Lady Alroy, deeply veiled and walking very fast. On coming to the last house in the street, she went up the steps, took out a latchkey, and let herself in. "Here is the mystery," I said to myself; and I hurried on and examined the house. It seemed a sort of place for letting lodgings. On the doorstep lay her handkerchief, which she had dropped. I picked it up and put it in my pocket. Then I began to consider what I should do. I came to the conclusion that I had no right to spy on her, and I drove down to the club. At six I called to see her. She was lying on a sofa, in a tea-gown of silver tissue looped up by some strange moonstones that she always wore. She was looking quite lovely. "I am so glad to see you," she said; "I have not been out all day." I stared at her in amazement, and pulling the handkerchief out of my pocket, handed it to her. "You dropped this in Cumnor Street this afternoon, Lady Alroy," I said very calmly. She looked at me in terror, but made no attempt to take the handkerchief. "What were you doing there?" I asked. "What right have you to question me?" she answered. "The right of a man who loves you," I replied; "I came here to ask you to be my wife." She hid her face in her hands, and burst into floods of tears. "You must tell me," I continued. She stood up, and, looking me straight in the face, said, "Lord Murchison, there is nothing to tell you." – "You went to meet someone," I cried; "this is your mystery." She grew dreadfully white, and said, "I went to meet no one." – "Can't you tell the truth?" I exclaimed. "I have told it," she replied. I was mad, frantic; I don't know what I said, but I said terrible things to her. Finally I rushed out of the house. She wrote me a letter the next day; I sent it back unopened, and started for Norway with Alan Colville. After a month I came back, and the first thing I saw in the *Morning Post* was the death of Lady Alroy. She had caught a chill at the opera, and had died in five days of congestion of the lungs. I shut myself up and saw no one. I had loved her so much, I had loved her so madly. Good God! how I had loved that woman!'

'You went to the street, to the house in it?' I said.

'Yes,' he answered. 'One day I went to Cumnor Street. I could not help it; I was tortured with doubt. I knocked at the door, and a respectable looking woman opened it to me. I asked her if she had any rooms to let. "Well, sir," she replied, "the drawing-rooms are supposed to be let; but I have not seen the lady for three months, and as rent is owing on them, you can have them." – "Is this the lady?" I said, showing the photograph. "That's her, sure enough," she exclaimed; "and when is she coming back, sir?" – "The lady is dead," I replied. "Oh, sir, I hope not!" said the woman; "she was my best lodger. She paid me three guineas a week merely to sit in my drawing-rooms now and then." – "She met someone here?" I said; but the woman assured me that it was not so, that she always came alone, and saw no one. "What on earth did she do here?" I cried. "She simply sat in the drawing-room, sir, reading books, and sometimes had tea," the woman answered. I did not know what to say, so I gave her a sovereign and went away. Now, what do you think it all meant? You don't believe the woman was telling the truth?'

'I do.'

'Then why did Lady Alroy go there?'

'My dear Gerald,' I answered, 'Lady Alroy was simply a woman with a mania for mystery. She took those rooms for the pleasure of going there with her veil down, and imagining she was a heroine. She had a passion for secrecy, but she herself was merely a sphinx without a secret.'

'Do you really think so?'

'I am sure of it,' I replied.

He took out the morocco case, opened it, and looked at the photograph. 'I wonder?' he said at last.

BRAM STOKER

BRAM STOKER (1847–1912) was born in Dublin of a middle-class family. After graduating from Trinity College, Dublin, where he took honours in science, he entered the Irish Civil Service. But his interest in the theatre led him to undertake the role of drama reviewer for a local paper; this in turn led to short-story writing. In 1876 he began a friendship with the great Victorian actor Henry Irving and two years later he moved to England to act as his business manager at the Lyceum Theatre which had been acquired by Irving. Stoker was to serve Henry Irving, who was later knighted, for twenty-seven years, until the actor's death in Bradford in 1905.

Stoker's most famous work is the great vampire novel *Dracula*. Since its first publication in 1897, the book has never been out of print and has been translated into countless languages. There have been films, plays and even musicals based on this remarkable tale. Stoker was never able to match the success of *Dracula* with his other novels, such as *The Jewel of the Seven Stars*, *The Lair of the White Worm* or *The Lady of the Shroud*; these all trailed in the wake of his vampire classic. However, Stoker's shorter fiction, such as 'The Judge's House', is still very effective. The style is straight-forward and appears to lack artifice and yet the story has great power to chill.

'The Judge's House', written in 1891, is a ghost story which starts in a quiet, unthreatening manner with a mathematics scholar, Malcolm-son, requiring some peaceful lodgings where he can prepare for his examination without distraction. However, as soon as he enters the old 'Judge's House', in the quiet market town of Benchurch, the reader is made aware that all is not quite as it should be. By subtle means, Stoker alerts us to the growing danger that threatens the scholar and we are slowly drawn into a story that is punctuated by dramatic moments. Tension and suspense are built up almost without the reader being conscious of them and by the time we reach the final pages we are completely gripped by the story. It is true to say that there is an inevitability about the climax but this strangely enhances our involvement with the tale rather than detracting from it. 'The

Judge's House' is a model chilling ghost story and not one to be read alone on a dark and stormy night.

The Judge's House

WHEN THE TIME for his examination drew near Malcolm Malcolmson made up his mind to go somewhere to read by himself. He feared the attractions of the seaside, and also he feared completely rural isolation, for of old he knew its charms, and so he determined to find some unpretentious little town where there would be nothing to distract him. He refrained from asking suggestions from any of his friends for he argued that each would recommend some place of which he had knowledge, and where he had already acquaintances. As Malcolmson wished to avoid friends he had no wish to encumber himself with the attention of friends' friends, and so he determined to look out for a place for himself. He packed a portmanteau with some clothes and all the books he required, and then took ticket for the first name on the local timetable which he did not know.

When at the end of three hours' journey he alighted at Benchurch, he felt satisfied that he had so far obliterated his tracks as to be sure of having a peaceful opportunity of pursuing his studies. He went straight to the one inn which the sleepy little place contained, and put up for the night. Benchurch was a market town, and once in three weeks was crowded to excess, but for the remainder of the twenty-one days it was as attractive as a desert. Malcolmson looked around the day after his arrival to try to find quarters more isolated than even so quiet an inn as the Good Traveller afforded. There was only one place which took his fancy, and it certainly satisfied his wildest ideas regarding quiet; in fact, quiet was not the proper word to apply to it – desolation was the only term conveying any suitable idea of its isolation. It was an old rambling heavy-built house of the Jacobean style, with heavy gables and windows, unusually small, and set higher than was customary in such houses, and was surrounded with a high brick wall massively built. Indeed, on examination, it looked more like a fortified house than an ordinary dwelling. But all these things pleased Malcolmson. 'Here,' he thought, 'is the very spot I have been looking for, and if I can only get opportunity of using it I shall be happy.' His joy was increased when he realised beyond doubt that it was not at present inhabited.

From the post-office he got the name of the agent, who was rarely surprised at the application to rent a part of the old house. Mr Carnford, the local lawyer and agent, was a genial old gentleman and frankly confessed his delight at anyone being willing to live in the house.

'To tell you the truth,' said he, 'I should be only too happy, on behalf of the owners, to let anyone have the house rent free for a term of years if only to accustom the people here to see it inhabited. It has been so long empty that some kind of absurd prejudice has grown up about it, and this can be best put down by its occupation – if only,' he added with a sly glance at Malcolmson, 'by a scholar like yourself, who wants it quiet for a time.'

Malcolmson thought it needless to ask the agent about the 'absurd prejudice'; he knew he would get more information, if he should require it, on that subject from other quarters. He paid his three months' rent, got a receipt, and the name of an old woman who would probably undertake to 'do' for him, and came away with the keys in his pocket. He then went to the landlady of the inn, who was a cheerful and most kindly person, and asked her advice as to such stores and provisions as he would be likely to require. She threw up her hands in amazement when he told her where he was going to settle himself.

'Not in the Judge's House!' she said, and grew pale as she spoke. He explained the locality of the house, saying that he did not know its name. When he had finished she answered: 'Aye, sure enough – sure enough the very place! It is the Judge's House sure enough.'

He asked her to tell him about the place, why so called, and what there was against it. She told him that it was so called locally because it had been many years before – how long she could not say, as she was herself from another part of the country, but she thought it must have been a hundred years or more – the abode of a judge who was held in great terror on account of his harsh sentences and his hostility to prisoners at assizes. As to what there was against the house itself she could not tell. She had often asked, but no one could inform her; but there was a general feeling that there was *something*, and for her own part she would not take all the money in Drinkwater's Bank to stay in the house an hour by herself. Then she apologised to Malcolmson for her disturbing talk.

'It is too bad of me, sir, and you – and a young gentleman, too – if you will pardon me saying it, going to live there all alone. If you were my boy – and you'll excuse me for saying it – you wouldn't sleep there a night, not if I had to go there myself and pull the big alarm bell that's on the roof!'

The good creature was so manifestly in earnest, and was so kindly in her intentions, that Malcolmson, although amused, was touched. He told her kindly how much he appreciated her interest in him, and added: 'But, my dear Mrs Witham, indeed you need not be concerned about me! A man who is reading for the Mathematical Tripos has too much to think of to be disturbed by any of these mysterious *somethings*, and his work is of too exact and prosaic a kind to allow of his having any corner in his mind for mysteries of any kind. Harmonical Progression, Permutations and Combinations and Elliptic Functions have sufficient mysteries for me!'

Mrs Witham kindly undertook to see after his commissions, and he went himself to look for the old woman who had been recommended to him. When he returned to the Judge's House with her, after an interval of a couple of hours, he found Mrs Witham herself waiting with several men and boys carrying parcels, and an upholsterer's man with a bed in a cart, for she said, though tables and chairs might be all very well, a bed that hadn't been aired for mayhap fifty years was not proper for young bones to lie on. She was evidently curious to see the inside of the house, and though manifestly so afraid of the *somethings* that at the slightest sound she clutched on to Malcolmson, whom she never left for a moment, went over the whole place.

After his examination of the house, Malcolmson decided to take up his abode in the great dining-room, which was big enough to serve for all his requirements; and Mrs Witham, with the aid of the charwoman, Mrs Dempster, proceeded to arrange matters. When the hampers were brought in and unpacked, Malcolmson saw that with much kind forethought she had sent from her own kitchen sufficient provisions to last for a few days. Before going she expressed all sorts of kind wishes; and at the door turned and said: 'And perhaps, sir, as the room is big and draughty it might be well to have one of those big screens put round your bed at night – though, truth to tell, I would die myself if I were to be so shut in with all kinds of – of *things*, that put their heads round the sides, or over the top, and look on me!' The image which she had called up was too much for her nerves, and she fled incontinently.

Mrs Dempster sniffed in a superior manner as the landlady disappeared, and remarked that for her own part she wasn't afraid of all the bogies[1] in the kingdom.

'I'll tell you what it is, sir,' she said; 'bogies is all kinds and sorts of things – except bogies! Rats and mice, and beetles; and creaky doors, and loose slates, and broken panes, and stiff drawer handles that stay out when you pull them and then fall down in the middle of the night. Look at the wainscot of the room! It is old – hundreds of years old! Do you think there's no rats and beetles there! And do you imagine, sir, that you won't see none of them! Rats is bogies, I tell you, and bogies is rats; and don't you get to think anything else!'

'Mrs Dempster,' said Malcolmson gravely, making her a polite bow, 'you know more than a Senior Wrangler!² And let me say that, as a mark of esteem for your indubitable soundness of head and heart, I shall, when I go, give you possession of this house, and let you stay here by yourself for the last two months of my tenancy, for four weeks will serve my purpose.'

'Thank you kindly, sir!' she answered, 'but I couldn't sleep away from home a night. I am in Greenhow's Charity, and if I slept a night away from my rooms I should lose all I have got to live on. The rules is very strict; and there's too many watching for a vacancy for me to run any risks in the matter. Only for that, sir, I'd gladly come here and attend on you altogether during your stay.'

'My good woman,' said Malcolmson hastily, 'I have come here on purpose to obtain solitude; and believe me I am grateful to the late Greenhow for having so organised his admirable charity – whatever it is – that I am perforce denied the opportunity of suffering from such a form of temptation! St Anthony himself could not be more rigid on the point!'

The old woman laughed harshly. 'Ah, you young gentlemen,' she said, 'you don't fear for naught; and belike you'll get all the solitude you want here.' She set to work with her cleaning; and by nightfall, when Malcolmson returned from his walk – he always had one of his books to study as he walked – he found the room swept and tidied, a fire burning in the old hearth, the lamp lit, and the table spread for supper with Mrs Witham's excellent fare. 'This is comfort, indeed,' he said, as he rubbed his hands.

When he had finished his supper, and lifted the tray to the other end of the great oak dining-table, he got out his books again, put fresh wood on the fire, trimmed his lamp, and set himself down to a spell of real hard work. He went on without pause till about eleven o'clock, when he knocked off for a bit to fix his fire and lamp, and to make himself a cup of tea. He had always been a tea-drinker, and during his college life had sat late at work and had taken tea late. The rest was a great luxury to him and he enjoyed it with a sense of delicious, voluptuous ease. The renewed fire leaped and sparkled and threw quaint shadows through the great old room; and as he sipped his hot tea he revelled in the sense of isolation from his kind. Then it was that he began to notice for the first time what a noise the rats were making.

'Surely,' he thought, 'they cannot have been at it all the time I was reading. Had they been, I must have noticed it!' Presently, when the noise increased, he satisfied himself that it was really new. It was evident that at first the rats had been frightened at the presence of a stranger, and the light of fire and lamp; but that as the time went on they had grown bolder and were now disporting themselves as was their wont.

How busy they were! and hark to the strange noises! Up and down behind the old wainscot, over the ceiling and under the floor they raced, and gnawed, and scratched! Malcolmson smiled to himself as he recalled to mind the saying of Mrs Dempster, 'Bogies is rats, and rats is bogies!' The tea began to have its effect of intellectual and nervous stimulus, he saw with joy another long spell of work to be done before the night was past, and in the sense of security which it gave him, he allowed himself the luxury of a good look round the room. He took his lamp in one hand and went all around, wondering that so quaint and beautiful an old house had been so long neglected. The carving of the oak on the panels of the wainscot was fine, and on and round the doors and windows it was beautiful and of rare merit. There were some old pictures on the walls, but they were coated so thick with dust and dirt that he could not distinguish any detail of them, though he held his lamp as high as he could over his head. Here and there as he went round he saw some crack or hole blocked for a moment by the face of a rat with its bright eyes glittering in the light, but in an instant it was gone, and a squeak and a scamper followed.

The thing that most struck him, however, was the rope of the great alarm bell on the roof, which hung down in a corner of the room on the right-hand side of the fireplace. He pulled up close to the hearth a great high-backed carved oak chair, and sat down to his last cup of tea. When this was done, he made up the fire and went back to his work, sitting at the corner of the table, having the fire to his left. For a while the rats disturbed him somewhat with their perpetual scampering, but he got accustomed to the noise as one does to the ticking of a clock or to the roar of moving water; and he became so immersed in his work that everything in the world, except the problem which he was trying to solve, passed away from him.

He suddenly looked up, his problem was still unsolved, and there was in the air that sense of the hour before the dawn, which is so dread to doubtful life. The noise of the rats had ceased. Indeed it seemed to him that it must have ceased but lately and that it was the sudden cessation which had disturbed him. The fire had fallen low, but still it threw out a deep red glow. As he looked he started in spite of his *sang froid*.[3]

There on the great high-backed carved oak chair by the right side of the fireplace sat an enormous rat, steadily glaring at him with baleful eyes. He made a motion to it as though to hunt it away, but it did not stir. Then he made the motion of throwing something. Still it did not stir, but showed its great white teeth angrily, and its cruel eyes shone in the lamplight with an added vindictiveness.

Malcolmson felt amazed, and seizing the poker from the hearth ran at it to kill it. Before, however, he could strike it, the rat, with a squeak that sounded like the concentration of hate, jumped upon the floor, and, running up the rope of the alarm bell, disappeared in the darkness beyond the range of the green-shaded lamp. Instantly, strange to say, the noisy scampering of the rats in the wainscot began again.

By this time Malcolmson's mind was quite off the problem; and as a shrill cockcrow outside told him of the approach of morning, he went to bed and to sleep.

He slept so sound that he was not even waked by Mrs Dempster coming in to make up his room. It was only when she had tidied up the place and got his breakfast ready and tapped on the screen which closed in his bed that he woke. He was a little tired still after his night's hard work, but a strong cup of tea soon freshened him up, and, taking his book, he went out for his morning walk, bringing with him a few sandwiches lest he should not care to return till dinner time. He found a quiet walk between high elms some way outside the town and here he spent the greater part of the day studying his Laplace.

On his return he looked in to see Mrs Witham and to thank her for her kindness. When she saw him coming through the diamond-paned bay-window of her sanctum she came out to meet him and asked him in. She looked at him searchingly and shook her head as she said: 'You must not overdo it, sir. You are paler this morning than you should be. Too late hours and too hard work on the brain isn't good for any man! But tell me, sir, how did you pass the night? Well, I hope? But, my heart! sir, I was glad when Mrs Dempster told me this morning that you were all right and sleeping sound when she went in.'

'Oh, I was all right,' he answered, smiling, 'the *somethings* didn't worry me, as yet. Only the rats; and they had a circus, I tell you, all over the place. There was one wicked looking old devil that sat up on my own chair by the fire, and wouldn't go till I took the poker to him, and then he ran up the rope of the alarm bell and got to somewhere up the wall or the ceiling – I couldn't see where, it was so dark.'

'Mercy on us,' said Mrs Witham, 'an old devil, and sitting on a chair by the fireside! Take care, sir! take care! There's many a true word spoken in jest.'

'How do you mean? 'Pon my word, I don't understand.'

'An old devil! The old devil, perhaps. There! sir, you needn't laugh,' for Malcolmson had broken into a hearty peal. 'You young folks thinks it easy to laugh at things that makes older ones shudder. Never mind, sir! never mind! Please God, you'll laugh all the time. It's what I wish you myself!' and the good lady beamed all over in sympathy with his enjoyment, her fears gone for a moment.

'Oh, forgive me!' said Malcolmson presently. 'Don't think me rude but the idea was too much for me – that the old devil himself was on the chair last night!' And at the thought he laughed again. Then he went home to dinner.

This evening the scampering of the rats began earlier; indeed it had been going on before his arrival, and only ceased whilst his presence by its freshness disturbed them. After dinner he sat by the fire for a while and had a smoke; and then, having cleared his table, began to work as before. Tonight the rats disturbed him more than they had done on the previous night. How they scampered up and down and under and over! How they squeaked, and scratched, and gnawed! How they, getting bolder by degrees, came to the mouths of their holes and to the chinks and cracks and crannies in the wainscoting till their eyes shone like tiny lamps as the firelight rose and fell. But to him, now doubtless accustomed to them, their eyes were not wicked; only their playfulness touched him. Sometimes the boldest of them made sallies out on the floor or along the mouldings of the wainscot. Now and again as they disturbed him Malcolmson made a sound to frighten them, smiting the table with his hand or giving a fierce 'Hsh, hsh' so that they fled straightway to their holes.

And so the early part of the night wore on; and despite the noise Malcolmson got more and more immersed in his work.

All at once he stopped, as on the previous night, being overcome by a sudden sense of silence. There was not the faintest sound of gnaw, or scratch, or squeak. The silence was as of the grave. He remembered the odd occurrence of the previous night, and instinctively he looked at the chair standing close by the fireside. And then a very odd sensation thrilled through him.

There, on the great old high-backed carved oak chair beside the fireplace sat the same enormous rat, steadily glaring at him with baleful eyes.

Instinctively he took the nearest thing to his hand, a book of logarithms, and flung it at it. The book was badly aimed and the rat did not stir, so again the poker performance of the previous night was repeated; and again the rat, being closely pursued, fled up the rope of the alarm bell. Strangely, too, the departure of this rat was instantly followed by the renewal of the noise made by the general rat community. On this occasion, as on the previous one, Malcolmson could not see at what part of the room the rat disappeared, for the green shade of his lamp left the upper part of the room in darkness, and the fire had burned low.

On looking at his watch he found it was close on midnight; and, not sorry for the *divertissement*, he made up his fire and made himself his nightly pot of tea. He had got through a good spell of work, and thought himself entitled to a cigarette; and so he sat on the great carved oak chair before the fire and enjoyed it. Whilst smoking he began to think that he would like to know where the rat disappeared to, for he had certain ideas for the morrow not entirely disconnected with a rat-trap. Accordingly he lit another lamp and placed it so that it would shine well into the right-hand corner of the wall by the fireplace. Then he got all the books he had with him, and placed them handy to throw at the vermin. Finally he lifted the rope of the alarm bell and placed the end of it on the table, fixing the extreme end under the lamp. As he handled it he could not help noticing how pliable it was, especially for so strong a rope, and one not in use. 'You could hang a man with it,' he thought to himself. When his preparations were made he looked around, and said complacently: 'There now, my friend, I think we shall learn something of you this time!' He began his work again, and though as before somewhat disturbed at first by the noise of the rats, soon lost himself in his propositions and problems.

Again he was called to his immediate surroundings suddenly. This time it might not have been the sudden silence only which took his attention; there was a slight movement of the rope, and the lamp moved. Without stirring, he looked to see if his pile of books was within range, and then cast his eye along the rope. As he looked he saw the great rat drop from the rope on to the oak armchair and sit there glaring at him. He raised a book in his right hand, and taking careful aim, flung it at the rat. The latter, with a quick movement, sprang aside and dodged the missile. He then took another book, and a third, and flung them one after another at the rat, but each time unsuccessfully. At last, as he stood with a book poised in his hand to throw, the rat squeaked and seemed afraid. This made Malcolmson more than ever eager to strike, and the book flew and struck the rat a resounding blow. It gave a terrified squeak, and turning on its pursuer a look of terrible malevolence, ran up the chair back and made a great jump to the rope of the alarm bell and ran up it like lightning. The lamp rocked under the sudden strain, but it was a heavy one and did not topple over. Malcolmson kept his eyes on the rat, and saw it by the light of the second lamp leap to a moulding of the wainscot and disappear through a hole in one of the great pictures which hung on the wall, obscured and invisible through its coating of dirt and dust.

'I shall look up my friend's habitation in the morning,' said the student, as he went over to collect his books. 'The third picture from the fireplace; I shall not forget.' He picked up the books one by one, commenting on them as he lifted them. '*Conic Sections* he does not mind, nor *Cycloidal Oscillations*, nor the *Principia*, nor *Quaternions*, nor *Thermodynamics*. Now for the book that fetched him!' Malcolmson took it up and looked at it. As he did so he started, and a sudden pallor overspread his face. He looked round uneasily and shivered slightly, as he murmured to himself, 'The Bible my mother gave me! What an odd coincidence.'

He sat down to work again, and the rats in the wainscot renewed their gambols. They did not disturb him, however; somehow their presence gave him a sense of companionship. But he could not attend to his work, and after striving to master the subject on which he was engaged gave it up in despair, and went to bed as the first streak of dawn stole in through the eastern window.

He slept heavily but uneasily, and dreamed much; and when Mrs Dempster woke him late in the morning he seemed ill at ease, and for a few minutes did not seem to realise exactly where he was. His first request rather surprised the servant.

'Mrs Dempster, when I am out today I wish you would get the steps and dust or wash those pictures – specially that one the third from the fireplace – I want to see what they are.'

Late in the afternoon Malcolmson worked at his books in the shaded walk, and the cheerfulness of the previous day came back to him as the day wore on, and he found that his reading was progressing well. He had worked out to a satisfactory conclusion all the problems which had as yet baffled him, and it was in a state of jubilation that he paid a visit to Mrs Witham at the Good Traveller. He found a stranger in the cosy sitting-room with the landlady, who was introduced to him as Dr Thornhill. She was not quite at ease, and this, combined with the doctor's plunging at once into a series of questions, made Malcolmson come to the conclusion that his presence was not an accident, so without preliminary he said: 'Dr Thornhill, I shall with pleasure answer you any question you may choose to ask me if you will answer me one question first.'

The doctor seemed surprised, but he smiled and answered at once. 'Done! What is it?'

'Did Mrs Witham ask you to come here and see me and advise me?'

Dr Thornhill for a moment was taken aback, and Mrs Witham got fiery red and turned away; but the doctor was a frank and ready man, and he answered at once and openly: 'She did: but she didn't intend you to know it. I suppose it was my clumsy haste that made you suspect. She told me that she did not like the idea of your being in that house all by yourself, and that she thought you took too much strong tea. In fact, she wants me to advise you if possible to give up the tea and the very late hours. I was a keen student in my time so I suppose I may take the liberty of a college man, and without offence, advise you not quite as a stranger.'

Malcolmson with a bright smile held out his hand. 'Shake! as they say in America,' he said. 'I must thank you for your kindness and Mrs Witham too, and your kindness deserves a return on my part. I promise to take no more strong tea – no tea at all till you let me – and I shall go to bed tonight at one o'clock at latest. Will that do.'

'Capital,' said the doctor. 'Now tell us all that you noticed in the old house,' and so Malcolmson then and there told in minute detail all that had happened in the last two nights. He was interrupted every now and then by some exclamation from Mrs Witham, till finally when he told of the episode of the Bible the landlady's pent-up emotions found vent in a shriek; and it was not till a stiff glass of brandy and water had been administered that she grew composed again. Dr Thornhill listened with a face of growing gravity, and when the narrative was complete and Mrs Witham had been restored he asked: 'The rat always went up the rope of the alarm bell?'

'Always.'

'I suppose you know,' said the doctor after a pause, 'what the rope is?'

'No!'

'It is,' said the doctor slowly, 'the very rope which the hangman used for all the victims of the judge's judicial rancour!' Here he was interrupted by another scream from Mrs Witham, and steps had to he taken for her recovery. Malcolmson, having looked at his watch and found that it was close to his dinner hour, had gone home before her complete recovery.

When Mrs Witham was herself again she almost assailed the doctor with angry questions as to what he meant by putting such horrible ideas into the poor young man's mind. 'He has quite enough there already to upset him,' she added.

Dr Thornhill replied: 'My dear madam, I had a distinct purpose in it! I wanted to draw his attention to the bell rope, and to fix it there. It may be that he is in a highly overwrought state and has been studying too much, although I am bound to say that he seems as sound and healthy a young man, mentally and bodily, as ever I saw – but then the rats – and that suggestion of the devil . . . ' The doctor shook his head and went on, 'I would have offered to go and stay the night with him but I felt sure it would have been a cause of offence. He may get in the night some strange fright or hallucination; and if he does I want him to pull that rope. All alone as he is it will give us warning, and we may reach him in time to be of service. I shall be sitting up pretty late tonight and shall keep my ears open. Do not be alarmed if Benchurch gets a surprise before morning.'

'Oh, doctor, what do you mean? What do you mean?'

'I mean this: that possibly – nay more, probably – we shall hear the great alarm bell from the Judge's House tonight,' and the doctor made about as effective an exit as could be thought of.

When Malcolmson arrived home he found that it was a little after his usual time, and Mrs Dempster had gone away – the rules of Greenhow's Charity were not to be neglected. He was glad to see that the place was bright and tidy with a cheerful fire and a well-trimmed lamp. The evening was colder than might have been expected in April, and a heavy wind was blowing with such rapidly increasing strength that there was every promise of a storm during the night. For a few minutes after his entrance the noise of the rats ceased; but so soon as they became accustomed to his presence they began again. He was glad to hear them, for he felt once more the feeling of companionship in their noise, and his mind ran back to the strange fact that they only ceased to manifest themselves when that other – the great rat with the baleful eyes – came upon the scene. The reading-lamp only was lit and its green shade kept the ceiling and the upper part of the room in darkness, so that the cheerful light from the hearth spreading over the floor and shining on the white cloth laid over the end of the table was warm and cheery. Malcolmson sat down to his dinner with a good appetite and a buoyant spirit. After his dinner and a cigarette he sat steadily down to work, determined not to let anything disturb him, for he remembered his promise to the doctor, and made up his mind to make the best of the time at his disposal.

For an hour or so he worked all right, and then his thoughts began to wander from his books. The actual circumstances around him, the calls on his physical attention, and his nervous susceptibility were not to be denied. By this time the wind had become a gale, and the gale a storm. The old house, solid though it was, seemed to shake to its foundations, and the storm roared and raged through its many chimneys and its queer old gables, producing strange, unearthly sounds in the empty rooms and corridors. Even the great alarm bell on the roof must have felt the force of the wind, for the rope rose and fell slightly, as though the bell were moved a little from time to time, and the limber rope fell on the oak floor with a hard and hollow sound.

As Malcolmson listened to it he bethought himself of the doctor's words, 'It is the rope which the hangman used for the victims of the judge's judicial rancour,' and he went over to the corner of the fireplace and took it in his hand to look at it. There seemed a sort of deadly interest in it, and as he stood there he lost himself for a moment in speculation as to who these victims were, and the grim wish of the judge to have such a ghastly relic ever under his eyes. As he stood there, the swaying of the bell on the roof still lifted the rope now and again; but presently there came a new sensation – a sort of tremor in the rope, as though something was moving along it.

Looking up instinctively, Malcolmson saw the great rat coming slowly down towards him, glaring at him steadily. He dropped the rope and started back with a muttered curse, and the rat, turning, ran up the rope again and disappeared, and at the same instant Malcolmson became conscious that the noise of the rats, which had ceased for a while, began again.

All this set him thinking, and it occurred to him that he had not investigated the lair of the rat or looked at the pictures, as he had intended. He lit the other lamp without the shade and, holding it up, went and stood opposite the third picture from the fireplace on the right-hand side where he had seen the rat disappear on the previous night.

At the first glance he started back so suddenly that he almost dropped the lamp, and a deadly pallor overspread his face. His knees shook and heavy drops of sweat came on his forehead and he trembled like an aspen. But he was young and plucky, and pulled himself together, and after the pause of a few seconds stepped forward again, raised the lamp, and examined the picture which had been dusted and washed and now stood out clearly.

It was of a judge dressed in his robes of scarlet and ermine. His face was strong and merciless, evil, crafty and vindictive, with a sensual mouth and a hooked nose of ruddy colour, shaped like the beak of a bird of prey. The rest of the face was of a cadaverous colour. The eyes were of peculiar brilliance and had a terribly malignant expression. As he looked at them, Malcolmson grew cold, for he saw there the very counterpart of the eyes of the great rat. The lamp almost fell from his hand when he saw the rat with its baleful eyes peering out through the hole in the corner of the picture and noted the sudden cessation of the noise of the other rats. However, he pulled himself together and went on with his examination of the picture.

The judge was seated in a great high-backed carved oak chair on the right-hand side of a great stone fireplace where, in the corner, a rope hung down from the ceiling, its end lying coiled on the floor. With a feeling of something like horror, Malcolmson recognised the scene of the room as it stood and gazed around him in an awestruck manner as though he expected to find some strange presence behind him. Then he looked over to the corner of the fireplace – and with a loud cry he let the lamp fall from his hand.

There, in the judge's armchair, with the rope hanging behind, sat the rat with the judge's baleful eyes, now intensified and with a fiendish leer. Save for the howling of the storm without there was silence.

The fallen lamp recalled Malcolmson to himself. Fortunately it was of metal, and so the oil was not spilt. However, the practical need of attending to it settled at once his nervous apprehensions. When he had turned it out, he wiped his brow and thought for a moment.

'This will not do,' he said to himself. 'If I go on like this I shall become a crazy fool. This must stop! I promised the doctor I would not take tea. Faith, he was pretty right! My nerves must have been getting into a queer state. Funny I did not notice it. I never felt better in my life. However, it is all right now, and I shall not be such a fool again.'

Then he mixed himself a good stiff glass of brandy and water and resolutely sat down to his work.

It was nearly an hour later when he looked up from his book, disturbed by the sudden stillness. Without, the wind howled and roared louder than ever, and the rain drove in sheets against the windows, beating like hail on the glass; but within there was no sound whatever save the echo of the wind as it roared in the great chimney, and now and then a hiss as a few raindrops found their way down the chimney in a lull of the storm. The fire had fallen low and had ceased to flame, though it threw out a red glow. Malcolmson listened attentively, and presently heard a thin, squeaking noise, very faint. It came from the corner of the room where the rope hung down, and he thought it was the creaking of the rope on the floor as the swaying of the bell raised and lowered it. Looking up, however, he saw in the dim light the great rat clinging to the rope and gnawing it. The rope was already nearly gnawed through – he could see the lighter colour where the strands were laid bare. As he looked the job was completed, and the severed end of the rope fell clattering on the oaken floor, whilst for an instant the great rat remained like a knob or tassel at the end of the rope, which now began to sway to and fro. Malcolmson felt for a moment another pang of terror as he thought that now the possibility of calling the outer world to his assistance was cut off, but an intense anger took its place, and seizing the book he was reading he hurled it at the rat. The blow was well aimed, but before the missile could reach it the rat dropped off and struck the floor with a soft thud. Malcolmson instantly rushed over towards it, but it darted away and disappeared in the darkness of the shadows of the room.

Malcolmson felt that his work was over for the night, and determined then and there to vary the monotony of the proceedings by a hunt for the rat, taking off the green shade of the lamp so as to ensure a wider spreading light. As he did so the gloom of the upper part of the room was relieved, and in the new flood of light, great by comparison with the previous darkness, the pictures on the wall stood out boldly. From where he stood, Malcolmson saw right opposite to him the third picture on the wall from the right of the fireplace. He rubbed his eyes in surprise, and then a great fear began to come upon him. In the centre of the picture was a great irregular patch of brown canvas, as fresh as when it was stretched on the frame. The background was as before, with chair and chimney-corner and rope, but the figure of the judge had disappeared.

Malcolmson, almost in a chill of horror, turned slowly round, and then he began to shake and tremble like a man in a palsy. His strength seemed to have left him, and he was incapable of action or movement, hardly even of thought. He could only see and hear.

There, on the great high-backed carved oak chair, sat the judge in his robes of scarlet and ermine, with his baleful eyes glaring

vindictively and a smile of triumph on the resolute, cruel mouth as
he lifted with his hands a *black cap*. Malcolmson felt as if the blood
was running from his heart, as one does in moments of prolonged
suspense. There was a singing in his ears. Without, he could hear the
roar and howl of the tempest, and through it, swept on the storm,
came the striking of midnight by the great chimes in the market-
place. He stood for a space of time that seemed to him endless, still
as a statue and with wide-open, horror-struck eyes, breathless. As
the clock struck, so the smile of triumph on the judge's face
intensified, and at the last stroke of midnight he placed the black cap
on his head.

Slowly and deliberately the judge rose from his chair and picked up
the piece of rope of the alarm bell which lay on the floor, drew it
through his hands as if he enjoyed its touch, and then deliberately
began to knot one end of it, fashioning it into a noose. This he
tightened and tested with his foot, pulling hard at it till he was
satisfied and then making a running noose of it, which he held in his
hand. Then he began to move along the table on the opposite side to
Malcolmson, keeping his eyes on him until he had passed him, when
with a quick movement he stood in front of the door. Malcolmson
then began to feel that he was trapped, and tried to think of what he
should do. There was some fascination in the judge's eyes, which he
never took off him, and he had, perforce, to look. He saw the judge
approach – still keeping between him and the door – and raise the
noose and throw it towards him as if to entangle him. With a great
effort he made a quick movement to one side, and saw the rope fall
beside him, and heard it strike the oaken floor. Again the judge raised
the noose and tried to ensnare him, ever keeping his baleful eyes fixed
on him, and each time by a mighty effort the student just managed to
evade it. So this went on for many times, the judge seeming never
discouraged nor discomposed at failure, but playing as a cat does with
a mouse. At last in despair, which had reached its climax, Malcolmson
cast a quick glance round him. The lamp seemed to have blazed up,
and there was a fairly good light in the room. At the many rat holes
and in the chinks and crannies of the wainscot he saw the rats' eyes;
and this aspect, that was purely physical, gave him a gleam of
comfort. He looked up and saw that the rope of the great alarm bell
was laden with rats. Every inch of it was covered with them, and more
and more were pouring through the small circular hole in the ceiling
whence it emerged, so that with their weight the bell was beginning
to sway.

Hark! it had swayed till the clapper had touched the bell. The sound was but a tiny one, but the bell was only beginning to sway and it would increase.

At the sound the judge, who had been keeping his eyes fixed on Malcolmson, looked up, and a scowl of diabolical anger overspread his face. His eyes fairly glowed like hot coals, and he stamped his foot with a sound that seemed to make the house shake. A dreadful peal of thunder broke overhead as he raised the rope again, whilst the rats kept running up and down the bell-rope as though working against time. This time, instead of throwing it, he drew close to his victim, and held open the noose as he approached. As he came closer there seemed something paralysing in his very presence, and Malcolmson stood rigid as a corpse. He felt the judge's icy fingers touch his throat as he adjusted the rope. The noose tightened – tightened. Then the judge, taking the rigid form of the student in his arms, carried him over and placed him standing in the oak chair, and stepping up beside him, put his hand up and caught the end of the swaying rope of the alarm bell. As he raised his hand the rats fled squeaking, and disappeared through the hole in the ceiling. Taking the end of the noose which was round Malcolmson's neck he tied it to the hanging bell-rope, and then descending, pulled away the chair.

When the alarm bell of the Judge's House began to sound a crowd soon assembled. Lights and torches of various kinds appeared, and soon a silent crowd was hurrying to the spot. They knocked loudly at the door, but there was no reply. Then they burst in the door, and poured into the great dining-room, the doctor at the head.

There at the end of the rope of the great alarm hell hung the body of the student, and on the face of the judge in the picture was a malignant smile.

GUY DE MAUPASSANT

GUY DE MAUPASSANT (1850–93) is generally regarded as the French master of the short story. He was born into a minor aristocratic family in Normandy and had his own private income. He studied in Rouen and Paris but with the outbreak of war the family lost their fortune and Guy was forced to become a poorly paid civil servant. Paris became his home. Here, despite his lowly salary, he enjoyed life to the full. He possessed boundless energy and vitality. He was an enthusiastic oarsman and was well known for his romantic escapades with young women.

Encouraged by the great French novelist Gustave Flaubert, a childhood friend of his mother, he took up writing and gradually found success. He joined the group of naturalistic authors at whose head was the formidable Emile Zola; these writers wanted to document the life and suffering of ordinary working people in an accurate, realistic and detached way. Maupassant's writing career lasted only a relatively short time – eleven years of intensive work – and yet in that period he produced over three hundred short stories and six novels, as well as plays and travel writing.

It all came to an end when he contracted the venereal disease syphilis during one of his illicit sexual liaisons. This brought about his mental deterioration and he ended his short life in a private asylum.

'The Necklace' is a classic Maupassant story with the surprising and in this case shocking twist at the end. In essence, this is a moral tale in which fate seems to contrive to make the central character, Madame Loisel, pay a heavy penalty for her 'sins' – those of pride and wanting a better and more glamorous life. In typical Maupassant fashion, the author gives no indication as to his own feelings in the matter and does not attempt to influence the reader's view. We must make up our own minds. However, as in real life, the question of who is to blame for Madame Loisel's fate is not answered easily. Life, Maupassant seems to be saying, is never a matter of black and white. The author is also aware that while there are virtues in being content with one's lot, this attitude stifles ambition and vision. The question the modern reader must ask themselves is who do you feel most sympathy for at the end – and why?

The Necklace

SHE WAS ONE of those pretty and charming girls who, by some freak of destiny, are born into families that have always held subordinate appointments. Possessing neither dowry nor expectations, she had no hope of meeting some man of wealth and distinction, who would understand her, fall in love with her and wed her. So she consented to marry a minor clerk in the Ministry of Public Instruction.

She dressed plainly, because she could not afford to be elegant, but she felt as unhappy as if she had married beneath her. Women are dependent neither on caste nor ancestry. With them, beauty, grace and charm take the place of birth and breeding. In their case, natural delicacy, instinctive refinement and adaptability constitute their claims to aristocracy and raise girls of the lower classes to an equality with the greatest of great ladies. She was eternally restive under the conviction that she had been born to enjoy every refinement and luxury. Depressed by her humble surroundings, the sordid walls of her dwelling, its worn furniture and shabby hangings were a torment to her. Details which another woman of her class would scarcely have noticed, tortured her and filled her with resentment. The sight of her little Breton maid-of-all-work roused in her forlorn repinings[1] and frantic yearnings. She pictured to herself silent antechambers, upholstered in oriental tapestry, lighted by great bronze standard lamps, while two tall footmen in knee breeches slumbered in huge armchairs, overcome by the oppressive heat from the stove. She dreamed of spacious drawing-rooms with hangings of antique silk, and beautiful tables laden with priceless ornaments; of fragrant and coquettish boudoirs,[2] exquisitely adapted for afternoon chats with intimate friends, men of note and distinction, whose attentions are coveted by every woman.

She would sit down to dinner at the round table, its cloth already three days old, while her husband, seated opposite to her, removed the lid from the soup tureen and exclaimed, 'Pot au feu![3] How splendid! My favourite soup!' But her own thoughts were dallying with the idea of exquisite dinners and shining silver, in rooms whose tapestried walls were gay with antique figures and grotesque birds in fairy forests. She would dream of delicious dishes served on wonderful plate, of soft, whispered nothings, which evoke a sphinx-like smile, while one trifles with the pink flesh of a trout or the wing of a plump pullet.

She had no pretty gowns, no jewels, nothing – and yet she cared for nothing else. She felt that it was for such things as these that she had been born. What joy it would have given her to attract, to charm, to be envied by women, courted by men! She had a wealthy friend who had been at school at the same convent, but after a time she refused to go and see her because she suffered so acutely after each visit. She spent whole days in tears of grief, regret, despair and misery.

One evening her husband returned home in triumph with a large envelope in his hand.

'Here is something for you,' he cried.

Hastily she tore open the envelope and drew out a printed card with the following inscription:

The Minister of Public Instruction
and Madame Ramponneau
have the honour to request the company of
Monsieur and Madame Loisel
At Home
at the Education Office on
Monday the 18th January

Instead of being delighted, as her husband had hoped, she flung the invitation irritably on the table, exclaiming: 'What good is that to me?'

'Why, my dear, I thought you would be pleased. You never go anywhere, and this is a really splendid chance for you. I had no end of trouble in getting it. Everybody is trying to get an invitation. It's very select, and only a few invitations are issued to the clerks. You will see all the officials there.'

She looked at him in exasperation, and exclaimed petulantly: 'What do you expect me to wear at a reception like that?'

He had not considered the matter, but he replied hesitatingly: 'Why, that dress you always wear to the theatre seems to me very nice indeed . . . '

He broke off. To his horror and consternation he saw that his wife was in tears. Two large drops were rolling slowly down her cheeks.

'What on earth is the matter?' he gasped.

With a violent effort she controlled her emotion, and drying her wet cheeks said in a calm voice: 'Nothing. Only I haven't a frock, and so I can't go to the reception. Give your invitation to some friend in your office whose wife is better dressed than I am.'

He was greatly distressed.

'Let us talk it over, Matilda. How much do you think a proper frock would cost, something quite simple that would come in useful for other occasions afterwards?'

She considered the matter for a few moments, busy with her calculations, and wondering how large a sum she might venture to name without shocking the little clerk's instincts of economy and provoking a prompt refusal.

'I hardly know,' she said at last, doubtfully, 'but I think I could manage with four hundred francs.'

He turned a little pale. She had named the exact sum that he had saved for buying a gun and making up Sunday shooting parties the following summer with some friends who were going to shoot larks in the plain of Nanterre.

But he replied: 'Very well, I'll give you four hundred francs. But mind you buy a really handsome gown.'

The day of the party drew near. But although her gown was finished, Madame Loisel seemed depressed and dissatisfied.

'What is the matter?' asked her husband one evening. 'You haven't been at all yourself the last three days.'

She answered: 'It vexes me to think that I haven't any jewellery to wear, not even a brooch. I shall feel like a perfect pauper. I would almost rather not go to the party.'

'You can wear some fresh flowers. They are very fashionable this year. For ten francs you can get two or three splendid roses.'

She was not convinced. 'No, there is nothing more humiliating than to have an air of poverty among a crowd of rich women.'

'How silly you are!' exclaimed her husband. 'Why don't you ask your friend, Madame Forestier, to lend you some jewellery? You know her quite well enough for that.'

She uttered a cry of joy.

'Yes, of course, it never occurred to me.'

The next day she paid her friend a visit and explained her predicament.

Madame Forestier went to her wardrobe, took out a large jewel-case and placed it open before her friend.

'Help yourself, my dear.'

Madame Loisel saw some bracelets, a pearl necklace, a Venetian cross exquisitely worked in gold and jewels. She tried on these ornaments in front of the mirror and hesitated, reluctant to take them off and give them back.

'Have you nothing else?' she kept asking.

'Oh yes, look for yourself. I don't know what you would prefer.'

At length she discovered a black-satin case containing a superb diamond necklace, and her heart began to beat with frantic desire. With trembling hands she took it out, fastened it over her high-necked gown, and stood gazing at herself in rapture.

Then in an agony of doubt, she said: 'Will you lend me this? I shouldn't want anything else.'

'Yes, certainly.'

She threw her arms round her friend's neck, kissed her effusively, and then fled with her treasure.

It was the night of the reception. Madame Loisel's triumph was complete. All smiles and graciousness, in her exquisite gown, she was the prettiest woman in the room. Her head was in a whirl of joy. The men stared at her and enquired her name and begged for an introduction, while the junior staff asked her for waltzes. She even attracted the attention of the minister himself.

Carried away by her enjoyment, glorying in her beauty and her success, she threw herself ecstatically into the dance. She moved as in a beatific dream, wherein were mingled all the homage and admiration she had evoked, all the desires she had kindled, all that complete and perfect triumph so dear to a woman's heart.

It was close on four before she could tear herself away. Ever since midnight her husband had been dozing in a little, deserted drawing-room together with three other men whose wives were enjoying themselves immensely.

He threw her outdoor wraps round her shoulders – unpretentious, everyday garments, whose shabbiness contrasted strangely with the elegance of her ballgown. Conscious of the incongruity, she was eager to be gone, in order to escape the notice of the other women in their luxurious furs. Loisel tried to restrain her.

'Wait here while I fetch a cab. You will catch cold outside.'

But she would not listen to him, and hurried down the staircase. They went out into the street, but there was no cab to be seen. They continued their search, vainly hailing drivers whom they caught sight of in the distance. Shivering with cold and in desperation, they made their way towards the Seine. At last, on the quay, they found one of those old vehicles which are only seen in Paris after nightfall, as if ashamed to display their shabbiness by daylight.

The cab took them to their door in the Rue des Martyrs, and they gloomily climbed the stairs to their dwelling. All was over for her. As for him, he was thinking that he would have to be in the office by ten o'clock.

She took off her wraps in front of the mirror for the sake of one last glance at herself in all her glory. But suddenly she uttered a cry. The diamonds were no longer round her neck.

'What is the matter?' asked her husband, who was already half undressed.

She turned to him in horror. 'I . . . I . . . have lost Madame Forestier's necklace.'

He started in dismay. 'What? Lost the necklace? Impossible.'

They searched the pleats of the gown, the folds of the cloak and all the pockets, but in vain.

'You are sure you had it on when you came away from the ball?'

'Yes, I remember feeling it in the lobby at the Education Office.'

'But if you had lost it in the street, we should have heard it drop. It must be in the cab.'

'Yes. I expect it is. Did you take the number?'

'No. Did you?'

'No.'

They gazed at each other, utterly appalled. In the end, Loisel put on his clothes again.

'I will go over the ground that we covered on foot and see if I cannot find it.'

He left the house. Lacking the strength to go to bed, unable to think, she collapsed into a chair and remained there in her evening gown, without a fire.

About seven o'clock her husband returned. He had not found the diamonds.

He applied to the police; advertised a reward in the newspapers, made enquiries of all the hackney-cab offices; he visited every place that seemed to hold out a vestige of hope.

His wife waited all day long in the same distracted condition, overwhelmed by this appalling calamity.

Loisel returned home in the evening, pale and hollow checked. His efforts had been in vain.

'You must write to your friend,' he said, 'and tell her that you have broken the catch of the necklace and that you are having it mended. That will give us time to think things over.'

She wrote a letter to his dictation.

After a week had elapsed, they gave up all hope. Loisel, who looked five years older, said: 'We must take steps to replace the diamonds.'

On the following day they took the empty case to the jeweller, whose name was inside the lid. He consulted his books.

'The necklace was not bought here, madame; I can only have supplied the case.'

They went from jeweller to jeweller in an endeavour to find a necklace exactly like the one they had lost, comparing their recollections. Both of them were ill with grief and despair.

At last in a shop in the Palais Royal they found a diamond necklace, which seemed to them exactly like the other. Its price was forty thousand francs. The jeweller agreed to sell it to them for thirty-six. They begged him not to dispose of it for three days, and they stipulated for the right to sell it back for thirty-four thousand francs, if the original necklace was found before the end of February.

Loisel had eighteen thousand francs left to him by his father. The balance of the sum he proposed to borrow. He raised loans in all quarters, a thousand francs from one man, five hundred from another, five louis[4] here, three louis there. He gave promissory notes, agreed to exorbitant terms, had dealings with usurers and with all the moneylending hordes. He compromised his whole future, and had to risk his signature, hardly knowing if he would be able to honour it. Overwhelmed by the prospect of future suffering, the black misery which was about to come upon him, the physical privations and moral torments, he went to fetch the new necklace and laid his thirty-six thousand francs down on the jeweller's counter.

When Madame Loisel brought back the necklace, Madame Forestier said reproachfully: 'You ought to have returned it sooner; I might have wanted to wear it.'

To Madame Loisel's relief she did not open the case. Supposing she had noticed the exchange, what would she have thought? What would she have said? Perhaps she would have taken her for a thief.

Madame Loisel now became acquainted with the horrors of extreme poverty. She made up her mind to it, and played her part heroically. This appalling debt had to be paid, and pay it she would. The maid was dismissed; the flat was given up and they moved to a garret. She undertook all the rough household work and the odious duties of the kitchen. She washed up after meals and ruined her pink fingernails scrubbing greasy dishes and saucepans. She washed the linen, the shirts and the dusters, and hung them out on the line to dry. Every morning she carried down the sweepings to the street, and brought up the water, pausing for breath at each landing. Dressed like a working woman, she went with her basket on her arm to the greengrocer, the grocer and the butcher, bargaining, wrangling and fighting for every farthing.

Each month some of the promissory notes had to be redeemed, and others renewed, in order to gain time.

Her husband spent his evenings working at some tradesman's accounts, and at night he would often copy papers at five sous a page.

This existence went on for ten years.

At the end of that time they had paid off everything to the last penny, including the usurious[5] rates and the accumulations of interest.

Madame Loisel now looked an old woman. She had become the typical poor man's wife, rough, coarse, hard-bitten. Her hair was neglected; her skirts hung awry; and her hands were red. Her voice was no longer gentle, and she washed down the floors vigorously. But now and then, when her husband was at the office, she would sit by the window, and her thoughts would wander back to that faraway evening, the evening of her beauty and her triumph.

What would have been the end of it if she had not lost the necklace? Who could say? Who could say? How strange, how variable are the chances of life! How small a thing can serve to save or ruin you!

One Sunday she went for a stroll in the Champs Elysées, for the sake of relaxation after the week's work, and she caught sight of a lady with a child. She recognised Madame Forestier, who looked as young, as pretty, and as attractive as ever. Madame Loisel felt a thrill of emotion. Should she speak to her? Why not? Now that the debt was paid, why should she not tell her the whole story? She went up to her.

'Good-morning, Jeanne.'

Her friend did not recognise her and was surprised at being addressed so familiarly by this homely person.

'I am afraid I do not know you – you must have made a mistake,' she said hesitatingly.

'No. I am Matilda Loisel.'

Her friend uttered a cry.

'Oh, my poor, dear Matilda, how you have changed!'

'Yes, I have been through a very hard time since I saw you last, no end of trouble, and all through you.'

'Through me? What do you mean?'

'You remember the diamond necklace you lent me to wear at the reception at the Education Office?'

'Yes. Well?'

'Well, I lost it.'

'I don't understand; you brought it back to me.'

'What I brought you back was another one, exactly like it. And for the last ten years we have been paying for it. You will understand that it was not an easy matter for people like us, who hadn't a penny. However, it's all over now. I can't tell you what a relief it is.'

Madame Forestier stopped dead.

'You mean to say that you bought a diamond necklace to replace mine?'

'Yes. And you never noticed it? They were certainly very much alike.'

She smiled with ingenuous pride and satisfaction.

Madame Forestier seized both her hands in great distress.

'Oh, my poor, dear Matilda. Why, my diamonds were only imitation. At the most they were worth five hundred francs!'

ANTON CHEKHOV

ANTON CHEKHOV (1860–1904) was born the son of a tradesman and the grandson of serfs. He studied medicine at Moscow University where he began writing humorous short stories for magazines. These made his name as a writer, and although he never abandoned this genre, many of his later stories, written when he had experienced more of the trials and tribulations of life, grew more serious and tended to be pessimistic. 'The Kiss' falls into this latter category.

However, Chekhov's great claim to fame lies in the theatre and although he wrote many stories it is now as a dramatist that he is best remembered. His plays, which include *The Seagull, Uncle Vanya, The Three Sisters* and *The Cherry Orchard*, are still performed with regularity all over the world.

Although his plays have overshadowed his prose work, Chekhov remains a master of the art of the short story. His later tales, like those of Guy de Maupassant, reveal in an unsentimental fashion the vagaries and cruel ironies of life. He shows a melancholy tenderness for his awkward heroes, such as Riabovitch in 'The Kiss', despite their inability to take action to better their lot. They stand on the sidelines and let life happen to them and accept whatever fate gives them without stir. With heroes like these, the author also provides the figure of an idealised woman, like the unknown lady in 'The Kiss'. Her mistaken amorous gesture becomes the main focus in Riabovitch's life in this half-ironical, half-pathetic tale. Chekhov pities more than he condemns such dreamy 'failures in life' as personified by his sad hero. In modern parlance Riabovitch could be referred to as 'a wimp', but his final action is both brave and decisive. However, we are still left wondering if it is also a foolish one.

The Kiss

AT EIGHT O'CLOCK in the evening of 20th May the six batteries of the U reserve artillery on its way to camp stopped for the night in the village of Mestechko. During the bustle, when some officers were busy with the guns and others scattered over the square hearing the reports of the quartermasters, a horseman in civilian clothes appeared from behind the church on a curious, small light bay[1] with a beautiful neck and a clipped tail, which ran sideways rather than straight, and threw out its legs in short frisky movements as though they were being lashed with a whip. The horseman drew up by a group of officers and, raising his hat, said: 'His Excellency General von Rabbek, the squire here, would be glad if you gentlemen would come and take tea with him.'

The horse frisked and backed sideways; the horseman once more raised his hat and, turning, disappeared behind the church with his strange-looking animal.

'Damn!' some of the officers grumbled, departing to their quarters. 'A fellow wants to sleep, and here comes this von Rabbek with his tea! We know what that means!'

And every officer in the six batteries vividly recalled an incident that had happened to them last year during manoeuvres when, together with the officers of a certain Cossack regiment, they were invited to tea in this manner by a certain count and retired officer, and how the cordial, hospitable count had entertained them royally and insisted on their spending the night in his house instead of at their quarters. It was all very nice, of course, and nothing better could have been desired, only the count was overmuch pleased with the society of the young men. Until daybreak he wearied them with episodes of his own happy past, led them from room to room to show them his costly pictures, old engravings and rare pieces of armour; he even read them letters he had received from various celebrities, and the tired officers listened and looked, inwardly longing for their beds and yawning cautiously behind their palms; when at last their host released them it was too late to go to bed.

Was von Rabbek by any chance such another? However, there was nothing to be done. The officers washed and dressed and set off together to find the squire's house. In the square by the church they were told that they could cut down to the river by a path behind the church, and then along the bank till they came to the squire's own garden, and the avenue would bring them to the door, or they could ride along the road that turned off half a verst up by the squire's barns. The officers chose the latter.

'Who is this von Rabbek?' they asked each other on the way. 'Is he the man who commanded the U cavalry division in Plevna?'

'No, that was not von Rabbek, but simply Rabbe, without the von.'

'What lovely weather it is!'

At the first barn the road divided in two – the one straight ahead vanished into the evening darkness, the other to the right led to the squire's house. The officers turned to the right and lowered their voices. On either side of the road stretched the stone barns with red roofs, massive and sombre, like the barracks of a provincial town.

'A good sign, gentlemen,' one of the officers remarked. 'Our setter is in front, which means that he scents game!'

Ahead of us all was Lieutenant Lobitko, tall and broad shouldered, with clean upper lip. He was twenty-five, though his full round face did not show it. He was famous in the brigade for his knack of sensing the presence of women in a place, even at a distance. He turned round and said: 'Yes, I am sure there are women here; I feel it by instinct.'

At the door of the house the officers were met by von Rabbek himself, a handsome old man of sixty, in civilian clothes. Shaking hands with his guests, he said that he was pleased and happy to see them, but begged them to excuse him for not having invited them to stay the night; his two sisters and their children had come, as well as his brothers and some neighbours, and in consequence he had not a single spare room.

The general was affability itself, but from the expression of his face it was obvious that he was not quite as overjoyed with his guests as the count of last year, and that he had invited them merely out of a sense of politeness. And this was made quite clear to them as they walked up the carpeted stairs, listening to their host, and saw the footmen hurrying to light the lamps in the hall and on the staircase. They felt that they were a nuisance in the house. Under a roof where two sisters and brothers and neighbours had gathered together, perhaps for the celebration of some family event, how could the family be pleased with the presence of nineteen strangers?

At the drawing-room door the guests were received by a tall, graceful old lady with an oval-shaped face and dark brows, who resembled the Empress Eugénie. With a gracious smile she welcomed them, apologising for not being able to ask them to stay the night. By the smile that disappeared from her face the moment she turned away, it was plain that the lady had seen many officers in her day and that she had no use for them now, and that if she had invited them to her house and was offering her excuses, it was only because her breeding and position demanded it of her.

When the officers entered the dining-room about a dozen men and women, old and young, were sitting at one end of a long table having tea. Behind their chairs, enveloped in cigar smoke, was a group of men, in the midst of whom a thin young man with red mustachios was speaking in English in a loud voice. Behind the group, through a door, was a view of a brightly lighted room with pale blue furniture.

'Gentlemen, there are so many of you that it is impossible to introduce you all!' the general said aloud with an effort at gaiety. 'Please introduce yourselves in a homely way.'

The officers, some with solemn countenances, others with strained smiles, and all feeling extremely uncomfortable, bowed and seated themselves at the table. There was one among them who felt more uncomfortable than the rest – the staff officer Riabovitch, a round-shouldered little man in spectacles.

At the moment when some of his comrades put on a serious expression and others constrained themselves to smile, his face, lynx-like[2] mustachios, spectacles and all, seemed to say, 'I am the shyest, most modest, most colourless officer in the whole brigade!' When he first entered the room and sat down by the table, he could not fix his attention on any one particular object or face – faces, garments, cut-glass decanters of cognac, the steam from the glasses, the stucco cornices – all mingled into a single impression that confused Riabovitch and aroused in him a desire to hide his head. Like a lecturer facing his audience for the first time, he saw the objects before his eyes, but seemed to comprehend nothing. (This condition, when a subject sees without comprehending, is known among physiologists as 'psychological blindness'.) Becoming used to his surroundings after a while, Riabovitch began to look about him. Being a shy man unused to society, he was first of all struck by the unusual courage of his new acquaintance – von Rabbek, his wife, two elderly ladies, a girl in a lilac dress, a young man with red whiskers, that turned out to be Rabbek's youngest son, who had very cleverly, as though they had rehearsed the thing beforehand, distributed themselves among the officers and begun an enthusiastic discussion in which the guests could not help but join. The lilac girl maintained warmly that life in the artillery was much easier than in the cavalry or infantry, while Rabbek and one of the old ladies defended an opposite view. A cross-conversation arose. Riabovitch looked at the lilac girl discussing a subject she knew nothing about and that she was not the least interested in, and watched the artificial smiles playing over her face.

Von Rabbek and his wife cleverly drew the officers into the discussion, keeping a careful eye meanwhile on their guests' glasses and plates to see that all were eating and drinking. The more Riabovitch looked and listened, the more he liked this insincere though excellently disciplined family.

After tea the officers went into the drawing-room. Lieutenant Lobitko's instinct had not failed him; there were many girls and young women in the room. The setter lieutenant stood near a fair young girl in a black dress, bending gallantly towards her as though he were leaning on an invisible sword. He smiled and moved his shoulders coquettishly. He must have been talking some interesting nonsense, no doubt, for the fair girl looked condescendingly at his round face and said indifferently, 'Really?' By this apathetic 'really' the setter, had he been wise, might have known that she was not very much entertained.

Someone began to play a melancholy valse[3] on the piano; the sad air floating through the wide-open windows made everyone remember that it was May and that the weather was beautiful, and that the scent of lilac and rose and young poplars was in the air.

Riabovitch, who in addition to the music was under the influence of the cognac he had drunk, leant against the window, smiling. He began to follow the movements of the women, and it seemed to him that the scent of rose and lilac and poplar did not come from the garden but from their faces and dresses.

Von Rabbek's son invited a tall, thin girl to dance, and took two or three turns round the room. Lobitko glided over the polished floor to the girl in lilac and whirled her away across the room. The dancing began . . . Riabovitch stood by the door among the non-dancing men and watched. He had never once danced in his life, nor had it ever fallen to his lot to put his arm around the waist of a respectable woman The idea that a man in the sight of all should take a strange young girl by the waist and offer his shoulder for her arm to rest on was very pleasing to Riabovitch, but he could never imagine himself in the position of such a man. There had been a time when he had envied the courage and daring of his comrades, and his heart had sickened at the consciousness that he was shy and round-shouldered and colourless and that he had lynx-like mustachios, but with the years he became reconciled; as he now gazed at the dancing couples and at those talking in loud assured voices he no longer envied them, he was affected only by a feeling of sadness.

When the quadrille was about to begin young von Rabbek came up to the non-dancing men and invited a couple of the officers to a game of billiards. The officers followed him out of the drawing-room. Riabovitch, from want of something to do and a desire to participate in some way in the general bustle, went after them. They walked through the drawing-room, then along a narrow glass corridor and into another room, where three sleepy footmen jumped up hastily from a couch at their appearance, and, passing through a host of other rooms, they at last entered the billiard-room. The game began.

Riabovitch, who never played at anything but cards, stood by the table looking indifferently at the players, while they, coats unbuttoned, cues in hand, walked about joking and calling out incomprehensible words. The players took no notice of him, only now and again when someone accidentally hit him with an elbow or a cue they turned with a polite, 'Pardon!' The first game had scarcely finished when he grew tired of it, and it seemed to him that he was not wanted there and was in the way. Again he was drawn to the ballroom and went out.

On his way back he met with a little adventure. About halfway he observed that he was not going in the right direction. He remembered quite well that he should have passed through a room where there were three sleepy footmen, but he had gone through six rooms and the footmen seemed to have vanished. Seeing his mistake, he went back a little way, and turning to the right entered a dimly lighted room which he did not remember to have seen on his way to the billiard-room; standing still for a moment, he resolutely opened the first door that met his gaze and found himself in a dark room. In front of him through the cracks in a door a bright light shone through, and from behind the door came the muffled strains of a sad melody. Here, as in the ballroom, the windows were wide open and there was a scent of poplar, lilac and rose . . .

Riabovitch stopped in perplexity. At this moment he heard a hurried footstep and the rustle of a dress, a woman's voice full of emotion whispered, 'At last!' and two soft, fragrant arms, unmistakably a woman's, were put around his neck; a warm cheek was laid against his own, and at the same moment there was the sound of a kiss. But instantly the woman gave a faint cry and, it seemed to Riabovitch, jumped away from him in horror. He, too, nearly cried out and made a rush towards the bright crack in the door . . .

When he returned to the ballroom his heart beat fast and his hands trembled so visibly that he hastily hid them behind his back. For the first few moments he was torn by shame and terror. It seemed to him that everyone in the room must know that he had just been embraced and kissed by a woman, and he cast an anxious glance around, but being convinced that all were dancing and chatting calmly as before, he abandoned himself to the enjoyment of the sensation experienced for the first time in his life. Something strange had happened to him . . . His neck, that had only just been encircled by two soft, fresh arms, seemed to him to be anointed with oil; on his cheek near the left ear, where the strange unknown had kissed him, was a pleasant sensation of cold as from peppermint drops, and the more he rubbed the spot the greater this sensation became; from the crown of his head to the soles of his feet he was filled with a new strange feeling that grew and grew . . . He wanted to dance, to talk, to run out into the garden, to laugh aloud . . . He had quite forgotten that he was round-shouldered and colourless, that his appearance 'was indefinite' (as a lady of his acquaintance had said in a conversation with another woman, a conversation he happened to have overheard). When von Rabbek's wife passed him, he gave her such a broad, kindly smile that she stopped and looked at him in surprise.

'I do like your house!' he said, refixing his spectacles.

The general's wife smiled and remarked that the house had belonged to her father, then she went on to ask him if his parents were alive, and how long he had been in the service, and why he was so thin, and so on . . . After talking to him for a while she went on further, and Riabovitch began to smile still more broadly and kindly and to imagine that he was surrounded by the kindest of people . . .

At supper Riabovitch ate and drank mechanically everything that was placed before him. He did not hear a word that was being said and tried to puzzle out his recent adventure. The adventure was both mysterious and romantic, but not difficult to explain. Some girl or a married woman, perhaps, had arranged to meet some man in that dark room, and being in a state of nervous excitement because she had waited a long time, she had mistaken Riabovitch for her hero, particularly as Riabovitch had stopped in uncertainty when he had entered the room, as though he, too, were expecting to meet someone . . . In this way Riabovitch accounted for the kiss he had received.

'But who is she?' he thought, gazing round at the faces of the women. 'She must be young, for old women do not arrange meetings with men. And she must be intellectual; I felt it in the rustle of her dress, in the scent about her, in her voice . . . '

His gaze alighted on the girl in lilac and she seemed very attractive to him; she had beautiful shoulders and arms, an intelligent face, and a beautiful voice. Looking at her Riabovitch determined that she and none other should be his fair unknown . . . But she smiled in an artificial way and screwed up her long nose, which made her seem old; then he removed his gaze to the fair girl in the black dress. She was younger and simpler, had beautiful temples and a pretty manner of drinking out of her glass. Riabovitch now wanted her to be his unknown, but soon he found that her features were too flat, and turned his attention to her neighbour.

'One can't tell,' he thought musingly. 'If one could take the shoulders and arms of the girl in lilac and add the temples of the fair girl and the eyes of the one sitting on Lobitko's left then . . . '

In imagination he modelled the form of the girl who had kissed him, a form that he desired but could not see at the table.

After supper the guests, satisfied and a little the worse for drink, thanked their hosts and took their leave. Once more the general and his wife apologised for not being able to put them up for the night.

'Very glad to have met you, gentlemen!' the general said, quite sincerely this time. (Departing guests are treated more frankly than arriving ones.) 'Very glad! I hope you will come and see us on your way back! Quite simply, you know. Which way are you going? Are you riding? If not, go down by the garden, it is much nearer.'

The officers went out into the garden. After the bright light and the noise it seemed to them very dark and still in the garden. They walked to the gate without speaking. They were half-drunk, merry and contented, but the darkness and stillness made them pensive for a moment. No doubt the same thought had occurred to them as to Riabovitch. Would they, like Rabbek, one day possess a big house, a family, a garden, and would they have the opportunity of entertaining guests, even insincerely, and of making them drunk and contented?

Coming out of the gate, they began to talk all at once and to laugh without any cause. They were now walking along the path that led down to the river and ran along the water's edge, winding round bushes and overhanging willows. The bank and the path were scarcely visible, and the opposite bank was completely enveloped in darkness. Here and there in the dark water were the reflections of stars, and only by the way they trembled and swam asunder could one tell that the river was flowing swiftly. The air was still. Sleepy woodcocks called on the opposite bank, and on a bush a nightingale, disregarding the officers, poured out its song. One of them stopped by the bush and shook it, but the nightingale continued to sing.

'What a brave beggar!' approving voices exclaimed. 'Here we are, standing near him, and he takes no notice of us, the rogue!'

Towards the end the path began to ascend, and by the church it led out on to the road. Here the officers, out of breath with their walk uphill, sat down to smoke. A dim red light appeared on the opposite bank, and from want of something to do they spent a long time in speculating whether it was a campfire, a light in a window, or something else . . . Riabovitch also gazed at the light, and it seemed to him that it smiled and winked at him, as though it knew about the kiss.

Reaching his quarters, Riabovitch undressed quickly and went to bed. In the same hut were Lobitko and Lieutenant Mersliakov, the latter a quiet taciturn fellow, who was held to be a cultured man, and who always read *The Messenger of Europe*, which review he carried about with him everywhere. Lobitko undressed and paced the room from end to end with a dissatisfied air, then he sent the orderly for beer. Mersliakov got into bed, at the head of which he placed a candle, then buried himself in the pages of the review.

'I wonder who she was?' Riabovitch thought, gazing at the grimy ceiling.

His neck still seemed to be anointed with oil, and a sensation of cold as of peppermint was still about his mouth. His imagination conjured up images of the shoulders and arms of the girl in lilac, the temples of the fair girl in black, her waist, garments, jewels. He tried to fix his attention on these images but they danced before his eyes, appearing and disappearing. When on shutting his eyes the images completely vanished, he could hear hasty footsteps, the rustle of a dress, the sound of a kiss, and a feeling of intense unreasoning joy took possession of him. As he abandoned himself to this feeling he heard the orderly return and say that no beer was to be had. Lobitko was much annoyed and again began to pace the room.

'Isn't he an idiot?' he said, stopping now by Riabovitch's bed, now by Mersliakov's. 'A man must be a dolt and a fool not to be able to get beer, what? The rascal!'

'Of course he can't get beer here,' Mersliakov remarked, without looking up from the pages of his journal.

'Why do you think so?' Lobitko persisted. 'I'll bet you anything I'll find some beer, and women too! I'll go this minute. . . You can call me any names you like if I don't find them!'

He took a long time in dressing and pulling on his long boots, then he lighted a cigarette and went out without another word.

'Rabbek, Grabbek, Labbek,' he mumbled, stopping in the passage. 'I don't feel like going alone, damn it! Riabovitch, won't you come for a stroll, eh?'

Receiving no reply, he came back, undressed slowly, and went to bed. Mersliakov sighed, threw his journal aside, and blew out the candle.

'Yes,' Lobitko muttered, smoking a cigarette in the darkness.

Riabovitch pulled the bedclothes over his head, and curling up began piecing together the disconnected images floating about in his brain, but he failed to obtain any result. He soon fell asleep, his last thought being that someone had caressed and made him happy. Some good, joyous thing had come into his life even though it was senseless. This thought did not leave him even in sleep.

When he awoke the feeling of oil on his neck and the sensation of cold as from peppermint around his lips had left him, but as yesterday a feeling of joy filled his heart. In ecstasy he gazed at the window-frames turned golden by the rising a sun, and listened to the noise in the street without. A loud conversation was going on under his very window. His battery-commander, Lebedetsky, who had only just caught up the brigade, was talking to a sergeant at the top of his voice from force of habit, never speaking in any other tone of voice.

'And what else?' the commander cried.

'Golubushka was hurt when she was shod, your honour; the surgeon applied some clay and vinegar. And last night, your honour, Mechanic Artiemev was drunk, and the lieutenant ordered him to be put on the reserve gun-carriage.'

The sergeant informed him also that Karpov had forgotten the new lanyards for the friction-tubes and the pegs for the tents, and that the officers had spent the evening at General von Rabbek's. During the conversation Lebedetsky's red beard appeared at the window. His short-sighted eyes peered at the sleepy faces of the officers; he greeted them.

'Is everything all right?' he asked.

'The saddle-horse galled his withers with the new yoke,' Lobitko replied with a yawn.

The commander sighed, deliberated for a while, then said aloud: 'I was thinking of going to Alexandra Evgrafovna – I must pay her a visit. Goodbye. I will catch you up by the evening.'

In a quarter of an hour the brigade had started on its way. When they had passed von Rabbek's barns Riabovitch looked at the house. The blinds were still down. The inmates were doubtless asleep. And she, too, slept – the girl who had kissed Riabovitch yesterday. He tried to picture her sleeping. There was the wide-open window of her bedroom, the green branches peeping in, the fresh morning air, the scent of poplar, lilac and rose, the bed, a chair with the dress she had worn yesterday thrown over it, slippers, a watch on the table – all these objects he saw clearly and precisely, but the girl's features, her sweet dreamy smile, the very thing he most desired to see, slipped his imagination as quicksilver slips through the fingers. About half a verst[4] further on he turned round; the yellow church, the house, the river and garden were bathed in light; the river looked beautiful with its bright green banks, reflections of the sky and silver patches of sunlight. Once more Riabovitch looked at the village, and a feeling of sadness came over him, as though he were leaving something very near and dear to him behind.

On the road, only the familiar scenes, void of interest, met the eye. To the right were fields of young rye and buckwheat and hopping rooks; in front, dust and the napes of human necks; behind, the same dust and faces. Ahead of the column marched four soldiers with guns – the vanguard. Next came the bandsmen. Vanguard and bandsmen, like mutes in a funeral procession, now and then ignoring the regulation intervals, marched too far ahead. Riabovitch with the fifth battery could see four batteries in front of him.

To a civilian, the marching brigade, long and cumbersome, presented a novel, interesting spectacle. It is hard to understand why a single gun needs so many men, or why so many strangely harnessed horses are needed to drag it, but to Riabovitch, who was familiar with all these things, it was extremely dull and uninteresting. He had learned years ago why a solid sergeant-major rides beside the officer in front of each battery and the drivers of leaders and wheelers behind them. Riabovitch knew why the near horses were called saddle-horses and the off horses led-horses, and he found it all intensely boring. On one of the wheelers rode a soldier, his back still covered with yesterday's dust and a clumsy ridiculous guard on his leg. Riabovitch knew the use of this guard and found it in no way ridiculous. The horsemen, every man of them, rode mechanically, with an occasional cry or flourish of the whip. The guns were not beautiful to look at. On the limbers were tarpaulin sacks full of oats, and the guns themselves, hung round with teapots, the soldiers' wallets and bags, looked like some harmless animals surrounded for some reason by horses and men. On the lee side of each gun, brandishing their arms, marched six gunners, and behind came more leaders, wheelers and more guns, each as ugly and uninspiring as the one in front. Behind the second followed a third and then a fourth, by the fourth an officer and so on. There were six batteries in the brigade, and each battery had four guns. The cavalcade stretched about half a verst along the road. At the end came a train of wagons, near which, with head bent in thought, walked the donkey Ulagar, who had been brought over from Turkey by a battery commander.

Riabovitch gazed indifferently at the necks in front and the faces behind; another day he would have closed his eyes and tried to doze, but now he abandoned himself to his new and pleasant thoughts. When the brigade had first started he tried to convince himself that the incident of the kiss was only a funny little adventure that could not be taken seriously, but he soon waved logic aside and abandoned himself to his dreams. . . . He imagined himself in the Rabbeks' drawing-room, now by the side of a girl resembling the one in lilac and the fair girl in black, now, when he closed his eyes, by the side of a strange girl with vague, elusive features. In thought he spoke to her, caressed her, drew her to his breast. He imagined himself going to the wars and leaving her behind, then the return and the supper with his wife and children.

'To the brakes!' rang the command before the descent of each hill. He too cried, 'To the brakes!' dreading each time that the cry would break the spell of his dream and bring him back to reality.

They passed a large country house. Riabovitch looked over the hedge into the garden. An avenue, long and straight as a rule, strewn with yellow gravel and planted with young birches, met the eye . . . With the ecstasy of a dreamer, he pictured tiny feminine feet walking along the yellow path and, unexpected, the image of the girl who had kissed him rose before his mind, the girl he had been unable to visualise yesterday at supper. This image became fixed in his brain and never afterwards left him.

At midday a loud command was heard from the rear of the column: 'Attention! Eyes right! Officers!'

In a carriage drawn by a pair of white horses was the brigade general He stopped by the second battery and called out something that no one understood. Several officers rode up, Riabovitch among them.

'Well, how goes it?' the general asked, blinking his reddened eyes. 'Are there any sick?'

Receiving a reply, the little general mused for a moment, then turned to one of the officers: 'The driver of your third gun wheeler has taken off his leg guard and hung it on the limber,[5] the blackguard. Punish him. He raised his eyes to Riabovitch and continued, 'And the breechings of your harness are too long.'

After a few more tiresome remarks the general turned to Lobitko with a smile.

'Why so sad today, Lieutenant Lobitko?' he asked. 'Are you sighing for Madame Lopukhova, eh? Gentlemen, Lobitko is sighing for Madame Lopukhova!'

Madame Lopukhova was a tall, portly lady, well on the wrong side of forty. The general, who had a weakness for large women of any age, suspected his officers of a like taste. The officers smiled respectfully. The general, pleased with his amusing sally, laughed aloud, then touched the coachman's back and saluted. The carriage rolled away.

'Though it seems to me like the wildest of dreams, beyond the range of possibility, it is really a very commonplace thing,' Riabovitch mused, gazing at the cloud of dust raised by the general's carriage. 'It is very usual and happens to everyone . . . Take the general, for instance; he must have fallen in love; now he is married and has children of his own. Captain Bachter is also married and loved, no doubt, for all that he has an ugly neck and no waist; and Salmanov is a rough fellow, too much of the Tartar, yet he had a love affair that ended in marriage. I am just as other men, and sooner or later the same fate will befall me . . . '

And the thought that he was an ordinary man and that his life was ordinary rejoiced and encouraged him. He gave free rein to his imagination and pictured *her* and his future happiness as he would like it to be.

When the brigade reached its destination and the officers rested in the tents, Riabovitch, Mersliakov and Lobitko were seated at supper round a box. Mersliakov ate slowly, reading *The Messenger of Europe* lying on his knee. Lobitko talked incessantly and kept on filling his glass with beer, and Riabovitch, whose head was in a whirl with his long daydreams, drank silently. After the third glass he grew tipsy and weak; an uncontrollable desire came over him to tell his colleagues of his new emotions.

'A funny incident happened to me at those Rabbeks',' he began, trying to give an indifferent, disdainful tone to his voice. ' I went into the billiard-room, you know.' . . . And he related the tale of the kiss in detail and was surprised that it took so little time in the telling – not more than a minute at most. It seemed to him that the story of the kiss would have taken at least till the morning in the telling. Lobitko, who was a confirmed liar, and thus believed no one else, looked at Riabovitch with an incredulous smile. Mersliakov raised his brows, and without looking up from his journal said: 'A strange thing, to be sure! to throw herself on a man's neck without a word. The girl must be neurotic, I should think.'

'No doubt,' Riabovitch agreed.

'A similar incident once happened to me,' Lobitko began. 'I was travelling to Kovna last year, second class. The carriage was packed with people; to sleep was impossible. I gave the conductor half a rouble and he took up my luggage and led me into a sleeping car. I lay down and covered myself with a blanket . . . It was quite dark, you know. Suddenly I felt someone touch me on the shoulder and breathe into my face. I put out my hand and felt an elbow . . . I opened my eyes, and would you believe it – there was a woman! Black eyes, lips as red as a fine salmon, nostrils breathing passion, a bosom like a buffer . . . '

'I can understand about the bosom,' Mersliakov interrupted him calmly, 'but how could you see the lips in the dark?'

Lobitko began to hedge and then to laugh at Mersliakov's lack of imagination. Riabovitch was offended; he walked away from the box, lay down and promised himself never to be communicative again.

The life of the camp began. Day followed day, each like every other. Riabovitch the whole time thought and felt and behaved like a man in love. Every morning, when the orderly brought his washing things and he poured the cold water over his head, he remembered that something sweet and precious had come into his life.

Sometimes, when his comrades began to talk of love and women, he drew nearer, listening, his face assuming the expression of a soldier hearing the tale of a battle in which he had fought. And on evenings when the officers, at the instigation of the setter, Lobitko, made Don Juan excursions into the village, Riabovitch, though he participated in them, was miserable and felt himself immeasurably to blame; in thought he asked forgiveness of *her* . . . In leisure hours, or on sleepless nights, when the desire usually came over him to recall his childhood, his father, mother, all that was near and dear to him, he invariably thought of Mestechko, the curious horse, Rabbek, his wife who looked like the Empress Eugénie, the dark room, the bright crack in the door . . .

On the 31st of August he returned from camp, not with the whole brigade, but with two batteries only; the whole way he was strangely excited, as though he were going home to his native place. Once more he longed to see the strange horse, the church, Rabbek's affected family, the dark room. An 'inner voice' that so often deceives those in love told him that he would see *her*. And he began to wonder how he would greet her, what he would say to her. Had she forgotten about the kiss? If the worst were to happen and he did not see her at all, he would, at any rate, walk through the dark room and remember . . .

Towards the evening, the familiar church and white barns appeared on the horizon. Riabovitch's heart beat fast. He did not hear what the officer who rode near him was saying, he forgot everything, and with a great longing gazed at the river sparkling in the distance, at the roof of the house, at the dovecot and circling doves, lighted up by the setting sun.

They arrived at the church; he listened to the quartermaster's report, expecting every moment to see the horseman appear who would invite them to the general's to tea, but the quartermaster had finished, the officers hastened to the village and still the horseman did not come . . .

'Rabbek will soon learn from the peasants that we are here and will send for us,' Riabovitch thought, entering the hut and failing to comprehend why his comrades had lighted the candles and why the orderlies were preparing the samovars.

He felt depressed. He lay down, then got up and looked out of the window to see if the horseman was coming. But no horseman was in sight. Once more he lay down, and unable to bear his anxiety, after a while he went out into the street and made his way to the church. The square by the church fence was dark and deserted. Three soldiers were standing together in silence at the crest of the hill. At sight of Riabovitch they started and gave the salute. He saluted in turn and began to descend the hill along the familiar path.

On the opposite bank the sky was a bright purple; the moon rose; two women, talking loudly, were pulling cabbage leaves in a kitchen-garden; beyond the kitchen-garden were the dark outlines of several huts . . . On this side it was the same as in May – there was the path, the bushes, the overhanging willows – only the song of the brave little nightingale was missing and the scent of poplar and young grass.

Riabovitch approached the garden and looked through the gate. It was dark and quiet within. The white trunks of the nearest birches were visible and a part of the avenue, the rest was a darkened mass. Riabovitch listened intently and peered into the darkness, but after half an hour of waiting and watching, and hearing no sound and seeing no light, he turned back.

He stopped by the river. Before him, gleaming in the darkness, was the general's bathing-hut and a sheet hanging on the rail of the little bridge. He went on to the bridge and without any reason put out his hand to touch the sheet . . . He gazed down into the water . . . The river flowed quickly and made a faint murmur by the stakes of the bathing-hut. The moon, large and red, was reflected near the left bank; tiny waves floated across it, extending the reflection, breaking it to pieces, as though they wished to carry it away . . .

'How senseless! how senseless!' Riabovitch thought, gazing at the quickly flowing water. 'How senseless it all is!'

Now that he no longer expected anything, the story of the kiss, his impatience, his vague hopes and disillusionment appeared to him in a true light. It seemed no longer strange to him that the general's horseman had not appeared and that he would never meet the girl who had kissed him in mistake for someone else; on the contrary it would have been strange if he had met her . . .

The water flew past him, whither and why no one knew. It had flown past in May. From a little stream it had poured into a great river, then into the sea; from the sea it had risen in mist, then come down in rain, and now perhaps the water flying past him was the very same he had seen in May. Why? Wherefore?

And the whole world and life itself seemed to Riabovitch to be one great, incomprehensible, senseless jest. He raised his eyes from the water and looked up at the sky; once more he remembered how fate, in the form of an unknown woman, had unexpectedly caressed him; he recalled his dreams and images of the summer, and his life appeared to him so poor, wretched and colourless . . .

When he returned to his quarters, not one of his colleagues was there. The orderly informed him that the officers had all gone to General 'Fontrabkin', who had sent a horseman for them . . . A feeling of joy for a moment sprang into Riabovitch's heart, but he instantly smothered it. As though to spite fate, who had treated him so badly, he did not go to the general's, but went instead to bed.

CHARLOTTE PERKINS GILMAN

CHARLOTTE PERKINS GILMAN (1860–1936) was born in Connecticut in the USA. She was an artistic and sensitive child who read avidly. After studying at art school, she earned her living designing greetings cards. She was of the new breed of women who wanted to be independent and to work for a living rather than accept a cosseted domestic life. She had a deep-seated concern about injustice and inequality and she campaigned for the cause of women's suffrage. Because of her strong views, she approached marriage with some apprehension. She wanted more from life than simply playing the subservient role of wife and mother. However, she married Charles Stetson, a handsome artist, in 1884. From the start of this union, Charlotte was prone to bouts of depression and when she gave birth to a daughter she fell into such a state of deep post-natal despair that her husband insisted on her seeing a specialist in such disorders. The doctor recommended a complete rest and she was advised ' . . . never touch pen, brush or pencil as long as you live'. The strictures of the supposed cure drove poor Charlotte mad. When she emerged from this nightmare, she believed that her personality had changed irrevocably and that she was left to live 'a crippled life'. Elements of this shattering experience are captured in 'The Yellow Wallpaper'. It is the most disturbing story in the whole collection, describing as it does a sensitive young woman's slow and seemingly inevitable descent into madness. The central character, haunted by the unsettling pattern of the wallpaper in her bedroom, describes convincingly how the twilight world of the insane gradually takes on a chilling reality. The restraints placed upon her by her apparently well-meaning husband and his sister serve only to aid the poor girl's slide into insanity.

Although Charlotte Perkins Gilman wrote over two hundred short stories and nine novels, this story is her most famous and frequently published fiction. Its power to shock and frighten is still as potent today as it was when it was first published.

When she was dying from inoperable cancer, Charlotte took her last defiant act of independence: she committed suicide, preferring, as she explained in her last note, 'chloroform to cancer'.

The Yellow Wallpaper

IT IS VERY SELDOM that mere ordinary people like John and myself secure ancestral halls for the summer.

A colonial mansion, a hereditary estate, I would say a haunted house and reach the height of romantic felicity – but that would be asking too much of fate!

Still I will proudly declare that there is something queer about it.

Else, why should it be let so cheaply? And why have stood so long untenanted?

John laughs at me, of course, but one expects that.

John is practical in the extreme. He has no patience with faith, an intense horror of superstition, and he scoffs openly at any talk of things not to be felt and seen and put down in figures.

John is a physician and *perhaps* – I would not say it to a living soul, of course, but this is dead paper and a great relief to my mind – *perhaps* that is one reason I do not get well faster.

You see, he does not believe I am sick! And what can one do?

If a physician of high standing, and one's own husband, assures friends and relatives that there is really nothing the matter with one but temporary nervous depression – a slight hysterical tendency – what is one to do?

My brother is also a physician, and also of high standing, and he says the same thing.

So I take phosphates or phosphites[1] – whichever it is – and tonics, and air and exercise, and journeys, and am absolutely forbidden to 'work' until I am well again.

Personally, I disagree with their ideas.

Personally, I believe that congenial work, with excitement and change, would do me good.

But what is one to do?

I did write for a while in spite of them; but it *does* exhaust me a good deal – having to be so sly about it, or else meet with heavy opposition.

I sometimes fancy that in my condition, if I had less opposition and more society and stimulus – but John says the very worst thing I can do is to think about my condition, and I confess it always makes me feel bad.

So I will let it alone and talk about the house.

The most beautiful place! It is quite alone, standing well back from the road, quite three miles from the village. It makes me think of English places that you read about, for there are hedges and walls and gates that lock, and lots of separate little houses for the gardeners and people.

There is a *delicious* garden! I never saw such a garden – large and shady, full of box-bordered paths and lined with long grape-covered arbours with seats under them.

There were greenhouses, but they are all broken now.

There was some legal trouble, I believe, something about the heirs and co-heirs; anyhow, the place has been empty for years.

That spoils my ghostliness, I am afraid, but I don't care – there is something strange about the house – I can feel it.

I even said so to John one moonlight evening, but he said what I felt was a draught, and shut the window.

I get unreasonably angry with John sometimes. I'm sure I never used to be so sensitive. I think it is due to this nervous condition.

But John says if I feel so I shall neglect proper self-control; so I take pains to control myself – before him, at least, and that makes me very tired.

I don't like our room a bit. I wanted one downstairs that opened on to the piazza[2] – and had roses all over the window, and such pretty old-fashioned chintz hangings! But John would not hear of it.

He said there was only one window and not room for two beds, and no near room for him if he took another.

He is very careful and loving, and hardly lets me stir without special direction.

I have a schedule prescription for each hour in the day; he takes all care from me, and so I feel basely ungrateful not to value it more.

He said he came here solely on my account, that I was to have perfect rest and all the air I could get. 'Your exercise depends on your strength, my dear,' said he, 'and your food somewhat on your appetite; but air you can absorb all the time.' So we took the nursery at the top of the house.

It is a big, airy room, the whole floor nearly, with windows that look all ways, and air and sunshine galore. It was a nursery first, and then playroom and gymnasium I should judge, for the windows are barred for little children, and there are rings and things in the walls.

The paint and paper look as if a boys' school had used it. It is stripped off – the paper – in great patches all around the head of my bed, about as far as I can reach, and in a great place on the other side of the room, low down. I never saw a worse paper in my life. One of those sprawling, flamboyant patterns committing every artistic sin.

It is dull enough to confuse the eye in following, pronounced enough constantly to irritate and provoke study, and when you follow the lame uncertain curves for a little distance they suddenly commit suicide – plunge off at outrageous angles, destroy themselves in unheard-of contradictions.

The colour is repellent, almost revolting: a smouldering unclean yellow, strangely faded by the slow-turning sunlight. It is a dull yet lurid orange in some places, a sickly sulphur tint in others.

No wonder the children hated it! I should hate it myself if I had to live in this room long.

There comes John, and I must put this away – he hates to have me write a word.

We have been here two weeks, and I haven't felt like writing before, since that first day.

I am sitting by the window now, up in this atrocious nursery, and there is nothing to hinder my writing as much as I please, save lack of strength.

John is away all day, and even some nights when his cases are serious.

I am glad my case is not serious!

But these nervous troubles are dreadfully depressing.

John does not know how much I really suffer. He knows there is no reason to suffer, and that satisfies him.

Of course it is only nervousness. It does weigh on me so not to do my duty in any way!

I meant to be such a help to John, such a real rest and comfort, and here I am a comparative burden already!

Nobody would believe what an effort it is to do what little I am able – to dress and entertain, and order things.

It is fortunate Mary is so good with the baby. Such a dear baby!

And yet I *cannot* be with him, it makes me so nervous.

I suppose John never was nervous in his life. He laughs at me so about this wallpaper!

At first he meant to repaper the room, but afterward he said that I was letting it get the better of me, and that nothing was worse for a nervous patient than to give way to such fancies.

He said that after the wallpaper was changed it would be the heavy bedstead, and then the barred windows, and then that gate at the head of the stairs, and so on.

'You know the place is doing you good,' he said, 'and really, dear, I don't care to renovate the house just for a three months' rental.'

'Then do let us go downstairs,' I said. 'There are such pretty rooms there.'

Then he took me in his arms and called me a blessed little goose, and said he would go down the cellar, if I wished, and have it whitewashed into the bargain.

But he is right enough about the beds and windows and things.

It is as airy and comfortable a room as anyone need wish, and, of course, I would not be so silly as to make him uncomfortable just for a whim.

I'm really getting quite fond of the big room, all but that horrid paper.

Out of one window I can see the garden – those mysterious deep-shaded arbours, the riotous old-fashioned flowers, and bushes and gnarly trees.

Out of another I get a lovely view of the bay and a little private wharf belonging to the estate. There is a beautiful shaded lane that runs down there from the house. I always fancy I see people walking in these numerous paths and arbors, but John has cautioned me not to give way to fancy in the least. He says that with my imaginative power and habit of story-making, a nervous weakness like mine is sure to lead to all manner of excited fancies, and that I ought to use my will and good sense to check the tendency. So I try.

I think sometimes that if I were only well enough to write a little it would relieve the press of ideas and rest me.

But I find I get pretty tired when I try.

It is so discouraging not to have any advice and companionship about my work. When I get really well, John says we will ask Cousin Henry and Julia down for a long visit; but he says he would as soon put fireworks in my pillowcase as to let me have those stimulating people about now.

I wish I could get well faster.

But I must not think about that. This paper looks to me as if it *knew* what a vicious influence it had!

There is a recurrent spot where the pattern lolls like a broken neck and two bulbous eyes stare at you upside down.

I get positively angry with the impertinence of it and the everlastingness. Up and down and sideways they crawl, and those absurd unblinking eyes are everywhere. There is one place where two breadths didn't match, and the eyes go all up and down the line, one a little higher than the other.

I never saw so much expression in an inanimate thing before, and we all know how much expression they have! I used to lie awake as a child and get more entertainment and terror out of blank walls and plain furniture than most children could find in a toy-store.

I remember what a kindly wink the knobs of our big old bureau used to have, and there was one chair that always seemed like a strong friend.

I used to feel that if any of the other things looked too fierce I could always hop into that chair and be safe.

The furniture in this room is no worse than inharmonious, however, for we had to bring it all from downstairs. I suppose when this was used as a playroom they had to take the nursery things out, and no wonder! I never saw such ravages as the children have made here.

The wallpaper, as I said before, is torn off in spots, and it sticketh closer than a brother – they must have had perseverance as well as hatred.

Then the floor is scratched and gouged and splintered, the plaster itself is dug out here and there, and this great heavy bed, which is all we found in the room, looks as if it had been through the wars.

But I don't mind it a bit – only the paper.

There comes John's sister. Such a dear girl as she is, and so careful of me! I must not let her find me writing.

She is a perfect and enthusiastic housekeeper, and hopes for no better profession. I verily believe she thinks it is the writing which made me sick!

But I can write when she is out, and see her a long way off from these windows.

There is one that commands the road, a lovely shaded winding road, and one that just looks off over the country. A lovely country, too, full of great elms and velvet meadows.

This wallpaper has a kind of sub-pattern in a different shade, a particularly irritating one, for you can only see it in certain lights, and not clearly then.

But in the places where it isn't faded and where the sun is just so – I can see a strange, provoking, formless sort of figure that seems to skulk about behind that silly and conspicuous front design.

There's sister on the stairs!

Well, the Fourth of July is over! The people are all gone, and I am tired out. John thought it might do me good to see a little company, so we just had Mother and Nellie and the children down for a week.

Of course I didn't do a thing. Jennie sees to everything now.

But it tired me all the same.

John says if I don't pick up faster he shall send me to Weir Mitchell in the fall.

But I don't want to go there at all. I had a friend who was in his hands once, and she says he is just like John and my brother, only more so!

Besides, it is such an undertaking to go so far.

I don't feel as if it was worthwhile to turn my hand over for anything, and I'm getting dreadfully fretful and querulous.

I cry at nothing, and cry most of the time

Of course I don't when John is here, or anybody else, but when I am alone.

And I am alone a good deal just now. John is kept in town very often by serious cases, and Jennie is good and lets me alone when I want her to.

So I walk a little in the garden or down that lovely lane, sit on the porch under the roses, and lie down up here a good deal.

I'm getting really fond of the room in spite of the wallpaper. Perhaps *because* of the wallpaper.

It dwells on my mind so!

I lie here on this great immovable bed – it is nailed down, I believe – and follow that pattern about by the hour. It is as good as gymnastics, I assure you. I start, we'll say, at the bottom, down in the corner over there where it has not been touched, and I determine for the thousandth time that I *will* follow that pointless pattern to some sort of a conclusion.

I know a little of the principle of design, and I know this thing was not arranged on any laws of radiation, or alternation, or repetition, or symmetry, or anything else that I ever heard of.

It is repeated, of course, by the breadths, but not otherwise.

Looked at in one way, each breadth stands alone: the bloated curves and flourishes – a kind of 'debased Romanesque' with delirium tremens[3] – go waddling up and down in isolated columns of fatuity.[4]

But, on the other hand, they connect diagonally, and the sprawling outlines run off in great slanting waves of optic horror, like a lot of wallowing seaweeds in full chase.

The whole thing goes horizontally, too, at least it seems so, and I exhaust myself trying to distinguish the order of its going in that direction.

They have used a horizontal breadth for a frieze, and that adds wonderfully to the confusion.

There is one end of the room where it is almost intact, and there, when the crosslights fade and the low sun shines directly upon it, I can almost fancy radiation after all – the interminable grotesque seems to form around a common centre and rush off in headlong plunges of equal distraction.

It makes me tired to follow it. I will take a nap, I guess.

I don't know why I should write this.

I don't want to.

I don't feel able.

And I know John would think it absurd. But I must say what I feel and think in some way – it is such a relief!

But the effort is getting to be greater than the relief.

Half the time now I am awfully lazy, and lie down ever so much. John says I mustn't lose my strength, and has me take cod liver oil and lots of tonics and things, to say nothing of ale and wine and rare meat.

Dear John! He loves me very dearly, and hates to have me sick. I tried to have a real earnest reasonable talk with him the other day, and tell him how I wish he would let me go and make a visit to Cousin Henry and Julia.

But he said I wasn't able to go, nor able to stand it after I got there; and I did not make out a very good case for myself, for I was crying before I had finished.

It is getting to be a great effort for me to think straight. Just this nervous weakness, I suppose.

And dear John gathered me up in his arms, and just carried me upstairs and laid me on the bed, and sat by me and read to me till it tired my head.

He said I was his darling and his comfort and all he had and that I must take care of myself for his sake, and keep well.

He says no one but myself can help me out of it, that I must use my will and self-control and not let any silly fancies run away with me.

There's one comfort – the baby is well and happy, and does not have to occupy this nursery with the horrid wallpaper.

If we had not used it, that blessed child would have! What a fortunate escape! Why, I wouldn't have a child of mine, an impressionable little thing, live in such a room for worlds.

I never thought of it before, but it is lucky that John kept me here after all; I can stand it so much easier than a baby, you see.

Of course I never mention it to them any more – I am too wise – but I keep watch for it all the same.

There are things in that wallpaper that nobody knows about but me, or ever will.

Behind that outside pattern the dim shapes get clearer every day.

It is always the same shape, only very numerous.

And it is like a woman stooping down and creeping about behind that pattern. I don't like it a bit. I wonder – I begin to think – I wish John would take me away from here!

It is so hard to talk with John about my case, because he is so wise, and because he loves me so.

But I tried it last night.

It was moonlight. The moon shines in all around just as the sun does.

I hate to see it sometimes, it creeps so slowly, and always comes in by one window or another.

John was asleep and I hated to waken him, so I kept still and watched the moonlight on that undulating wallpaper till I felt creepy.

The faint figure behind seemed to shake the pattern, just as if she wanted to get out.

I got up softly and went to feel and see if the paper *did* move, and when I came back John was awake.

'What is it, little girl?' he said. 'Don't go walking about like that – you'll get cold.'

I thought it was a good time to talk, so I told him that I really was not gaining here, and that I wished he would take me away.

'Why, darling!' said he. 'Our lease will be up in three weeks, and I can't see how to leave before.

'The repairs are not done at home, and I cannot possibly leave town just now. Of course, if you were in any danger, I could and would, but you really are better, dear, whether you can see it or not. I am a doctor, dear, and I know. You are gaining flesh and colour, your appetite is better, I feel really much easier about you.'

'I don't weigh a bit more,' said I, 'nor as much; and my appetite may be better in the evening when you are here but it is worse in the morning when you are away!'

'Bless her little heart!' said he with a big hug. 'She shall be as sick as she pleases! But now let's improve the shining hours by going to sleep, and talk about it in the morning!'

'And you won't go away?' I asked gloomily.

'Why, how can I, dear? It is only three weeks more and then we will take a nice little trip of a few days while Jennie is getting the house ready. Really, dear, you are better!'

'Better in body perhaps – ' I began, and stopped short, for he sat up straight and looked at me with such a stern, reproachful look that I could not say another word.

'My darling,' said he, 'I beg of you, for my sake and for our child's sake, as well as for your own, that you will never for one instant let that idea enter your mind! There is nothing so dangerous, so fascinating, to a temperament like yours. It is a false and foolish fancy. Can you not trust me as a physician when I tell you so?'

So of course I said no more on that score, and we went to sleep before long. He thought I was asleep first, but I wasn't, and lay there for hours trying to decide whether that front pattern and the back pattern really did move together or separately.

On a pattern like this, by daylight, there is a lack of sequence, a defiance of law, that is a constant irritant to a normal mind.

The colour is hideous enough, and unreliable enough, and infuriating enough, but the pattern is torturing.

You think you have mastered it, but just as you get well under way in following, it turns a back-somersault and there you are. It slaps you in the face, knocks you down, and tramples upon you. It is like a bad dream.

The outside pattern is a florid arabesque, reminding one of a fungus. If you can imagine a toadstool in joints, an interminable string of toadstools, budding and sprouting in endless convolutions – why, that is something like it.

That is, sometimes!

There is one marked peculiarity about this paper, a thing nobody seems to notice but myself, and that is that it changes as the light changes.

When the sun shoots in through the east window – I always watch for that first long, straight ray – it changes so quickly that I never can quite believe it.

That is why I watch it always.

By moonlight – the moon shines in all night when there is a moon – I wouldn't know it was the same paper.

At night in any kind of light, in twilight, candlelight, lamplight, and worst of all by moonlight, it becomes bars! The outside patterns, I mean, and the woman behind it as plain as can be.

I didn't realise for a long time what the thing was that showed behind, that dim sub-pattern, but now I am quite sure it is a woman.

By daylight she is subdued, quiet. I fancy it is the pattern that keeps her so still. It is so puzzling. It keeps me quiet by the hour.

I lie down ever so much now. John says it is good for me, and to sleep all I can.

Indeed he started the habit by making me lie down for an hour after each meal.

It is a very bad habit, I am convinced, for you see, I don't sleep.

And that cultivates deceit, for I don't tell them I'm awake – oh, no!

The fact is I am getting a little afraid of John.

He seems very queer sometimes, and even Jennie has an inexplicable look.

It strikes me occasionally, just as a scientific hypothesis, that perhaps it is the paper!

I have watched John when he did not know I was looking, and come into the room suddenly on the most innocent excuses, and I've caught him several times *looking at the paper!* And Jennie too. I caught Jennie with her hand on it once.

She didn't know I was in the room, and when I asked her in a quiet, a very quiet voice, with the most restrained manner possible, what she was doing with the paper, she turned around as if she had been caught stealing, and looked quite angry – asked me why I should frighten her so!

Then she said that the paper stained everything it touched, that she had found yellow smooches[5] on all my clothes and John's and she wished we would be more careful!

Did not that sound innocent? But I know she was studying that pattern, and I am determined that nobody shall find it out but myself!

Life is very much more exciting now than it used to be. You see, I have something more to expect, to look forward to, to watch. I really do eat better, and am more quiet than I was.

John is so pleased to see me improve! He laughed a little the other day, and said I seemed to be flourishing in spite of my wallpaper.

I turned it off with a laugh. I had no intention of telling him it was *because* of the wallpaper – he would make fun of me. He might even want to take me away.

I don't want to leave now until I have found it out. There is a week more, and I think that will be enough.

I'm feeling so much better!

I don't sleep much at night, for it is so interesting to watch developments; but I sleep a good deal during the daytime.

In the daytime it is tiresome and perplexing.

There are always new shoots on the fungus, and new shades of yellow all over it. I cannot keep count of them, though I have tried conscientiously.

It is the strangest yellow, that wallpaper! It makes me think of all the yellow things I ever saw – not beautiful ones like buttercups, but old, foul, bad yellow things.

But there is something else about that paper – the smell! I noticed it the moment we came into the room, but with so much air and sun it was not bad. Now we have had a week of fog and rain, and whether the windows are open or not, the smell is here.

It creeps all over the house.

I find it hovering in the dining-room, skulking in the parlour, hiding in the hall, lying in wait for me on the stairs.

It gets into my hair.

Even when I go to ride, if I turn my head suddenly and surprise it – there is that smell!

Such a peculiar odour, too! I have spent hours in trying to analyse it, to find what it smelled like.

It is not bad – at first – and very gentle, but quite the subtlest, most enduring odour I ever met.

In this damp weather it is awful. I wake up in the night and find it hanging over me.

It used to disturb me at first. I thought seriously of burning the house – to reach the smell.

But now I am used to it. The only thing I can think of that it is like is the *colour* of the paper! A yellow smell.

There is a very funny mark on this wall, low down, near the mopboard.[6] A streak that runs round the room. It goes behind every piece of furniture, except the bed, a long, straight, even *smooch*, as if it had been rubbed over and over.

I wonder how it was done and who did it, and what they did it for. Round and round and round – round and round and round – it makes me dizzy!

I really have discovered something at last.

Through watching so much at night, when it changes so, I have finally found out.

The front pattern *does* move – and no wonder! The woman behind shakes it!

Sometimes I think there are a great many women behind, and sometimes only one, and she crawls around fast, and her crawling shakes it all over.

Then in the very bright spots she keeps still, and in the very shady spots she just takes hold of the bars and shakes them hard.

And she is all the time trying to climb through. But nobody could climb through that pattern – it strangles so; I think that is why it has so many heads.

They get through, and then the pattern strangles them off and turns them upside down, and makes their eyes white!

If those heads were covered or taken off it would not be half so bad.

I think that woman gets out in the daytime!

And I'll tell you why – privately – I've seen her!

I can see her out of every one of my windows!

It is the same woman, I know, for she is always creeping, and most women do not creep by daylight.

I see her in that long shaded lane, creeping up and down. I see her in those dark grape arbours, creeping all around the garden.

I see her on that long road under the trees, creeping along, and when a carriage comes she hides under the blackberry vines.

I don't blame her a bit. It must be very humiliating to be caught creeping by daylight!

I always lock the door when I creep by daylight. I can't do it at night, for I know John would suspect something at once.

And John is so queer now that I don't want to irritate him. I wish he would take another room! Besides, I don't want anybody to get that woman out at night but myself.

I often wonder if I could see her out of all the windows at once.

But, turn as fast as I can, I can only see out of one at one time.

And though I always see her, she *may* be able to creep faster than I can turn! I have watched her sometimes away off in the open country, creeping as fast as a cloud shadow in a wind.

If only that top pattern could be gotten off from the under one! I mean to try it, little by little.

I have found out another funny thing, but I shan't tell it this time! It does not do to trust people too much.

There are only two more days to get this paper off, and I believe John is beginning to notice. I don't like the look in his eyes.

And I heard him ask Jennie a lot of professional questions about me. She had a very good report to give.

She said I slept a good deal in the daytime.

John knows I don't sleep very well at night, for all I'm so quiet!

He asked me all sorts of questions, too, and pretended to be very loving and kind.

As if I couldn't see through him!

Still, I don't wonder he acts so, sleeping under this paper for three months.

It only interests me, but I feel sure John and Jennie are affected by it.

Hurrah! This is the last day, but it is enough. John is to stay in town overnight, and won't be out until this evening.

Jennie wanted to sleep with me – the sly thing; but I told her I should undoubtedly rest better for a night all alone.

That was clever, for really I wasn't alone a bit! As soon as it was moonlight and that poor thing began to crawl and shake the pattern, I got up and ran to help her.

I pulled and she shook. I shook and she pulled, and before morning we had peeled off yards of that paper

A strip about as high as my head and half around the room.

And then when the sun came and that awful pattern began to laugh at me, I declared I would finish it today!

We go away tomorrow, and they are moving all my furniture down again to leave things as they were before.

Jennie looked at the wall in amazement, but I told her merrily that I did it out of pure spite at the vicious thing.

She laughed and said she wouldn't mind doing it herself, but I must not get tired.

How she betrayed herself that time!

But I am here, and no person touches this paper but Me – not *alive!*

She tried to get me out of the room – it was too patent! But I said it was so quiet and empty and clean now that I believed I would lie down again and sleep all I could, and not to wake me even for dinner – I would call when I woke.

So now she is gone, and the servants are gone, and the things are gone, and there is nothing left but that great bedstead nailed down, with the canvas mattress we found on it.

We shall sleep downstairs tonight, and take the boat home tomorrow.

I quite enjoy the room, now it is bare again.

How those children did tear about here!

This bedstead is fairly gnawed!

But I must get to work.

I have locked the door and thrown the key down into the front path.

I don't want to go out, and I don't want to have anybody come in, till John comes.

I want to astonish him.

I've got a rope up here that even Jennie did not find. If that woman does get out, and tries to get away, I can tie her!

But I forgot I could not reach far without anything to stand on!

This bed will *not* move!

I tried to lift and push it until I was lame, and then I got so angry I bit off a little piece at one corner – but it hurt my teeth.

Then I peeled off all the paper I could reach standing on the floor. It sticks horribly and the pattern just enjoys it! All those strangled heads and bulbous eyes and waddling fungus growths just shriek with derision!

I am getting angry enough to do something desperate. To jump out of the window would be admirable exercise, but the bars are too strong even to try.

Besides I wouldn't do it. Of course not. I know well enough that a step like that is improper and might be misconstrued.

I don't like to *look* out of the windows even – there are so many of those creeping women, and they creep so fast.

I wonder if they all come out of that wallpaper as I did?

But I am securely fastened now by my well-hidden rope – you don't get *me* out in the road there!

I suppose I shall have to get back behind the pattern when it comes night, and that is hard!

It is so pleasant to be out in this great room and creep around as I please!

I don't want to go outside. I won't, even if Jennie asks me to.

For outside you have to creep on the ground, and everything is green instead of yellow.

But here I can creep smoothly on the floor, and my shoulder just fits in that long smooch around the wall, so I cannot lose my way.

Why, there's John at the door!

It is no use, young man, you can't open it!

How he does call and pound!

Now he's crying to Jennie for an axe.

It would be a shame to break down that beautiful door!

'John, dear!' said I in the gentlest voice. 'The key is down by the front steps, under a plantain leaf!'

That silenced him for a few moments.

Then he said, very quietly indeed, 'Open the door, my darling!'

'I can't,' said I. 'The key is down by the front door under a plantain leaf!' And then I said it again, several times, very gently and slowly, and said it so often that he had to go and see, and he got it of course, and came in. He stopped short by the door.

'What is the matter?' he cried. 'For God's sake, what are you doing!'

I kept on creeping just the same, but I looked at him over my shoulder.

'I've got out at last,' said I, 'in spite of you and Jane. And I've pulled off most of the paper, so you can't put me back!'

Now why should that man have fainted? But he did, and right across my path by the wall, so that I had to creep over him every time!

CHARLES LAMB

CHARLES LAMB (1775–1834) and his sister Mary Anne (1764–1847) wrote a number of books for children, the most famous being *Tales from Shakespeare*. This retelling of the plots of Shakespeare's plays in story form still remains the best work of its kind.

Lamb worked as a clerk at East India House in London and his meagre earnings, along with what Mary could earn by needlework, was the main income of the family. The strain on Mary unbalanced her mind and in 1796 she stabbed her mother to death. Mary was confined to a lunatic asylum for a time but on her release she returned home to live with Charles. Sadly she never fully recovered from her illness, having only what Charles referred to as bouts of 'serenity'.

It was the year of his mother's death that poems and then stories by Charles Lamb began to appear in print. In 1807, during a period when Mary was at ease with herself, they collaborated on *Tales from Shakespeare*. There were several other collaborations, including *Poetry for Children* in 1809.

Charles Lamb was devoted to his sister and he never married, but in the 1820s he and Mary adopted an orphan girl, Emma Isola.

In all, he lived a sad life, yet the dismal and tragic circumstances did not hinder his wit or his sense of humour, as is demonstrated by 'Juke Judkins' Courtship'. This is a subtle and whimsical tale told in the first person by Juke Judkins himself. The real amusement comes from his pompous assertions about his kindnesses and generous nature for these confessions clearly reveal that he is a selfish and tight-fisted soul. The cleverness in the writing is shown in the way that Jukins constantly presents the reader with evidence of his miserly ways while attempting to demonstrate his canny and clever nature. Lamb shows how such traits can be traced back to childhood and how, in Judkins' case, the more dominant parent helped to form his unpleasant nature. He is a timeless character: we all know a Juke Judkins, someone who is too blind to see that what he perceives as his virtues are in fact his failings.

Juke Judkins' Courtship

I AM THE ONLY SON of a considerable brazier[1] in Birmingham, who, dying in 1803, left me successor to the business, with no other encumbrance than a sort of rent-charge, which I am enjoined to pay out of it, of ninety-three pounds sterling per annum to his widow, my mother; and which the improving state of the concern, I bless God, has hitherto enabled me to discharge with punctuality. (I say, I am enjoined to pay the said sum, but not strictly obligated; that is to say, as the will is worded, I believe the law would relieve me from the payment of it; but the wishes of a dying parent should in some sort have the effect of law.) So that, though the annual profits of my business, on an average of the last three or four years, would appear to an indifferent observer, who should inspect my shop-books, to amount to the sum of one thousand three hundred and three pounds, odd shilling, the real proceeds in that time have fallen short of that sum to the amount of the aforesaid payment of ninety-three pounds sterling annually.

I was always my father's favourite. He took a delight to the very last in recounting the little sagacious tricks and innocent artifices[2] of my childhood. One manifestation thereof I never heard him repeat without tears of joy trickling down his cheeks. It seems that when I quitted the parental roof (August 27, 1788), being then six years and not quite a month old, to proceed to the Free School at Warwick, where my father was a sort of trustee, my mother – as mothers are usually provident on these occasions – had stuffed the pockets of the coach, which was to convey me and six more children of my own growth that were going to be entered along with me at the same seminary, with a prodigious quantity of gingerbread, which I remembered my father said was more than was needed: and so indeed it was; for, if I had been to eat it all myself, it would have got stale and mouldy before it had been half spent. The consideration whereof set me upon my contrivances how I might secure to myself as much of the gingerbread as would keep good for the next two or three days, and yet none of the rest in manner be wasted.

I had a little pair of pocket-compasses, which I usually carried about me for the purpose of making draughts and measurements, at which I was always very ingenious, of the various engines and mechanical inventions in which such a town as Birmingham abounded. By means of these, and a small penknife which my father had given me, I cut out the one half of the cake, calculating that the remainder would reasonably serve my turn; and subdividing it into many little slices, which were curious to see for the neatness and niceness of their proportion, I sold it out in so many pennyworths to my young companions as served us all the way to Warwick, which is a distance of some twenty miles from this town; and very merry, I assure you, we made ourselves with it, feasting all the way. By this honest stratagem I put double the prime cost of the gingerbread into my purse, and secured as much as I thought would keep good and moist for my next two or three days' eating.

When I told this to my parents on their first visit to me at Warwick, my father (good man) patted me on the cheek, and stroked my head, and seemed as if he could never make enough of me; but my mother unaccountably burst into tears, and said, 'it was a very niggardly action', or some such expression, and that 'she would rather it would please God to take me' – meaning (God help me) that I should die – 'than that she should live to see me grow up *a mean man*', which shows the difference of parent from parent, and how some mothers are more harsh and intolerant to their children than some fathers, when we might expect quite the contrary.

My father, however, loaded me with presents from that time, which made me the envy of my schoolfellows. As I felt this growing disposition in them, I naturally sought to avert it by all the means in my power; and from that time I used to eat my little packages of fruit, and other nice things, in a corner, so privately that I was never found out. Once, I remember, I had a huge apple sent me, of that sort which they call cats'-heads. I concealed this all day under my pillow; and at night, but not before I had ascertained that my bedfellow was sound asleep – which I did by pinching him rather smartly two or three times, which he seemed to perceive no more than a dead person, though once or twice he made a motion as if he would turn, which frightened me – I say, when I had made all sure, I fell to work upon my apple; and, though it was as big as an ordinary man's two fists, I made shift to get through it before it was time to get up. And a more delicious feast I never made; thinking all night what a good parent I had (I mean my father) to send me so many nice things, when the poor lad that lay by me had no parent or friend in the world to send him anything nice; and thinking of his desolate condition, I munched and munched as silently as I could, that I might not set him a-longing if he overheard me.

And yet, for all this considerateness and attention to other people's feelings, I was never much a favourite with my school-fellows; which I have often wondered at, seeing that I never defrauded any one of them of the value of a halfpenny, or told stories of them to their master, as some little lying boys would do, but was ready to do any of them all the services in my power, that were consistent with my own well-doing. I think nobody can be expected to go further than that.

But I am detaining my reader too long in recording my juvenile days. It is time I should go forward to a season when it became natural that I should have some thoughts of marrying, and, as they say, settling in the world. Nevertheless, my reflections on what I may call the boyish period of my life may have their use to some readers. It is pleasant to trace the man in the boy; to observe shoots of generosity in those young years; and to watch the progress of liberal sentiments, and what I may call a genteel way of thinking, which is discernible in some children at a very early age, and usually lays the foundation of all that is praiseworthy in the manly character afterwards.

With the warmest inclinations towards that way of life, and a serious conviction of its superior advantages over a single one, it has been the strange infelicity of my lot never to have entered into the respectable estate of matrimony.

Yet I was once very near it.

I courted a young woman in my twenty-seventh year; for so early I began to feel symptoms of the tender passion! She was well-to-do in the world, as they call it; but yet not such a fortune as, all things considered, perhaps I might have pretended to. It was not my own choice altogether; but my mother very strongly pressed me to it. She was always putting it to me that I had 'comings-in sufficient' – that I 'need not stand upon a portion';[3] though the young woman, to do her justice, had considerable expectations, which yet did not quite come up to my mark, as I told you before.

My mother had this saying always in her mouth, that I had 'money enough', that it was time I enlarged my housekeeping, and to show a spirit befitting my circumstances. In short, what with her importunities, and my own desires in part cooperating – for, as I said, I was not yet quite twenty-seven – a time when the youthful feelings may be pardoned if they show a little impetuosity – I resolved, I say, upon all these considerations, to set about the business of courting in right earnest. I was a young man then; and having a spice of romance in my character (as the reader has doubtless observed long ago), such as that sex is apt to be taken with, I had reason in no long time to think that my addresses were anything but disagreeable. Certainly the happiest part of a young man's life is the time when he is going a-courting. All the generous impulses are then awake, and he feels a double existence in participating his hopes and wishes with another being.

Return yet again for a brief moment, ye visionary views, transient enchantments! ye moonlight rambles with Cleora in the Silent Walk at Vauxhall (NB – about a mile from Birmingham, and resembling the gardens of that name near London, only that the price of admission is lower), when the nightingale has suspended her notes in June to listen to our loving discourses, while the moon was overhead (for we generally used to take our tea at Cleora's mother's before we set out, not so much to save expenses as to avoid the publicity of a repast in the gardens – coming in much about the time of half-price, as they call it), ye soft intercommunions of soul, when, exchanging mutual vows, we prattled of coming felicities! [4] The loving disputes we have had under those trees, when this house (planning our future settlement) was rejected, because, though cheap, it was dull; and the other house was given up because, though agreeably situated, it was too high-rented! – one was too much in the heart of the town, another was too far from business.

These minutiae will seem impertinent to the aged and prudent. I write them only to the young. Young lovers, and passionate as being young (such were Cleora and I then), alone can understand me. After some weeks wasted, as I may now call it, in this sort of amorous colloquy, [5] we at length fixed upon the house in the High Street, No. 203, just vacated by the death of Mr Hutton of this town, for our future residence. I had all the time lived in lodgings (only renting a shop for business) to be near my mother – near, I say, not in the same house; for that would have been to introduce confusion into our housekeeping, which it was desirable to keep separate. Oh, the loving wrangles, the endearing differences, I had with Cleora, before we could quite make up our minds to the house that was to receive us ! – I pretending, for argument's sake, the rent was too high, and she insisting that the taxes were moderate in proportion: and love at last reconciling us in the same choice. I think at that time, moderately speaking, she might have had anything out of me for asking. I do not, nor shall ever, regret that my character at that time was marked with a tinge of prodigality. [6] Age comes fast enough upon us, and, in its good time, will prune away all that is inconvenient in these excesses. Perhaps it is right that it should do so.

Matters, as I said, were ripening to a conclusion between us, only the house was yet not absolutely taken, some necessary arrangements, which the ardour of my youthful impetuosity could hardly brook at that time (love and youth will be precipitate)[7] – some preliminary arrangements, I say, with the landlord, respecting fixtures – very necessary things to be considered in a young man about to settle in the world, though not very accordant with the impatient state of my then passions – some obstacles about the valuation of the fixtures – had hitherto precluded (and I shall always think providentially) my final closes with his offer; when one of those accidents which, unimportant in themselves, often arise to give a turn to the most serious intentions of our life intervened and put an end at once to my projects of wiving and of housekeeping.

I was never much given to theatrical entertainments; that is, at no time of my life was I ever what they call a regular playgoer; but on some occasion of a benefit-night, which was expected to be very productive, and indeed turned out so, Cleora expressing a desire to be present, I could do no less than offer, as I did very willingly, to squire her and her mother to the pit. At that time it was not customary in our town for tradesfolk, except some of the very topping ones, to sit, as they now do, in the boxes.

At the time appointed I waited upon the ladies, who had brought with them a young man, a distant relation, whom, it seems, they had invited to be of the party. This a little disconcerted me, as I had about me barely silver enough to pay for our three selves at the door and did not at first know that their relation had proposed paying for himself. However, to do the young man justice, he not only paid for himself, but for the old lady besides; leaving me only to pay for two, as it were. In our passage to the theatre the notice of Cleora was attracted to some orange wenches that stood about the doors vending their commodities. She was leaning on my arm and I could feel her every now and then giving me a nudge, as it is called, which I afterwards discovered were hints that I should buy some oranges.

It seems it is a custom at Birmingham, and perhaps in other places, when a gentleman treats ladies to the play – especially when a full night is expected and the house will be inconveniently warm – to provide them with this kind of fruit, oranges being esteemed for their cooling property. But how could I guess at that, never having treated ladies to a play before, and being, as I said, quite a novice at entertainments of this kind?

At last, she spoke plain out, and begged that I would buy some of 'those oranges', pointing to a particular barrow. But, when I came to examine the fruit, I did not think the quality of it was answerable to the price. In this way I handled several baskets of them; but something in them all displeased me. Some had thin rinds, and some were plainly over-ripe, which is as great a fault as not being ripe enough; and I could not (what they call) make a bargain.

While I stood haggling with the woman, secretly determining to put off my purchase till I should get within the theatre, where I expected we should have better choice, the young man, the cousin (who, it seems, had left us without my missing him), came running to us with his pockets stuffed out with oranges, inside and out, as they say. It seems, not liking the look of the barrow-fruit any more than myself, he had slipped away to an eminent fruiterer's, about three doors distant, which I never had the sense to think of, and had laid out a matter of two shillings on some of the best St Michael's I think I ever tasted.

What a little hinge, as I said before, the most important affairs in life may turn upon! The mere inadvertence to the fact that there was an eminent fruiterer's within three doors of us, though we had just passed it without the thought once occurring to me, which he had taken advantage of, lost me the affection of my Cleora. From that time she visibly cooled towards me; and her partiality was as visibly transferred to this cousin. I was long unable to account for this change in her behaviour; when one day, accidently discoursing of oranges to my mother, alone, she let drop a sort of reproach to me, as if I had offended Cleora by my *nearness*, [8] as she called it, that evening.

Even now, when Cleora has been wedded some years to that same officious relation, as I may call him, I can hardly be persuaded that such a trifle could have been the motive for her inconstancy; for could she suppose that I would sacrifice my dearest hopes in her to the paltry sum of two shillings, when I was going to treat her to the play, and her mother too (an expense of more than four times that amount), if the young man had not interfered to pay for the latter, as I mentioned?

But the caprices of the sex are past finding out; and I begin to think my mother was in the right, for doubtless women know women better than we can pretend to know them.

O. HENRY

WILLIAM SYDNEY PORTER (1862–1910), who signed his work with the *nom de plume* O. Henry, is one of the greatest and most prolific American short-story writers of any age. He was the son of a doctor and as a young man moved to Texas for his health. After working on a ranch for a couple of years, he was employed at the bank in Austin. Later he married and became a journalist on the *Houston Post*. Then something very disconcerting happened. He was accused of embezzling money from the Austin bank. Rather than face the charge, he fled to South America. However, on learning that his wife was dying, he returned home. After her death he served a short prison sentence. While in gaol he began to write short stories that began appearing in various magazines and periodicals. Soon after his release, he settled in New York, which was always a city of wonder and romance to him. There he lived out his life, but sadly, despite his enormous success, it was marred by ill-health, debts and alcoholism.

Many of O. Henry's stories are set in New York and examine the lives of those who lived and worked in this fabulous city, but 'One Dollar's Worth' deals with the life he knew as a young man in Texas, when that territory was still the Wild West. Like so many skilful writers, he makes the plot of this charming tale deceptively simple, but on closer inspection the reader can observe a very careful and clever underlying design. The use of the comparisons between the two sets of lovers is expertly counterbalanced with the fact that the fake silver dollar, which is the central focus of the story, saves the lives and happiness of both pairs. O. Henry also interweaves ideas of sacrifice and the perception that some lives are perceived as being cheap: the treatment of the Mexican natives is mirrored in the slaughter of the plovers. At first glance, this story may seem a simple meal, but take a closer look: it is a feast.

One Dollar's Worth

THE JUDGE of the United States court of the district lying along the Rio Grande border found the following letter one morning in his mail:

> Judge – When you sent me up for four years you made a talk. Among other hard things, you called me a rattlesnake. Maybe I am one – anyhow, you hear me rattling now. One year after I got to the pen,[1] my daughter died of – well, they said it was poverty and the disgrace together. You've got a daughter, judge, and I'm going to make you know how it feels to lose one. And I'm going to bite that district attorney that spoke against me. I'm free now, and I guess I've turned to rattlesnake all right. I feel like one. I don't say much, but this is my rattle. Look out what I strike.
>
> Yours respectfully,
>
> RATTLESNAKE

Judge Derwent threw the letter carelessly aside. It was nothing new to receive such epistles from desperate men whom he had been called upon to judge. He felt no alarm. Later on he showed the letter to Littlefield, the young district attorney, for Littlefield's name was included in the threat, and the judge was punctilious in matters between himself and his fellow men.

Littlefield honoured the rattle of the writer, as far as it concerned himself, with a smile of contempt; but he frowned a little over the reference to the judge's daughter, for he and Nancy Derwent were to be married in the fall.

Littlefield went to the clerk of the court and looked over the records with him. They decided that the letter might have been sent by Mexico Sam, a half-breed border desperado who has been imprisoned for manslaughter four years before. Then official duties crowded the matter from his mind, and the rattle of the revengeful serpent was forgotten.

Court was in session at Brownsville. Most of the cases to be tried were charges of smuggling, counterfeiting, post-office robberies and violations of federal laws along the border. One case was that of a young Mexican, Rafael Ortiz, who had been rounded up by a clever deputy marshal in the act of passing a counterfeit silver dollar. He had been suspected of many such deviations from rectitude, but this was the first time that anything provable had been fixed upon him. Ortiz languished cosily in jail, smoking brown cigarettes and waiting for trial. Kilpatrick, the deputy, brought the counterfeit dollar and handed it to the district attorney in his office in the courthouse. The deputy and a reputable druggist were prepared to swear that Ortiz paid for a bottle of medicine with it. The coin was a poor counterfeit, soft, dull-looking, and made principally of lead. It was the day before the morning on which the docket² would reach the case of Ortiz, and the district attorney was preparing himself for the trial.

'Not much need of having in high-priced experts to prove the coin's queer, is there, Kil?' smiled Littlefield, as he thumped the dollar down upon the table, where it fell with no more ring than would have come from a lump of putty.

'I guess the Greaser's³ as good as behind the bars,' said the deputy, easing up his holsters. 'You've got him dead. If it had been just one time, these Mexicans can't tell good money from bad; but this little yaller rascal belongs to a gang of counterfeiters, I know. This is the first time I've been able to catch him doing the trick. He's got a girl down there in them Mexican jacals⁴ on the river bank. I seen her one day when I was watching him. She's as pretty as a red heifer in a flower bed.'

Littlefield shoved the counterfeit dollar into his pocket, and slipped his memoranda of the case into an envelope. Just then a bright, winsome face, as frank and jolly as a boy's, appeared in the doorway, and in walked Nancy Derwent.

'Oh, Bob, didn't court adjourn at twelve today until tomorrow?' she asked of Littlefield.

'It did,' said the district attorney, 'and I'm very glad of it. I've got a lot of rulings to look up, and – '

'Now, that's just like you. I wonder you and father don't turn to law books or rulings or something! I want you to take me out plover-shooting⁵ this afternoon. Long Prairie is just alive with them. Don't say no, please! I want to try my new twelve-bore hammerless. I've sent to the livery stable to engage Fly and Bess for the buckboard; they stand fire so nicely. I was sure you would go.'

They were to be married in the fall. The glamour was at its height. The plovers won the day – or rather, the afternoon – over the calf-bound authorities.⁶ Littlefield began to put his papers away.

There was a knock at the door. Kilpatrick answered it. A beautiful, dark-eyed girl with a skin tinged with the faintest lemon colour walked into the room. A black shawl was thrown over her head and wound once around her neck.

She began to talk in Spanish, a voluble, mournful stream of melancholy music. Littlefield did not understand Spanish. The deputy did, and he translated her talk by portions, at intervals holding up his hands to check the flow of her words.

'She came to see you, Mr Littlefield. Her name's Joya Treviñas. She wants to see you about – well she's mixed up with that Rafael Ortiz. She's his – she's his girl. She says he's innocent. She says she made the money and got him to pass it. Don't you believe her, Mr Littlefield. That's the way with these Mexican girls; they'll lie, steal, or kill for a fellow when they get stuck on him. Never trust a woman that's in love!'

'Mr Kilpatrick!'

Nancy Derwent's indignant exclamation caused the deputy to flounder for a moment in attempting to explain that he had misquoted his own sentiments, and then he went on with the translation. 'She says she's willing to take his place in the jail if you'll let him out. She says she was down sick with the fever, and the doctor said she'd die if she didn't have medicine. That's why he passed the lead dollar on the drugstore. She says it saved her life. This Rafael seems to be her honey, all right; there's a lot of stuff in her talk about love and such things that you don't want to hear.'

It was an old story to the district attorney.

'Tell her,' said he, 'that I can do nothing. The case comes up in the morning, and he will have to make his fight before the court.'

Nancy Derwent was not so hardened. She was looking with sympathetic interest at Joya Treviñas and at Littlefield alternately. The deputy repeated the district attorney's words to the girl. She spoke a sentence or two in a low voice, pulled her shawl closely about her face, and left the room.

'What did she say then?' asked the district attorney.

'Nothing special,' said the deputy. 'She said: "If the life of the one" – let's see how it went – "*Si la vida de ella a quien tu amas* – if the life of the girl you love is ever in danger, remember Rafael Ortiz." '

Kilpatrick strolled out through the corridor in the direction of the marshal's office.

'Can't you do anything for them, Bob?' asked Nancy. 'It's such a little thing – just one counterfeit dollar – to ruin the happiness of two lives! She was in danger of death, and he did it to save her. Doesn't the law know the feeling of pity?'

'It hasn't a place in jurisprudence, Nan,' said Littlefield, 'especially *in re*[7] the district attorney's duty. I'll promise you that the prosecution will not be vindictive; but the man is as good as convicted when the case is called. Witnesses will swear to his passing the bad dollar which I have in my pocket at this momet as Exhibit A. There are no Mexicans on the jury, and it will vote Mr Greaser guilty without leaving the box.'

The plover-shooting was fine that afternoon, and in the excitement of the sport the case of Rafael and the grief of Joya Treviñas were forgotten. The district attorney and Nancy Derwent drove out from the town three miles along a smooth, grassy road, and then struck across a rolling prairie toward a heavy line of timber on Piedra Creek. Beyond this creek lay Long Prairie, the favourite haunt of the plover. As they were nearing the creek they heard the galloping of a horse to their right, and saw a man with black hair and a swarthy face riding toward the woods at a tangent, as if he had come up behind them.

'I've seen that fellow somewhere,' said Littlefield, who had a memory for faces, 'but I can't exactly place him. Some ranchman, I suppose, taking a short cut home.'

They spent an hour on Long Prairie, shooting from the buckboard. Nancy Derwent, an active, outdoor Western girl, was pleased with her twelve-bore. She had bagged within two brace of her companion's score.

They had started homeward at a gentle trot, when within a hundred yards of Piedra Creek a man rode out of the timber directly toward them.

'It looks like the man we saw coming over,' remarked Miss Derwent.

As the distance between them lessened, the district attorney suddenly pulled up his team sharply, with his eyes fixed upon the advancing horseman. That individual had drawn a Winchester from its scabbard on his saddle and thrown it over his arm.

'Now I know you, Mexico Sam!' muttered Littlefield to himself. 'It *was* you who shook your rattles in that gentle epistle.'

Mexico Sam did not leave things long in doubt. He had a nice eye in all matters relating to firearms, so when he was within good rifle range, but outside of danger from no. 8 shot, he threw up his Winchester and opened fire upon the occupants of the buckboard.

The first shot cracked the back of the seat within the two-inch space between the shoulders of Littlefield and Miss Derwent. The next went through the dashboard and Littlefield's trouser leg.

The district attorney hustled Nancy out of the buckboard to the ground. She was a little pale, but asked no questions. She had the frontier instinct that accepts conditions in an emergency without superfluous argument. They kept their guns in hand, and Littlefield hastily gathered some handfuls of cartridges from the pasteboard box on the seat and crowded them into his pockets.

'Keep behind the horses, Nancy,' he commanded. 'That fellow is a ruffian I sent to prison once. He's trying to get even. He knows our shot won't hurt him at that distance.'

'All right, Bob,' said Nancy, steadily. 'I'm not afraid. But you come close, too. Whoa, Bess; stand still, now!'

She stroked Bess's mane. Littlefield stood with his gun ready, praying that the desperado would come within range.

But Mexico Sam was playing his vendetta along safe lines. He was a bird of different feather from the plover. His accurate eye drew an imaginary line of circumference around the area of danger from bird-shot, and upon this line he rode. His horse wheeled to the right, and as his victims rounded to the safe side of their equine breastwork he sent a ball through the district attorney's hat. Once he miscalculated in making a detour, and overstepped his margin. Littlefield's gun flashed, and Mexico Sam ducked his head to the harmless patter of the shot. A few of them stung his horse, which pranced promptly back to the safety line.

The desperado fired again. A little cry came from Nancy Derwent. Littlefield whirled, with blazing eyes, and saw the blood trickling down her cheek.

'I'm not hurt, Bob – only a splinter struck me. I think he hit one of the wheel-spokes.'

'Lord!' groaned Littlefield. 'If I only had a charge of buckshot!'

The ruffian got his horse still, and took careful aim. Fly gave a snort and fell in the harness, struck in the neck. Bess, now disabused of the idea that plover were being fired at, broke her traces and galloped wildly away. Mexican Sam sent a ball neatly through the fullness of Nancy Derwent's shooting jacket.

'Lie down – lie down!' snapped Littlefield. 'Close to the horse – flat on the ground – so.' He almost threw her upon the grass against the back of the recumbent Fly. Oddly enough, at that moment the words of the Mexican girl returned to his mind: 'If the life of the girl you love is ever in danger, remember Rafael Ortiz.'

Littlefield uttered an exclamation.

'Open fire on him, Nan, across the horse's back! Fire as fast as you can! You can't hurt him, but keep him dodging shot for one minute while I try to work a little scheme.'

Nancy gave a quick glance at Littlefield, and saw him take out his pocket-knife and open it. Then she turned her face to obey orders, keeping up a rapid fire at the enemy.

Mexico Sam waited patiently until this innocuous fusillade ceased. He had plenty of time, and she did not care to risk the chance of a bird-shot in his eye if it could be avoided by a little caution. He pulled his heavy Stetson low down over his face until the shots ceased. Then he drew a little nearer, and fired with careful aim at what he could see of his victims above the fallen horse.

Neither of them moved. He urged his horse a few steps nearer. He saw the district attorney rise to one knee, and deliberately level his shotgun. He pulled his hat down and awaited the harmless rattle of the tiny pellets.

The shotgun blazed with a heavy report. Mexico Sam sighed, turned limp all over, and slowly fell from his horse – a dead rattlesnake.

At ten o'clock the next morning court opened, and the case of the United States versus Rafael Ortiz was called. The district attorney, with his arm in a sling, rose and addressed the court.

'May it please your honour,' he said, 'I desire to enter a *nol. pros.*[8] in this case. Even though the defendant should be guilty, there is not sufficient evidence in the hands of the government to secure a conviction. The piece of counterfeit coin upon the identify of which the case was built is not now available as evidence. I ask, therefore, that the case be stricken off.'

At the noon recess, Kilpatrick strolled into the district attorney's office.

'I've just been down to take a squint at old Mexico Sam,' said the deputy. 'They've got him laid out. Old Mexico was a tough outfit, I reckon. The boys was wonderin' down there what you shot him with. Some said it must have been nails. I never see a gun carry anything to make holes like he had.'

'I shot him,' said the district attorney, 'with Exhibit A of your counterfeiting case. Lucky thing for me – and somebody else – that it was as bad money as it was! It sliced up into slugs very nicely. Say, Kil, can't you go down to the jacals and find where that Mexican girl lives? Miss Derwent wants to know.'

NOTES TO THE TEXT

The Black Veil
1 *native place* the place where he had been born
2 *fallen off* left their home and their mother never to return
3 *dissolution* in this sense, the man's death
4 *Burke nor Bishop* referring to criminals who sold corpses to doctors for the purpose of experimentation
5 *chafed* rubbed
6 *avocations* occupations

The Withered Arm
1 *supernumerary* in this instance, milkers who were not employed on a regular basis
2 *tisty-tosty* local expression meaning attractive
3 *barton* farmyard
4 *laved* to lave means to wash or bathe
5 *lineaments* facial features
6 *incubus* evil spirit that descends on sleepers
7 *chimmer* chamber; in this instance, bedroom
8 *unconscious usurpation* Gertrude's ignorance that her marriage blocked any chance of Rhoda being reconciled with Lodge
9 *patron* Gertrude is seen by Rhoda as her patron, i.e. someone who helps and supports her
10 *furze* spiky green plant
11 *garniture* trimmings
12 *prosiness* tedium
13 *nostrums* patent medicines
14 *desuetude* disuse
15 *commonage* common land (the rights to)
16 *turbary* the right of digging turf on common land
17 *draught animal* horse used to pulling a plough
18 *rencounter* a meeting with someone again

The Terribly Strange Bed
1 *blackguard* in this sense the word refers to the disreputable nature of the gambling establishment
2 *piece of pasteboard* playing card

3 *sou*   small coin
4 *sacré mille bombes!*   exclamation of excitement
5 *surtout*   frock coat
6 *Voyage autour de ma Chambre*   a trip around my room
7 *Childe Harold*   a poem by the nineteenth-century poet Lord Byron
8 *entresol*   a low storey in a building between the first and ground floor
9 *Prefecture*   a large police station
10 *sub-prefect*   police officer one rank down from the chief
11 *posse comitatus*   a body of men
12 *procès-verbal*   written account

The Bottle Imp

1 *lockfast*   secured with a lock
2 *Captain Cook*   famous sailor who discovered Australia
3 *Prester John*   a legendary medieval Christian emperor
4 *pilot-coat*   a seaman's coat
5 *forecastle*   forward part of the ship where the sailors live
6 *ava*   a delicacy from Samoa
7 *papaia*   exotic fruit of the pawpaw family
8 *Chinese Evil*   leprosy
9 *Haoles*   white people, i.e. not natives
10 *sunder*   to keep apart
11 *farthing*   coin that was worth a quarter of a penny
12 *wroth*   angry
13 *calaboose*   prison
14 *belaying pin*   a wooden or iron pin used on ships
15 *make a catspaw*   fool me
16 *flat*   dim

The Red-Headed League

1 *Omne ignotum pro magnifico*   the unknown is always thought to be magnificent
2 *at scratch*   from the beginning
3 *billet*   position
4 *rubber*   a game of cards
5 *smasher*   a maker of counterfeit coins
6 *crack a crib*   thieves' slang for committing a burglary
7 *napoleons*   French gold coins
8 *partie carrée*   a game or match
9 *skirts*   the tails of his jacket

10 *ennui* boredom
11 *L'homme c'est rien – l'oeuvre c'est tout* the man is nothing, the work is everything

The Stolen Bacillus

1 *bacteriologist* a scientist who studies bacteria – germs. A bacillus is a single bacterium that can cause disease by entering the body.
2 *rhetoric* speech used to persuade
3 *ethnology* ethnic background
4 *incontinently* immediately
5 *screw of a horse* worn-out nag
6 *ostler boy* stablehand
7 *Vive l'anarchie!* Long live anarchy!

The Squire's Story

1 *wainscoted* the lower half of the rooms were panelled with wood
2 *piqued* prided
3 *aut a huntsman aut nullus* if you are not a huntsman you are nothing
4 *Reynard* the fox
5 *laggards* those who had lagged behind the rest
6 *asseverations* solemn, serious declarations
7 *fain to equivocate* was led to hide the truth of where he had been
8 *buffo stories* highly comic stories
9 *dissenter* a supporter of Oliver Cromwell against Charles I. See note 16.
10 *Mordecai* biblical character who would bow down to no one
11 *Griselda* model of enduring patience
12 *Dogberries and Verges* representatives of law and order in Shakespeare's *Much Ado About Nothing*
13 *durance* stay
14 *making extracts* writing out extracts
15 *posset* a hot-drink remedy for a cold made with curdled milk and spices; in this instance, treacle was also included
16 *Church-and-King-and-down-with-the-Rump* a reference to the causes of the English Civil War. The horse was named after a cry given by the supporters of King Charles I and the loyal members of his Parliament.

The Journey to Panama

1 *wont* usual behaviour
2 *physiognomy* the features of the face

3 *citizens of the new Southern flag*   reference to the Southern States of America that had separated from the North. At the time of the story both sides were involved in a civil war (1861–5).
4 *Isthmus*   a narrow piece of land joining two larger pieces of land
5 *auri sacre fames*   cursed hunger for wealth
6 *viands*   items of food
7 *Honi soit qui mal y pense*   shame to him who evil thinks
8 *Cerebus*   a three-headed dog who guarded the realm of the dead in Hades. Miss Viner is alluding to Mr and Mrs Grumpy and their daughter.

The Sphinx Without a Secret

1 *clairvoyante*   someone with exceptional insight
2 *Gioconda*   someone possessing a puzzling, mystifying character, after the painting *La Gioconda* by Leonardo da Vinci which featured a lady with a very enigmatic smile
3 *ma belle inconnue*   my beautiful unknown

The Judge's House

1 *bogies*   evil spirits
2 *Senior Wrangler*   a senior mathematician
3 *sang froid*   composure, coolness under unnerving circumstances

The Necklace

1 *repinings*   discontent
2 *coquettish boudoirs*   attractive and seductive lady's private rooms
3 *pot au feu*   literally 'pot on the fire' – a simple meal
4 *louis*   in this context, a French coin
5 *usurious*   the rates charged by the moneylenders

The Kiss

1 *bay*   reddish-brown horse with a black mane and tail
2 *lynx-like*   like the whiskers of a lynx, which is a large cat
3 *valse*   waltz
4 *verst*   a Russian measure of length, about two thirds of a mile
5 *limber*   detachable front of a gun carriage

The Yellow Wallpaper

1 *Phosphates or phosphites*   effervescent drinks which act as a tonic
2 *piazza*   veranda
3 *'debased Romanesque' with delirium tremens*   The design resembled a pattern similar to the Romanesque style of art but its

characteristics had been exaggerated in a crude fashion to create a disturbing effect.

4 *columns of fatuity*   stupid or silly columns in the pattern
5 *smooches*   marks
6 *mopboard*   skirting board

Juke Judkin's Courtship

1 *brazier*   a worker in brass
2 *sagacious tricks and innocent artifices*   wise tricks and simple cunning actions
3 *'need not stand upon a portion'*   he should not be prevented from courting the girl because her wealth was less than his
4 *felicities*   the wedding and married life
5 *amorous colloquy*   loving conversations
6 *prodigality*   extravagance
7 *precipitate*   in a hurry
8 *nearness*   extreme caution when spending money

One Dollar's Worth

1 *pen*   abbreviation for penitentiary, the state prison
2 *docket*   a list recording the cases and the individuals to be tried in court
3 *Greaser*   slang expression for a Mexican
4 *jacals*   settlements
5 *plover-shooting*   a plover is a medium-sized wading bird
6 *the calf-bound authorities*   the law books
7 *in re*   in the matter of, concerning
8 *nol. pros.*   *nolle prosequi* – a legal term meaning to stop the proceedings